T0147957

CONCEALED IN DESTINY

Ken Coats

iUniverse, Inc.
Bloomington

Concealed in Destiny

iUniverse books may be ordered through booksellers or by contacting:

iUniverse
1663 Liberty Drive
Bloomington, IN 47403
www.iuniverse.com
1-800-Authors (1-800-288-4677)

ISBN: 978-1-4620-8333-6 (sc)
ISBN: 978-1-4620-8335-0 (hc)
ISBN: 978-1-4620-8334-3 (e)

Registration Number: TXu 1-606-522

Printed in the United States of America

iUniverse rev. date:2/9/2012

CONCEALED IN DESTINY

CHAPTER 1

Night came early, and it was ugly. Rain, which was wind-whipped into stinging pellets, raked the ship's bow as it plowed through tall, rolling waves agitated from their quiet undulations three hours earlier. Rick Scanlon stared through the wall of water cascading down the windows of the pilothouse. The winter storm had caught up with his freighter just as a dim line of lights appeared across the eastern horizon ahead, marking the coastline of San Francisco. There were some unusual lines in his dark features when he looked up at the ship's clock. The time was 1830 hours.

His ship, a bulk carrier named *Raleigh*, moved through the water at quarter speed while it was rendezvousing with the pilot boat, which contained the current harbor pilot on duty. The launch was just now pulling in close to the leeward side of the freighter. Illuminated by large searchlights on the small boat, the *Raleigh* and the launch paced each other side-by-side, over and through the tall, undulating waves while Rick watched two of his deckhands drop a Jacob's ladder over the side.

The rope ladder with wooden slats for rungs unwound down the side of the *Raleigh* while it careened against its slippery hull. As he stood on an elevated platform attached to the side of the station boat and the boat nudged the *Raleigh's* hull, the pilot stepped off onto the ladder while he timed his departure to coincide with the crest of a twenty-foot wave.

Turbulence begets technique, Rick thought. Only harbor pilots who were skilled in their profession could make such a risky transfer so easily.

On the bridge ten minutes later, after he was escorted by Charley Gibson, one of the deckhands, the pilot introduced himself as Hugh Langton while he hung up his weather gear. A slender man who appeared to be in his fifties, Langton first checked the *Raleigh's* papers and took enough time for a general knowledge of the ship's tonnage and engine power before he ordered, "Four degrees to starboard!"

"Four degrees to starboard!" Helmsman Bob Greely responded.

Fifteen seconds later when the cargo ship's rudder reached its new position, Greely repeated, "Four degrees to starboard!"

The maneuver was only for Langton to get a feel for the vessel under the current conditions. When the *Raleigh* finally turned to the new heading, Langton was satisfied with the feel of the vessel under the current conditions of the ocean.

"Can you keep her in the lane tonight?" Rick asked, nodding toward the two rows of lit buoys, which marked a wide channel ahead of his ship.

"The storm is making the steering a bit sluggish, but we still should be docking at Oakland to give you and your crew plenty of shore time this evening," Langton replied.

"That's what I like to hear," Rick said and then moved on to the back of the wheelhouse, where Gibson was drinking coffee. He stood by the cup storage locker, which was nothing more than rows of individual niches in the bulkhead.

"I'd hand you one poured, captain, but I can't reach your cup," Gibson said, nodding upward to the lone cup on the top row just as the ship's first mate, Jess Williams, entered the pilothouse. Water spilled down his yellow slicker into small pools tracing his footsteps across the deck.

As he looked over at the pilot, Jess said, "Glad to see you got her heading for the gate." His voice echoed inside the darkened bridge. "As you know, there's bound to be quite a swell running just outside the channel in the shoal water."

"No problem. I've checked the *Raleigh's* steering with your helmsman," Langton replied, nodding toward Bob Greely. Then with a half-smile, he added, "Just another day at the office."

"Good! Let's get this old bucket into port! I'm ready for a drink!" Jess said. He left the pilot and Greely at the wheel and moved on back to join Rick and Gibson. As he hung up his slicker, he found his own cup from the bulkhead niche. When he turned to the young deckhand, he asked, "Ready for some dry land, Gib?"

"Yeah, I was thinking about what you told me earlier today. A trip to Big Irene's should fix me up, right?"

"One way or the other," Jess said. His smile revealed a missing tooth when he looked over at Rick. "Coming with us, skipper? Irene was asking about you the last time I was there."

"Got other plans tonight," Rick said. Then, as if he was testing his own memory, he added, "I haven't been to her place since I got back from Desert Storm, and that's been a while. She still got her upstairs business?"

"Yeah, and Irene tells me you used to keep her girls up there pretty happy."

"Well, I'll probably go back again when I'm gray-haired and have trouble getting it up."

"Ah, go to hell," Jess snorted.

Each man balanced himself against the *Raleigh's* motion by holding onto the bulkhead's bracing structure. The talking continued between Jess and Gib, but Rick only half-listened to the conversation. His thoughts were on his ship's overdue mortgage payment. The bank had sent him three e-mail notices during their homeward voyage from Japan. *With the bank's gluttony for their money,* he thought to himself, *the income from this recent cargo delivery will slip through my hands as quickly as the fish a zookeeper feeds to a sea lion.*

CHAPTER 2

THE STORM WAS CAUSING the commuter plane, a thirty-seat, turbo-jet plane, to be late in arriving at the Oakland International Airport. Despite the erratic motion of the plane, the young female flight attendant was doing her best to comfort her passengers. She had just retrieved a pillow from the aisle for one of them when a pamphlet landed at her feet. The attendant picked it up and then noticed a blonde woman several seats forward raise her hand. With effort, the attendant moved up the aisle and handed the pamphlet to the passenger.

Dr. Patricia Kendall accepted the medical journal with a sincere thank-you accompanied by a smile. She started reading the journal again, but the print zigzagging from the plane's motion discouraged her. She tossed the pamphlet in the vacant seat beside her on top of the *Reno Gazette-Journal*. A small headline in the newspaper proclaiming Presidents' Day weekend peeked out from under the pamphlet.

Two hours ago on the way to the airport in Reno, her parents had tried to persuade her to leave the following morning, but she had insisted on making this 6:00 p.m. flight. Tomorrow, she would have a first-period lecture at the university followed by two knee arthroscopies at the hospital. Relying on an early morning flight to meet the day's work schedule was too uncertain.

The weather could have made this brief holiday a lot more enjoyable, she told herself while she watched the rain hit the window of the regional jet. It had rained the entire three days she had been home. Being the youngest and only single member of a five-sibling family, she felt it was her duty to visit her aging parents as often as possible.

The incessant raindrops against the plane's window formed continual pools of water. She glanced again at the words written on the back of the seat in front of her: "Use seat bottom cushion for flotation." The message, which was not only beneficial for the present conditions, brought memories of her career as a flight attendant. After college, her desire for travel had trumped her medical aspirations, which had been simmering in her mind since childhood. But after two years as a flight attendant, the constant travel and hectic schedules had become more than she had bargained for.

Or maybe it had been Larry. She hadn't thought about him for a long time. He was a handsome pilot who had been ten years older than her and every girl's dream. When their relationship grew serious, the rumors started about his dalliances. Most of the gossip came from other flight attendants who were probably jealous of her. Then on a flight together, he told her that the woman who was meeting him when they landed in Miami was his sister, but after landing, she noticed the greeting between Larry and his so-called sibling was not like brother and sister. She learned later it had been his wife.

The betrayal had hurt deeply and made her extremely wary of future relationships, of which she had had several, but none serious. The deceit, now that she thought about it, had helped her make the career change. She knew she was fortunate in graduating early from both high school and college. The flight attendant experience had not been much of a detriment in prolonging the start of her medical practice. Now thirty-two years old, she had been an orthopedist for three years.

The pilot's voice over the PA system interrupted her thoughts. "We will start our approach to Oakland International Airport in about eight minutes." There was a pause. "Sorry the weather isn't more cooperative. Mother Nature's not in one of her better moods tonight."

Three rows behind Pat, Hokusai Utamaro looked up at the overhead compartment, where he had stuffed his bag and hiking boots. The door was ajar. One of his boots had begun to make its appearance due to the motion of the buffeting plane. His condition prevented him from immediately attending to the door. The hot dog he had eaten just before he had boarded the plane was churning his insides. When the flight attendant got up to recover a pillow form the aisle, Hok started to signal her but changed his mind.

Wearily, he started to unbuckle his own seat belt when the pilot's voice stopped him. Instead, his attention focused on a white paper bag.

It was barely visible in the expandable pocket on the back of the seat in front of him.

As Hok reached for the bag to have it close at hand, he looked around at the other passengers in the cabin. There were probably twenty men plus an attractive blonde woman and the flight attendant, a pretty brunette who reminded him of his girlfriend, Kara. He had spent the holiday weekend with her and her parents at the family home in Virginia City. Kara, a college classmate at Stanford, was one of the reasons he had remained in America after graduation instead of returning to his home in Hong Kong. The other reason was his job with an import firm in San Francisco, doing business in the Far East. His thoughts were interrupted by another jolt of the plane. In desperation, Hok buried his face in the bag.

After he announced the approach time, Captain Jeff Dunniger studied the fuel gage on the instrument panel. The fifty-knot headwind plus the extensive vectoring had taken their toll on his fuel supply.

The blond features of the copilot, Arnold Wilcox, were set in a perpetual frown. His white-knuckled hand rested firmly on the yoke control while the rain-soaked gale pitched the small jet about like a steel ball seesawing through bumper pins.

Dunniger contemplated the remaining fuel before he glanced again at his radio frequency selector. When air traffic control notified him that he would be delayed in heavy traffic on his approach, he didn't wait any longer to declare a fuel emergency.

"Metro 469," the crisp voice of approach control responded. "You are number four on the approach. Plan the ILS Runway 11 approach!"

"Roger," Dunniger acknowledged and then listened to the ATC sequence, specifically a B-737 onto short final followed by an A-320 and then a B-767 as they were switched over to the tower controller.

Three minutes later, Dunniger called again. "This is Metro 469 on ten-mile final. Are we cleared for the approach?"

"Metro 469," ATC answered, "fly heading 080. You are two from PLAZA. Maintain 1,800 until established and cleared for the ILS 11 approach."

Deep furrows lined Dunniger's face as he studied his instrument panel. When satisfied with his position, he stared out at the black night while he called the tower. "Cleared the ILS 11 approach … and thanks for the help."

Dunniger felt air filling his lungs, but there was little time to relax. He and Wilcox fought a whipsawed aircraft, trying to keep it coupled with the instrument landing system. As he realized he needed to keep his passengers as calm as possible, Dunniger kept his composure with effort when he announced over the loudspeaker, "We are starting our approach to Oakland International Airport." His brief message left a hollow echo inside the cabin.

At that instant, the pilot of the B-767 was rolling out on the runway and reported gains and losses of twenty knots on final. "Damn!" the controller swore silently. There was a significant wind shear in the path of the approaching airplanes.

"We are a dot low!" Wilcox said loud enough to be heard above the sound of the rain pounding the cockpit windows.

His remark was just ahead of the tower's notification: "Metro 469! The B-767 ahead of you just reported gains and losses of twenty knots on final!"

Before Dunniger could acknowledge the call, his aircraft dropped like an overloaded elevator. Instinctively, he shouted, "What the hell!"

Jolted by the sudden movement, Wilcox yelled, "Bring it up!"

★ ★ ★

The airport's Doppler radar failed to detect a layered slice of air in the path of the approaching aircraft. The easterly gale wind had quickly accelerated to a speed of eighty knots.

Pat heard a gagging cough behind her. A seat belt unsnapped and was followed by quick footsteps. Pat had already pulled her own seat belt tighter when the pilot's voice had announced the start of the approach to landing.

Then the plane fell abruptly. It dropped as if attracted by a magnet. On impulse, Pat glanced out the window. *Are those lights down there?* The thought flashed across her mind just as a sudden jolt of the plane jerked her forward with a blinding force.

CHAPTER 3

THE *RALEIGH* STEAMED UNDER the Golden Gate Bridge and on past Alcatraz and then Treasure Island, and now it was about to clear the Bay Bridge. It had not been an easy trip. Sweat beads glistened on Bob Greely's brow, and not from physical exertion. The storm's intensity had kept him more alert than the job had usually needed.

At the front of the bridge with Greely and Langton, Rick stared at the rain slamming against the windows in sporadic sheets of water. "This is the first time I've entered port here during a heavy storm," he said, turning to Langton. "I'm surprised. I thought we would have more protection from the storm inside the harbor."

"Some of these storms out of the north will sweep right down the bay's channel from the Marin headlands to San Mateo," answered the harbor pilot.

"Like this mother," Greely injected dryly.

"Yes, this one is a good example," Langton continued. "But the storm has kept the traffic in the bay light, and that is in our favor. However, we will anchor tonight near your designated docking area and take the *Raleigh* dockside tomorrow when the storm has hopefully abated."

When Lee Holman, a steward from the galley, brought in a fresh container of coffee, Rick moved to the back of the bridge for a refill. "Are you seeing your fashion model tonight, captain?" the tow-headed steward asked while he set the hot container on a bulkhead shelf.

"Yeah, I guess so," Rick answered absently before he realized what he had said. "How the hell did you know about her?"

"Me and Gib saw you one night. Remember, Gib?" Holman said, glancing at Gibson, who was still on the bridge near Jess. "You and a brunette were in one of them big limos," Holman continued. "The next day, we saw her picture on a magazine cover."

"That's right, captain," Gib confirmed. "Wow! When I get to be a shipmaster, that's the way I want to live!"

"You're right, boy! The only merchant sailor who can afford to live like that is the captain," Jess added dryly.

"Wait a minute, you beetle-brained assholes," Rick snapped. "It's none of your damn business, but that limo belonged—" A sound outside the wheelhouse cut him off.

It started with a loud hum vibrating the bridge's windows and then accelerated into a whirring roar. Suddenly, it appeared off the port side, a flying shadow with widely spaced eyes. It skimmed the bow, creating tiny runners of sparks, and then ploughed a long, deep furrow in the water off the starboard bow before it disappeared into the blustery night.

"What the hell's going on up there?" The *Raleigh's* chief engineer, Swede Sorenson, yelled over the ship's PA system.

"Not sure, Swede!" Rick shouted into the ship's microphone near the wheel. "We've been hit! It was an airplane, I think! Stand by!"

When he turned back to Langton, Rick asked quickly, "Are we clear to maneuver?"

"Yes, within reason!" The pilot answered, clearing his throat. "We passed the bridge's pylons a while ago! Whattaya have in mind?"

"We're going to see what hit us! If you will guide the ship close to where that plane is, I'll prepare the crew to take on the stranded passengers!" Rick didn't wait for the pilot's confirmation. "Jess!" he yelled over his shoulder, "get a Mayday call to channel sixteen!" Then he turned back to Langton and said, "Is two nautical miles from the Bay Bridge a good guess?"

"Yes!"

"Two nau—"

"I heard him, skipper!" Jess interrupted while he switched on the radio near the helm.

Rick watched the *Raleigh* make a slow, arcing turn to get windward of the plane and create a lee while he listened to Jess's call.

"Mayday! Mayday! Mayday! This is the MV *Raleigh* about two nautical miles east of the Bay Bridge. A plane just hit our bow deck and then fell into the water off our starboard side, over!"

"Motor vessel *Raleigh.* This is Coast Guard Station Oakland. Switch and answer on channel twenty-two, over."

"Roger that. Switching and answering on twenty-two."

But Rick didn't hear the answering chatter. He was on the ship's PA system. "All hands not on watch go topside! Prepare to take aboard stranded passengers from an airplane! Take all lifejackets available! Prepare to launch all lifeboats and rafts!"

When Rick clicked off the PA system, Langton shouted, "Captain, the strong wind will set the ship down on the plane! We can't get too close! How quickly can you anchor?"

"We are going to find out!" Rick replied. "Can you man the radio? I want Jess to come with me!"

With Langton's answering nod, Rick and Jess each grabbed some weather gear and left the bridge. On the way out, Rick yelled over his shoulder, "Gib, get your weather gear on and man the searchlight in the forward lookout station!"

Near the starboard bow down on the main deck, Rick and Jess watched a half-submerged airplane come into view from the searchlight's beam.

"It's slowly sinking!" Rick shouted, standing close to Jess. The rain, which was swept by the strong wind, tattooed their slickers in sporadic waves.

"I think you're right!" Jess answered. "We ain't got time to anchor if we're going to help, but what can we do—"

"Captain!" A yell from a deckhand moving toward them interrupted Jess. "All lifeboats and rafts are about ready to launch!"

"Good!" Rick shouted his reply. "Make it two men per craft with a tow line out from the Raleigh!"

"Aye, captain!" the deckhand yelled over his shoulder while he headed aft in a stumbling run.

Just then a door opened above one of the plane's wings. Rick and Jess, who were watching intently, saw a passenger crawl out on the wing and then hold desperately to the wing when the plane dipped suddenly from waves.

"Jess!" Rick shouted while he kept his eyes on the frantic passenger. "I want you to get me to that plane with the derrick!"

CHAPTER 4

Pat's feet were cold! Something sloshed around them! The howling wind just outside the plane had her in a different world until she recognized the sound of the groans and moans all around her. Now she remembered the plane's breath-catching, sudden drop and then the jolting impact and the shooting stars that filled her mind.

Pat instinctively felt her forehead. A sharp pain knifed through her body when she touched a large lump over her right temple. There was blood on her fingers, but her injury was soon forgotten. She had to move. There were others who would need her help.

When she forced herself to think rationally, she realized the plane had ditched in the bay with a loud, jarring crash, but the writhing cries of the suffering kept her attention. This time, she got all the way up on her feet by holding onto the seat in front of her. She fought a sudden weakness before she moved a heavy foot out into the aisle. Conscious of the hard rain pelting the cabin's exterior, she started forward while she shouted with as much voice as she could summon, "We must get out of this plane! Bring your seat cushions!"

Shadowed heads that were outlined in the light from outside the airplane began to stir. At the seat by the over-wing exit on the right side of the aisle, Pat grabbed the passenger's shoulder while she yelled close to his ear, "Can you hear me?" When his head nodded slowly, Pat said, "The lever above the window, pull it down and push out the exit door!" As the man started to rise, Pat turned to her left, but that passenger was already following her instructions and opening his exit.

Moving on, Pat found a male passenger slumped over in his seat. As she leaned close in the darkened interior, she could hear his raspy breathing. When she leaned him back against the seat, she could feel a jagged piece of metal imbedded in his rib cage. Blood oozed from the wound. She stopped two men moving toward the exits. "Carry this man off the plane!" she ordered. "Use care. He has a chest injury!"

The door to the cockpit opened. A wave of water surged into the cabin. Clearly, the plane was sinking nose-first. One of the pilots, his right arm-hanging limp, mumbled through a bloody handkerchief that he held to his nose, "The captain is hurt! Can someone help him?"

Pat waded past the uniformed man and on into the cabin. The pilot lay slumped over the instrument panel. Red water lapped at his waist. When she leaned him back in his seat, she saw that a lacerated bone was sticking through a pool of blood near his left clavicle. Quickly, she removed his tie and then used it to make a sling for his arm.

"Try to hold him still with your good arm!" Pat directed the copilot, who had followed her into the cockpit. "I'll get help for both of you."

Back in the cabin, two male passengers at the front of the plane were just getting up from their seats.

"Help the pilots!" she yelled. "Both are injured!" She moved on past the men and headed toward the back of the plane, but her steps became slower. She was aware of the rising water in the cabin, yet her feet seemed to be moving through poured concrete. A searing pain flashed behind her eyes. Unconsciously, she rubbed the side of her head with the injury, which was still bleeding. She started to sit down, but there was a body slumped over in the seat. When she leaned the person back in the seat a thick film with a putrid odor covered the face. With handfuls of water, Pat uncovered the face of a man. His eyes blinked open.

"My shoulder," the man grunted, holding his left arm.

"Can you move?" Pat asked. When he nodded, Pat helped him out into the aisle and started him forward. When he was moving freely, she turned back and checked to make sure there were no other passengers left on the plane.

Most of the noises were now coming from outside the cabin. Pat was almost to the rear of the plane. Her progress was slow. Just when she realized she was walking uphill, her foot struck something. When she reached under the water, she felt the heel of a woman's shoe, and it was still attached to the foot. She heard something behind her. As she looked around, two men approached.

"Quickly!" Pat gasped, pointing below the water's surface. "A woman is under there!"

When the men lifted the lifeless body of the flight attendant above the water level, Pat breathed heavily and ordered, "Please get her out of this plane as soon as you can! Do either of you know CPR?"

"I do!" the trailing man, who was holding his half of the body, yelled over his shoulder.

"Good!" Pat said. "Start just as soon as you can!"

At the exit, the trailing man, still with his back to Pat, called, "Are you still behind?"

"Don't worry about me!" Pat shouted. The water in the plane, which was nearly chest high, had impeded her progress. As she felt for the tops of the seats, she propelled herself forward with each heavy step.

Suddenly, the light outside intensified along with a new and different type of noise. "It's a helicopter from the police department or coast guard," she heard the man yell as he left the plane.

Pat stopped before she got to the exit. The cold air spilling in through the exit was a godsend. She struggled to make the final steps. Then just as she reached for the frame of the exit opening, the plane tipped abruptly, submerging her under a wall of water.

CHAPTER 5

Rick descended over the top of the airplane. With one foot in the large hook connected to the derrick line, he balanced himself upright while he held onto the line. When he stepped off on one of the wings, he quickly helped an injured pilot through the adjoining exit just as the first lifeboat arrived from the *Raleigh*.

The two men in the boat steadied it against the plane with boat hooks while Rick waited for three other passengers who were already on the wing to get into the boat. Then as he struggled to stay on the slippery wing, Rick lifted the pilot into the arms of the passengers seated in the boat.

A man with a chest injury was next. He was followed by another pilot holding his right arm while being pushed through the exit. With both injured men on their backs, Rick wrapped an arm around each one to prevent them from sliding off the wing. But he soon had help from the other passengers who were now steadily leaving the exits.

Despite the incessant waves crashing against the downed plane, the passengers were scrambling into the *Raleigh's* lifeboats and rafts without anyone falling into the bay. When the steady flow of passengers coming through the exits began to ebb, Rick ordered two extra seamen in one of the boats to enter the plane.

Todd Johnson, one of the seamen, had no sooner entered the plane when Rick heard him yell, "Captain, here comes an injured man!"

The passenger cried out when Rick touched his shoulder. "Push him through on his back!" Rick ordered.

When the man turned and started through the second time, Rick lifted him from the waist and pulled him through the exit. Only grunts and groans came from the man as Rick moved him over to a waiting boat.

The first helicopter from the coast guard arrived. It whirled overhead with its floodlight illuminating the area. Then Todd Johnson came scrambling through the exit near Rick.

"We're bringing out the flight attendant, captain!" he shouted.

"How many more?" Rick asked.

"Only one, a woman! She is right behind us! We've got to get some air into this flight attendant!" Todd answered while he quickly positioned himself to administer CPR on the plane's wing.

But the other woman had not made an appearance at the exit. On hands and knees, Rick moved over to the exit and looked inside. The water level was at the top of the seats. At that instant, the plane tilted abruptly, pitching Rick headfirst inside the airplane. He felt the jarring impact of his head striking something solid.

As the plane steadied, Rick struggled to his feet. The shooting stars in back of his eyeballs faded into a sharp pain above his left ear. By instinct, he started to touch the hurt but stopped when something moved against his leg. He reached under the water and pulled up a lifeless body. It was a woman. Quickly, he squeezed open her mouth, and with his cheek firmly pressed against the woman's nose, he started blowing into her mouth. As he paused between each repeated breath, he soon felt the return rush of air on his face.

She was light in his arms even though her clinging blouse revealed full development. The gloomy interior of the plane failed to hide a cut on her forehead. When her eyelids fluttered open, two large brown eyes stared at him. Tiny furrows suddenly etched her features. She started to speak, but he stopped her with a light squeeze.

"Everyone is okay. You are the last one off the plane," he said softly. She rewarded him with a tired smile before her eyes closed again. He felt her relax in his arms.

"Hey, skipper, are you okay? I saw you dive into the plane!" Rick's fixation with the woman in his arms was broken when Todd Johnson yelled through the plane's exit door.

"Yeah I'm all right. Here comes the last passenger," Rick replied while he lifted the woman up to his deckhand.

After Rick crawled through the exit, he paused, unsure if the sudden dizziness overpowering him had been caused from the plane's movement in the water or the throbbing hurt above his ear. While he rested on one knee, the whirling sensation in his brain soon stopped and watched the coast guard handle the plane's passengers.

The area around the ditched plane and the *Raleigh* was now lit by powerful searchlights from two coast guard cutters and three helicopters. The injured were being hoisted up to the hovering aircraft while the rest of the passengers were being placed aboard the cutters.

On the *Raleigh's* main deck, Jess watched Rick crawl through the plane's exit and then stop his forward progress as if uncertain of his whereabouts. When Jess noticed the blood covering Rick's left ear, he immediately sent one of the of the *Raleigh's* deckhands standing nearby to the captain's quarters to get a change of clothes for Rick.

Watching carefully, Jess waited until Rick began to study all the activity going on around him before he yelled through his bullhorn, "Hey, skipper, are you okay?"

Just then a man on one of the coast guard cutters with a bullhorn at his mouth yelled to Jess, "We have all the plane's passengers aboard our boats—"

"All but one!" Jess cut him off just as the deckhand returned with a bag in his hand. "Wes, take the bag on down to the skipper!" Jess ordered. Then turning back to face the man on the cutter, Jess yelled through his own bullhorn, "Our captain has a gash in his head and appears to need some medical attention. He's there on the plane's wing!" Jess paused momentarily before he asked, "Where are you taking all the passengers?"

"San Francisco General Hospital!" the man on the cutter said.

"All right!" Jess answered. He aimed his bullhorn toward Rick and yelled, "We'll know where to get in touch with you, skipper!"

Rick waved a limp hand with blood on the fingers.

CHAPTER 6

FROM THE BAY TO the hospital, the news media made its presence felt with picture-taking and interviewing of all survivors physically able to pose or talk. The news of the successful rescue of the plane's passengers after the accident in the bay was airing on all the local TV and radio stations in San Francisco soon after their admittance at the hospital. By the time all the injured passengers had been treated and assigned to their hospital rooms, the severity and trauma of the accident had dwindled to personal experiences associated with the rescue.

★ ★ ★

After the Novocain injection in ER, Rick's head felt strangely numb. As he lay on the bed, he had a hard time concentrating on the nurse's chatter. "Dr. Kendall is an orthopedic surgeon. We see her often here at this hospital, which is buzzing right now about her handling of the passengers after the plane crash," a tall, willowy nurse said excitedly while she assisted a man in a white coat as they placed a small bandage over Rick's head wound.

"Eh, who is Dr. Kendall?" Rick asked in a wondering voice.

"Oh, I thought you knew!" the nurse went on giddily. Dr. Kendall is the one you helped out of the plane. Everyone is talking about how the captain of the ship saved the doctor's life. It's just like a fairy-tale ending."

When the bandaging was completed, the man in the white coat said with a slight chuckle, "This patch above your ear is no fairy tale." Then he handed Rick his business card and added, "I'm Dr. Phillips. If you have any trouble recovering from your wound, please call me."

"Okay, doc," Rick answered, "but I don't see any lit candles, so I shouldn't be too worried, right?"

"Six stitches were required," the doctor said with a smile touching his lips. "Your hair line should cover what my tailoring missed." Then he pointed to a bag sitting on the floor and added, "That bag came with you. If there's a change of clothes in it and you want to shower, there's a place just down the hall." He paused as he moved over to a wall cabinet and got a plastic head cap. He placed the cap on the bag, turned back to Rick, and said, "Be sure you wear this in the shower."

Preparing to leave, the doctor evidently felt it was necessary to add his praises of Dr. Kendall. "Captain, the person you saved did a super job on the injured, especially under the circumstances." He paused and then continued, "It's ironic, but I heard recently that she is planning to take time off from her practice to study medical care for catastrophic accidents. And she is going to China for her study."

When the two left his cubicle, Rick got off the small bed. Despite the numbness lingering about his ear, he felt fine. As he headed for the shower, he realized he owed Jess a big thanks for sending along the change of clothes.

After his shower, the talk about Dr. Kendall lingered on his mind. Or was it the feel of her in his arms back on the airplane? He smiled inwardly while he stepped out into a wide corridor. The emergency area in this hospital was huge. His chances of seeing her again were mighty slim.

★ ★ ★

Pat's self-control was running thin. Two nurses and a doctor, all women, kept interrupting each other while dressing her head injury.

"The captain of that ship is gorgeous, Dr. Kendall," one of the nurses babbled. "And ironically, he has a head injury also. I was told who he was by the nurse attending Dr. Phillips's area here in ER, so I went to see for myself."

"ER is all abuzz about him. He's tall and dark, and he's—" the other nurse started.

"Virile-looking!" the attending doctor finished the sentence.

"Not you too, Sarah!" Pat voiced her astonishment.

"I had to see for myself what all the excitement was about," Sarah replied. "After all, here in ER, we seldom have this kind of passion to stir our environment."

"Remember ladies," Pat spoke curtly. She had heard enough of the prattle. "Looks can be deceiving. Most of those types are too self-centered, too shallow, at least for my interest." She paused, allowing a thin smile to cross her face. "Don't get me wrong. I'm certainly grateful that he and his ship were in the bay tonight."

After he found his way around the various cubicle sections and followed the exit signs out of ER, Rick got lucky. He saw her again. She was wearing the usual surgery scrubs and a narrow bandage was wrapped around her head. Her back was to him as she leaned on the counter at a nurse's station. She was studying something on a clipboard in her hand.

He turned and walked in her direction. Despite the loose-fitting scrubs, her leaning position outlined long, slender legs under the pants. His dinner date with the model crossed his mind but only for a moment. Two steps away and just loud enough for her to hear, he said, "I understand you are the Florence Nightingale of the airways."

Pat didn't turn immediately. She didn't have to. The wall mirror in the nurse's station was in her line of vision. A tall man with broad shoulders stood behind her. The bandage above his left ear was partially hidden by curly dark hair that looked slightly wet. White teeth showed through lips that parted into a smile. *The nurses are right about his appearance*, she thought, *but you can't tell a book by its cover.*

"And you must be the brave knight of the seaways," Pat countered as she turned around to meet him.

Her eyes locked on his during the long pause that followed before she held out her hand. "Thanks for saving my life, captain. I realize that is small compensation, but right now, I can't think of anything else to say."

"I can!" Rick said, shaking her hand.

But her gaze had moved up to his bandaged head. "I hope your injury wasn't serious?"

"Only a scratch, and I'm glad to see that you required no major cosmetic surgery." His eyes, full of smiles, remained leveled on hers.

"Captain," Pat said and placed the clipboard back on the counter before she continued, "The other passengers have been asking to meet you, and it will only take a few minutes. Please, if you will come with me?" She started down the hall.

Rick caught up with her quickly. "But doctor, I'm really more interested in knowing you better, maybe over dinner. How can I reach you?"

About as subtle as his ship's derrick, Pat thought, but she stopped. "Of course, I'll accept a dinner invitation with you, captain, but as my guest." She reached for a card in the pocket of her blouse. "Please call me at your convenience." She handed him the card and then turned and entered a cubicle where a doctor and nurse were bandaging Hok's shoulder.

"Mr. Hokusai Utamaro, this is Rick Scanlon, the captain of the ship's crew that got us safely out of the plane tonight." Pat made the introduction.

As he extended his free hand to Rick, the man said, "Please ... call me Hok. It's much easier."

Rick shook the hand of an Asian man whose broad smile changed to a deeply earnest expression when he said, "Captain, I'm sincerely thankful for you and your crew saving my life tonight." He paused. His dark eyes blinked several times before he added, "With the water pouring in and my sore shoulder, I didn't think I was going to get out of that plane before it sank. We passengers cannot thank you and your crew enough for being in the bay tonight—"

"Excuse me, Hok," Pat interrupted. "But the other passengers want to meet the captain, so we must move on."

"I understand," Hok said. "Before you go, captain, I'm curious. You do any business in Hong Kong?"

"Not as much as I would like. Why do you ask?"

"Maybe I can be of help. We have been looking for shippers for that area." His white teeth showed when he added, "Being from Hong Kong was influential in getting my job with an import firm here in San Francisco." Hok turned to the nurse and asked, "Would you please get my wallet from my coat? I think it's with the rest of my stuff in the box under my bed."

After the nurse handed Hok his wallet, Rick exchanged business cards with him and then started to leave, but Hok was persistent. "I feel sure you will be hearing from my firm."

"I hope so," Rick replied. "And the next time we meet, I hope neither of us is wrapped in bandages." He turned and left the room with Pat as Hok handed his wallet back to the nurse.

Then while the nurse returned the wallet to Hok's stuff under the bed, he asked, "Will you please get my cell phone from my coat pocket?" After the nurse handed Hok the phone, he waited until she had left the room before he dialed a number.

"Willard, this is Hok. In case you are aware of the plane crash in the bay tonight, I was one of the passengers rescued—"

Hok paused for a while, the phone still to his ear. Finally, he said, "Here in Frisco's General Hospital." There was another long pause before he said, "A sore shoulder that I hope will allow me to take the day off tomorrow." Then after a short pause, he said, "The other reason I'm calling is I believe the shipper that you were asking about has been found."

CHAPTER 7

After meeting the rest of the plane's passengers, Rick called his date on his way out of the hospital. He listened to Sheila Winthrop's shrill voice. "No! I haven't been watching the news!" It grated on his ear like an out of tune guitar. "I'm watching an old Marilyn Monroe movie on the tube! I've been sitting here in my new cocktail dress all night, waiting for you!"

"Sorry to spoil your evening. You'll have to believe me. An airplane hit my ship in the bay tonight, and that is what has caused my delay." He paused momentarily. "Save the dress for another occasion. I'll bring pizza or something. Let's stay in tonight, okay?"

"Well! That's not my idea of an exciting evening! And I think you could have called me sooner about the accident!" The banging of the receiver still rang in his ear as he left the hospital.

Sheila Winthrop is probably the only person in the entire city unaware of the accident in the bay tonight, Rick thought. As he hailed a cab near the hospital, his thoughts remained on Shelia. *I wouldn't bother with her tonight except it's been awhile since I've even seen a woman let alone being with one, but that's the way of life for a seafarer,* he rationalized quietly. An hour later in front of Sheila's apartment building, Rick paid the cabdriver and then entered the building, carrying a large pizza carton.

When Rick got off the elevator on Sheila's floor, her face was set like stone when she opened her door to his knock. "It's about time!" she snapped and then turned abruptly and moved on back toward her living room, leaving Rick to close the door.

"Better late than never," Rick muttered, barely audible. He headed on to Sheila's kitchen, where he placed the pizza on the table. After he fixed two quick scotch and sodas from Sheila's liquor supply, he took the drinks to the living room.

He held onto one of the drinks and set the other on an end table by the couch where he sat down. As he looked over at Sheila, who sat rigidly in a nearby cushioned chair, Rick said, "When you feel the urge, tell me, and I will hand you your drink." He paused a few moments and then added, "This way, I'll feel more confident that I won't get your drink tossed in my face."

The brief levity helped. A smile touched her lips. It was the break in the chilly atmosphere Rick was looking for. He took a long swallow from his drink before he said, "I've got to admit your ability to select clothes that become you never wavers. That dress, what there is of it, is stunning."

Sheila's petulant mood vanished. She rose from her chair and pirouetted in front of him. The dress she wore was black and exposed more of her than the dress which contained spaghetti shoulder straps for style, in her case, and not for need to hold the garment in place.

"I'm glad you like it." She had smoky eyes and a voice to match when the mood was right. "I'll wear this for you tomorrow night."

Rick set his drink on the lamp table by his chair and then rose slowly and pulled her close. "Sorry, but I can't make it tomorrow night. The airplane accident has changed my work schedule."

"What! Not again! I've had—"

But his kiss sealed her lips, and the embrace lingered. Tense shoulder muscles gradually relaxed under Rick's hands. Soft moans stirred from deep in her throat. When tongues began their slow exploration, he reached for the fastener in back of the dress. After a slight pull of the zipper, the dress slipped easily to the floor. She wore nothing underneath.

Her hands had also been busy. After they moved into the bedroom, there were two separate piles of clothes left on the floor. With long, slender legs wrapped around his waist, all thoughts of the rescue and Dr. Pat Kendall faded from Rick's mind.

CHAPTER 8

"ISN'T IT ABOUT TIME the *Raleigh* joined the Smitzer fleet?" Sam Pollster, general manager of Oakland-based Smitzer Shipping, said from behind his desk.

It was the following morning after the ship's arrival in Oakland. The GM and Rick had spent an hour talking about the rescue in the bay before they got down to business. His secretary had just entered with Rick's check and had left it on Sam's desk. He scrawled his name across the bottom of the certificate before he handed it to Rick.

"Not yet," Rick replied, glancing at the amount before pocketing the check. "I still like the feel of her deck under my feet," he said, emphasizing the word *my*. Then as he rose to leave, he added, "But thanks for the offer. Hell, you never know. I may change my mind one of these days."

Late in the afternoon of that same day, Rick was tempted to call Sam. Stacks of papers piled like meld cards in a canasta game lay on his desk. He was in his quarters aboard the *Raleigh*, trying to decide which bills he could pay and which he could hold a while longer without alarming his creditors. *And I wanted to be an independent mariner,* he told himself for the hundredth time, but lately, that thought was weighing heavier on his mind.

His sea legs had come from a four-year hitch in the US Navy, spending most of his time aboard a carrier. Starting out as a seaman in the deck gang, he had asked for and received a transfer to the bridge crew as his interest in seamanship and navigation increased. Radar bearings, plotting courses, depth soundings, and celestial observations intrigued him.

For those interested and those who could qualify, the navy offered specialty programs. Rick had taken advantage of one of them, their diving school at the Naval Diving and Salvage Training Center at Panama City, Florida, where he had learned the basic scuba skills, including dive planning, decompression chamber operations, and salvage work. This diver training had occurred near the end of his navy tenure.

When he left the navy, he and a shipmate named Jake Flowers, who had attended the diver and salvage school with him, returned to Florida, bought a two-hundred-foot-long, shallow-draft ship, and went into the salvage business. With a five-man crew, they contracted with the coast guard and anyone else who wanted the ocean depths probed for wrecks along both coasts of Florida during the mid-90s. But after ship payments and crew's salaries, they were barely eking out a living.

Then one week while docked in the Keys, their luck had changed. The crew had become acquainted with an old fisherman crippled from a war wound at Omaha Beach, or so he said. Lester was his name, and he claimed he had only the one name. He fished every day off the end of the pier close to where the salvage ship was docked. It wasn't long before the crew was inviting Lester aboard for lunch, and this gesture was reciprocated with his catch of the day handed over to the ship's cook. And Lester was a good fisherman, too good in the minds of the crew when the frequency of the daily fish meal began to lose its appeal.

But Rick soon noticed that Lester's daily visits were growing longer, and he was seen all over the ship, examining the diving equipment, looking into the crew's quarters, checking out the engine room and the galley. Then near the end of the week-long idle period when Rick and Jake were alone on the bridge, Lester asked them to join him for a drink at Sloppy Joe's that evening.

But Lester was not alone in the bar when Jake and Rick had arrived at sundown. A dark-featured man with oily black hair and dressed in a white suit sat with Lester at a corner table.

"This is Cesar Rodriguez from Honduras," Lester said when Rick and Jake sat down. "He wants to buy your ship."

Momentarily stunned by the offer, Rick and Jake could only stare in surprise at Rodriguez, who appeared to be about their age.

"Why our ship?" Rick was first to speak.

Rodriguez did not answer immediately. He reached in his pocket for a long, slender cigar, then after he lit it, he watched the smoke curl up toward the ceiling before he shifted his gaze to Jake and then to Rick. "I in seafood business." His broken English came from a syrupy voice oozing deep within his throat. "We ship lobster tails to Miami. Your ship is size I need. Will you sell?"

"How much you pay?" Jake, still reeling from surprise with the chance to sell, mimicked Rodriguez's language pattern.

"I show you price on paper," Rodriguez said after he removed a pen and piece of paper from his inside coat pocket. He wrote something on the paper while he positioned his free hand to block the vision of Rick and Jake. Then after he folded the paper, he moved it across the table between Rick and Jake. Rick opened the paper. The figure was $400,000.00 with the added words, "Cash—no paperwork." It was considerably more than their ship was worth. Jake opened his mouth, but a sharp kick against his shin snapped his jaws shut.

"May I use your pen?" Rick asked. After he took the pen, he played Rodriguez's game. With his free hand, he shielded his writing and started by crossing out the figure on the sheet and replacing it with $800,000.00. Then he wrote in large letters, "Cash tonight—no paperwork and you have bought yourself a ship." Rick waited for a nod from Jake. It was slow in coming, and when it did, it was accompanied with a frown and gradually widening eyes.

Rick refolded the paper and handed it back to Rodriguez, who studied the writing for a few minutes. With his voice edged in irritation, he said, "Be off ship by midnight. I pay you at dock."

When the sale was completed as planned, Rick and Jake gave each crew member a thousand-dollar bonus and then rented rooms for everyone in a hotel on shore for the rest of the night. Over coffee the following morning in the hotel's coffee shop when Jake was finally alone with Rick, he asked, "Now that our partnership has been dissolved and you are moving on while I'm staying, tell me something. How the hell did you figure that Rodriguez would go for the bigger number?"

"Well, as you know, since the salvage work lately has been so lousy, we have been thinking about getting out of the business. Since I had already sent our ship's certificate back to the Coast Guard documentation center, there was nothing further to link our name with the ship. And secondly, we both had a damn good idea that the seafood business was not this guy's main business, right?" With Jake's nod, Rick continued,

"About the time that Lester started coming aboard for lunch, the coast guard had sunk a ship out in the gulf that was about the size of ours. I got this over the Internet on Keysnews.com. It wasn't an easy job for the coast guard. They had quite a gun battle before the ship went down, but according to the news account, a large amount of dope was found aboard the sunken wreck."

Rick waited for a refill by the waitress before he continued, "I was gambling that Rodriguez and Lester were part of the drug smuggling operation. But I felt it was worth the gamble, especially when Rodriguez wanted to deal in cash without any entitlements or legal documents."

Jake studied Rick for a few moments and then said, "You do like a challenge, don't you?"

The remark stunned Rick momentarily. It brought to mind his high school English class in which Rick was generally the only one to finish the various pop quizzes in the allotted time required. At the end of the term, Rick's habit had prompted the teacher to say, "Since you seldom have the assigned lessons completed on time, you do like a challenge, don't you?"

The clinking of Jake's coffee cup against its saucer halted Rick's musing. After swallowing the last of his coffee, Jake said, "Well, ex-partner, thanks to you I'm out of debt, and for the first time in my life, I've got some money." He paused briefly and then asked, "What are you going to do with your share?"

"Buy another ship," Rick replied. "Only this time, I'm going for the cargo business. What about you?"

"Not me," Jake answered. "I'm hanging around Florida for a while. Maybe do a little gambling over in the Bahamas."

CHAPTER 9

THAT WAS FIVE YEARS *ago,* Rick mused. *I should have stayed in Florida with Jake.* But his reverie was interrupted by the telephone.

"Hello!" Rick answered.

"Rick Scanlon?"

"Yes! Speaking."

"I'm Willard Dallworth, business manager of Pacific Rim Importers. Hok Utamaro is with our company. I am calling for two reasons. First, I want to congratulate you and your crew for the gallant rescue of the airplane passengers in the Bay three nights ago. It was certainly fortunate for Hok and the other passengers and crew of the plane that you and your ship happened to be where you were when they crashed." After a slight pause, he continued, "And the second reason is regarding business. Hok tells me you might be interested in doing some shipping out of Hong Kong. Is that correct?" There was a subtle change in his voice. It held a note of confidentiality. It sounded as if he had moved the phone closer to his mouth.

"Yeah, I could be," Rick answered.

"I know of a lucrative shipping contract with a Hong Kong firm," Dallworth continued. "However, there are some risks that I won't care to discuss over the telephone. Are you still interested?"

"I am accustomed to taking risks. Shipping is a risky business," Rick answered soberly while he glanced at the stack of bills. "What about this contract?"

"I would like to talk with you about it at the Federal Building here in San Francisco. It's at 450 Golden Gate Avenue. Are you familiar with the location?"

"Just a minute," Rick replied, pausing to study a large map of the bay area mounted on the wall above his desk. "Is it about three or four blocks off Market Street?"

"That's it," Dallworth said. "Can you meet me there at ten o'clock in the morning?"

"Yes."

"I have a better idea," Dallworth said. "It would be more convenient to meet at Peat's Coffee Shop at the corner of Van Ness and Turk, which is near the Federal Building. Will that work for you?"

"Yes," Rick answered and then voiced the thought, "I assume Hok will be with you. Otherwise how—"

"No, Hok will not be with me," Dallworth interrupted. "But he gave me a lengthy description of your appearance. However, just in case of a delay in our get-together, here is my cell number, and I would appreciate yours if you have one." The conversation ended with the exchange of cell numbers.

With his left arm in a sling, Hok sat across from Dallworth while he listened to the phone conversation. When his boss hung up, Hok said, "Well, it's a start, right?"

"Yes," Dallworth answered. "And thanks again, Hok, for suggesting this shipper. If the rumors we are both hearing about his financial condition are true, he should be the man who can help the DEA with this drug matter."

Hok studied his boss for a few moments before he asked, "Willard, I'm curious. How did you get involved in this drug situation?"

"Your question is certainly reasonable now that I have you implicated," Dallworth answered, a thin smile crossing his face. "A fraternity brother of mine from college is the DEA agent here in San Francisco. We have kept in touch over the years, not socially but with the Christmas card thing and an occasional phone call."

Dallworth paused to take a brief call from his secretary before he continued, "Evidently, there are a lot of drugs being shipped to our country along the California coast. This fraternity brother asked for my help because of my experience with shippers. He feels he can stop most of this drug trafficking by nailing a drug dealer in Hong Kong. And since you're from there is why I asked you to get involved with me." Dallworth stopped talking but kept looking at Hok. With an elbow propped on the arm of his chair and his chin resting on his hand, he was silent for several moments. "Hok, what I'm about to tell you I want your promise to keep just between you and me, okay?"

"Okay," Hok answered hesitantly. "I'm listening."

"Well, it's just an intuition of mine and based only on rumors while at college, but this frat brother, whose name is Ed Broadman, is supposed to be of the Islam faith. He has the looks of a Muslim but not the name. His roommate at college claimed that Broadman made phone calls speaking in Pashto, which I believe is the native language of most Afghans. These calls were made only when Broadman thought his roommate was out of earshot." Dallworth paused momentarily with deep furrows lining his face. "It seems to me that from rumors and the news media, the more of these drug lords are caught, the hotter the drug trafficking is becoming along the California coast. It makes me wonder if this guy Broadman is who he claims to be."

A thin smile masked Dallworth's wrinkled brow when he added, "I know my hunch is judging the character of this man by profiling rather than fact, but I'm not getting into the deep water with him until I know more about him, understand?"

With a nod from Hok, Dallworth added, "Now that you know my feelings, do you have any objections about getting involved?"

Before Hok could reply, Dallworth's phone rang again. After he answered, he covered the mouthpiece with his other hand, "Hok, you will have to excuse me. My secretary is adamant that I take this phone call."

Hok rose to leave. "Willard, before I go, I want you to know as long as you are paying my salary, I have no objections."

CHAPTER 10

Rick left early for his appointment the following morning. It was a bright, sunny, winter day, the kind of day with just the right temperature to put some spring in his steps as he walked along the pier to where he could catch a cab.

Ten minutes after he had started his walk, he heard his name called. It came from someone on the bow of a small ship moored at the dock. Rick looked up, shielding his eyes from the sun's rays.

"Don't you remember your ex-partner?" The voice came from Jake Flowers.

"Well, I'll be damned!" Rick declared. "As I live and—"

"Continue to borrow!" Jake ended the adage.

"Man, you're way ahead of me!"

"Come aboard for a cup," Jake said, motioning toward the gangplank. "I want you to see a real salvage ship."

The cup of coffee lasted for more than an hour. The state-of-the-art vessel contained facilities to maximize the efficiency for deploying and retrieving divers while equipping them with numerous observation tools and cutting torches to aid in their salvage work at the ocean floor. The ship also had the latest navigational/communications systems and computers to provide the crew with information about the ever-changing ocean depths.

"My share from the sale of our old salvage boat dwindled down to zero in about six months," Jake said. He and Rick were finishing their coffee in the galley after they had inspected the salvage ship from the engine room to the bridge. "But it was fun while it lasted. And the

Bahamas is a nice place to be in the winter. I would still be there if they didn't have those damn casinos. So when my money ran out, I got the chance to skipper this beauty." Jake paused, looking into his coffee cup for a few moments before continuing, "Things were going well for me until the owner went broke."

"You say the owner used this ship as a hobby?" Rick asked. "I like his style."

"He was in some kind of hi-tech stuff here in Silicon Valley, but his firm went down the drain like many of the dot-coms did a few years ago. My job now is trying to sell this boat for the bonding company," Jake replied.

"What kind of interest have you had?"

"A few lookers but no offers in the three weeks it's been for sale," Jake answered. Then as he eyed Rick, he asked, "Why don't you sell that old bucket of yours and get back in the salvage business?" With a smile, he then added, "And take me on as your first mate."

Rick drained his coffee cup and prepared to leave. "The idea is appealing. I still have a hankering for the salvage business, but right now, with the heavy mortgage on the *Raleigh*, this probably isn't a good time to sell. I'll—"

"Wait a minute," Jake interrupted. "The *Raleigh* is a big freighter and worth a lot more than this salvage ship right now because of the heavy demand in the shipping business. I'd be willing to wager that you could put a hell of a dent in your mortgage by making the switch."

Rick leveled his eyes on Jake while thinking, *Jake, you always were a good salesman. That's how you talked me into the salvage business years ago.* A smile creased Rick's face when he said, "Ah, what the hell? Give me your business card."

Rick was twenty minutes late getting to the coffee shop on Van Ness and Turk. He had called Dallworth on his cell during the cab ride. Immediately after he entered the café, a man sitting at a corner table stood up and waved Rick on back to the other empty chair at his table. "I am Willard Dallworth," the man who appeared to be in his midforties said when Rick reached the table. They shook hands and then sat down.

"And I am Rick Scanlon and apologize again for being late."

"No problem. As you can see with laptops and restaurants equipped for hi-tech, time is seldom wasted," Dallworth answered, closing his computer and placing it on the floor by his chair.

True to his words, after they had exchanged business cards, Dallworth began explaining the purpose of their meeting. "One of my fraternity brothers from college is the Drug Enforcement Agency's special agent in charge here in San Francisco. His name is Ed Broadman. He is looking for a shipper to help him bust a drug ring supplying the West Coast traffickers."

Dallworth paused for a drink of coffee. He was a stocky-built man with a rubicund face that seemed to glow as he talked. "This dope syndicate operates out of Hong Kong," he continued. "And fronts as Imperial Salvage of Hong Kong. We have done some business with them. Three shiploads of scrap metal so far." A fleeting smile crossed his face. "Apparently, my firm has been doing more business than I realized, but Broadman will tell you about that. He is expecting us at the Federal Building in the agency's fourteenth-floor offices." Dallworth eyed Rick intently. "That is, if you are still interested."

Questions buzzed in Rick's head like persistent bees, but the *Raleigh's* insufferable mortgage burned his brain with greater tenacity. He studied Dallworth for a few moments and then asked, "I'm assuming the payment for this kind of venture will be worthwhile?"

"I can assure you of that," Dallworth replied.

Rick swallowed the rest of his coffee before he got up from his chair. "Let's go," he said.

On the way out of the coffee shop, there was a newsstand near the cash register. "Drug Shipment Seized near Fisherman's Wharf" emblazoned the chronicle's headline. Dallworth pointed to one of the men pictured on the front page. "That's the guy we are going to see," he said.

Rick got only a quick glance at a tall man in the picture before Dallworth picked up his change and headed out the door.

CHAPTER 11

FROM THE RESTAURANT, THE Federal Building was approximately three blocks away. They walked briskly along busy Golden Gate Avenue while discussing the plight of the San Francisco 49ers. By the time they had reached the entrance to the Federal Building, both were in agreement that the team needed considerable improvement before they were of playoff caliber.

Entering the busy ground floor lobby, they had to wait several minutes for an available elevator. At the fourteenth floor, they stepped off the elevator and entered a smaller lobby containing a couch and two lounge chairs and a smiling receptionist sitting behind a desk.

"We are Dallworth and Scanlon," Willard said. "We are running a bit late for our ten o'clock appointment to see Mr. Broadman. However, I did notify his secretary that we wouldn't be on time."

"Yes, I was told by her that you would be late." The receptionist's smile deepened. She pressed one key on her telephone before she picked up the receiver and announced, "Mr. Dallworth and Mr. Scanlon are here."

She cradled the receiver and directed them down a long, quiet corridor to a waiting room where the wall-to-wall carpeting made the room appear larger than it was. A gray-haired woman at a polished mahogany desk looked up from her computer. The name Silvia Harding was etched in a nameplate near her telephone.

"Good morning, Mr. Dallworth," she said, with a thin smile.

Willard acknowledged her greeting while he pointed to a stack of papers on her desk. "I hope my old fraternity brother isn't keeping you on overload these days."

"No more than usual," she replied. With the same meager smile still creasing her face, she turned to Rick and said, "I assume this is Mr. Scanlon."

"That's right," Willard answered.

With the acknowledgment, she ushered them through a door that opened into a corner office overlooking the city's midtown.

"Mr. Broadman will be with you soon. Please sit down." She motioned to four straight-back, cushioned chairs arranged in a semicircle facing a large desk clearly designed for an executive. A telephone, scratch pad, and large manila envelope were the only items on the wide surface of the desk. Seascapes and pictures of the president and the DEA director hung on the fabric-covered walls.

"Mr. Broadman likes coffee about this time. May I bring you gentlemen some or possibly tea or a soft drink?"

"Coffee, black, is fine for me," Willard said.

"Same," Rick said.

The secretary soon returned with a tray containing three cups of coffee. She placed two of the cups on a small table between Willard and Rick and set the third one on the desk. Then, she left the room.

Although sitting in the chair was more comfortable than its austere appearance implied, Rick had a strange feeling he was being watched. The room's silence compounded his suspicion, but his concern was short-lived. From behind him, a door opened and closed.

"Good to see you again, Willard." A tall, square-shouldered man extended his hand to Dallworth.

"The feeling is mutual, Ed," Dallworth said then, nodding toward Rick. "Shake hands with Rick Scanlon, the guy I called you about."

Broadman had a firm grip and white teeth that dazzled from a baked-brown face. His dark eyes were the same color as his hair, which had a polished look from the morning sun streaming through the window. There was a slightly awkward gait to his walk as he moved on around and sat at his desk.

"Congratulations on your job yesterday at the wharf," Dallworth said, referring to the newspaper article he and Rick had seen at the coffee shop. "All our wars are not being fought these days in the Middle East, right?"

"Thanks, Willard. Yes, and for us to win this particular war, we have to hit the syndicates," Broadman answered, wasting no time in addressing the reason for this meeting. "One of them is a legitimate company, or I should say it fronts as a legal operation. But the type of business it does is an excellent ploy for shipping drugs without detection to the States." He paused to open the large envelope on his desk.

Broadman's speaking voice reminded Rick of a man wading through water that covered a treacherous bottom. The DEA official pronounced each word slowly and distinctly as if making sure his intellectual progress was clear before moving on to the next thought.

"Could it be they are using the type of shipping I heard about recently?" Willard interjected.

"What's that?"

"Submarines!"

Broadman's hands stopped moving on the envelope. For an instant, he seemed to stare at Willard without seeing him. Then with his eyes switching back and forth from Willard to the envelope, he continued opening it, but his hand movements were much slower. "We have heard those rumors but have nothing yet to substantiate them. I am curious. Where did you hear your rumor?"

"My brother-in-law is a navigator on a scientific research submarine with the weather bureau. They sail out of San Diego. He told me that a couple of times, they have detected a mysterious sub but that it has always been either too fast or too sly for them to get any kind of identification."

Willard's answer seemed to satisfy Broadman. There was no more fumbling around with the contents of the envelope. He pulled out a handful of pictures and looked at them briefly. Then he got up from his chair and walked back around to the front of his desk to face Willard and Rick. But this time, his uneven movement was noticeable. He walked with a slight limp.

Broadman handed Rick three pictures of an obese-looking Chinese man dressed in a business suit. The size of the man obscured his age, but Rick guessed he was in his late fifties.

"That is Fuchou, owner of Imperial Salvage of Hong Kong," Broadman said. "He has only the one name. He is a junkyard broker, buying scrap metal wherever available in the world and selling it to metal-fabricating companies in China and Japan. Our plan is for Willard to arrange a sale of scrap metal to Fuchou and you do the hauling." Broadman paused momentarily before he asked, "You are an independent hauler, right?"

"Yes," Rick answered, looking at Broadman. "Why? Is that important?"

"Fuchou has always asked for an independent hauler," Willard broke in. "We don't know why. It could be that some independent haulers don't mind getting involved in the drug trade. It also could be because the corporate shippers generally try harder not to return with empty holds, which impedes Fuchou's drug operation." Willard turned to Broadman and then said, "But Ed can tell you about that."

"After Willard called us about you," Broadman continued, "we did some investigating on your recent hauling. Break-bulk-type shipping is convenient for the drug trade. Hauling scrap metal to Japan, as you have been doing, and returning with only ballast water in the holds is ideally suited for this clandestine operation."

Rick's skeptical look caused Broadman to stop talking momentarily while he moved back behind his desk and sat in his chair. "We believe the dope is sealed in tubes and placed inside the cargo holds after, as in your case, the scrap metal is removed and before the holds are refilled with ballast water for the return trip to the States."

When Broadman paused to clear his throat, Rick said, "We usually discharge ballast water before entering the bay to allow the ship easier access over the bar." As he eyed Broadman gravely, Rick continued, "Even though some ballast water usually remains in the holds, these tubes containing the dope will probably be exposed."

"We are aware of that," Broadman said. "However, we understand there is usually a considerable amount of sediment in the bottom of these holds that doesn't get discharged. Am I correct?"

"That's true," Rick confirmed. "So you are saying these tubes are buried in the sediment, but how is this done without the crew being aware of it?"

"This Fuchou is clever," Broadman answered. "Our reports are he usually throws a party for the crew immediately after the ship is unloaded and before the holds are refilled with ballast water. At the time of the party, the two or three members of the crew staying aboard to watch the ship are not forgotten. A couple of Fuchou's henchmen, with permission from the captain at the party, will take the watch plenty of the party refreshments, especially the liquor. Then while the watch is distracted with this unexpected benevolence, some more of Fuchou's men will steal aboard the ship and store or more probably bury the dope in the hold's sediment."

CHAPTER 12

RICK REFLECTED ON WHAT Broadman had said. *If I had the courage of my own convictions, I would walk out of here right now,* he thought, but curiosity trumped his morality. "What happens back here in the States? How does the dope leave the ship without being detected?"

"Needless to say, all kinds of people are involved in the drug business. Some could be from this office or from the coast guard or even the harbor patrol, but at any rate, after the ship docks, we think the dope is removed from the holds at night and stored under the pier near the ship. Later, possibly a day or two, a boat, maybe a tug, will dock in the vicinity of the ship. That night, the stored contraband will be taken aboard the tug, which will leave the following morning." Broadman paused for another drink of coffee before he continued, "With your help, our objective is to catch the distributors here in the States and nail Fuchou at the same time."

"But Fuchou is particular for us to use the shipper he recommends," Dallworth interjected. "And it has always been a foreign hauler, never an American. However, we are fortunate that Hok has already done some scrap metal business with this Fuchou and will be available to do some lobbying in your behalf."

When Dallworth paused for a drink of coffee, Broadman added, "The chronicle's broad coverage of the rescue in the bay included a brief paragraph regarding your present economic status. This, we believe, should be another reason for Fuchou to consider you as a hauler."

A long silence hung in the air. Broadman and Dallworth studied Rick while they awaited his reaction. Neither could be sure of what he was thinking. In the meantime, Rick was trying to organize the scattered thoughts in his mind. *I wouldn't be in a thousand miles of this drug situation if money wasn't so damn critical,* and that thought burned his brain.

Then with an almost uncanny ability, Broadman seemed to read Rick's thoughts. "I mentioned that we did some investigating about your shipping business," he said, keeping his eyes on Rick. "We certainly intend to make this venture worthwhile to you." Rick's matching stare and continued silence forced Broadman to add, "We need you just as much as you need us."

Rick had to define what was before him and what was expected of him. There would be a risk to this type of shipping contract, but there was also the risk of bankruptcy hovering over his head like a dark cloud. He finally broke the long silence. "Okay, so you are asking me to put my ass on the line? What's in it for me? And it had better be worthwhile."

"A million dollars … plus expenses," Broadman replied.

"One million!" Rick blared. Abruptly, he leaned forward and returned Broadman's stare. "You haven't told me the whole story, right?"

"I have not," Broadman answered. "The last shipper we hired for this scam is with his ship somewhere on the bottom of the Philippine Sea. Our contact in Hong Kong claimed the dope had been stored properly in the ship's holds before being filled with ballast water. We believe that greed was the main reason for the mission's failure. Off the coast of Taiwan, the dope was being hijacked onto a small sailing boat when detected by one of Fuchou's planes."

Broadman paused for another drink of coffee before he continued, "To give you an idea of the type of operation you will be dealing with, Fuchou has a fleet of airplanes and torpedo boats that ply the southeastern coast of China and the Taiwan Strait. In the case of our hired shipper, the pilot of one of Fuchou's planes contacted one of the torpedo boats in the area and the two vessels in the act of confiscating the dope were sunk in short order." Broadman paused and then looked Rick squarely in the eye before he asked, "Are you still interested?"

Rick barely listened. Dollar signs floated behind his eyeballs. He turned to Dallworth. "Willard, I will get some help from you in soliciting this shipping business, right?"

Dallworth nodded. "As I already mentioned, Hok will be helping, and I will make the initial contact by telephone. I will also call two other Hong Kong firms requiring break-bulk-type shippers who we have been doing business with. I'll write letters of recommendation, including a newspaper clipping of your rescue. You can present the letters to each of the three firms during your personal calls."

Rick's puzzled look prompted Broadman to add, "We will expect you to solicit business from the companies that Willard is talking about. There is the possibility that you can pick up additional business with these two legitimate firms, but they are to be used only as a cover, understand?"

Rick nodded, but said nothing. *This will give my crew a chance for some well-earned time off,* he was thinking, *since it's going to take time to get the business settled in Hong Kong before any shipment of scrap metal. But how is my crew going to feel about the potential danger in this type of voyage? The promise of extra pay should solve that problem*, he reasoned. And knowing his crew as well as he did, he felt confident that no one would tip off Fuchou as to their venture.

Broadman and Dallworth waited. The only break in the long silence was Broadman reaching for his coffee cup. Finally, Rick turned to Dallworth. "Willard, I'll be ready to leave for Hong Kong just as soon as you and Hok make the initial contacts."

CHAPTER 13

As soon as Scanlon and Dallworth left, Ed Broadman reached inside a draw of his desk and pulled out the morning edition of the chronicle. Their visit had interrupted his reading.

Quickly, he scanned the article on the drug bust until he came to the paragraph about the Afghan drug kingpin, Ahmad Sattar. According to the paper, this man was responsible for shipping over a billion dollars' worth of heroin to the United States since the year 2000. The article indicated that drug trafficking on the West Coast had been reduced 30 percent since the start of the new century, and this particular drug lord was now in hiding.

A smile creased Broadman's face. *The 30 percent statistic is certainly correct for some drug lords but not all*, he thought while he glanced at the date on his telephone console. *Has it really been thirty years since I met my revered benefactor and moved to America?* He leaned back in his chair and propped his lame leg on a small footstool he kept handy behind his desk.

* * *

Faisal Hasan awakened from his sleep. There was pain in his leg. He listened. *Ah, yes, there it is.* Raindrops splattered on the tin roof. Rain always brought the dull ache. He got out of bed. Walking helped relieve some of the pain. Five years ago, the polio had been bad, but there had been little money. A teenager, Faisal lived with his father in the desolate mountain area east of Kandahar, Afghanistan.

He smiled through clinched teeth, thinking about what his father had told him yesterday. "When I thirteen like you, I live with pain!" his father had said while he was taking another drink of cheap wine. Then he showed Faisal the bullet hole in his arm for the hundredth time. It had happened when he was in the army. They were freedom fighters, he often said, fighting to take down an oppressive government.

But Faisal knew it was really a guerilla army made up of Afghans and other Muslims who were primarily mercenaries from Saudi Arabia, Algeria, and Egypt. He had read about it in a book. This army was organized to overthrow the Marxist government in control of Afghanistan at the time and supported by the USSR. But when the guerillas were successful in driving out the Russian invaders and overthrowing the Marxist government, the resulting regime of Nazi-type Muslims had left the majority of Afghans in worse shape than before the uprising had started.

In the history book Faisal was reading, he noted that the freedom fighters were supported with billions of dollars from both Saudi Arabia and the United States. The help from Saudi Arabia did not surprise Faisal nearly as much as the aid from the United States, who, Faisal felt sure, was not a Muslim country. Later, he was to learn that America's support was due to their paranoia of Communism.

Faisal's mother had died when he was born, and the three older brothers had left home long ago, except for Bashir, who was back for one night last month. Bashir wore a new suit. He said he was on his way to the Orient to work on a gambling ship. Faisal could not recall when Bashir was without a deck of cards. Long after going to bed that night, Faisal could hear his dad and Bashir playing cards. The meager meals were even more frequent for a long time after Bashir had left.

Faisal hobbled over to an opening in the wall where a window used to be. A cool breeze came with the rain. Water had begun to puddle in the road thirty feet away. There was a loud clap of thunder followed by lightening. It streaked across the sky, outlining Doc Hakim's house on top of the distant hill. *I wonder if Doc is listening to the rain,* Faisal speculated quietly. They fished together now, but for a long time, he didn't like Doc. That was when he used to come to the house and drink with his father. The night the pain in his leg was the worst, Doc was drinking at the house. He took care of the leg, but Doc never drank after that.

Suddenly, two lights appeared through the rain. They seemed to be stationary in the road as the raindrops on the roof muffled all other sounds except the thunder.

Faisal was nearly hypnotized by the lights while he wondered if the car would ever pass in front of the house. Finally, there was a slight movement in the two lights. He listened hard. First, there was the faint rumble of a motor and then more movement of the lights. They moved up and down and sometimes sideways as the rumble grew louder.

It was a big car. It was almost even with the house when the sky brightened for an instant. Four heads were outlined in the car, two in front and two in the back. Just as the car passed the house, there was a crash of thunder and two other sounds, each a second apart, but they were muted by the thunder. Gradually, the car's sound faded, absorbed by the incessant raindrops on the roof.

Faisal turned to go back to bed, and then he stopped, remembering those two distinct sounds. Suddenly, he realized they had been gunshots. He turned around just as another bolt of lightning streaked the sky. There was something lying beside the road. It was shaped like a body.

Faisal slipped on his pants and crawled through the window opening. A man lay in the ditch. Despite the rain, blood was rapidly changing the color of his white shirt. His breathing sounded like razor blades rubbing together, but the man was too big to move. Quickly, Faisal tore the man's shirt in two and tied the pieces as tight as he could over the wound in the man's chest.

After he made sure the man was still breathing, Faisal got up and headed toward Doc Hakim's house. Two hours later, the wounded man was in one of Doc's bedrooms. Faisal spent the night there in an adjacent bedroom.

The next morning, Faisal returned to his home without learning who the wounded man was. But about a month later, he found out when he lost both his father and Doc Hakim on the same night. Faisal had awoken, coughing. Then he felt the blast of heat. He had just enough time to crawl through the window of his bedroom before the roof fell in. He couldn't stand, so he kept crawling. In the distance, there was another fire, and it was on top of the hill.

The sounds were far away, too far to be distinguishable. The darkness behind Faisal's eyes was soothing. Gradually, the sounds turned into shuffling footsteps mixed with low voices. Faisal woke up to daylight and staring eyes from men standing near his bed. One of them, a big man, placed a gentle hand on Faisal's shoulder, and he recognized the man immediately. Under his shirt's open collar, there was still a bandage. He leaned down and said, "We arrived too late to save your father and Dr. Hakim."

Faisal stayed only a few days at Ahmad Sattar's large home outside Kandahar before he became the only passenger on a plane loaded with boxes labeled, "Pistachio Nuts."

For the next ten years, Faisal's home was in Clearwater, Florida, with Floyd and Sarah Broadman, who were a retired couple with the same dark features as Faisal. Every few months, a courier delivered a box to the home. The package was just like the pistachio boxes that had come to America with Facial. Adoption papers were signed during his second year in Clearwater, and Faisal became Edward Broadman.

He returned to Afghanistan only once. When Ed was eighteen, he spent the entire summer at Ahmad's farm near Kandahar. Ahmad had two sons, Rahab and Malak, who were as big as their father and helped in the drug business only when they had to. Their interests were primarily drinking and brawling.

But Ed was intrigued by the entire heroin process. The planting, cultivation, and harvesting of the opium poppy plant as well as the morphine extraction and ultimate conversion to the heroin base held his complete interest. He often traveled with Ahmad to the poppy fields and the refinement labs and finally to the distribution centers.

He soon learned that the last phase was the one with the greatest risk and the most difficult to control. The distribution network consisted of individual groups that constantly changed. There was no cohesive organization like the Cosa Nostra.

Although he returned to Afghanistan only the one time, Ed kept in touch with Ahmad by telephone. During his senior year at the University of Miami, Ed was interviewed for a job with the Drug Enforcement Agency. When he was accepted, he and Ahmad devised a plan, and the plan had worked.

At the time when Ed had started with the agency, Afghanistan had been home to many drug traffickers. Competition among the various groups was often violent. With leads from Ahmad regarding the routing and conveyance of his competitors' contraband, Ed's record for apprehending drug shipments was unmatched. And one by one, Ahmad 's enemies in drug trafficking had either dropped out of business or had been persuaded to work for him by the enforcement efforts of Rahab and Malak.

Five years after Ed had started with the DEA, Ahmad Sattar had become the leader in the opium drug trade. His title had been created by the news media. Out of respect for their livelihood and out of fear as well as hate, Ahmad Sattar became the godfather to thousands of Afghans.

CHAPTER 14

THE RINGING OF THE telephone interrupted Broadman's reverie. "There is someone calling from Hong Kong," Sylvia's voice echoed over the receiver when he picked it up.

"Who is it?" Broadman asked.

"He wouldn't give his name. He said he had information in connection with your drug bust yesterday."

"Let one of the agents take it!" Broadman's voice was edged with irritation.

"The man says this information is for your ears only," Sylvia persisted.

"All right, I'll take it on the hotline!" Broadman replaced the receiver on his desktop phone and reached in a drawer for the receiver of another telephone.

"Hello!" Broadman said into the receiver. The following moment of silence became an eternity. Suddenly, Broadman knew he was a man being warned, but he wasn't sure why.

"Little brother." The words were in Pashto. "It has been too long. Much too long."

Broadman froze, breaking into a cold sweat. "Not too long for me, Bashir. How did you find me?"

"I have kept in touch with a few people around Kandahar," Bashir said, his voice low and threatening. "I know of your association with Sattar and how it began. I know where you work. I can make trouble for you, but that's not why I called."

Broadman felt the hammering inside his chest. "What do you want?"

"The irritation in your voice hurts me, Faisal. You are being unkind." Bashir's words seeped through the receiver as smoothly as palm oil in the hands of a masseur. Then his tone abruptly changed. "Your question is stupid! I want money but not for the purposes you think!"

"I'll be the judge of that!" Broadman snapped. Thoughts raced through his brain. *This is a kill job for Rahab and Malak.* But he then realized that they were probably in hiding with Ahmad.

"I want five hundred thousand dollars to buy you and your godfather a treasure map."

Broadman was stunned. His murderous thoughts jolted to a stop. "A treasure map! You are making the joke!"

"No joke, little brother. And Sattar can use the treasure since the American troops are now putting the squeeze on his drug operation."

Broadman riveted his attention on Bashir's words. He realized his brother had been updated on Ahmad 's current problem. "All right, I'm listening. What about this map?"

"That's better, little brother. When your godfather's drug operation is hurting, I knew you would listen for ways to help it."

"Come on! About the map!"

"A drug pusher named Kuang, who is a sailor on a Chinese freighter, on the dock one night watched two men fight another man for a body belt. Just before the guy with the belt was knifed, the belt was ripped from his body and thrown to the dock. Kuang, thinking the belt contained money, grabbed it and took off while the other two men were busy tossing the dead body into the bay. Kuang didn't know what he had until reading about the murder in the paper the next day. The dead man found in the bay was the son of the only survivor from a Japanese hospital ship that was sunk by an American submarine during WWII. And here's the kicker, Faisal. This ship was carrying treasure plundered by the Japs from their conquered territories."

There was interference on the line. Broadman waited anxiously for it to clear. He must learn Bashir's whereabouts in Hong Kong. Rahab and Malak would have to come out of hiding, pronto. He could send them by submarine. From what Dallworth was saying, it would be prudent to move the sub away from the coastal waters of California. Their new Russian Kilo 636 submarine, which was to be used for drug shipments to Western Europe, was still being outfitted in the Severodvinsk Navy yard in northwestern Russia. The crew, which had been handpicked by Ahmad, had already been sent to the Russian seaport on the White Sea for sub training.

"Kuang took the map, since it's really a navigation chart to his ship's captain, but it was of little use," Bashir went on when the static cleared. "The map is in code, and they have been unable to find a cartographer who can decipher it."

"Then why are you calling me?" Broadman asked bitterly.

"Because you have access to cartographers."

He is right, Broadman confirmed silently. The CIA had the finest cartographers in the world. Despite the urgency of keeping his identity concealed, his curiosity was aroused. "How much treasure is supposed to be in the sunken ship?"

"A billion dollars or more!"

"What!"

"That's right, little brother. This is a haul."

Thoughts flashed across Broadman's mind like fireflies at nighttime. Besides the use of cartographers, he also had access to naval records to review the history of sunken ships during the war with Japan. He didn't trust Bashir, but he knew he had to keep his brother on the hook until Rahab and Malak could dispose of him. He would use this time interval by trying to confirm that there was such a treasure and why it had not been discovered during the past sixty years.

"I will make no commitments until I check out the authenticity of your story," Broadman said while another thought crossed his mind. "And what is your expected payment if this transaction is completed successfully?"

"The money must be in cash, and my take is 10 percent of the purchase price." When there was no response after a long pause, Bashir asked, "How long will you need for your checking?"

Broadman hesitated. He wasn't sure of the time required for the research. "Give me your telephone number, and I will call you my answer as soon as I have completed my investigation."

"Don't play games with me, little brother. You will not have your hounds on my tail until I'm ready." The cold implacability was still in Bashir's voice. "I will call you in two days for your answer."

The phone clicked in Broadman's ear.

CHAPTER 15

BROADMAN WAS CORNERED. HE forced himself to think rationally and carefully. He realized Bashir had kept updated on the events in their home country. After the Americans had invaded Afghanistan, Ahmad and his sons had crossed the border into Pakistan and set up their base of operations near Quetta, the capital of the Baluchistan Province.

Their poppy farms and process centers had been allowed to flourish under the Taliban in exchange for weapons and manpower provided by Ahmad. But when the Taliban had been driven back into the mountains by the Americans, his drug operation had been placed in peril. Ahmad had to form his own guerrilla army and continue the war against the Americans to assure the survival of his drug operation.

But Broadman was ready when Bashir called two days after the previous call. He had personally spent hours researching naval records on ships sunk in the Pacific near the end of World War II, many of which were still classified. Bashir's accounting corresponded with the research. Two Japanese hospital ships had left Singapore bound for Japan on March 25, 1945. Five days later, as Bashir claimed, the one hospital ship, the *Jawa Maru*, was sunk near the entrance to the Taiwan Strait by an American submarine called the *USS Swordfish*, whose captain was nearly court-martialed for the flagrant violation.

The other hospital ship, the *Asaka Maru*, was still unaccounted for, and its last sighting was by one of our torpedo boats near Batan. But during Broadman's research, what convinced him of the treasure's possibility was the extent of the Japanese plundering in World War II. They even had a code name for it called "the Golden Lilly." Billions of dollars' worth of gold, silver, gems, artwork, jewelry, and platinum had been looted from their occupied nations of Southeast Asia and shipped back to Japan.

To simplify the logistics of transporting and handling this vast amount of plunder, much of it had been stored in warehouses in Manila for shipment to Japan; however, with the heavy blockade of Japan by the American submarines beginning late in 1943, the Japanese Navy had to devise clandestine methods of getting the loot back to the homeland. What they couldn't send by hospital ships, they stored in warehouses and buried in caves in and around Manila.

"Have you checked out my story?" Bashir's strident voice sounded over the phone

"Yes."

"Are you sending the money?"

"I will send the money by courier," Broadman spoke slowly. "The money will be in a large briefcase that will match his other piece of luggage."

"Wait, Faisal, how does the courier get that quantity of bills through customs in normal-sized luggage?"

"That is my problem, but be assured the briefcase is specially designed to avoid detection of the money," Broadman replied. "Before the briefcase is exchanged for the map, the courier will examine the document for its authenticity."

"So the courier will be a cartographer?" Bashir asked.

"No!" Broadman answered emphatically. "The document is to be folded so its contents are not revealed. Is that clear?"

"Yes."

"The courier will understand the rudiments on how to examine the parchment to determine if it cannot be copied. If the map is genuine, the courier will call me from his cell phone, and I will tell him how the money can be revealed to complete the transaction."

"And my commission. How do—"

"It will be included with the rest of the money in the briefcase," Broadman interrupted.

"When will the courier be here in Hong Kong?"

"He will arrive in two weeks." Broadman paused briefly before he continued, "The drop must be in a public place. You name the place and time. Keep in mind it will be checked out."

Transmission static distorted Bashir's voice momentarily. When it cleared, he said, "Your lack of trust grieves me, little brother."

This insolence rattled Broadman's patience. He remained silent, waiting for the information, but his mind was working overtime. He had things to do and a short time to do them. He had the courier in mind, but the man would have to be informed of the delivery process without being made aware of the plot.

The long silence ended. Bashir spoke slowly, making sure there was no interference, "The meeting place will be at the Dragon Head Bar in Kowloon. Its address is 34 Canton Road. And the phone number is 4522 6669."

"Just a minute!" Broadman ordered while he wrote the address on a scratch pad. "For this deal to be permanent, you will call me in one week at this same time, and I will explain how the money for map transfer is to be made in the bar. Remember, no call, no deal. Is that clear?"

"Yes."

"All right! When and what time for the meeting?"

"Two weeks from now on Saturday at 4:30 p.m." There was a click in Broadman's receiver.

CHAPTER 16

RICK WAS IN HIS private quarters aboard the *Raleigh*. It had been two days since his meeting with Broadman and Dallworth. He had already spoken to the crew about his planned trip to Hong Kong and the risk involved if a shipping contract was successful. No one had refused to make the voyage. All agreed the payback would be worth the gamble.

His preparations for making the trip had kept Rick so busy that he had forgotten to call Hok and thank him for arranging the potential business. He dialed Hok's number. After he heard Hok's greeting, Rick said, "This is Rick Scanlon. Hok, I certainly want to thank—"

"When are you leaving?" Hok's clear voice cut him off.

"In two weeks," Rick laughed. "Hok, I know you are in on the deal but at least give me a chance to thank you for recommending the *Raleigh's* services to your boss."

"You are welcome. I was glad to do it. And I want you to know that I will do my best to pave the way for your welcome by Fuchou."

"Thanks, Hok. I have a feeling I'm going to need all the help I can get."

"Only time will tell," Hok answered. "I will now plan on leaving for Hong Kong in about ten days. Hold just a minute please." After a short pause, he continued, "The cell phone number on your business card is current, right?"

"Yes."

"Please let my secretary know where you will be staying in Hong Kong. Incidentally, my grandparents want to meet you."

"Your grandparents?" Rick questioned, unsure he had heard correctly.

"Yes, my own parents were killed in an automobile accident when I was hardly old enough to remember them. Needless to say, I am eternally grateful to my grandparents for raising me. Their home in Hong Kong is the only home that I have ever known. Since you are responsible for me still breathing, they are anxious to meet you."

"Well, I hope you haven't overdone the rescue thing. See you in Hong Kong," Rick said. When he hung up the phone, his arm brushed some papers to the floor. Dr. Pat Kendall's business card was among them. He picked it up and thought about the date he had set with her for the following night. Then his phone rang again.

"May I speak to Rick Scanlon?" Ed Broadman's stern voice sounded through the receiver.

"Speaking."

The DEA official wasted little time. "I need someone to make a drop for me in Hong Kong and since you are—"

"Wait a minute," Rick broke in. "Why me?"

"Because I believe you can use an extra hundred thousand dollars."

Rick was quiet for a few moments. *If this offer is too good to be true, it probably is,* he thought. "Doesn't your organization have people who do this kind of activity as part of their regular job?"

"Yes!" Broadman snapped in reply. There was a long pause. "I'm asking you because of the convenience." His words, which were accompanied by a heavy intake of breath, were smoother and slower. "I'm offering you the job because you are already scheduled to go to Hong Kong in two weeks." Broadman paused for several moments before he asked, "Why should this be a burden to you?"

Rick answered hesitantly, "Well, that's just it. I don't want it to be a burden. But you are right. I can use the money. Okay, tell me more about this delivery."

"It's a highly secretive mission. Any leaks on your part, and the deal is off. Is that understood?"

"In that case, I want to know what I'll be carrying."

"Money!" Broadman replied curtly.

Questions raced through Rick's mind. *Why not wire the money? Is it really money? Is this guy on the level?"* Rick tried to find his mind, but it kept wandering back to the hundred thousand. "All right," he finally answered, "but where?"

"Come to my office at 10:00 a.m. tomorrow morning, and you will be informed of the details! Is that satisfactory with you?"

"Yes," Rick replied.

"Remember, no leaks. Good day!"

The phone clicked in Rick's ear.

CHAPTER 17

Rick's relationship with the model had never been serious. They got together when convenient for each other. And it seemed to be the case with all women of his acquaintance. Not that he lacked any social life when the opportunity was available, but his long sea voyages had prevented any lasting relationship to develop.

His feelings for Pat seemed different, and it surprised him. *Was it just because of the way they met at the accident, or was there something else about her that attracted him?* He was going to find out.

For his dinner date with her, he chose a restaurant styled for comfort with the type of atmosphere that encouraged leisurely dining and casual conversation. They sat at a window table high above the city. The moon was a huge yellow ball surrounded by a blanket of twinkling stars that turned the bay into an emerald sea.

For several moments, Pat studied the view outside. "That has to be heaven upside down," she said, nodding toward the window.

"That assessment is certainly more poetical than medical. Do you have any more of them?" Rick asked.

"Who knows? My inspirations are spontaneous." Her teeth dazzled in the candlelight that heightened her angular features. She tasted her drink and then asked, "Was that your ship that picked us up in the bay?"

"Mine and the bank's."

"Regardless, I am eternally grateful that you happened along the other evening." Her eyes were unblinking.

"That makes two of us," Rick said. Then after he offered her one of the two olives speared on the toothpick in his martini, he added, "That had to be a strange way for you to go to work, right?"

"Maybe that's why the hospital approved my sabbatical." Her words were almost a whisper. She glanced toward the window again before she asked, "Is San Francisco your home base—or is port more correct?"

"Yes."

"I'm envious. I enjoy traveling, but I never seem to have the time for it. Tell me about the places you have been. What's your favorite country that you have visited?"

"China."

"Oh!" Suddenly, her eyes were fixed in studious attention. "Tell me about China."

He took another swallow from his martini and then noticed a slight scattering of freckles across Pat's nose. He liked the idea that she didn't try to hide them with extra makeup. He cleared his throat and then started, "Well, the country is thousands of years old and looks its age in many areas. But it is going modern and in a hurry. Construction cranes standing like tall trees dot the landscapes of all the major cities that I have seen recently, such as Beijing, Shanghai, and Hong Kong. Coke signs and the golden arches are popping up everywhere along with lots of Wal-Mart's. But what I really like most about the country is the people. They give me the feeling they like Americans."

Rick paused, fascinated by Pat's rapt attention. Although she remained quiet, her eyes did the talking. They missed nothing while they sparkled or stared, reflecting her mood, never allowing him the privilege of knowing her mind. And he was trying hard to learn.

The ice tinkled in his glass when he took another swallow from his drink. Then he noticed the band members assembling on the stage in the opposite corner of the room. *Maybe the dance floor is the breakthrough for me,* he thought while he quietly waited for the music to begin. When it did, the number was just right, a slow, dreamy tune, the kind meant for dancing "with" and not "at" each other. Pat's shoulders automatically began a slight swaying to the music's tempo.

Nodding in the direction of the dance floor, he asked, "May I see your moves?"

Ignoring any verbal response to the crude invitation, Pat stood and headed toward the dance floor. *No surprises yet,* she thought.

"I like the way you fit," he said moments later while they danced to the rhythm of the music. Her head was close to his shoulder. "And your perfume is exciting. I must warn you. I like girls a hell of a lot better than boys."

"Could have fooled me," Pat answered. But she was pleasantly surprised at his nimble footwork. He was a tall, sinewy man. With her hand on his back, she could feel the firmness of his body, yet the fluidity in his muscles was almost sensuous in their movements.

"Did you take lessons or give them?" she asked.

"Uh!"

"Don't be coy. You know what I mean. You are an excellent dancer. I didn't think a man of the sea would be skilled at ballroom dancing."

"Oh! Sorry, my mind wasn't on dancing," Rick responded.

"Really! What was it on? Or should I even ask?"

"I was wondering if you could cook."

"What?" Pat cried, moving her head from his shoulder and looking up at Rick just as the song ended.

He was slow in answering while he continued to hold her. Another song started, but the tempo of the music had barely changed. Her thin dress offered little resistance to his hand as he pulled her close and continued dancing.

"Well, about the cooking part," he began. "I hate to cook, and since I like everything about you so far, if I know you can cook, it's an important stimulant to the beginning of our relationship."

His smile was impish. His eyes twinkled while she listened to his explanation. *As ridiculous as his reasoning sounds, it's probably true in his way of thinking,* Pat thought while she moved her head back to his shoulder.

They danced, oblivious to the other dancers on the floor, both absorbed in their own thoughts. It was that kind of music and that kind of atmosphere to forget the cares of the world and enjoy the moment.

"Does it bother your dancing when I breathe in your ear?" he asked.

"Better your breath than your tongue," she replied while moving her head from his shoulder. "I enjoy dancing, but it has been a while since I've been on a dance floor, as you can probably tell."

"I don't believe it," he countered. With their eyes inches apart and the roguish grin still tugging his lips, he added, "Believe me, you've still got the right moves."

When the music stopped, they headed back to their table. On the way, there was a table with two elderly couples, both smiling broadly as Pat and Rick approached. One of the ladies reached out and stopped Pat. "You two dance divinely. The best couple on the floor," she said while the others at the table confirmed with polite clapping.

"Why, thank you," Pat answered with a smile conveying her pleasure as she moved past.

Rick, following her, leaned down and said to the lady, "I taught her everything she knows."

The men at the table picked up on the comment immediately and said, "Hear, hear," while they intensified their clapping.

Back at their own table, the lady's compliment still on Pat's mind, she regarded Rick with a faintly amusing expression before she asked, "You never did answer my question. Where did you learn to dance so well?"

"It was a long time ago," he began. "I had a paper route in Chicago, where I grew up. On my route was the Homestead, a place for men to visit, not for a twelve-year-old boy," Rick said and then paused momentarily, a brief smile flashing across his face before he continued, "One of the employees held two jobs. She also taught ballroom dancing. For some unknown reason, she took an interest in me, and since I was about her same height at that time, she would take me to her dance classes."

He paused for another swallow of his martini while he thought, *She also taught me a few other things, but this isn't the right time to discuss them.* "So that's how—"

"She must have been an interesting partner," Pat interrupted. Her coy smile turned into laughter, not a loud kind but a warm, controlled voice.

"Your laugh becomes you," Rick said. It was a knee-jerk remark, prompting him to the realization he could live a long time with that laugh. "Okay, that's enough about me," Rick declared. "Now let me hear about why you wanted to be a doctor."

She let him have that long look again before she answered, "Well, for sure, my background is not as interesting as yours. My father built us kids a tree house in our backyard. Since I was the youngest of the family, the tree house was not as sturdy as it had once been by the time I was nine or ten. One day, a neighborhood boy named Francis and I were playing in the tree house. Francis was overweight and too big to be in the tree house. He fell through the floor and broke his arm."

She tasted her drink before she continued, "It was a compound fracture. A fragment of the ulna bone in his right arm protruded through the skin. Since both my parents were gone at the time, I rushed to the house and called 911. While waiting for the ambulance to arrive, Francis, of course, was in terrible pain. His loud crying was enough to alert the neighborhood, but no one came. It was one of those days when all the neighbors were either gone or inside and couldn't hear the wailing. I still recall that the jagged bone and the bleeding didn't bother me. It was the pain that Francis had to endure, and I was unable to do anything about stopping it."

She paused, glancing out at the bay for a few moments. "I did go back to the house for towels to wrap around the wound. When the ambulance came, I marveled at how quickly the medics had Francis sedated, stopping his crying. I was almost as relieved as Francis. That incident inspired me to relieve pain and suffering by becoming a doctor."

A long silence hung between them before Rick said, "Francis's pain was the medical profession's gain. As for me, I wouldn't have been that sympathetic. He shouldn't have had his fat ass up in the tree house."

You are being insensitive, Pat thought with a sidelong glance at Rick, but she said nothing.

★ ★ ★

A misty rain diffused the glare of the streetlights lining the cab's route. Pat lived in a high-rise on a quiet street in Oakland. A doorman with an umbrella stood beside the cab ten seconds after it had stopped at the curb.

"Thanks for a fine evening, captain," Pat said, starting to get out of the cab. "I've enjoyed—"

"I wouldn't object to coming up for a while," Rick interrupted.

"Not tonight. I've a busy day tomorrow."

"And I thought you'd be unable to resist my charm," Rick persisted.

"Your charm is not my primary consideration." A note of irritation edged her voice. "I'm trying to tell you that I'm leaving on a long trip in a couple of days, and I am busy with my travel plans."

"If you will pardon my curiosity, may I ask where to and for how long?"

"Beijing, and my return plans are indefinite at the present time."

What luck! flashed through Rick's mind. He leaned closer and said, "Now I know why the questions about China. It happens that I'm going to be in Hong Kong about the same time. Maybe we could get together if I know how to reach you."

Pat started to say no and then caught herself. It would be rude to refuse his invitation, and anyway, enough people had told her she was too involved in her work.

She searched in her purse for a card. "I'm sure I wouldn't mind seeing an American friend in China," she said and then wrote the address on the back of the card before she handed it to him.

"Thanks," Rick said. "Maybe together we will improve the China and US governments' relationship."

Pat got out of the cab and then turned, and with a slightly amused expression, she said, "Maybe together we'll just have a Chinese or Peking duck."

CHAPTER 18

Rick had to wait in line to register. Broadman had reserved a room for Rick in a hotel in Kowloon instead of Hong Kong Island, which was just across the bay. "For convenience in conducting your business," he had told Rick.

The lobby of the Kimberly Hotel in midtown Kowloon had the appearance of a fire sale on luggage. Arriving and departing guests rubbed elbows with each other. When he finally reached the front desk, there was a message from Hok waiting for him. It was an invitation to dinner that night at his grandparents' home.

After he had checked into his room and the bellhop had left, Rick examined his luggage. It was the first chance he had to really look at it. Back in the States, Rick had arrived at the airport, with his clothes packed in disposable luggage bags as instructed by Broadman. A DEA agent was waiting for him at the planned meeting area near the ticket counter of Rick's scheduled airline. The agent, who had a large, upright, roller bag plus a matching briefcase designed for riding on top of the carry-on luggage, motioned for Rick to follow him to the nearest men's room. In one of the stalls, Rick repacked while the agent got rid of Rick's disposable bags. At the departure gate, the agent stayed close by until Rick actually boarded his plane.

According to Broadman, the luggage was manufactured of EVA foam to create extra light carry-on baggage, but the briefcase held Rick's greatest interest. He had packed it with a laptop plus business documents and papers in large envelopes. The extra space—and there was plenty of it—contained socks, underwear, and handkerchiefs. According to

Broadman, the money was inside the lining of the briefcase. *Well,* Rick thought, reaching for the telephone to call Hok, *it has certainly fooled customs at both airports.*

Rick had an hour before Hok would pick him up. Under the shower, he thought about the drop he was to make the next day at the Dragon Head Bar on Canton Road in Kowloon. He was supposed to meet his contact at 4:30 p.m. Rick remembered Ed Broadman's crisp instructions: "You will place the briefcase on your table which should be located against a wall and away from the room's main pedestrian traffic. A man will approach. He will say in a foreign language that will probably be unfamiliar to you, 'Will you share your table?' You will not answer. When he repeats in English, you will allow him to sit. He will remove a folded document from a large unsealed envelope and place it on the table. You will test the authenticity of this folded document with these two ink pens filled with the chemicals for that purpose. I have already showed you the procedure. If the test is positive, you will call me on your cell phone. I will explain how the liner in the briefcase can be opened to reveal the money. Then give the briefcase to the man. He will place the document back in the envelope. After sealing the envelope, he will hand it to you. You will keep the document in your possession and deliver it to me when you return to San Francisco."

When he left the bathroom with a towel wrapped around his waist, Rick's thoughts were still on the briefcase. *I wonder how much money is inside this thing,* he pondered while he opened the bag to retrieve his underwear. Curiously, he felt all around the liner, which was of the same material as the bag's exterior but with compartmentalized dividers subtly stitched to the sides and revealing no storage room behind the liner.

Must be a lot of travelers with large bags full of valuables, Rick thought and laughed to himself, noticing the size of the room's safety deposit box as he placed the briefcase inside its housing. Twenty minutes later, he left the room.

In the lobby, Rick sat near a window facing the front of the hotel and waited for Hok to arrive. The wait was short as he watched Hok pull out of the traffic and stop his car under the portico.

"Good to see you again, Hok!" Rick greeted Hok while he got into his car. "And I commend you for being punctual. I had little time to view the street scene from the hotel's lobby."

"This ride will make up for that," Hok said and laughed. "My grandparents live here on the Kowloon Peninsula but a distance from downtown."

Hok headed in the direction of the Hong Kong International Airport and then turned in a northerly direction. After they passed the large Queen Elizabeth hospital, they drove past the huge King's Park, which Hok said was the home of the famous Kowloon Cricket Club. Fifteen minutes later, they reached the residential area named Ho Man Tin, where his grandparents lived in a small two-story condo.

Hok's grandparents spoke English fluently, but they were a contrasting couple. She was Chinese with an expressive, happy face while he was Japanese and somber with a speaking voice just loud enough to be heard.

"Welcome to our home. We are honored by your presence," Asawa Utamaro said with a bow when Rick met him. Hok's grandfather had been with the Japanese intelligence during World War II. Since then, he had made his living as a cartographer working out of his home, where some of his awards for mapmaking hung on the walls.

"It's the other way around," Rick said after he glanced at the inscriptions under the awards.

The elder Japanese's handshake was firm as he caught the subtle complement. During Hoksai's recent telephone calls, he had had nothing but praise for this man. Asawa's eyes were clear and penetrating as he studied the American.

The living room, where Rick sat with Hok and his father, contained several family mementos. A picture of Asawa was on one of the tables. He wore a uniform with medals pinned to his chest.

"Mr. Utamaro, you must've had some interesting experiences during the war," Rick said, pointing to the picture. "Would you mind telling me some of them?"

Asawa sat quietly for several moments, and then he reached over and opened a drawer in the table. After a brief search, he pulled out a yellowed newspaper clipping. The headline in English read, "Americans Capture Cryptographer." There was a picture of Asawa standing between two American soldiers.

"I was treated well as a prisoner, which surprised me." A smile crossed Asawa's face when he finally answered, "You Americans made a friend out of an enemy."

"That's one of the reasons why my grandparents do not object to me living in America," Hok said with a laugh.

A moment later, his grandmother appeared at the door. Dinner was ready.

At the table, Rick met Hok's cousin, Hsiang, who had brought a friend named Kuang. "They don't speak English," Hok said. "They are from the same part of Beijing that my mother came from. They are shipmates and are on a two-week leave from a small freighter that sails the coast of China from here up to the Taiwan Strait."

"That's interesting," Rick said, looking at the two young men across the table. "How is the shipping business with them?" A long scar etched the face of Kuang, who was the taller of the two men.

Hok asked the question in Chinese and then listened to Hsiang's reply. "They are busy and working a lot of overtime," Hok repeated. "Recently, most of their hauling is around the Shanghai area."

The long silence that followed was broken finally by Hok's grandmother. "Mr. Scanlon, I hope you enjoy your visit. Is this your first trip to Hong Kong?"

"No I have been here before and for the same reason," Rick answered, "but this time, I hope to be more successful in picking up some shipping business."

"Who are some of the firms you will be calling on?" Asawa asked.

"Asian Metalworks, Ling Hue Bridge and Iron Company, and Imperial Salvage." The last name slipped out before Rick had realized it.

An abrupt silence filled the room. Hok's grandparents exchanged startled looks. Hsiang's movements never slowed, but Kuang's chopsticks stopped an instant between his mouth and his plate.

Three pairs of eyes pinned Rick. Asawa spoke first. "May I ask who you are seeing at Imperial Salvage?"

Rick stared at Hok, who made a slight turn of his head. When he realized his mistake, Rick instinctively felt he had to continue with his blunder. "A man named Fuchou. Why? Is there something about this company I should know?"

"Fuchou is well known. He controls the drug trafficking in Hong Kong." There was a subtle note of disapproval in Asawa's voice.

"I have never pretended to be a saint," Rick said, clearing his throat, "but I have a ship and crew to keep afloat. If Fuchou's money is good and his cargo's legitimate, I'll haul it."

Kuang was listening hard, though he was pretending not to. He understood English, but speaking the language was difficult. With his chopsticks, he picked at the food on his plate.

Hok had told his grandparents that he and Rick just happened to be in Hong Kong at the same time, checking on work for their respective businesses. "Maybe I can help," he said while he looked steadily at Rick. "My firm has done some legitimate business," he said and paused with a brief smile before he continued, "with Imperial Salvage. The owner likes for vendors to call in the afternoon. I'll be glad to make a date ... say about 2:00 p.m. tomorrow, and introduce you to him."

"I would like that, Hok, and the timing is right," Rick answered, eyeing Hok intently, "since I have another engagement later in the afternoon."

CHAPTER 19

HONG KONG HAS GOT to be having an unusually hot day for this time of year, Rick thought while the sun beamed its hot rays against the sidewalk leading to the Imperial Salvage's office building.

Rick had arrived by cab. Hok had had to take his grandmother to the hospital. Her heart condition was a bit unstable. Rick got the call from Hok about noon. They decided to go ahead with this appointment but without Hok.

The cab had left Rick at the guarded gate in the tall security fence surrounding the company's huge storage yard containing mountainous piles of scrap metal. He had to show the guard both his passport plus Dallworth's signed letter of introduction before he was allowed through the gate. By the time Rick reached the entrance door, sweat beads lined his brow as he entered the building for his appointment at two o'clock.

A smiling receptionist sitting at a desk near the back of the room looked at Rick's card and then asked him to have a seat in one the several chairs available. He walked over to one of the chairs but didn't sit down immediately. Imperial Salvage had a large reception room with décor primarily of ocean scenery. Pictures of seascapes and sailing ships covered the walls. A floor-to-ceiling, glass-enclosed aquarium several feet in diameter and filled with a variety of swimming fish and sea urchins stood near one wall. It was a unique display in a reception room, especially for this kind of business.

Rick decided to have a closer look at the aquarium and walked on over to it. He moved slowly around the large glass tank, studying the aquatic animals and plants, and to his surprise, mounted on the wall near the back of the aquarium, there was a tiger's head.

At that moment, the front door swung open, and two barrel-chested men entered with heavy footsteps. Behind the aquarium and out of sight of the men, Rick noticed the receptionist's practiced smile changed instantly to a disquieting stare as they approached her desk. Sweat beads were showing on the brows of the men. After a short pause, she mumbled something into the mouthpiece and then looked at the men and said, "Mr. Baltasar and Mr. Domingo, you may go in now."

The receptionist's face was set like stone as she watched them leave the reception room. When Rick's movement startled her from her reverie, she babbled quickly, "Oh, Mr. Scanlon! Those men had a prior appointment."

Only a person with acute skills of perception would have caught the slight change in one of the tiger's eyes as the two men walked on down the hall from the reception room.

Fuchou watched Ahmad Sattar's two sons approach his office door while his attention was fixed on a TV screen recessed into the back of his desk. He smiled inwardly, because he understood why they were traveling with aliases, but Spanish names did not quite fit their complexions. *The strength of Ahmad's two sons is below their necks*, he concluded silently.

Fuchou's office was anything but a scrap metal company's office. Tall windows were covered completely with a thinly woven, translucent material that protected the office's privacy but also allowed maximum daylight to filter into the room. The expensive-looking artwork, which was randomly spaced on the walls, was complemented further by the floor's thick carpet. A handcrafted oak desk was at one end of the room. Four leather-bound chairs faced the desk. An ornamental birdcage housing a sleeping yellow parrot with black wings provided an interesting distraction to the room's elegance. The office furnishings contrasted sharply with Fuchou's appearance. His massive bulk sat quietly in a large cushioned chair behind his desk.

In the mid-90s, Fuchou had made a deal with Ahmad Sattar, who supplied the heroin, and Fuchou sold it on a fifty-fifty basis. However, after the Afghanistan War started with the Americans, Sattar demanded more money for the white powder, which prompted Fuchou to find other sources of supply, but there had been consequences.

Suddenly, a frown clouded Fuchou's features. He twisted the dial near the TV screen and studied the American shipper in the reception room. Was he who he was supposed to be? Recently, Fuchou's drug shipments to America's West Coast had been intercepted and not always by their troublesome DEA. Sattar's organizational method was the same as a Colombian Warlord's Plata O Plomo—money or lead. The muscle behind the offer was Sattar's, but the brain to ferret out the drug dealers who were not part of his cartel, Fuchou believed, had to belong to someone else.

The American waiting in the reception room could learn Asian patience, Fuchou reasoned. He turned off the monitor just before his office door opened.

"Bashir Hasan did not come home last night!" The taller brother, Rahab, spoke immediately after he entered the office. He seated himself in one of the visitor's chairs without wasting time.

"Did you try the casino where he works?" Fuchou asked.

"He left before we got there!" Malak, the younger brother, snapped his words while he sat in another visitor's chair.

"Hasan was not to be found in any of the bars you suggested," Rahab continued, a trace of suspicion entering his voice.

Fuchou took his time answering. He reached up to lightly tap the birdcage, but the sleeping parrot was undisturbed. "Be patient. Some men do not use the same bed every night," Fuchou said. "My source of information is trustworthy."

Fuchou continued to study his pet bird, but his mind was on Hasan, a faro dealer on the gambling ship permanently anchored in the harbor. He was a frequent user of the white powder. Fuchou's information on Hasan's living habits had come from one of his best drug pushers, a man named Kuang.

When the Sattar brothers had come to his office yesterday, Fuchou had given them the information they had requested. He would determine later if his cooperation helped relieve the pressure on his drug shipments to America; however, he did value self-preservation. After he had met the Sattar brothers, Fuchou had made sure the automatic in his desk drawer was loaded and in working condition.

Fuchou was especially wary of the taller Sattar. His size was imposing but not as intimidating as his eyes. They were dark coals like the eyes of a tiger. Whatever thoughts were behind them never came through.

Rahab watched the slow, deliberate movements of the fat slob behind the desk. *Two bullets,* Rahab spoke silently. *One in each of his slanted eyes will settle the account of this independent drug dealer.*

But Rahab's mind soon returned to why he and his brother were here. Faisal's plan was for them to be at the Dragon Head Bar today at 4:30 p.m. After the exchange, they were to tail Hasan, and when the opportunity was right, they would kill him and take the money. But they did not have pictures of either participant in the exchange, only physical descriptions, and in a large crowded room, their quarry might not be so easy to identify.

Their plane had arrived late, and they had missed the chance to be on the lookout for the American when he had checked into his hotel. The plan also called for them to take the map from the American, but because they knew he would be in the Hong Kong area for several days, their initial priority, according to Faisal, was Hasan.

"Try Hasan's place this afternoon," Fuchou said, interrupting Rahab's reverie. "He's probably sleeping off a bad night."

CHAPTER 20

THE SOUND OF THE magazine slapping against the tabletop when it left Rick's hand drew the receptionist's attention. "How much longer before my two o'clock appointment?" Rick asked, his voice brittle with sarcasm as he pointed to the office clock. The time was nearly three o'clock.

"I'm sorry, Mr. Scanlon," the receptionist replied. "The meeting is taking longer than expected."

Rick waited another ten minutes, and then saying nothing to the receptionist, he walked out. A block from Imperial Salvage, he hailed a cab. Forty minutes later while the driver waited, Rick hurried into his hotel for the briefcase containing the money.

"The Dragon Head Bar!" Rick snapped his instruction to the driver after getting back into the cab.

They were soon part of the traffic again, but it wasn't long before Rick could tell by the driver's head movement that he was being watched in the rearview mirror. Then, with a wide grin creasing his face, the driver said, "The Dragon Head good place to go after hard day."

Just what I need, Rick thought, *a cabdriver who doubles as a psychiatrist.* When the cab stopped in front of the bar, the driver turned to Rick. "You relax inside. You soon forget trouble. You—"

"I'll determine that!" Rick interrupted the verbal therapy. He paid the driver and got out of the cab.

The dark interior of the bar caused him to pause for a few moments. When his eyes refocused, he saw that there were no vacant tables in the crowded room with a noise level of bedlam proportion. He started for the bar just as a man got up from a table and headed in the general direction of the door. The vacated table was nearly hidden along the wall on the far side of the room.

On the way to the table, Rick passed a cage full of restless parakeets. Their chirping was hardly discernable over the loud clamoring of the beer-swilling customers. Chinese dockhands and sailors dressed in denim shirts and dungarees sat at the tables. They jabbered in a staccato speech that was punctuated by screeching chair legs on the wooden floor.

Within seconds after he had sat down, Rick ordered a draft from a dark-haired waitress. Her brief uniform was a close fit to her olive skin. When she leaned over to wipe the table, he got a view of most of her.

That cabdriver was right. The thought racing through Rick's mind prompted him to say, "Hong Kong has some interesting sights."

"You haven't seen those sights before?" she asked. Her words poured forth in English barely understandable.

"Well, those that I haven't, I am interested in seeing."

A laugh bubbled from her throat as she left to wait on four sailors banging empty beer mugs on their table.

CHAPTER 21

Kuang hurried along Arran Street on the north side of Kowloon. He was anxious to complete his errand as he left the hot, sun-baked sidewalk and entered the Wing Po Hotel. *At least it's shaded from the sun*, Kuang thought, looking around at the lobby's couch and two chairs. Grimy, padded material was showing through the fabric covering the furniture's armrests. A desk clerk remained seated in back of the wooden counter containing three paperback books and a newspaper. He looked up from his magazine and asked with little breath in his voice, "Can I help you?"

"I am meeting a friend on the third floor," Kuang answered while he continued to the elevator adjacent to the desk.

"Have good day," the clerk said before he continued reading his magazine. His eyes were his only movement.

The meeting with Bashir was set for four o'clock. Kuang read 3:55 on a wall clock as he entered the elevator and pressed the button for the third floor. Underneath his shirt, he felt the sweat between his skin and the treasure map. It was inside the same wide leather belt he had picked up from the dock when the dead Japanese had been tossed in the bay.

When he left the elevator, Kuang headed in the direction of Bashir's room. The door numbers indicated that it would be located at the end of the long hall. Kuang smiled to himself, thinking of the money he would get for the map. After today, there would be no more drug business. Suddenly, his thoughts changed, which caused him to slow his pace. *Could he trust Bashir to have the money?* he asked himself.

Kuang had met Bashir in a waterfront bar here in Kowloon. The Afghan went there to drink while Kuang was there to sell drugs. Bashir soon became one of Kuang's better customers.

Liquor and dope consumed together changed Bashir. He became surly and quarrelsome. Sober, he could be very friendly. Once when a woman photographer was in the bar, he had her snap a picture of himself and Kuang posing together.

Although his only apparent income was from a faro dealer's salary, Bashir always had money. It led Kuang to believe that some of the gamblers' losses at Bashir's table did not always go to the casino. This suspicion made the rumors all the more believable, because he knew that Bashir also bet heavily on the horses.

He must be down on his luck, Kuang thought, noticing that the paint-chipped walls in the corridor matched the lobby's interior condition. The dingy living quarters added to Kuang's worries.

CHAPTER 22

Bashir Hasan paced back and forth in his hotel room as though it were a cage. An hour ago, he had broken the seal on a liter of scotch, and it was now half empty. He glanced at his watch again while questions buzzed in his head like swirling bees. *Would Kuang have the map as he promised? Would the courier that Faisal was sending with the money be on time? Since Faisal doesn't trust me, who else will be at the Dragon Head Bar to witness the drop?* His mental burden ended abruptly when he heard a knock on the door.

Bashir swung open the door. As Kuang entered, the smell of liquor hung in the room like a transparent fog.

"Do you have the chart?" Bashir snapped. His bloodshot eyes suddenly grew wary when he saw Kuang's empty hands.

Kuang nodded but said nothing.

"Let's see it!"

"Where money?" Kuang made no move to show the map.

"I'm picking up the hundred thousand dollars we agreed on this afternoon." Bashir's voice grated like sand on a boardwalk. He jerked his wrist upward to glance at his watch. "I'll get the money after I see the map!"

"Have money brought here." Kuang studied Bashir intently.

"I'm getting the money from my bank on Canton Road," Bashir replied, but his eyes blinked.

The reaction was enough to confirm Kuang's suspicion that the money was not coming from a bank, but where was it coming from? "Have bank bring me money!" he persisted.

With eyes narrowed, Bashir backed slowly to a lamp table near the window. "I don't like this game you are playing!" His words iced in accusation. "You have ten seconds to show me a map!" He reached into the drawer of the table and pulled out a .32-caliber automatic. A silencer jutted from the end of the barrel.

The sight of the gun momentarily startled Kuang. He stared hard at Bashir. There was more than ferocity behind the Afghan's eyes. There was desperation. Kuang reached for his belt.

"Slow!" Bashir hissed. Two hands aimed the gun at Kuang.

His stare never leaving Bashir's face, Kuang began to unbutton his shirt. While pulling the shirt out of his pants, Kuang eased his hand under the loose garment to the sheath in the back. He eased his hands underneath the loose garment to the sheath in the back. When Bashir's eyes focused on the wide belt, Kuang felt the hilt of the dagger. An instant later, his hand blurred. The dagger, flipped with an underhanded motion, creased the side of Bashir's throat. His hands jerked upward from the shock of the searing cut. His gun discharged into the ceiling.

Seizing the opening, Kuang rammed his shoulder into Bashir's unprotected midsection. The charge drove them both against the table, splintering it while sending them crashing to the floor. The table lamp flipped in the air and struck Kuang on the head, scattering broken glass across the room.

The gun lay on the floor. With the stunned Kuang lying on top of him, Bashir could not reach the gun. He finally struggled out from under Kuang's motionless body by rolling him over on his back, but by the time Bashir got his hand on the gun, Kuang had him by the wrist. The movement had awakened him.

Sprawled on his back against a piece of the table, Kuang couldn't exert the full strength of his arm against the weight of the hovering Bashir. The gun inched downward as sweat streaked the men's faces. Out of the corner of his eye, Kuang saw the gun come into view.

The lamp cord, which had tangled around his other wrist and tugged ramrod straight by his straining arm, broke suddenly. His free hand fell on a large piece of jagged glass. An instant later, he slammed it against Bashir's face while part of the glass pierced his throat. Bashir coughed, gurgled a hoarse breath, and then collapsed.

Kuang crawled out from under Bashir's lifeless body, but he didn't get up immediately. He took a few moments to allow the hammering inside his chest to stop. When his gasping breaths normalized, allowing him to think rationally again, he was now sure the money wasn't here, but where was it?

The thought of the money triggered the Asian's greed. Quickly, he searched Bashir's clothing. In his wallet, there were fifty-seven dollars, which Kuang stuffed in his own pocket. In another pocket, there was a handwritten note with the words "Dragon Head Bar 4:30 p.m.," and what really caught his eye was the date, which was today.

Kuang was familiar with the bar. It was a sailor's hangout. *If it is the place for the drop, how will I recognize the person with the money?* The thought flashed across his mind. But when he glanced again at Bashir's motionless body, he knew he had no other choice but go to the Dragon Head Bar.

★ ★ ★

"Stop here!" Rahab Sattar ordered. He and Malak were in the backseat of a cab that rolled to a stop against the curb on Arran Street. Rahab swung open the door, knocking over two bicycles parked on the sidewalk. He paid the fare, and the two brothers headed toward the Wing Po Hotel one block away. They walked fast, paying little attention to the other pedestrians along the sidewalk.

"Go in same way as yesterday?" Malak asked while he stepped around a man pushing a cart filled with mussels.

The pungent odor of the shellfish assailed Rahab's nostrils as he nodded his assent, but he kept his eyes fixed on an opening ninety feet ahead in the wall of storefronts. When they arrived at the opening, they turned and walked down an alley extending the length of the Wing Po Hotel.

The two brothers didn't slacken their pace as they weaved a path between garbage cans stacked near the back entrance. They entered the building and climbed three flights of stairs to the floor with Bashir's room. With no one in the corridor but he and his brother, Rahab removed a pair of gloves and a small knife from his coat pocket. Moments later, the two were inside the room and standing over a man choking to death in his own blood.

Rahab, unconcerned with the gravity of the man's wound, glanced around the room and noticed the gun lying on the floor. He kneeled down and held the man in a sitting position while he spoke in his ear. "Can you hear me?"

Bashir's eyelids opened, but only the whites of his eyes showed. The pupils gradually rolled into place as Rahab continued his questioning.

"Faisal Hasan sent us! Are you Bashir, his brother?"

Bashir could only respond with a gurgled mouthful of blood.

"What happened?" Rahab persisted.

With an unsteady hand, Bashir gestured toward some scattered papers among the pieces of wood and glass covering the floor.

Malak quickly shuffled through the papers while he watched Bashir, whose dull stare fixed on a white piece of stiff paper with some writing on the back. When Malak turned over the piece of paper, it was a snapshot of two men. One of the men was Bashir.

Rahab jerked the picture out of Malak's hand and held it in Bashir's face and then pointed to the other man in the photograph. "Is this the man who stuck you?"

Bashir nodded.

"Why?"

Bashir coughed up another mouthful of blood with the words, "Has treasure map."

Malak noticed another piece of paper near an open wallet on the floor. When he read the handwriting on the paper, he handed it to Rahab.

As he read the words "Dragon Head Bar," Rahab quickly held the paper in front of Bashir's face. "Is this your handwriting?" he snapped.

When Bashir gave a feeble nod, Rahab stood up and allowed Bashir's head to thud against the carpet. Rahab picked up the gun and took a few moments to examine it. Then he held the gun against Bashir's head. The percussion sound from the two bullets entering Bashir's brain was slightly audible.

Paying no attention to the blood spilling out of Bashir's head, Malak asked, "Do you think this man with the map is at the Dragon Head Bar?"

"We are going to find out," Rahab answered while he shoved the picture in his pocket.

CHAPTER 23

HSIANG WAS THIRSTY. HE felt the heat from the pavement through his sandals as he put the two cans of paint in the trunk of the Volkswagen. He had purposely made this his last stop on ship's business for Captain Yang. The paint store was across the street from his favorite place to relieve his thirst, the Dragon Head Bar.

While he was crossing the street, Hsiang recognized two sailors from a coast guard cutter that had anchored earlier in the day near Captain Yang's ship. The two sailors turned and entered the Dragon Head.

Lots of people were about. Hsiang glanced along the sidewalk as he stepped up on the curb. One of the pedestrians resembled Kuang, but the distance was too great to identify the approaching figure. *If that is Kuang, he is in a hurry*, Hsiang mused, watching the distant figure dart around other people in his path. His curiosity aroused, Hsiang stepped into a colonnaded entry to a small novelty shop and waited.

It only took a couple of minutes to recognize the oncoming man as Kuang. *Why the hurry?* Hsiang pondered. He had not seen Kuang since last night at the Utamaro's house. When Kuang was thirty feet away, Hsiang stepped out of the store's entrance and hollered, "Kuang! Why such hurry?"

Hsiang's sudden appearance caused Kuang to stop abruptly in front of a man carrying a bag over his shoulder. The man grumbled, nearly dropping the bag before moving on past, while Kuang's startled expression changed instantly to a deep frown.

"Come, let us have beer," Hsiang said, walking on ahead to hold the door open to the bar. "You look like you need one."

Sweat glued Kuang's shirt to his back as he moved toward the bar's entrance, but his features remained clouded in a frown.

★ ★ ★

Rick finished his first drink in a hurry. The beer was good, and it was cold. He had just set the empty mug on the table when the waitress was back with another frosty beer.

"What kept you?" he asked.

She ignored the question but nodded toward the briefcase on the table. "You guard the bag? What do you carry in it?"

As he leaned back in his chair, he turned slightly and faced her, his eyes leveling on hers. "It is a collection of rare specimens of plants and animals that I use in my medical practice."

"Oh! You are doctor?"

"No, pharmaceuticals are closer to my specialty."

She glanced at Rick with a flash of curiosity. "What is in the collection?"

"Petals from the most delicate orchids found in the deepest part of the Congo River Valley, eyeteeth from only pack leaders of Belgian tigers, and swatches of wool from virgin sheep living in the highest part of the Himalayas," Rick answered, his eyes remaining locked on hers.

With a heavy frown, she asked, "What use for?"

Rick leaned closer to speak confidentially. "I make strong medicine of these specimens," he replied with only the hint of a smile creasing his face.

She was distracted momentarily by two men holding empty beer mugs in the air. She leaned down. "That medicine make good girls bad." A quiet laugh echoed from her throat when she turned and left the table.

Rick took a swallow from his second beer and then glanced at his watch. The time was 4:45. *Maybe I should make myself more visible,* he thought while he looked around the room. The bright daylight drew his attention when the door opened. Two husky men, one tall and the other of average height, entered the bar. Rick recognized them immediately as the two who had received the preferred treatment at the Imperial Salvage Company about three hours ago. They were still dressed in the same baggy pants with deep pockets and gray T-shirts, which were now showing sweat stains.

The two men stopped just inside the door. After they paused for a few moments, their heads began turning from side to side, quickly at first and then slowly. Their lips moved, and their glances darted from table to table. Their inspection required several minutes before they started moving. Each man took a separate path toward the long bar at the back of the room.

Something inside Rick told him to keep out of their sight. When the shorter one drew close, Rick bent over and wiped some dust from his shoe. By the time he raised up again, the two were at the bar.

Rick continued watching them. When their drinks came, they didn't turn around, but their eyes remained focused toward the long mirror over the back bar. With lips moving occasionally and heads turning only a fraction at a time, they kept their vigil while they stood at the bar.

They should have tried the beer, Rick thought. The two men had hardly touched their drinks. When they did, it was more of a quick sip than a swallow. Suddenly, the taller man's glass stopped halfway to his mouth. The image of his features froze in the mirror's reflection.

Rick turned. Hok's cousin, Hsiang, and his buddy, Kuang, came into the bar. After they paused briefly to look around the room, they continued over to an empty table along the opposite wall from where Rick was sitting. *Hok's cousin is a little guy,* Rick thought while he noticed how much shorter he was than his friend.

When Rick's gaze turned again to the back of the room, the taller man set his drink on the bar. He said something to his buddy, and then the two started in the direction of Hsiang and Kuang.

Casually, the two men from the bar moved around the tables and standing drinkers in their path, but their attention was fixed on Hsiang and Kuang. When he stopped beside Hsiang's chair, the taller man spoke first. The tight movements of his lips were brief, but the eyes of both Asians changed from a startled took to a cobralike, darting glare.

Each man from the bar kept one hand in his respective pants' pocket. The taller man withdrew his hand, but it was a momentary gesture for Kuang's eyes only. The two Asians rose slowly from their chairs. Then all four men started toward the door.

Watching the two seamen apparently being forced from the room placed Rick in a dilemma. Thoughts raced across his mind. *I want to help Hok's cousin, but I'm on a secret mission. If I blow this money drop, I'll lose the hundred thousand that I can really use. Maybe I'd better stay out of it. But he's so small.*

It was Hsiang's size that goaded Rick into action. He could see that they would pass by the table with the parakeets, whose owner was in a spirited conversation with three other Chinese at an adjacent table. Rick, now completely absorbed in his new mission, left the briefcase on the table while he got up and moved toward the caged birds. He got there in plenty of time to intercept the departing group.

He leaned down by the cage as if to take a closer look while he listened to make sure his inspection was not interrupting the noisy chatter near him. Then Rick casually tapped the cage with his fingers while he moved his hand toward the latch. When the four men were almost parallel to the cage, Rick slid back the latch and opened the door. It faced the approaching party.

A flying ball of feathers shot out of the crowded cage. Its flight path pointed directly toward the heads of the four men. Instantly, the rest of the parakeets followed, wings beating to the cadence of a thousand trip-hammers.

The taller man withdrew his pocketed right hand to shield his face against the rocketing parakeets. Rick took two quick steps and drove a hard right fist into the man's stomach. An instant later, his nose was a bloody pulp from Rick's smashing left hook. The blow knocked the man over the table occupied by the group near the parakeet's cage. The jabbering suddenly changed to a chorus of shouts and yells as the seated men scrambled to get away from the falling body.

Kuang, who was guarded by the taller man, ran for the front door immediately after he heard the impact of Rick's first punch. Hsiang was not as fortunate in escaping from the shorter man, who used only one hand to ward off the parakeets' flying attacks while he fired his concealed pistol. The force of the bullet, which struck Hsiang in the back, knocked him through the door.

Surrounded by the shouting bar patrons, Rick saw the shorter man running for the front door. When he reached the empty birdcage, Rick raised it over his head and hurled it at the departing captor. The metal cage caught the man in the back of the head, smashing him against the wall near the door. Rick moved in on the dazed man and landed a savage right hand that sent him and a table crashing to the floor.

With the two captors on the floor, Rick turned and moved quickly back to his table, grabbed the briefcase, and then ran on outside the bar. Hsiang was across the street and slumped over the hood of a parked car.

Kuang was nowhere in sight. Rick crossed the street and helped Hsiang enter the passenger side of the car.

"To ship," Hsiang said weakly. He held the keys in a bloody hand.

Rick got in the driver's side after he tossed the briefcase in the backseat, but after he started the car, he couldn't move because of a line of cars blocking his access to the street. By the time he did get the car out into the traffic, he saw the two thugs he had fought with through the rearview mirror. They had just left the bar. One looked in Rick's direction while the other hailed a cab.

CHAPTER 24

RICK WEAVED THE CAR as fast as he could through the late afternoon traffic while he watched for any cabs on his tail. He was heading toward the waterfront, or at least he hoped so. They were headed in the direction that Hsiang had indicated with a limp arm before he had slumped against the passenger door. *Damn stupid of me to get this involved*, Rick swore silently when he glanced at the briefcase in the backseat. *Not only do I have two hoodlums on my ass, but I just blew a hundred thousand.* The groans from Hsiang stopped Rick's musing. *Will he be physically able to identify his ship?* The thought prompted Rick to ask, "Why are we going to your ship? We should be going to the nearest hospital."

"Ship first," Hsiang grunted his answer without opening his eyes.

Although Hsiang's direction signal was weakly applied, it proved effective. Fifteen minutes later, they were at the waterfront, and then Rick slowed the car. The abrupt change in speed caused Hsiang to open his eyes.

"We are at the waterfront. I'm trying to get you to your ship," Rick said.

"Ship," Hsiang answered, but it was an effort for him to keep his eyes open.

Rick steered the car around piles of cargo while his glances switched between Hsiang and the ships at dockside. He passed a Dutch freighter unloading its cargo of wheat. The next ship was a British Frigate being moored to a pier adjacent to the Dutch freighter. As they moved past an unidentified freighter being loaded with rice, Hsiang's glazed eyes momentarily sparkled when he pointed to the next ship at the dock.

Rick stopped at the gangplank of a small cargo ship that was flying a China flag.

He got out of the car and hurried around to the passenger's side. When he opened the door, he had to grab Hsiang before the man fell to the dock. His shirt seeped with blood. Rick reached for his briefcase and then he picked up Hsiang. Thankful the wounded man was relatively small so he could carry both aboard the freighter.

The ship was quiet, and the sound of Rick's footsteps echoed along the main deck. He headed toward an open doorway at midship. Just before he got there, a tall, gray-haired, Chinese man with whiskers stepped through the doorway and onto the main deck. His stare quickly changed from curiosity to concern when he saw the injured Hsiang.

"Come," the man said while he gestured for Rick to follow him back through the door and to a compartment at the end of a passageway. A brass nameplate was on the door, and after it was opened, Rick saw a stiff-billed cap hanging from a hook on the back of the door.

"I met Hsiang and his buddy, Kuang, last night," Rick said while he placed Hsiang on the only bunk in the room. "About two hours ago, I happened to be in the same bar where it appeared to me—"

Rick was interrupted by a heavy groan from Hsiang. When the tall man leaned close, Hsiang muttered what he had to say between raspy breaths. And it took him a while, but when he finished, the older man's response was brief. He laid his hand on Hsiang's shoulder and then turned around and faced Rick.

"Hsiang should be in a hospital, but he insisted on coming here first," Rick said while he picked up the briefcase. "I'll leave now."

"No!" the man said while he shook hands with Rick. "I Captain Yang. Hsiang told me about you." He nodded toward the prostrated Hsiang. "You are brave man to help him and Kuang. Men you fight are after map."

This jolted Rick. *Could this map be the document he was to pick up for Broadman?* The thought flashed across his mind. He was cautious. "So there is some kind of a map involved?"

"Kuang brought to me when found it. Kuang say it navigation chart showing location of treasure from ship sunk near Taiwan Strait. Happened during WWII. Map printed in code on material like animal hide. I no help."

"Then Kuang has the map?" Rick asked. His voice pitched higher from this new revelation.

The captain nodded.

But Rick was trying to organize the scattered threads of his thoughts. *If this is the document, why the hell is a DEA man interested in a treasure map? Is this Broadman for real?*

Another groan from Hsiang caused a deep frown to cloud the captain's face. "Men you fight follow you here?" he asked.

"I think so."

"Must get underway. Please help Hsiang."

"But I'm not a doc—" Rick's protest was unheeded as the captain moved over to an intercom sitting on a small desk. He flipped a switch and spoke in short syllables. In less than a minute, Rick heard running footsteps in the passageway outside the door. The ship soon backed away from the dock and headed rapidly out into the main channel.

While the captain was calling the ship's crew to their workstations, Rick thought, *I've learned who has the document, so I still have a chance to earn the hundred thousand. I'm safe from those two gunmen, so I'll do what I can for Hsiang.* He moved over to the bunk and removed Hsiang's bloody shirt. The bullet had passed completely through the body and apparently had punctured part of the lung. Hsiang's cramped position in the car had kept the opening to the lung partially closed, but now he began coughing up frothy red blood.

There was a knock at the door. A young Chinese sailor brought in a bucket of hot water and some towels, and then he left. When Rick turned around, there were bandages, tape, and sulfa powder on the desk. Rick saw the medical supplies, turned to the captain, and said, "Are you a doctor?"

"No," the captain said and shook his head. Then he pointed to Rick and then to the bandages and finally to Hsiang.

"But I'm not a doctor!" Rick tried to explain just as Hsiang coughed up another mouthful of blood.

"Please," the captain pleaded. He took both of Rick's hands in his own and placed them on Hsiang's chest.

How the hell can a bankrupt cargo hauler get himself into a spot like this? The question flashed in Rick's mind. His only medical training was in first aid, but when he looked at Hsiang choking in his own blood, he knew he had to do something.

The first thing he did was thoroughly clean the wound before he dusted it with sulfa powder. Then he applied a compress and made sure the edges of the wound were held together. When the captain turned

Hsiang on his side, Rick dressed the back where the bullet had entered. The rib cage was completely covered with an airtight pressure bandage. Finally, Hsiang was propped up on pillows, allowing him to breathe easier.

When Rick turned around, the captain motioned him to a basin of clean water sitting on a nearby table. After he washed his hands, Rick dried them on a white towel beside the basin. Then after he rolled down his sleeves, he turned to face the captain again.

The captain remained silent for several moments before he reached out with both hands and grasped Rick's arms. His chin whiskers trembled briefly when a smile creased his face. Turning, he motioned for Rick to follow him. They left the compartment and walked along the passageway, which now smelled of freshly cooked food. The tantalizing aroma led them to the ship's galley, where a single setting was laid out at one of the long tables. Heat vapors drifted slowly above bowls of rice, steamed clams, and a large cup of tea.

The captain motioned for Rick to sit. "Thank you," Rick said without hesitation. He smiled inwardly when he reached for the utensils. Wrapped in a napkin were a set of chop sticks and a fork.

A man stood near the stove in the galley area. The captain said something to him before he left.

While he ate, Rick made two calls on his cell phone. The first one was to Hok, who listened quietly while Rick explained his afternoon's progress, starting at Fuchou's office and then describing the incident at the bar and ending on Captain Yang's ship.

"Where are you headed now?" Hok asked when Rick finally ended his long account.

"I don't know." Rick answered. "I was hoping you might have an idea."

"No, I don't either, but you are in good hands. Hsiang speaks well of Captain Yang. Let's keep in touch. I'll pick you up when you say so."

The second call was the one that left Rick the most skeptical when he talked with Broadman. To Rick's surprise, Broadman did not seem too upset about him blowing the money drop. He told Rick to hold onto the briefcase and return it when he came back to San Francisco. Then Broadman asked a few questions about the description of the man with the map. And when he asked, "Was he the bigger of the two men being forced from the bar?" Rick suspected that Broadman had already been informed of the aborted money drop before the call.

After Rick had consumed a second helping of clams and a refill of his tea cup, the man who had been waiting patiently by the galley stove motioned for Rick to follow him. He led Rick down a ladder to another compartment one deck below with an empty bunk that Rick soon put to use.

CHAPTER 25

RICK OPENED HIS EYES to a dark stillness. Moments past before he realized the ship had stopped. Lying quietly, he began trying to organize the scattered threads of his thoughts just as a knock sounded at the door. It opened to a sailor framed in the light from the passageway. He motioned with his hand for Rick to follow him.

After he grabbed his briefcase, Rick crawled out of the bunk and followed the man up a ladder to the main deck blanketed by a moonless night. Captain Yang appeared out of the darkness and signaled for Rick to follow him down the gangplank and onto a wooden pier. When he stopped briefly, the captain spoke in a low voice to someone ahead. Whoever it was left with hurried footsteps.

Rick and the captain followed at a slower pace and climbed an embankment to a path that twisted through treelike bushes before it led to an open area. A shadowy outline of a small building appeared in the distance. Its windows were lit holes puncturing the night.

Just before they reached the cabin, a door swung open, lighting a path to the entrance. The next instant, a tall, slender man built like the captain and about the same age appeared in the doorway. Hugging each other briefly, they both jabbered with an explosion of enthusiasm. *At least I'm in a friendly neighborhood*, Rick reasoned. The man soon turned, and with a broad smile, he bowed slightly and spoke in broken English, "I, Jilin Yang, the captain's older brother. Come in, please."

The two men continued talking while Rick glanced around the living quarters of the cabin. A small kitchen was at one end of the room. The other end contained a faded couch and chair along with a wooden desk in one of the corners. Although devoid of any decorations, the room was spotlessly clean.

Rick's attention kept returning to the captain's brother. He seemed familiar, but there wasn't time to find out about him when he said, "You both must be tired from ordeal today. Come." He motioned for Rick and the captain to follow him through a hallway to three small bedrooms in the back of the cabin.

The comfortable bed offset the short night. Rick felt rested the next morning when he returned to the main room of the cabin where both the Yangs were having tea. The elder Yang rose immediately. "Come … join us for tea." He motioned for Rick to take a vacant chair at the table while he poured an extra cup of tea.

"Thank you," Rick said. "I've got to admit since I've been over here in your part of the world, I'm beginning to enjoy tea almost as much as coffee."

"Sorry." Jilin Yang said while he stood from the table. "I do have coffee. I make you—"

"No," Rick interrupted. "Honest, the tea is fine. Sit back down. What is more important to me right now is getting word to a Japanese friend who will pick me up. That is, if I can tell him where I'm at."

"I see," Jilin answered. A brief smile crossed his face. "Do you have cell phone?"

"Yes."

"Will your friend be in car?"

"Yes."

"You are eighty kilometers from Hong Kong. Call your friend. I tell him how to get here."

The call was made, and Hok assured Rick that he would be there by midafternoon. The long wait that followed was anything but dull for Rick. The name "Jilin Yang" kept rolling over in his mind until he finally said to him, "Your name has a familiar ring. Are you some kind of government official?"

"My brother is Dr. Yang," the captain said while Jilin cleared his throat from a hot drink of tea. "He reported threat of grave health problem SARS when he believed our government was not."

"Now I recall," Rick said, turning to look at the doctor. "There was an article in *TIME Magazine* about you. And now the rest of the world is grateful for what you have done to stem the spread of this acute respiratory problem."

The impassive features of the doctor broke into a smile, nodding his thanks while leaving the table to make another pot of tea.

Rick still wasn't through. "Captain, you are going to have to pardon my curiosity, but why is the doctor here?"

"He staying in his summer place till storm of his revelation blows over. When SARS first known here in China, government claimed only few cases and people not to worry, but my brother knew better. That's when he wrote letter to Chinese Central Television, saying number of SARS cases reported by government very incorrect. To dispute government by signing his name to letter could mean jail or physical harm or both."

Dr. Yang returned to the table with a fresh pot of tea. After he filled everyone's cup, he looked at Rick. "I sure I not be here much longer. Heard from friends that government is relenting. Enough about me. Talk about your patient, Hsiang. Saw him early this morning. He rested well during night. Your bandaging done well. You make good doctor."

"Glad to hear he had a good night," Rick said. "And thank you for that analysis. Coming from you, that makes me feel better about Hsiang's condition."

When Rick turned to Captain Yang, he said, "That reminds me! Hsiang's friend, the other guy involved in that fracas yesterday, have you heard from him? He skipped after the fight yesterday."

"Kuang called early this morning," the captain replied while he handed Rick a newspaper showing a rough sketch of a man resembling Kuang. "He said not to believe what in paper."

It was a Chinese daily newspaper. After Rick studied the sketch for a few moments, he looked at the captain for an explanation.

"The paper say that man wanted for murder." The captain started in by pointing to the sketch. "Murder happened yesterday at Wing Po Hotel in Kowloon." The captain paused briefly before he continued, "I told Kuang he could be murdered yesterday at bar without your help. But he say, 'I don't trust American. Anybody do business with Fuchou, I don't trust.'"

"I can explain that Fuchou situation," Rick said curtly, noticing the skeptical looks from both Yangs. "I would like to talk with Kuang. If I knew how to reach—"

The captain shook his head. "Kuang said he going to home in Beijing. He has no phone, no address. He call me when safe to come back to ship."

Rick reflected for a few moments on what the captain had just told him. When he looked over at the briefcase sitting by a lounge chair, he thought, *My trip to Hong Kong has been anything but a financial success.*

CHAPTER 26

HOK ARRIVED IN THE midafternoon when he had said he would. Rick introduced him to the Yangs. Then they all went to see Hsiang, who appeared to be recovering well from the bullet wound. After a short visit, Rick and Hok headed back to Hong Kong. Their discussion on the trip back was primarily about the Yangs. Hok mentioned that he had read about the SARS situation and could understand why Dr. Yang was hiding out. When Hok switched the subject to the briefcase in the backseat, Rick said it was just to make an impression while he was soliciting shipping business.

It remained in Rick's hand when he got out of the car back at his hotel in Kowloon. He walked around to the driver's side and then leaned down and said to Hok, "Thanks a million for picking me up. Oh, by the way, I think now is a good time for me to take a day off of our shipping business and visit Beijing. It's been a while since I've seen that capital city."

"Give me a call when you get back, and by the way, tell Dr. Kendall I said hello," Hok answered, laughing loudly while driving out from under the Hotel's portico.

In his room, Rick was soon on the phone with Pat. "Remember a sailor from California?" Rick asked when he heard Pat's voice.

"Well, I do remember one. But since I'm alone in a foreign country, I had better know something about who you are. Please describe yourself."

"Modesty forbids me to—"

"Say no more! That word modesty, by you, signals instant recognition," Pat interrupted. But the brief static obscured the possibility of any gaiety that might have been in her voice.

What the hell! You never know unless you try, Rick thought as he continued, "I have no other business in Beijing but to see you. So If I hop on one of those big silver birds and head your way, will you have dinner with me tomorrow night?"

"Um, I can hardly say no to an invitation like that." Her words flowed amiably over the phone. "If you will call after arriving, I will make the dinner reservations." There was a pause, and then she said, "Unless, of course, you prefer to do so."

"No, I would appreciate you handling that chore," Rick said. "See you tomorrow night."

The following evening, they went to dinner at the Quanjude Roast Duck Restaurant in downtown Beijing. The room where they were seated was huge and plushy. *I should have selected the restaurant*, Rick mused, his mind on the size of the check to follow.

"Have you been here before?" he asked.

"No," Pat answered. "But I have heard only the highest of praises about this place since arriving in Beijing." Dressed in a thigh-high shimmer of black silk, her sparkling eyes relished the moment as they missed nothing in her survey of the restaurant's interior. "I am told it has a 130-year history and the restaurant's site was personally selected by one of China's premiers."

While reproaching himself quietly for his selfishness, Pat's smile blinded Rick with dazzling teeth. Her mood was not only priceless but delightfully contagious. *Enjoy it while it lasts*, Rick thought as the waiter arrived at their table.

"I am a bit disappointed," Pat said, studying the menu. "I have always wanted to eat Peking duck in Peking, China, but apparently, I am going to have to settle for Peking duck in Beijing, China. Peking duck sounds better than Beijing duck, don't you agree?" Pat asked, peering over the menu at Rick while suppressing the laughter in her voice.

Rick studied her intently and began singing, "You say tomato, and I say tomato," and then he end by saying, "Ah, but the proof of the title will be in the tasting."

Later and after the first taste, Pat raised her fork and declared, "Let the word go forth to friend and foe. Change names, never the recipe for Peking duck."

"I'll drink to that," Rick answered, raising his wine glass.

When they left the restaurant, the last rays of the day's sunset greeted them, which prompted Pat to say, "The weatherman's report today was not nearly as encouraging as the present conditions." She paused momentarily and then said, "However, the day isn't over yet."

"Apparently, the Chinese weathermen go to the same school as ours back home," Rick said. They walked hand-in-hand along the sidewalk. Lots of pedestrians were about, and the ever-present bicycle riders continued their mass movement along the street.

"Let's walk a while and enjoy what's left of this gorgeous day," Pat said.

"Good idea," Rick answered, giving her hand an extra squeeze. "A walk is just the finishing touch needed for our dinner."

They walked for a while, pausing occasionally to window-shop at the latest fashions in new store buildings and marveled at the number of tower cranes in the process of constructing more huge skyscrapers.

"It's obvious," Rick said while he looked up at one of the tall buildings nearly completed. "The upcoming Olympics is not the only reason for the building boom taking place here in the heart of Beijing."

The streetlights were on by the time they headed back to where Rick had parked his rental.

"China's current accelerated economy has produced too many automobiles and too much smog," Pat said with a cough. They were standing at a stoplight, waiting for the traffic to clear before crossing the street.

"My thoughts exactly," Rick answered when they were finally able to cross the street. It was another ten minutes before they reached his car, which prompted Rick to say, "I've had enough walking for a while. How about you?"

"My thoughts exactly," Pat acknowledged with a slight cough, not in reference to the fog this time.

He ignored the mockery while he unlocked the passenger door for her. But when he straightened up, he said, "Well, doc, despite the dig, you have to admit we were lucky to find a parking spot as close to the restaurant as we did."

"And room to get out," Pat said. She was watching a man directly across the street, working diligently to steer his car clear of the curb and the two parked cars in front and behind him. While Rick was opening her door, she looked to see how the adjacent cars were parked next to their car. "At least we won't have the same problem as that man across the street," Pat said before she entered their car.

After he closed the door, Rick glanced over at the driver wedged into the tight parking place. *Car drivers can be damn inconsiderate of how they—* but his silent complaint stopped short when he recognized the driver. It was Kuang. The mind-boggling odds of seeing him here in Beijing froze Rick momentarily.

CHAPTER 27

SWEAT BEADS COVERED KUANG's forehead from rage and frustration. He glared at the pedestrians passing along the sidewalk while they gave his car a wide berth. He was envious of a couple directly across the street, getting into their car. They had plenty of parking room. Momentarily, his troubled mind focused on the tall man with the woman. He stared hard. It was Hok Utamaro's American friend, and mutual recognition was instantaneous. The American's look in Kuang's direction never wavered. Curiously, the American waved his hand, and a smile appeared on his face. Then he started watching the traffic as if he was trying to cross the street. Abruptly, Kuang changed tactics. His car's transmission erupted in course growls as he shifted repeatedly from forward to reverse and rammed the two parked cars in front and behind him. He wanted no part of the American. When he forced out enough room to turn into the street, he left the parking place in a wheel-spinning start.

As he watched Kuang's rapid departure, Rick yelled to Pat, "Fasten your seat belt!" Then he ran around the car and entered the driver's side.

"What is this all about?" Pat asked, staring at Rick, who jammed the key into the ignition and started the motor.

"Just a minute!" Rick snapped, watching for a break in the traffic. The next instant, he squealed the tires in a fast U-turn from the curb and raced after the other car.

"I'm waiting for an answer!" Pat, who was still adjusting her seat belt, shouted above the roar of the car's engine.

Thoughts raced through Rick's mind. *It's ridiculous enough to tell her I want to buy a treasure map from that man ahead, especially when he's trying to avoid me.* "That man ahead has a secret document stolen from our government!" Rick said. He yanked the steering wheel to miss some bicycle riders who peddled quickly and got out of the way.

"But what has that to do with you?" Pat yelled defiantly, bewildered by the sudden change of events.

"I work occasionally for the government!" *That's not too far from the truth,* Rick almost said aloud as he fought the steering wheel and skidded the car around a corner to keep Kuang in sight.

They were in the heart of the city, speeding along a street named "Wangfuijing" or something. After they made a quick left turn, they traveled only a few blocks before they entered an open area. It was surrounded by large buildings and museums with tall monuments rising from the central courtyard area. It was the famous Tiananmen Square.

Rick realized the torture he was putting Pat through before she spoke again, and this time her words were brittle. "Let me out anytime! You can play cops and robbers with that person ahead without me!"

"I can't," Rick countered. "I'll lose him if I stop!"

They moved rapidly across the enormous square that was paved with stone. The car bounced over a pothole. Pat said nothing. Her glare was enough.

As they left the square, they turned right and weaved their way through a network of narrow streets. Then they abruptly turned left onto a wide and straight street named Dongsi Beidajie. Rick floored the gas pedal, barely keeping pace with Kuang's taillights, which were hard to follow when they intermingled with the lights from other cars.

Kuang watched the trailing car in his rearview mirror. His frown deepened. This could be a long chase. When he glanced at his gas gage, he saw that his tank was only half filled. He had rented the car at the Beijing Airport. After he had made his escape at the Dragon Head Bar, he had gone directly to the airport in Hong Kong. Bashir's money had paid for the airline ticket and the rental.

Just before he had boarded his plane, there had been a news broadcast on the TV monitor in the airport's concourse about Bashir's murder. A suspect was being sought. The sketch artist's composite drawing on the screen resembled Kuang but in more of a caricature likeness. *It must have been that clerk at the Wing Po Hotel who identified me,* Kuang thought, but his attention returned to the road ahead. He was now approaching Ditan Park, an area he was quite familiar with.

Ditan Park was where the spring festival of the Chinese New Year was held. As a child, Kuang had come here often with his mother. Near the park, a horse-drawn wagon loaded with bags of rice and some leisurely peddling bicycle riders had slowed Kuang's progress considerably. In frustration, he pressed his horn loud and long, scattering the bicyclists while spooking the team of horses. The hard stares were of no concern to him as he drove past. The car directly behind had his attention.

Though his eyes were fixed on the car ahead, Rick was well aware of a pair of eyes on him. In retrospect, he wished he had left Pat downtown. She could have taken a cab home. *But if I had stopped, that guy ahead would have been long gone*, he thought.

Rick groped in vain for the words to soften her resentment, but his mind kept returning to the job at hand. He stayed with the government alibi.

"That man ahead has secret plans of a new guidance system for space-launched missiles. He is trying to pass them to—"

"I don't want to hear about it!" Pat interrupted. Her words snapped like icicles hitting concrete.

"But it's your patriotic duty!"

"My patriotism has nothing to do with this! When this chase started, you could have been more considerate of my welfare instead of your own self-interests!"

Rick remained silent. He concentrated on his driving. He had to. Kuang had made a hard left turn, burning rubber with his skidding tires. From the tall trees towering under a darkened sky, Kuang was following a perimeter street bordering a park. He passed the car directly ahead of him, barely missing a head-on collision with an approaching car, which led a string of cars in close procession.

By the time Rick could get around the car in his path, Kuang's taillights had disappeared. Rick slammed on his brakes. He made a skidding U-turn in the middle of the street and raced back to a park entrance he remembered, maneuvering around the cars ahead. His tires squealed from the sharp turn into the park, where there appeared to be commercial buildings on each side of the street.

Strange for buildings of this kind to be in a park, Rick thought, but his mind was distracted for only an instant. The taillights of Kuang's car were directly ahead. They weren't moving. A three-car collision had blocked the street near a tall apartment complex.

But as Rick braked his own car, he could see Kuang cramp the steering wheel of his car to make a hard right turn. Then Rick watched Kuang's car bound over the street curb and up a short flight of concrete steps onto a boardwalk in front of the buildings. Then the car made an abrupt left turn, bypassing the wreck cars while smashing through a newspaper kiosk just before getting back on the street. It was soon out of sight after the car had driven farther into the park.

Quickly, Rick decided to follow the same bypassing maneuver, but his rental was built closer to the ground than Kuang's car was. When he passed over the steps, he felt the car take a sudden jolt before they reached the walk. He passed the wreck, drove back onto the street, and entered the park. A single red light on his dashboard was the first warning signal followed quickly by a second red light before smoke began billowing from under the hood. A moment later, the engine died. When the car rolled to a stop, Rick shifted to the parking gear out of habit—or at least he tried to. The gear shift moved with little effort. He realized the car's transmission was disabled.

"Damn it!" He swore and banged his hands on the steering wheel while the taillights ahead soon disappeared. Rick leaned back against the seat. *What the hell do I do now*? he thought, disgusted. *This certainly wasn't the evening I had planned*. He didn't look at Pat. Instead, he glanced out at the dark stillness, but nothing stirred. Finally, he turned to her and said, "I don't suppose you would care for a walk in the park, would you?"

But Pat remained tight-lipped, which surprised Rick. He had expected a tongue-lashing from her. Instead, she glared straight ahead at the windshield. Gradually, they both became aware of the silence outside the car. The trees were ghostlike. There was no movement. Not even a leaf stirred. The funeral stillness about the park made the small undulations scattered throughout the grass-covered grounds appear like burial plots.

When the car that they had been following disappeared, all sounds vanished with it. A puzzling strangeness existed. Everything around them seemed frozen in time. Then it happened. The ground shook with the first stirring of a tremor. Small undulations scattered throughout the grass-covered grounds.

"What is it?" Pat cried, turning to Rick, who was already reaching for her.

"It's an earthquake! Come on! Quickly!"

They left the car. Rick held onto Pat's hand. They ran and stumbled with each step toward an open area between the tall trees. Their branches shook as if warning Rick and Pat not to come any closer.

I have lost them! Kuang chortled to himself. After he had glanced through the rearview mirror several times, he began to relax. He was familiar with the park's winding streets. Growing up in Beijing, he had often bicycled in this area. Kuang slowed his car, made a sharp left turn at an unlighted intersection, and drove out of the park. When he rounded a corner, he approached the park's entrance, near where he had previously dodged the three-car crash. He had just accelerated his car's speed to pass by when he felt the ground shake.

Kuang knew instantly what was happening. He jammed the brakes hard, sending the car into a skidding turn toward the park's entrance, and then he sought out open spaces for protection. But the street in the path of his headlights rippled upward, forcing his car to turn sharply, and he was now heading directly for the tall apartment complex.

CHAPTER 28

The ground erupted under Rick and Pat, and they each fell. Before they could get up, the ground wavered again. The sound of trees snapping and splintering filled the air.

"Stay down!" Rick shouted. He held one arm across Pat's shoulders. Her face was buried in the grass. Suddenly, the ground tipped again, causing her and Rick to tumble backward violently from the sharp incline

Echoing above the noise of falling trees was a low rumble so intense it sounded as destructive as the heaving ground. The uprooted trees left Rick and Pat a hazy view of the apartments. The tall buildings staggered on their foundations at first and then began swaying as if in a tribal dance. Undecided when and where to fall, they lunged and ripped at each other in a fight for survival before one after the other toppled to the ground in a thunderous roar.

Finally, the shock waves subsided, allowing Rick and Pat time to regain their feet. Their movements trancelike, they continued toward the remains of the apartment complex. By the time they reached the area, a massive dust cloud had just cleared the huge piles of broken wood and masonry. There was no sound or sign of life.

Fires broke out. Small fires from leaking gas kindled into flames by the splintered wood. Flickering shadows began ghost-dancing over the instantly created cemetery. A bare leg extended from underneath a fragmented piece of a brick wall. Beside a twisted steel girder lay a severed arm. A male body stretched grotesquely halfway through a window frame as if the man had tried to hurdle the sill.

Suddenly, a baby's cry sounded. It came from somewhere behind the mountains of rubble. Rick and Pat quickly made their way to an area of small housing units adjacent to the apartment complex. The infant's cry came from under one of the flattened units. It was near an exterior masonry wall left standing from a toppled apartment building.

Rick picked up a splintered board and began to dig through the rubble. He moved a broken section of the roof and disturbed a form wrapped in clothing.

"I think I've found a body!" he yelled to Pat, who was moving some pieces of wood on the other side of the roof section. When she got around to where Rick was, he had just climbed down from the debris carrying the mangled body of a woman. He placed it on the ground and then turned and went back to work. The infant's cry was louder.

Pat took only enough time to salvage a torn sheet to cover the victim before she returned to help Rick, who shoved and clawed a tunnel through the ruins. He removed a broken table, and after he dug out a splintered chair, there was just enough light from the area's spontaneous fires for him to see the child, which was still in its crib.

The crying intensified when Rick started crawling toward the child through a passageway made by the fallen roof structure. As he inched his way slowly through the rubble, he called, "Don't cry, kid! I'll have you out soon." He cursed under his breath when the infant howled louder. There was nothing wrong with the kid's lungs.

Rick stopped to blink away a grimy sweat bead in his eye. When he started forward again, a sharp nail scraped across his lower rib cage just as he reached the baby's crib, which was built of heavy wood. Fortunately, the child had been saved from a crushing death by its crib. Rick had to pry apart the thick slats to get to the baby. In the meager light, the work was slow.

He could find only two of the upright pieces that would move. Finally, he worked the howling infant through the opening. "You are okay now, kid." Rick hugged the child. "We are both going to feel a hell of a lot better when we get out of here." He kept speaking to the child in a low voice while backing out of the narrow tunnel.

Five minutes later, Rick sat on a piece of the broken table, watching Pat and the infant. She had the baby tucked in her arms, whispering in its ear. The crying soon quieted.

A baby's cry registered in the depths of Kuang's mind. He opened his eyes and stared into the darkness. The cry was stronger. It was nearby. To his left, there was a tall masonry wall rising high above him.

Kuang lay sprawled beside his car, which was buried under the same crumbled masonry he could feel touching his body. He wiped the grime from his face and then got to his feet and looked around the corner of the wall. The shadowy figure of Rick Scanlon carrying a baby moved down from a huge pile of building debris. He handed the noisy kid to a woman.

That must be the woman I saw in Scanlon's car that has been following me, Kuang reasoned. He watched the two comforting the squalling kid while his eyelids gradually hooded into slits. Because of these two foreigners, he had been chased for an hour and almost killed in an earthquake. The intensity of his rage burned inside his brain. He reached for his dagger.

Pat stood, snuggling the baby in her arms. The infant's crying had changed to hungry whimpers. *This child is alive by some miracle,* she thought, looking up at Rick. In the dim light, she saw blood on his face and an ugly scratch through a rip in his shirt.

"Let's go back to our car," he said, stepping down from the pile of splintered wood. "It will be more comfortable in the park to wait out the night." He leaned over the baby. "Is it a boy or a girl?"

"A girl," Pat answered. "And she needs changing. When we get back to—" she started, but a darting shadow interrupted her. "Rick!" Her scream was instinctive, and it came an instant ahead of a flashing knife aimed at his back.

Pat's shrill cry caused Rick to pivot automatically. The knife missed its real target but not by much. It sliced a long gash across his shoulder.

"Kuang, wait a minute!" Rick yelled, but when he shifted his weight, he stumbled over a piece of broken concrete. Kuang sprang at Rick and struck again with his knife. Rick moved just enough for the blade to miss, and it snapped in two when it hit the concrete. Now realizing he couldn't stop Kuang with words, Rick fought for his life.

Arms flailing, each man tried to establish a choking hold as they grappled over the rubble and up to the base of the masonry wall. A rip in the attacker's shirt revealed a wide belt around his waist, but the exposure was momentary as Pat, terrified, watched the struggle. Suddenly, a second tremor started and with a greater force than the first one.

With the ground trembling, Pat clutched the baby tighter while she tried to stay on her feet. She was becoming frantic for Rick's safety as he fought with the man near a brick wall. The rumble of the earthquake echoed above the grunts and curses of the two men, but Pat's attention was averted momentarily when a looming shadow appeared over the rubble. It moved slowly at first, and then it accelerated like a leopard springing for its prey.

She glanced up, and then by pure instinct, she cried out, "Rick! The wall!" A moment later, the ground rose abruptly, and she fell backward with the baby.

Rick heard Pat's scream just before he and Kuang catapulted upright onto their feet. The sudden shift in the ground level gave Rick the advantage. He was at the end of the wall while Kuang was closer to the middle, but the desperate Kuang fought harder. He grazed Rick's ear with the brick in his hand an instant before Rick's left fist caught Kuang on the jaw.

The tremor ended as the wall toppled with a heavy crash against the ground. Another dust cloud rose above the ruins of the apartment complex.

Rick heard a baby's cry. He stared into a black hole as sharp rocks dug into his back. Stars danced across the back of his eyes when he got to his feet. After he waited for a few moments until his vision cleared, he moved over to the hapless infant now lying on Pat's stomach. He held the baby in one arm and got Pat into a sitting position.

"How do you feel?" he asked when her eyes opened.

"Dizzy," Pat replied.

"You should. You got a lump on the back of your head. Sit awhile. I'll take care of the baby." When Rick reached for the fussing infant, it squirmed in his arms as he stood up and began to move about.

Near the base of the toppled wall, Kuang's leg protruded through some brick and mortar fragments. Rick bent down to have a closer look. The infant cried louder when Rick had to change his holding position to move the debris covering the crushed body. His hand soon touched a wide leather belt under the rubble.

Quickly, he glanced in Pat's direction. She remained where he had left her. He turned back, and with one hand, he started digging and scratching in the crumbled masonry, but the belt was caught on something. His jerking motions increased the intensity of the child's crying. *Shut up, kid,* Rick growled to himself, but the bawling baby and his clawing in the masonry rubble did not muffle the approaching noise behind him. Instantly, he cradled the baby in his arm like a football. Then with his free hand, he jerked with all his strength and yanked the belt free.

A moment later, Pat's voice came from over his shoulder, "Let me take the baby."

Rick shoved the belt under his shirt. *That damn chart had better be there*, he swore silently. Then he turned and handed the baby to Pat.

The baby's howling was soon reduced to an occasional sniffle while Pat snuggled it in her arms. Nothing stirred as they rested on top of the rubble. *When the tall buildings collapsed, they must have automatically buried their occupants,* Rick thought. The flickering fires, which had been ignited from ruptured gas lines, were like eternal memorials for the dead. The eerie darkness gave Rick a creepy feeling. "Let's go back to our car. We should be more comfortable there for the night."

CHAPTER 29

The sky filled with the sound of a helicopter as the afternoon sun beamed its warm rays over the devastated park. The aircraft landed a short distance from where Rick, Pat, and the baby had spent the night. Three people climbed out of the helicopter—a gray-haired man wearing a Chinese officer's uniform and two younger men wearing what appeared to be enlisted men's uniforms.

The older man said, "I Colonel Zhang Cheung. We here to build field hospital soon as possible."

Rick's handshake included a slight nod of his head while he introduced himself then Dr. Kendall.

"Medical doctor?" the colonel questioned while he looked directly at Pat.

"Yes," she answered.

"Need people like you. Can you help with injured?"

"Yes, I would like to help."

When the baby started crying, the colonel asked, "Your baby? Is it hurt?"

"No, we found the baby in the rubble from that apartment complex." Pat pointed in the direction of the building. "The baby is not hurt, just hungry."

"We have nothing but water aboard—" He was interrupted by a shout from a third uniformed man who was approaching rapidly from the chopper. He conferred with the colonel in a fast cadence. When the soldier finished talking, the colonel turned to Rick and said, "Word by radio, trucks with tents can't get to park. Roads are blocked. Come … must hurry." He started running toward the helicopter.

Just before takeoff after everyone was aboard, the colonel handed Pat a bottle of water. "Hope baby can drink from bottle," he said. Pat thanked him and prepared to get some water into the fussy youngster.

When the helicopter was in the air and the engines quieted, Rick asked the colonel, "How severe was the earthquake?"

"Thousands dead. Most of city in ruins. No electricity. No water. No communication in or out of city. All power lines and cellular towers down." The colonel's eyes, rimmed in shadows, revealed the despair from the tragedy when he paused momentarily. "After we land, helicopter go for medical team to lay out field hospital in park."

Twenty minutes after liftoff, the pilot landed the chopper in an opening barely large enough to accommodate the helicopter. The scattered debris had almost hidden the street intersection near the landing area. A long line of army trucks were stopped in front of three buildings that had toppled into the street. A stalled bulldozer was just ahead of the trucks.

But it was the rescue workers that caught Pat's eye, and many of them were digging into the rubble, carrying dead bodies, or administering to bodies on the ground. With the baby, she followed the colonel and his men from the helicopter but then headed toward a first-aid station under construction while Rick continued on with the colonel.

The first-aid station was being set up by four soldiers. Injured people lined up and got in the way of the soldiers' work. Pat noticed boxes of medical supplies but no doctors or nurses.

"Can you speak English?" she asked, getting one of the soldier's attention.

The young man nodded and said, "I try." A frown etched his face.

"I'm a doctor. If you can find some milk for this baby, I'll start helping the injured."

The soldier understood. He handed some wooden pegs to one of his buddies and then reached for the baby. Pat went to work on the first patient in line, a man with a deep cut on his leg.

Rick followed Colonel Cheung and his men to the blocked intersection. He tugged at the belt under his shirt. It was sticking to his skin. During the night when Pat had been dozing with the baby, he had made sure there was a map inside the belt. In the moonlight, the parchment had looked like a map.

But that was soon forgotten. A man was standing among several five-gallon cans near the bulldozer while talking animatedly to the Colonel. Another man tightened a battery cable on the dozer's engine as if he was afraid of being electrocuted. They didn't hear Rick approach until he asked, "What's the trouble?"

"Operator sick from exhaustion. They truck drivers," Cheung nodded toward the two men. "They don't know American machine."

Rick studied the big D8 Caterpillar tractor. *Wonder if I can still operate one of those,* Rick questioned silently. His thoughts returned to salvage school, where he had learned to use a bulldozer for dock work as part of his training. "Mind if I have a look?" he finally asked.

The colonel's head nodded quickly while he motioned to the machine with his hand.

"Has the machine stopped because it ran out of fuel?" While he waited for the answer, Rick picked up one of the cans. It was empty.

Cheung interpreted after he had listened to one of the men. "Machine stopped cause of no fuel. Took all cans to fill machine. Then would not start."

The dozer's fuel injection lines could be air bound, Rick thought while he tried to remember the instructor's comments back at salvage school. *The dozer has a self-bleeding control system, the instructor had said, but if the machine has some age, this system may not always function properly, so you may have to manually bleed the air.*

Rick went over to a toolbox, got the tools he needed, and then went to work. After bleeding all eight fuel lines, he climbed up on the driver's seat. Ten minutes later, when all the black smoke had been exhausted from the engine, he began clearing a roadway for the trucks.

CHAPTER 30

When the caravan finally reached the park, there was no helicopter with the people to build the temporary hospital. Rick continued operating the bulldozer to clear the park's streets of uprooted trees. An hour later, he climbed down from the machine after he had been called by Colonel Cheung, who stood with Pat near the head of the truck column. A frown creased his weather-beaten features.

"Got word on radio. All medical teams working at damaged hospitals. Get them in operation first. Won't be here for hours." Cheung looked anxiously at Rick and Pat. "Could you two get field hospital started?"

A thin smile crossed Rick's face as he glanced over at Pat, who was nodding her agreement, before he answered, "Colonel, you don't leave us with too many options, but just one thing." Rick handed him Hok's name and telephone number on a piece of paper. "As soon as you have established some kind of communication center, would you let this man know where I am and that I want him to come and see me as quickly as possible?"

"Yes, telephone will be in place by tomorrow."

"That's the best news I have heard in a while," Rick replied. Then he remembered the briefcase. "Colonel, I have a room at the Jinglun Hotel. Are you familiar with it?"

Cheung nodded. "It in central business district. Earthquake do no damage there."

"That's good to know. Could you get word to the hotel to hold my room?"

"I call hotel for you," Cheung replied with another nod of his head.

"Thank you," Rick said, breathing a sigh of relief before turning to Pat. "Well, what are we waiting for? Let's build a hospital!" He picked up a stick and handed it to her. "Draw us a plan, doctor," he said while he pointed to a bare spot on the ground.

Pat reached for the stick hesitantly. "My only experience is from a first-aid training class during med school," she said, allowing her thoughts to drift back in time a few moments. Then she started sketching a rimless wheel in the loose dirt on the ground. She made the wheel's hub the main operating section and then drew five spokes extending from the hub to the wheel's rim, indicting recovery areas.

"Allow enough room in these areas to move around freely," Pat said, pointing to the spokes. "Privacy is not too important for these kinds of patients."

Rick answered with a nod before he turned to Cheung, "Okay, colonel, let's move your trucks carrying the largest tents to the center of that cleared field." Rick pointed to an open area in the park. After he looked at the rough sketch again, he added, "And have the other trucks separate into five lanes extending out from the center." An hour later, the park rang with the hammering of steel-driven stakes.

Only the sun's amber rays lit the horizon when Pat hurried over to where Rick was leveling an area of the park, making room for more recovery tents.

"Can you help get a generated started so we can have some lights?" she yelled to get Rick's attention.

By the time he stepped down from the machine, Pat was already retracing her steps. When he caught up with her, he noticed dark circles under her eyes.

"Better not overdo it, doc," he said. "Save a few for tomorrow."

"Huh." It was her only answer.

They walked in silence, weaving their way around the soldiers swinging sledgehammers. When they passed a truck loaded with cots, Pat slowed. With her hand, she motioned toward the cots and said, "I will admit I could use one of those before too long."

"The colonel has set up some tents for us close to where the soldiers are bivouacked. I'll show you after I get the generator started." He left to join Cheung and three other men gathered around the electrical unit.

By midnight, the care center and some ward tents had lights. Rick left a work schedule with a night crew and then went looking for Pat.

At the surgery ward's entrance, he stood for a few moments, admiring the efficiency of the medical staff that had arrived by helicopter just before dark. He counted three rows of operating stations with two people positioned at each station. Each row was identified by its specialty. The teams farthest away from him were busy removing damaged tissue and foreign matter from wounds before the doctors stitched them closed. One burn victim waited quietly for treatment.

Pat was treating spinal and abdominal injuries at the last station in the first row. She had just finished an operation for a torn urethra on a patient with a fractured pelvis when Rick approached her from behind. She leaned on the operating table while she waited for the next patient. She swayed slightly before she raised her hand to brush away something in front of her eyes. Suddenly, her knees buckled. She slumped against the table and started falling, but Rick was there.

He picked her up in his arms. With a nod of his head, he motioned to one of the nurses assisting Pat that he was taking her outside. The cherubic little nurse hurried on ahead to hold open the tent flap.

He was fifty yards from the care center before the cool night air began to revive Pat. When he felt her stir, Rick held her closer. The night was quiet in this area of the sprawling encampment. Stars on black velvet surrounded a full moon as he walked out from under a tall gingko tree where the leaves barely stirred.

A smile crossed Pat's features, but her eyes remained closed. Her look of contentment caused him to stop. He stared for a long time, unmindful of her weight in his arms.

CHAPTER 31

Hok arrived three days after the start of the field hospital. He found Rick working between a large metal tank and a much larger metal configuration near the care center. "Meeting you in strange places is getting to be a habit," he said, feeling grime in his palm after the brief handshake with Rick.

"Yeah," Rick answered, handing Hok a rag. "And the places aren't exactly on the tourist trail either." While Hok wiped his hand, Rick picked up two wrenches lying on the ground near some pieces of steel pipe and continued working. "Evidently, Colonel Cheung was able to reach you with my message?"

"Yes, I came as quickly as I could after his call. It isn't easy flying into Beijing these days." Hok paused, watching Rick install what appeared to be the final piece of pipe connecting the two metal objects. "I have heard some excellent reports on the job you and Dr. Kendall are doing here at this field hospital."

"All the credit belongs to Pat Kendall. She and a Dr. Duprey have organized the medical people who were available into an efficient health-care group."

When two men approached, Rick said, "Excuse me for a few minutes, Hok. I want to tell these guys how to operate this thing."

At the end of Rick's fifteen-minute show-and-tell demonstration, the two men nodded their heads, and then Rick turned to Hok and said, "Okay, we can go to my tent now. I have something I want to show you."

On the way, Hok asked, "Pardon my curiosity, but what was that 'thing' that you were telling those guys how to operate?"

A smile creased Rick's face. "I'm trying to provide some hot water as well as some heat to our hospital. The oil tank and boiler were brought in yesterday. I understand they were about the only usable things left of a grade school in the area. Fortunately, the earthquake happened in the evening."

Thirty minutes later, they were in Rick's tent, sitting on his cot, which was the only piece of furniture inside the enclosure. Rick removed the belt from underneath his shirt while he began telling Hok how he had gotten it. "This belt almost cost me my life. Ironically, if Kuang had only known I would've paid him for it, he would be alive today."

"Why did Kuang consider you an enemy?"

"That, I would like to know. He told Captain Yang he didn't trust anybody doing business with Fuchou. Incidentally, I would have told you sooner about my money-drop mission, but Broadman was emphatic about keeping it a secret."

Rick zipped open the belt and removed the document. After he spread it between them on the cot, he asked, "Do you have any idea why Broadman, a DEA agent, would be interested in a treasure map, if that's what this document is?"

Hok only glanced at the document. He reflected on the question a few moments before he answered, "Rick, you broke a secret. I'm going to break one that I promised to keep with my boss. He also has some doubts about trusting Broadman. He thinks he might be an Afghan affiliated with the Taliban." Hok paused a few moments, still looking directly at Rick. "If Broadman could be working to supply dope to the California coast from only Afghanistan while stopping shipments from all other sources—"

"And since our army's presence in Afghanistan," Rick interrupted, "has put the squeeze on the supply from that country, the Taliban is looking for extra money to support itself."

Absorbed in thought, a long silence hung between them. "This parchment feels funny. Is it for real?" Hok broke the stillness.

"It passed all the tests Broadman supplied me with to prove its authenticity," Rick said. Watching Hok intently, Rick then added, "I wouldn't mind trying a double cross on Broadman. How about you?"

Hok stared at Rick. "I'm not exactly following you."

"I haven't been in contact with Broadman since the earthquake, but I now have in my possession both the map and the money to pay for it." Rick paused momentarily. "I'm assuming the briefcase is still in my hotel room here in Beijing, so lets' think about this situation a moment. The map was Kuang's, but we are pretty sure, despite his feelings about me, had he known that I had the money to pay for it, he would at least have talked to me."

"So Kuang was not the original one with the map to meet you at the bar," Hok said.

"That's what I'm thinking."

"But how do you know if this is a treasure map?"

"Do you think your grandfather could tell us that?"

Hok's face clouded in a frown, a look that Rick hadn't seen before. "If anyone can decode this chart, I believe my grandfather can," he said, but the look remained.

He is concerned for his grandfather's safety, Rick thought. *He knows I am getting him involved in a risky scheme, but I have no other choice.*

"That should take care of one of our problems," Rick said. "The next step is to get a search permit from China. Do you think Captain Yang or his brother, the doctor, can help us?"

"Yes," Hok replied hesitantly while he stared at Rick. "Are you saying you want me included in your search for the treasure?"

Rick blanked, realizing the fault of his musing about Hok's concern, but he recovered quickly. "Hok, that chart is worthless to me without your help. Will a share of whatever success we have be satisfactory with you?"

A broad, tooth-filled smile cracked Hok's face. He held out his hand. "You are more than generous, especially since the only diving experience I've had is to examine an ancient shipwreck sunk along the California coast. But is your ship prepared for this kind of work?"

"No, however, I have an old partner who is trying to sell a well-equipped salvage vessel back in San Francisco. And I know an outfit back there that is interested in buying my ship. So if this map is genuine, I believe we can—" A noise at the entrance to the tent interrupted Rick.

"Rick, could you help with the bulldozer?" Pat asked. When she saw Hok, she walked inside. "Hi, Hok!" she said, her voice lifting. "Colonel Cheung told me you would be arriving today." They held each other in a quick embrace. "Hopefully," she said, still holding on to Hok while looking up at him, "we can meet someday without the result of a disaster."

"It's good to see you again, Dr. Kendall, and all in one piece." Hok hesitated, noticing unfamiliar lines in her face, which prompted him to say, "Resolved. Our next meeting shall be under nothing but pleasant conditions. And that reminds me, I bring a personal invitation from my grandparents for you to visit them before you leave China."

"Well, thank you, Hok, and please thank your grandparents for their offer, but I don't think I'll be doing any traveling for a while."

"Yes, I am well aware that your sabbatical here in Beijing has been short-lived," Hok said and smiled.

"Um, that's one way of putting it," she answered amiably while she glanced at Rick. He had inched closer to Hok after they had both rose from the cot when Pat had entered, but he had been unable to hide the body belt completely. One end was hanging over the cot.

When Pat noticed the loose end, something stirred in her memory. She moved to have a closer look. Her mood changed suddenly. She had seen that belt before, but where? An eel of fear wriggled inside her when she remembered. That belt was under the torn shirt of the man Rick had fought with. Then she saw the unfolded piece of paper. The creases in the paper were spaced about the same width as the body belt.

Pat looked up at Rick. Her eyes were concerned and angry when they locked on his. "Somehow, I believe the fight after the earthquake had something to do with that map or whatever it is there on the cot."

"It did." Rick's stare never wavered from hers.

"Then it must be a valuable piece of paper?"

"It could be."

Irritated by Rick's short answers, she leaned down to have a closer look at the chart. There was a long silence. Hok suddenly realized he was in the middle of a simmering squabble, and he wanted to leave; however, he was unable to think of a graceful retreat.

There was a grim set to Pat's jaw when she again faced Rick and said, "I'm not an engineer, but I don't believe that has anything to do with military hardware." Her voice tore at him. There was another pause while the frown etched into her features eased slightly. "I'm aware I wouldn't be alive today without you." She lessened the intensity of her voice, trying to control herself. "But that doesn't give you the right to risk my life in pursuing your own self-interests. I certainly do not appreciate your deception."

She is overreacting! Rick cursed under his breath, but with her eyes on his face, he was aware of her ability to understand his thoughts. "Look at it this way," Rick said and then paused to clear his throat. "With the earthquake happening, your medical skill has been essential in ramping up this field hospital into an efficient health-care unit. How about giving me some credit for being responsible in having you at the right place at the right time." Rick paused, hoping his segue was reasonable enough to lighten her attitude.

It only fanned the fire. Her strident tone of voice was instantaneous. "Evidently, it isn't logical to you that I would have volunteered my services wherever I might have been here in Beijing after the earthquake." She whirled, nodded curtly to Hok, and left. The snap of the tent flap matched the biting edge of her voice.

Walking rigidly back to surgery, Pat's fury spawned tears. And it wasn't as much from Rick's deceit about the map as it was from his apparent lack of recognizing her will in performing her medical obligations.

After becoming a doctor, her work has been her life, and his failure to not realize that made her fume. But her indignation was short-lived. Ahead of her at the surgery entrance, a nurse was motioning for her to hurry.

CHAPTER 32

When Pat stormed out of the tent, a thin smile tugged at Rick's mouth when he turned to Hok. "Needless to say, it was never my intent for her to know of this treasure situation." He paused a few moments before adding, "But we can't always control our intentions."

By the time Rick had finished the bulldozer work and made some adjustments to the water heater, the day was shot. He had planned to spend the day going to the hotel with Hok to get the briefcase. Instead, Hok had to stay the night after Rick had found him an extra cot.

A gray dawn had turned into a misty rain by the time they were ready to leave the following morning in Hok's rental car. Three hours later, after they had made many detours to avoid blocked-off streets, they finally drove out of the area damaged by the earthquake. Another thirty minutes, and they arrived at Rick's hotel. If the briefcase was still in Rick's room, Hok would take it back to the States after he left the map with his grandfather to decode, but two calls would be made first.

Up in Rick's room, with the briefcase still in the room's safe, Hok made the first call to his boss. Rick sat listening to Hok explain the history of the briefcase and the debacle at the bar, which had prompted their plan to hunt for the treasure if the map could be decoded. He said they felt no remorse about double-crossing Broadman. He mentioned why he was bringing back the briefcase instead of Rick and then asked Dallworth if he would deliver it to Broadman.

After Hok finished, Dallworth was silent for several minutes. The phone was on conference call. "Hok, now you understand why I've had my doubts about Broadman. Rick, has Hok mentioned to you about my feelings?"

"He has," Rick answered.

"All right. Hok, come on home with the briefcase. Yes, I will take it to Broadman. At the present time anyway, both you and I are innocent of the briefcase and its relation to any treasure map. Rick, I was thinking that with my delivery as well as bringing your 'too busy with the hospital and Dr. Kendall' excuse, you might appear more honorable to Broadman."

"That was our reasoning and thanks for your help." Rick answered.

"Glad to, but a word of caution. Broadman is no dummy. Rick, those two thugs you had to deal with at that bar could be his henchmen and still looking for you. Have you called Broadman since the earthquake?"

"No, I'm going to call as soon as we hang up."

"Then, Hok, I won't contact him until I see you with the briefcase. Good luck, and keep your tracks covered."

Five minutes later, Broadman was on the phone. "The earthquake here in Beijing has caused my delay in contacting you for a while," Rick started the conversation. "And I've been—"

"So that is why you haven't been answering your cell phone," Broadman interrupted, his voice edged in irritation. "What are you doing in Beijing? The business we sent you on is in Hong Kong."

"Give me a chance to explain," Rick answered curtly. "I came up here to see a lady doctor friend. We got caught in the earthquake. Since medical people and hospital facilities suddenly became urgently needed, we both are helping out." Rick paused momentarily. "That is the first reason for this call. The second reason is since the money drop has been botched, I'm sending the briefcase back with Willard Dallman's employee, Hokusai Utamaro, as soon as I can reach him by phone." Rick winked at Hok before he continued, "He knows nothing about its history—"

"Wait a minute!" Broadman's voice was brittle. "At airport security, won't he wonder why it contains only a computer and Hong Kong street maps? I'm assuming those items are still in the briefcase."

"They are. The only things missing are my socks and shorts. But he will be told it's your briefcase and you prepared the contents, which I have studied and no longer need for soliciting the shipping business. And the third and final reason for this call, I will be here in Beijing for a while longer in helping with a field hospital."

"How much longer?" Broadman iced the words. Then with a trace of suspicion entering his voice, he asked, "Where are you calling from now?"

"The Jinglun Hotel in Beijing, where I have a room and where the earthquake did no damage. That is why this must be a short call. I'm needed at the field hospital. I should not be here in Beijing more than two or three weeks. By then I'm sure you can reach me by cell phone. Have a good day."

Back at the field hospital three hours later, Hok was ready to leave again and this time for the airport. From the driver's seat of his rental, which was parked near Rick's tent, he said, "You're sure you don't want to go with me to check on this?" He tapped his shirt front, which showed a faint outline of the money belt.

Rick leaned against the car and shook his head. "I trust you, and I can be of more use here. Before leaving for home with the briefcase, call me for an update on your grandfather's progress. If my cell phone isn't working, leave a message with Colonel Cheung. You have his office phone number that I gave you?"

Hok nodded, and then with a wave of his hand, he drove off.

CHAPTER 33

BROADMAN HEARD THE CLICK of Scanlon's phone in his ear. He sat and reflected on the conversation. *Is the return of the briefcase a ploy?* he questioned. *Is Scanlon trying to deceive me with his show of integrity? Why isn't he returning it himself? Could it possibly have anything to do with the treasure map?*

He rose from his chair and moved slowly around his office while he thought about the treasure map and where it might be at the present time. Rahab had kept him updated because Kuang's name was on the back of the picture he had taken from Bashir's room. Two days after the bar fight, Kuang's rough sketch was in a Hong Kong newspaper. He was a murder suspect and last seen buying an airline ticket to Beijing.

Several days after the earthquake, the police beat section of the same paper listed his picture again as one of the victims who had died in the Beijing earthquake. The case was now closed. After a few telephone calls by his staff, Broadman learned that Kuang's body was found near the field hospital that Scanlon was involved with.

Could it be because he has the map? Broadman pondered. *And is planning to hunt for the treasure? But that isn't practical. The map is in code. And just who is this Hokusai Utamaro? Is he something more than an employee of Willard Dallworth?* He made a note to have his office do a background check on this man.

Two days later, the bio was on his desk. Broadman thumbed through the pages and saw nothing unusual until he read that his grandfather was a cartographer. It sparked his curiosity. He immediately called for the grandfather's bio. When he read it the following day, he said, "Aha, there's the connection!" He almost shouted out loud. *So the grandfather will be decoding the map! This is a job for Rahab!* From the report he read, he found the grandfather's address in Kowloon and then reached for his phone.

But his training as an agent caused him to pause and consider the whole situation before he made any rash decisions. *We don't know that the grandfather has the map,* Broadman mused. *And if he does, why not let him do the decoding and then take the map. In the meantime, my staff can keep a watch for any movement of Scanlon's ship, which I know is still docked here in San Francisco.*

Broadman was glad that Rahab was still in Hong Kong. After the debacle at the bar, Ahmad Sattar had ordered his two sons home, but Broadman had convinced his mentor to have Rahab stay awhile. And the belligerent Rahab had kept alert.

About three weeks after Scanlon's telephone call, his freighter was part of the Smitzer fleet. The agent who reported this transaction also claimed that Scanlon was the new owner of a smaller salvage ship that had been on the market for several months. A week later, the same agent reported that Scanlon's salvage ship left port bound for Kaohsiung, Taiwan.

But Broadman was skeptical, because he felt sure that Scanlon was still in China. The agent claimed his information had come from the harbormaster, who had become friendly with the man selling it. And it was this man who was skippering the ship to Taiwan. Then two days after that, Willard Dallworth delivered the briefcase.

"I'm surprised to see you with the briefcase, Willard. I was told that your man, Utamaro, would be delivering it."

"Ed, when a young man has been away from his girlfriend for a while, he has other things on his mind besides business."

"I understand," Broadman said. "But I would like to talk with him. Would you have him stop by my office?"

"Sorry, Ed. He has already gone back. His stay was short since I have some urgent work for him in Hong Kong."

Immediately after Dallworth left, Broadman had his agent check Utamaro's travel schedule at the airport. He had left the day before the return of the briefcase but not for Hong Kong. His destination had been Kaohsiung, Taiwan.

Over the years, Broadman had established an excellent relationship with counterparts in the Taiwan Police Department. Within an hour after his call, Broadman learned that Scanlon and Utamaro had reserved a suite at the Ambassador Hotel in downtown Kaohsiung and neither had checked in yet. With this information, Broadman immediately made two other phone calls—one to Ahmad Sattar and the other to Rahab.

CHAPTER 34

DURING HER LUNCH BREAK, Pat stopped at her tent to change shoes. She was about to leave when she saw an envelope on her cot. She had a premonition it was from Rick. That same voice inside her said he had gone.

Recently, there had been little time to think of him. The Park Hospital was the only medical facility in the area that was equipped to handle the severely injured. Thousands of these patients had arrived since her talk about the map in Rick's tent. That had been several weeks ago. She had seen Rick but only fleeting glances. He seemed to be working both day and night, which matched her work schedule. She assumed Hok's visit to the hospital was brief since she had only seen him the one time with Rick.

She sat down on the cot and studied the envelope. "Pat" was scrawled across its front in bold lettering. She had an inclination to toss the note without reading it, but this man had saved her life.

Why does he bring out the worst in me? she pondered. *Is it because he has few of the refined qualities she admired in a man like Francois Duprey?* Her thoughts shifted to the doctor and their talk two nights ago when they left surgery together.

"How about a walk with me around the lake? It's a good relaxer," Duprey said, holding the tent flap open for her.

"Is that a medical diagnosis, doctor?" she asked, stepping outside into the cool night air.

"No, it's a chance for me to try to tell you of my appreciation for the job you are doing here at the hospital."

They walked in amiable silence toward the lake, which was a distance from the main hospital area.

"Back in America, your practice will seem rather uneventful after China," Dupery said. They stopped to sit on two large rocks that were part of the shoreline.

"Under normal circumstances, the answer would be yes," Pat answered, "but on an airplane trip just before I left the States, my work was rather hectic."

"I forgot that. Yes, I heard of your airplane crash. You were rescued by this Rick Scanlon, who has also become a hero here in China." There was a splash in the middle of the lake. Francois waited for the ripples to recede before he added, "Are you in love with him?"

She stared at Francois. Had she heard correctly? "I beg your pardon?" she asked tersely.

"The American captain, Rick Scanlon, who saved your life. Are you in love with him?"

"No!" Pat answered. "My attitude toward Mr. Scanlon is just the opposite. I'm quite bitter with him for his dishonesty and his total disregard for my welfare while here in China." Puzzled, she stared at Francois. "What made you ask?"

"There is an old Chinese proverb; something about a life saved belongs to the saver. The two of you didn't appear like casual acquaintances the other evening when he carried you from surgery."

"But I thought—" She stopped. After she had fainted, she thought two of the nurses had taken her out of surgery. The next day, she could only catch a few words of their explanation on how she had gotten to her tent. She never remembered seeing Rick that evening, and no one else had mentioned her fainting spell. *Could that have been to save me from any embarrassment?* she reflected.

Now it's my turn, she thought, smiling to herself. "Why is it that you have never married?"

"I was in love once," he answered. "It was a long time ago when I was in med school in Paris. She was beautiful, a rising young artist. We shared a one-room flat on the Left Bank." His face was solemn when he turned to look again at the lake. "Amie smoked incessantly. We had known each other three years to the day when cancer took her." When he looked at Pat again, the easy smile returned. "So now I have my work and my memories."

"But are memories enough?"

"For me, they are."

The night was quiet. A shooting star generated a long flashing jet stream before it vanished. "Regarding my relationship with the man you mentioned," Pat said, "he has characteristics that I am not comfortable with. His soldier-of-fortune lifestyle and his recklessness are completely opposite to my nature."

"I have watched this man, Scanlon, work with people, and I have heard others, such as Colonel Cheung, assess his qualities." Duprey paused while swinging his legs to the ground before he helped Pat step down from her seat on the rock. When they turned to head back, he added, "I agree with Colonel Cheung. A man like this American Ship Captain is rare."

Pat continued to study the envelope while she thought about her talk with Francois. She recalled a warning bell during one part of the conversation. So it had been Rick who brought her here that night. Her clothes, she remembered, had been stained with blood and grime that had soaked all the way through to her skin, but she had awakened the next morning between clean sheets … in the nude.

She opened the envelope. The note was brief:

> Dear Pat:
>
> I have left to do some salvage work with Hok in the Taiwan Strait. I should return in about three weeks.
>
> Love,
> Rick

She immediately noticed the way it had been signed. *Does he expect me to take that literally?* she asked herself. After she stretched out on the cot, she read the message again, her thoughts drifting.

The early morning sun beamed its welcome rays on a nurse hurrying along a worn path to Pat's tent. At the entrance, the nurse started to call, but something stopped her. She stared, fascinated at the sleeping face. It seemed to emit a soft glow in the darkened interior of the tent. A smile touched Pat's lips just before her eyes opened.

"Dr. Kendall," the nurse said quietly, "more patients."

CHAPTER 35

THE NEWSPRINT BLURRED IN front of Rahab Sattar. He tossed the newspaper on the adjacent lamp table and shifted his weight in the cushioned chair.

The lobby of the Ambassador Hotel in downtown Kaohsiung, Taiwan, was busy. People moved continually across its carpeted floor while some like Rahab occupied the sofas and chairs, which were random spaced throughout the large room.

According to Fasial, this was check-in day for Scanlon, and since early this morning, Rahab had been diligent in his watch. He sat at the opposite end of the lobby from the entrance door, which started revolving again. For what seemed like the hundredth time in the past hour, his glance riveted in that direction. A bellhop carrying two pieces of luggage emerged from the divided door. As it continued rotating, the next section discharged a Japanese couple who were small enough to fit comfortably together in the door's pie-shaped configuration.

Rahab swore silently. He stood up but didn't move from in front of his chair. He turned his head slowly from side to side, stretching his neck and shoulder muscles. The disguise he wore wasn't helping his disposition. His scalp was hot under the tight hairpiece, and his heavy beard itched.

He was in this seaport on orders from Faisal, orders that had been confirmed later by a call from his father. The orders were simple: Take the navigation chart from Scanlon here at the hotel. The only problem was that Scanlon hadn't arrived.

Rahab didn't have to ask Faisal how he had learned of Scanlon's plans. The spidery DEA webbed a huge informational network, and Faisal's office in San Francisco was a central part of it.

A tall brunette caught Rahab's attention when she entered the lobby from the elevator area. She stopped near the front desk and said something to one of the desk clerks. When she continued toward the entrance door, his thoughts switched to Jamila al-Darda, whom, until yesterday, he hadn't seen since they were both teenagers. And now they shared a suite here at the hotel.

His father had mentioned in his phone conversation that he was sending Jamila to assist him in taking the map. Rahab had learned from Faisal that the white man he had fought at the Dragon Head Bar was an American named Rick Scanlon, but Jamila al-Darda troubled his mind as much as Scanlon. During the telephone conversation with his father, the mention of her name had surprised him. Then he almost dropped the phone when his father said he was sending her to help with the job here in Kaohsiung.

During the silence that followed, the pain suddenly returned to Rahab's stomach. The pain that had been dormant for years began wriggling once again in his bowels. *How had she gotten involved?* he wanted to asked, but it wasn't the time. This call had come from Pakistan. His father was still in hiding.

"Our road of life sometimes takes unexpected turns," his father had continued. "Do not burden yourself with unnecessary thoughts. Fill your mind with the job to do." There was a sound like ice rattling in a glass. "The chart is important to us. The salvage work will be a profitable diversion. We will let the DEA think they are winning the drug war."

When Rahab had met Jamila's plane, they had stopped for coffee at one of the airport's cafés before they took a taxi to the hotel here in Kaohsiung. Life had been good to Jamila during the past ten years since he had seen her. Her dark hair shimmered in soft curls around her shoulders, accentuating a clear, dusky complexion completely devoid of any makeup. The only enhancements to her features were tiny jeweled earrings and a slightly reddish hue to her full lips. Dressed in a gray sweater and black pants, her casual travel wear complimented the full maturity of her lithe, sensual body.

The Taliban had forbidden girls to be educated, but Jamila's mother had been a French Muslim and former schoolteacher. It was noticeably apparent from her speaking voice that Jamila was not lacking in education. "I have brought several disguises for you." She touched her shoulder bag, which hung over one of the chairs. "You are to choose whichever you feel will make you look like an exporter from London."

Rahab said nothing but silently cursed himself for being so thoughtless. He had forgotten that Scanlon would be able to recognize him. This disguise idea had to have been Faisal's. He had taught the technique to all members of the family.

"Do you know what Scanlon looks like?" Rahab asked gruffly.

She nodded. "Your father gave me his picture. It's a newspaper clipping."

Rahab's eyes leveled on hers. "I can speak English. Can you?"

She immediately switched to English. It was flawless. "I worked four years in the British Embassy in Kabul. I also made several trips to London on official business. I'm quite comfortable with the language, as well as the British customs."

"And if I'm to be an Englishman, how are we to register?" His voice had an edge. "Do we have names?"

"Charles and Jane Willoughby. I'm an interior decorator on vacation, traveling with my brother." The hint of a smile appeared in her eyes while her lips trailed playfully along the edge of her cup.

*Damn this woma*n! Rahab fought to control himself. He had the uneasy feeling she was still taunting him from their encounter that summer night years ago.

That night had been as hot as Jamila. They had gone swimming in the nude. Later, while they lay on the soft grass, they began fondling each other. Their excitement blazed and led to ultimate fulfillment, but immediately after he entered Jamila, his erection went soft. Quickly, she began to masturbate him, and when there was no response, she tried rousing him with her mouth, but it didn't help. Her emotions changed to scorn and eventually to laughter.

That had been his first experience with sex, and it was his last until a few years later when he went to a brothel in Mumbai, India; however, his malady still existed. When he finally went to a doctor, Rahab was told that an understanding woman could cure his humiliating problem. However, by that time, his attitude toward women had changed. He firmly believed that the Taliban's denial of virtually all women's rights was justified.

During the long silence, Rahab masked his emotions with stone-cold features. Then he got up from his chair and grabbed the shoulder bag. "I will be back soon!" he said bitterly without looking at her.

CHAPTER 36

JAMILA'S HEELS CLICKED IN a slow cadence on the sidewalk. She walked along the street leading back to her hotel, but she was in no hurry. Rahab would be there, watching for Scanlon. And if the American should happen along, she would recognize him. His image was committed to memory from the picture that Ahmad had showed her. She marveled at how well informed he was on American affairs. His contacts had to be exceptional.

The blare of a car horn interrupted her thoughts while her eyes again fixed in eagerness. The sights and sounds of this bustling seaport intrigued her. Changes were everywhere. On the streets, cars and bicycles competed for the right-of-way. Store windows displayed mannequins clad in bikinis, more daring than any she had ever worn on the Caribbean beaches while she had traveled with Ahmad. And two blocks back, she had passed one of the American's golden arches.

But the afternoon sun was hot. Just ahead was a welcome sight, the shade of a department store's portico. It gave her a chance to look at some cocktail dresses with Yves Saint Laurent labels that filled one of the windows. The hemlines of the dresses were teasingly high, but her attention wavered. The window reflected the image of two male pedestrians walking in opposite directions while looking her way. When they bumped into each other, a smile crossed her face.

Her thoughts shifted to Rahab. *Why didn't he look at her that way?* Since she had arrived, she had caught him staring at her several times, and when she met his eyes, he blinked as if washing away some self-conscious guilt before his normal glare returned. She dismissed the thought of his problem still existing. That was long ago, and besides, she felt sure it was the first time for him.

Jamila moved on when three Asian women stopped to look at the dresses. Ten minutes later, she arrived at her hotel. As she approached the entrance, some costume jewelry in one of the hotel's display windows caught her attention. She hesitated for a moment.

★ ★ ★

A line of cars stalling Rick's cab a half block from his hotel's entrance strained Rick's patience. He paid the fare, and with a bag in each hand, he started toward the hotel's entrance. He was unaware of the people along the broad sidewalk. The forthcoming salvage work was heavy on his mind. He would rent one of the hotel's security boxes when he registered for himself and Hok, who was arriving sometime this evening with the decoded navigation chart. The *Valiant* should be here in two days. That was the name he had given his newly purchased salvage ship, gambling that a name related to gallantry would engender more luck in its mission.

Jake Flowers had called over a week ago after he had gotten the ship underway from Honolulu. Rick's accountant in San Francisco, who was also his power of attorney, had said by phone that the two-ship transaction had been settled amicably by all parties. There had been a chuckle in the accountant's voice when he had said the representative from Rick's bank had seemed very pleased with the settlement.

Rick had decided to have his ship arrive here at Kaohsiung. It was the closest major port relative to the apparent site of the sunken treasure ship. The weather added to his crowded mind. He glanced up at the sky and then realized—perhaps too late—that the brunette directly ahead of him had stopped. His momentum pushed them both into one section of the revolving door. They had no choice but to remain confined together until the moving door discharged them into the hotel's lobby.

Instinctively, Jamila started to apologize in her native language, but the man behind her spoke first.

"Excuse my clumsiness!"

When she turned to face him, she switched to English and said, "No, it is my fault!" But her smile froze when she recognized him immediately.

"I'll accept on a fifty-fifty basis." Rick smiled, extending his hand.

Jamila's eyes blinked. "Fifty-fifty," she repeated, a catch in her throat. She felt the hammering inside her chest, but she looked up at him and smiled. "Since both of us came through the accident unhurt, I will take my leave. Good afternoon, sir."

"Good afternoon," Rick answered. An impish grin tugged at his mouth when he added, "And I hope we run into each other again soon."

Jamila flashed him a smile and then turned and started across the lobby to the elevators. Her image gradually faded from Rick's view as he walked over to the desk.

CHAPTER 37

Rahab saw Jamila emerge from the revolving door. She had a hangdog look as if she was at fault. When Rick Scanlon suddenly appeared from behind her, Rahab started, nearly bolting upright from his chair. Emotions seesawed across his mind. A bile of bitterness rose in his throat as he thought of the beating he had taken from this American and watched the brief conversation by the entrance door. His loathing gradually receded to irritation, noticing the attention Scanlon paid to Jamila as she walked across the lobby.

While Scanlon completed his registration at the desk, Rahab sat quietly, watching over the top of his paper. When the American, who was led by a bellhop pushing the luggage cart, started for the elevator lobby, Rahab rose from his chair. With the folded paper tucked under one arm, he casually followed to take a position well behind the waiting Scanlon. By the time Scanlon's elevator arrived, there were several other passengers taking the same elevator, including the disguised Rahab, who unobtrusively stationed himself against a side wall of the elevator's cab.

When Scanlon got off on six, Rahab excused himself and stepped between an elderly couple in his path and then left the elevator just before the doors closed. The bellhop asked Scanlon for his key at the door of room 615 as Rahab sauntered past. The long, quiet corridor turned a corner where Rahab restlessly waited, walking a few paces and then returning to glance back around the corner only to repeat his nervous vigil when there was no activity at 615. When the bellhop, a short, stocky, older Asian, finally emerged from the room, Rahab did not move from the corner until the hotel employee disappeared into the elevator.

Five minutes later, Rahab opened the door to his room on the eighth floor. In the living room separating the two-bedroom suite, Jamila stopped her pacing.

"I just saw Rick Scanlon down in the lobby!" she announced excitedly. "We literally ran into one another and—"

"I know! I saw you both from my surveillance location!" Rahab interrupted curtly, walking on past her to a credenza against one of the living room walls. The polished mahogany sideboard contained various bottles of liquor plus a bucket of ice cubes. He tossed a handful of the ice cubes into a tall glass before he filled it with vodka.

He turned around and faced Jamila, but his eyes did not see her. His thoughts were on a plan to search Scanlon's room for the navigation chart. He shook his glass several times before he took a healthy drink.

Jamila waited, realizing from Rahab's glazed eyes that he was deep in thought. *Does this son of the famous drug lord have the cunning skills of his father?* she asked herself.

But she would have to wait awhile to find out. Then Rahab set his drink back on the credenza and headed for the door. "Stay here! I will be back soon!" he snapped the words over his shoulder just before he left the room.

Down in the lobby, Rahab walked over to the front desk where he soon got the attention of a clerk who had just completed a telephone call.

"Can I help you," the young man asked cordially.

"Yes," Rahab spoke slowly, thinking the words out carefully before saying them. "I will be returning to Kaohsiung in about one month. I will be bringing several business partners with me. I would like several suites like my present one on the eighth floor but not as high up. Do you have similar suites like possibly on the sixth floor?"

"I believe we do, but let me make sure," the clerk replied, and then his fingers raced across the keyboard of an idle computer. After the clerk stopped, he studied the screen for a few moments before he said, "Yes, we do. As a matter of fact, the room arrangement on six is identical to eight." After he studied the screen again, he added, "Sir, I am sorry to have to tell you those rooms on floors six through eight are already reserved one month from now. There is a convention—"

"Not a problem," Rahab interrupted. "The business plans here in the city have not been confirmed with all of my associates, but I will remember to have my secretary call for reservations well in advance of our arrival date. Thank you."

Five minutes later, Rahab walked over to the credenza in his suite and picked up his drink, which was now sitting in a faint pool of water. Unmindful of the wet ring left on the sideboard's sparkling surface, Rahab sat in one of two cushioned chairs. "All right, here is my plan."

Jamila tossed her magazine onto the coffee table, and with lackluster eyes, she stared back at Rahab. But her outward appearances were deceiving. She was keenly interested to know if Rahab had a brain in his head. She waited.

"Scanlon is in room 615. It is a suite like this, according to the information I was able to gather from a desk clerk without drawing any suspicion of our motive." Rahab shot her an arrogant look, but she could see that the muscles of his face were beyond relaxation. He took another drink from his glass before he continued, "Your job is to meet Scanlon. Keep him busy long enough for me to search his room."

"That is easy for you to say." Jamila's voice was controlled. "And where is this meeting supposed to take place … and when?"

Rahab thought about his previous meeting with Scanlon and unconsciously touched his nose. "Try the hotel bar this evening." Then with his eyes locked on hers and his voice still unrelentingly cold, he added, "The way he watched you walking across the lobby, I don't think your job will be too difficult." With his drink still in his hand, Rahab rose from his chair. "I will be waiting here for your call," he said. "And be sure you call soon after making contact with Scanlon." Then he walked into his room and closed the door.

CHAPTER 38

JAMILA PREPARED FOR THE evening, starting with a scented bath. Despite the feeling of apprehension connected with her mission, she felt an additional warmth, thinking about the handsome American. No separate bedrooms for him, she felt sure. The thought made her breasts tingle in the foamy water. Languidly, she rubbed the nipples into rigid cones.

Two hours later, Jamila entered the hotel's cocktail lounge. She paused, looked around the dimly lit interior, and then moved to the only vacant table near the back of the crowded room. Her table was against the wall on the opposite side of the room from a long bar where there was standing room only. But the service was excellent. Her waitress had long dark hair and oval eyes filled with smiles. Three minutes after Jamila had ordered a martini, it sat on her table.

The nervous ache between her shoulder blades disappeared as the strong drink settled in her stomach. Faces in the crowd began to have features. She counted three other women in the room, but they weren't alone. *No competition so far*, she thought, *but unless my man shows, there will be no game.*

However, her presence had not gone unnoticed. She caught the glances of several men throughout the room. Normally, she would be uneasy sitting alone in a crowded bar, but she was comforted by the fact there was a considerable mixture of nationalities among the customers. A large black man in a white suit was sitting at a table with two Asian men wearing darker business suits. Two women with dark hair occupied a table with two blond men. And near the front of the room, there was a dark-skinned man with a large mustache pointed at the ends. He wore a red fez. The long tassel occasionally caught on his ear while he talked with two Asian men sitting at his table. A blonde white woman in a yellow dress sat in the fourth chair at the table.

Jamila finished her drink just as the waitress appeared with another.

"That man over there bought you a drink," the waitress nodded in the direction of a slender white man sitting alone. His smile wavered at Jamila's frown when she saw that he was not Rick Scanlon. Quickly, she recovered from her disappointment and smiled her thanks.

The complimentary drink was slightly bitter but not from its taste. *If Scanlon doesn't arrive soon*, Jamila thought, *I might be placed in an awkward position, should this gracious gentleman make an attempt to introduce himself.* Then as she glanced up at the front of the room, she breathed a deep sigh of relief. Scanlon had entered the lounge.

He paused, looking in the direction of the bar for a few moments before glancing around the room. He was in no hurry. He even stepped aside to let a couple that had entered behind him pass by.

But Jamila's eyes fixed on him. She felt the beating inside her chest. Would he recognize her from that distance? Then she knew. There was no change in his expression when he looked in her direction. He moved on over to the bar, where he had to stand, which gave her new hope. It would surely improve his chances of noticing her. She waited. Scanlon got his drink, turned, and again faced the room, but three other men stood near him, obstructing his view of her.

From the corner of her eye she saw the man who had bought her the drink stand up. He was looking her way. But her anxiety soon disappeared when she turned to avoid facing him. The waitress was approaching. Jamila stood up and met the waitress. "Will you hold my table? I'll return shortly." Her voice was steady, showing no emotion.

When the waitress nodded her agreement, Jamila picked up her purse, but instead of walking straight ahead toward the door, she took an angular path leading her along the bar. She had to move slowly, weaving her way through the standing customers. The three-man group was just ahead. They parted, allowing her to pass, but the bartender called out to Scanlon, who turned and faced the bar just as she drew close enough to hear Scanlon say, "Thanks, I wondered what happened to the olives."

Jamila hesitated for a moment before she continued to the corridor, where she soon found the ladies' room. After a brief repair of her makeup, she returned. This time, she deliberately crowded close to Scanlon as she passed.

A jumble of voices radiated in the air around Rick. At least three different languages were being spoken at the same time. A dark-skinned man in a white turban had just said something to Rick, who took a long drink of his martini while he tried to decipher what the words meant. But when he lowered his drink, a shoulder was under it.

"Oh that was clumsy of me!" Jamila said quickly.

Rick heard the woman's voice while he juggled his drink to keep from spilling it on her. "No, it was my fault," he apologized as he got his drink under control. When he recognized the tall brunette, he added quickly, "No, I am not sorry it happened. I was hoping to bump into you again." His eyes locked on hers while he thought, *Is she alone or not?* "Tell you what," he said. "I promise not to bore you with anymore cracks like that if you will have a drink with me."

Jamila looked Rick squarely in the eyes as her features changed into a dazzling smile. "All right, you may join me," she said. She then turned and headed for her table.

CHAPTER 39

After introductions at Jamila's table, Rick asked, "You aren't one of the natives. What brings you to this part of the world?"

"I am traveling with my brother who is in the export business. We are from London," she replied.

"That seems to be the business to be in today," Rick mumbled.

"How is that?"

"Uh, I was thinking out loud," Rick said, taking another swallow from his drink. *Jane Willoughby must be a Latin from London,* he thought. Only tiny dimples marred her dark features when she smiled. She had a strong chin and a nose just right for her features. She had that aristocratic look about her, Rick thought, watching from the rim of his glass.

"What do you do in London?"

"I am an interior decorator. I work with a firm on Bruton Place."

"Isn't that near Berkeley Square?"

Jamila's eyes blinked through her fixed stare. Scanlon's apparent knowledge of London caught her off guard. She strived to maintain her composure, but her showing emotions were different than those being concealed. She had to stay alert and not allow this American, despite his charms, to know too much about her. She proceeded cautiously. "Apparently you are familiar with London?"

"Not very," Rick said and shook his head. "I know it's big, noisy, and wet. It rained both times I was there."

Jamila's deep breath was instinctive. She picked up her cocktail for a drink before she asked, "And your business?" Before Rick could answer, she added, "Wait a minute. Let me guess? You search for oil, or maybe construction is your work."

"Uh-uh, not even close. I haul freight on a ship."

"Ah yes, I should have guessed it. A seafaring man." She tasted her drink again. "Do you spend a lot of time at sea?"

"As much as I can. My income depends on it."

"I always thought a sailor's life would be a lonely life and boring. What do you do when you aren't working?"

"We spend our idle time thinking and talking about women."

I am glad, she thought, flashing him a smile while she asked, "Doesn't that also get boring?"

"Never," Rick answered, watching her over the edge of his glass. "As much as we try, men have never been able to completely understand women."

"Really!" *Is he putting me on?* she wondered. His face was still impassive. *Well, the drinks are good as well as relaxing, and I'm doing my job, although I'll have to call soon.* "What do men find that is so mysterious about women?"

"I'm not sure. Part of it, I guess, we prefer it that way. We like the fact you are built differently. And since you are, we treat you differently, or I think most of us do."

"You mean put us on a pedestal?"

He nodded. "When you're wearing miniskirts."

She laughed, not loudly but in a warm controlled voice. *The kind of laugh you liked to spend some time with,* Rick thought and then asked, "Why don't we continue this discussion over dinner? I happen to know you English get just as hungry as we Americans."

"Now that you mentioned it, I am famished. I accept your invitation with pleasure, but first, I want to visit the ladies' room. If you will excuse me."

In the corridor just off the lobby, she called Rahab on her cell. "You took long enough to call!" he said. His hard raspy voice grated on her ear.

"I did not wish to make my actions appear suspicious!" she retaliated. "I am going to dinner with him! The rest is up to you!" She snapped the cover closed on her cell phone.

CHAPTER 40

As the evening hours passed, the function of the large room where Rick and Jamila were having dinner changed from dining to dancing. The orchestra helped mellow Jamila's mood. They played slow classical tunes during the early part of the evening. Now there was a livelier beat to the music as couples headed for the dance floor.

Instinctively, her shoulders began moving to the beat of a rumba.

When he noticed her reaction to the music, Rick asked, "Would you care to dance?"

"Yes!" Jamila answered promptly while rising from her chair. She enjoyed dancing and never missed an opportunity. In London, she had spent many evenings in the pubs, dancing to rock music. When she reached the dance floor, she immediately began the pronounced hip movement in perfect timing to the rhythmical beat of the Cuban music. Her dancing pleasure was soon amplified when combined with Rick's smooth footwork.

"You are an excellent dancer," she said, moving through a twirling maneuver in flawless timing with his lead.

"And you make my job easy," Rick answered. Her dancing was effortless, an untamed spirit choreographed in harmony with the music. He felt like an animal trainer with little to do. As the beat of the music increased, there was fluidity to her body like a leopard moving through the jungle.

I wonder if this Jane Willoughby is on the level, Rick pondered, enjoying the heady fragrance of her perfume when they held each other close. *Was this second meeting at the bar deliberate? She had seemed to pop up suddenly.*

I am glad this get-together is not in Beijing, But that was the last time his thoughts strayed during the rest of the evening.

Jamila could feel him through the thin material of her dress, and the occasional touches of her ear with the tip of his tongue were not unwelcomed. They didn't leave the dance floor until the band went on break.

Tall snifters of brandy awaited them at their table in the tiered room. The glow from the table lamps and the warm liqueur stoked smoldering fires. A toe began to move slowly up Rick's leg. Over the edge of her goblet, Jamila's eyes leveled with his. "Are American ship captains as virile as they appear to be in your movies?" she asked.

Rick waited until the silky foot reached its destination before he answered, "Now you know."

Her laugh was interrupted by the waiter. "Will there be anything else?" he inquired.

When Rick shook his head, Jamila whispered, "Why don't we go where we can be more comfortable?"

★ ★ ★

Rahab got off the elevator on the sixth floor and moved to Scanlon's room. At the door, he reached in his pocket for a knife with three stainless steel blades. It had been a gift from Faisal, who had also provided instructions on its use. He worked on the lock for a full minute before there was a slight but distinctive click.

Once inside, Rahab closed the door quietly by pressing his back against it. He made a quick visual survey of the suite, noticing immediately that both bedroom doors were open. All lights were on, but there was no noise. *I wonder if his partner has arrived,* Rahab thought.

When he learned that Scanlon was in a two-bedroom suite, Rahab knew that he would probably have to contend with both Scanlon and his partner, whomever that happened to be. He moved quickly to the bedroom on the right, his first choice.

The bed was undisturbed. When Rahab looked in the small closet, he immediately recognized the two bags that Scanlon had arrived with. They were sitting on the floor, only the larger bag folded open. With his special blade, he soon had the smaller bag opened. He kept the contents of both bags piled as they had been stored inside each bag. Rahab looked closely for any hidden compartments inside the liners of each bag. Minutes later, Rahab was convinced there was no chart in this bedroom.

When he returned to the living room, Rahab searched inside the credenza, which was similar to the one in his own suite. When he found nothing resembling a map in the sideboard, he looked around, making sure there was no in-room safe before he went into the second bedroom, which showed no signs of any current occupancy.

When he returned to the living room this time, he took a final look around, making sure that everything was back in its original place. He turned and reached for the doorknob when he heard a key being inserted into the door lock. Instantly, Rahab had to make a decision. Which bedroom would he hide in? He chose the one with the bags.

CHAPTER 41

As he followed the bellhop along the corridor, Hok yawned and scratched himself under his jacket. It had been a long day. The last leg of his flight from Tokyo had been uncomfortable from the strong headwinds that had hammered against the plane. He had called Rick earlier in the day to advise him of his late arrival.

The bellhop set Hok's two suitcases on the floor and reached in his pocket for the room key. Watching him, Hok felt another key slip down his sock to his instep. It was the key to one of the hotel's safety boxes, which he had rented on check-in. He smiled to himself. His grandfather had taught him the habit years ago. The safest place to hide a key was in your sock.

When the door swung open, the bellhop reached to turn on the lights out of habit. Then he stopped and reached for the bags instead. "You have a thoughtful roommate," the bellhop said over his shoulder and then moved into the lighted room. Still holding a bag in each hand, the bellhop turned to face Hok. "Which bedroom, sir?"

"That is fine. Right here," Hok answered, handing the short Asian man a tip. After the bellhop left, Hok noticed the doors were open and the lights were on in each of the adjoining rooms. *Well, let me see which one Rick is using,* Hok thought as he entered the room to his right. Seeing the clothes hanging in the closet prompted him to turn and head back to the middle room. After he picked up his bags, he walked into the other bedroom and began unpacking.

Rahab had remained hidden behind the opened door to the bedroom containing the clothes. When he heard Scanlon's partner return to the sitting room, he moved from behind the door and watched the man disappear into the vacant bedroom. Rahab silently moved across the middle room to the wall adjacent to the door opening. As he inched one eye around the door frame, he drew a blackjack from his pocket.

Hok tossed both of his bags on the bed. He exhaled another yawn, stretched his back muscles, and then bent over to start unpacking. With a shirt in one hand and some underwear in the other, he had just straightened up when shooting stars exploded behind his eyeballs.

Rahab grabbed the slumping body before it hit the floor. Then, with one hand, he shoved the suitcases out of the way before he dropped the body onto the bed. After he quickly checked the man's wallet, Rahab discovered his name was Hokusai Utamaro. The name triggered a memory. Fasial had mentioned an Asian partner that Scanlon was working with. But after a quick search, the navigation chart was not in either of the bags or in any of the man's pockets.

Was there any other key besides the room key? The question raced through Rahab's mind. Once more, he searched all of Utamaro's pockets. After he pulled off the man's shoes, Rahab felt inside each one before he slipped them back on the Asian man's feet. But there was no other key.

With the appearance of Utamaro, Rahab had to change his tactics. He stripped off the Asian's gold watch and put it in his pocket. After he had rifled through all the contents of the wallet, Rahab kept the cash and tossed the empty wallet and credit cards on the bed. He scattered some clothes about and pulled out two dresser drawers before he left the bedroom. In the sitting room, Rahab prepared to leave once again. When he opened the door, he turned out the lights before he removed his gloves. He shoved them into his pocket and then stepped out into the corridor.

CHAPTER 42

Rick paid the dinner check, and ten minutes later, he and Jamila entered her suite. She left him standing in the middle of the living room and walked over to a bedroom door. She opened it, glanced in the room, closed the door, and adjusted the latch before she returned to Rick.

As she wrapped her arms around his neck, she met his lips in a long, lingering kiss. He never kissed with his eyes closed. He was glad of the habit. The bedroom door latch was not in the same position as the one at the entrance door. He smiled to himself as thoughts flashed across his mind again for the hundredth time about why he had acquired certain habits. It was from his father's simple logic—since we are creatures of habit, make them work for you, not against you.

I'll play the game for a while longer, he thought, feeling the back of Jamila's dress for the zipper. He slowly pulled it down. They parted briefly when the dress became tangled at her feet. A tiny smile played at the corner of her lips as she turned and lifted her hair. When her brassiere fell to the floor, Rick reached around to her breasts. The nipples were rigid to his touch.

And I am supposed to be working, Jamila sighed, but her thoughts returned to Rahab. Despite their differences, she would do everything possible to make his search easier. Ahmad did not like failure. She had to keep this big American free of any suspicion as she turned to face him.

Her emotions struggled vainly with her playacting when he traced a path downward with his kisses. Part of her mind focused on his questioning look when she had pretended to lock Rahab's door. That look had been a little unsettling. If the chart wasn't in Scanlon's room, she wanted to be sure Rahab could search the clothes here in the living room. Her low moan echoed in her ear when Scanlon's kisses reached one of her nipples.

It is easy keeping this American entertained, she thought as the warm glow inside her intensified. She unzipped him, feeling inside, touching, but only with fingertips as she began to undress him, starting with his shirt, returning often to feel and slowly stroke, as if time was forever.

Finally, she realized that if Scanlon was carrying the navigation chart, it had to be in his jacket. She glanced over at the couch where he had tossed the garment. It would be Rahab's responsibility. She turned her full attention to Scanlon, continuing her slow movements, only stopping to examine the parts of his body that were more interesting to her.

And Rick was not idle. Her underwear peeled down with little more than a whisk of one hand while his exploring fingers searched teasingly. Despite the heady effect of the blood surging through his veins, Rick forced himself to think rationally.

She must have me mixed up with some rich guy who is married, he speculated. *I'll give the photographer my best smile when he comes barreling in through the unlocked bedroom door and maybe a moon shot if the conditions are right.* His brief smile was hidden. *And the clothes here in the living room,* his thoughts continued. *Someone's in for a surprise when he or she finds only the fifty bucks left in my wallet.*

Rick's musing was interrupted when Jamila led him into her bedroom. It was lit only by a small bedside lamp. She sat on the bed and then reached into a drawer in the nightstand. When she leaned back against the headboard, there was a joint between her lips. She lit the joint, and after she inhaled deeply, she offered it to Rick.

His mind and body were in a tug-of-war. He looked down at himself, wondering which would be his best side for the camera shot when the first intoxicating whiff of marijuana hit his brain. He reached for the joint. "That's good grass," he said after inhaling the toke.

Jamila took another long drag before she kissed Rick and permitted the smoke to intermingle in their mouths. The warm narcotic generated pinpoint fires beneath his skin.

When the roach became too hot, Jamila staggered slightly while taking the spent joint to the bathroom. Unconsciously, she had left the bathroom door ajar, which was in the line of sight to the living room door. About to leave, something drew her attention to the living room. She paused and allowed her eyes to focus properly. There was a shadowy outline of someone standing near her bedroom door. For several moments, she studied the person. It was Rahab. *How long has he been standing there?* The question chased the fog from her mind.

She continued to stare at Rahab's dim figure. *Why is he spying on us? Apparently, he didn't find the chart in Scanlon's room, but why isn't he searching the clothes in the living room?* Then when Rahab moved slightly, she knew. His pants were around his ankles; he was slowly stroking himself.

As she watched him, Jamila felt smoldering fires being rekindled. *He has his pleasure, and I have mine,* she thought. She picked up a jar of oil from the vanity. *Rahab will be on his knees in a few minutes,* she resolved before she left the bathroom. The sweet, acrid smell of marijuana floated like a warm cloud throughout the bedroom.

"You left me in an awkward position," Rick said.

"I like your position," she answered, dipping her fingers into the perfumed oil. "I intend to keep you that way for a while."

She began stroking him, leaning down often to tease him with her tongue while continuing her massage. He soon reached for her, numbing her lips with his kiss before taking the oil and rubbing the fragrant liquid over her breasts. She helped him by cupping each breast in her hand.

Rick massaged downward, feeling her hips rise, pressing herself against him as he kissed wherever his hand went.

As she thought of Rahab in the next room, she slowly changed positions with Rick, lowering herself over him. When she felt his warm breath, she leaned over to the bedside table for a vibrator. After she turned it on, she moved the instrument over the length of Rick's erection before she encircled him with her lips.

A while later, they lay in each other's arms, their hands moving idly over smooth skin, stopping only long enough to sustain the yearning with the touch of fingertips. Finally, Rick sat up and reached under his pillow. As he got into position, a smile touched her lips. "You didn't have to," she said. "I also believe in safe sex. I have a supply on hand."

"I'll remember that the next time," he answered. He then sealed her lips with his own and entered her slowly, but he didn't remain quiet. Her restless hips spurred him into action. He began to slam into her with deep, powerful strokes, driving himself to fulfillment.

With arms and legs cradling him, Jamila dug her fingers into his back. "Oh, yes! Yes!" she breathed in his ear.

Gasping breaths slowly eased. They luxuriated in the quiet aftermath, wrapped in each other's arms. When the tiny beads of sweat covering their bodies became evident, she whispered, "Let's go shower."

They were soon lathering each other in the shower as the warm spray covered them in a steamy cloud. As she gently stroked Rick with one hand, she reached around him with the other and inserted a finger deep inside.

"Love your technique," he choked.

An impish grin curled her lips. She turned off the shower and then stepped out and placed a large towel over the toilet seat. When Rick sat down facing her, she kneeled down and took him in her mouth. Within moments, he started pressing on the back of her head. She gave his testicles a tight squeeze and heard him gasp. After she reached into the drawer of the vanity, she fitted him with a condom before she straddled his legs.

As she eased her weight down until full penetration was completed, she remained quiet, her lips and tongue moving to explore his face. Shoulders still, her slow undulations held him captive while warm moist tongues continued their caresses. She cupped one of her breasts and forced it into his mouth. When Rick began to tense, she accelerated her movements until her rapid breathing became one continuous moan.

They remained in the same position afterward, chins resting comfortably on each other's shoulder. But there was still a smoldering fire. It was deep down. Tiny muscles were tantalizing Rick with their slow pulsations. "I like the way that moves. You have hidden talent," he said, giving her a light squeeze.

She brushed her hand across his jaw when she got up. After she covered herself in a towel, she stepped into the bedroom to finish drying. It was then that she remembered Rahab. She walked into the living room. He had gone, but when Jamila looked around, a smile crossed her face. There was a wet spot on the carpet near her bedroom door.

CHAPTER 43

As HE GOT OFF the elevator on the way to his room, a murky haze blurred Rick's mind. The long hours were finally taking their toll. His leaden footsteps got him through the door of his suite, but immediately after he turned on the lights, a heavy groan echoed in his ears. The agonizing sound cleared some of the lassitude from his mind but not enough to know where the gurgled moan originated. He listened. There it was again, and it came from Hok's room. His bedroom door was open.

Damn! I forgot about Hok, Rick swore. He turned and switched off the light, but the groans continued. Rick was guided to Hok's room by the light filtering through his open bathroom door. Still fully dressed, Hok was sprawled on his bed. After he walked into the room, Rick reached down and shook his partner. "Hok, are you all right?"

As he slowly rose to a sitting position, Hok felt the back of his head. He said nothing. When Rick turned on the bedside lamp, Hok blinked before he asked, "What time is it?"

"One o'clock. How long have you been here?"

"I got in around midnight," Hok's said. "I looked to see which room you had and then came into this one. I just started to unpack when something whacked me on the back of my head." He paused to gingerly pat the lump on his head before he added, "And that's all I remember."

"The chart! You did store it in the hotel's security box?"

"Yes." Hok reached inside his sock and pulled out the security box key.

His movement drew attention to a wallet lying on the bed. Rick picked up the wallet and handed it to Hok. "See if our sneaky visitor left you any money."

Hok looked inside and then slapped the wallet against his palm. "The thief took it all! I had two hundred dollars!" He tossed the empty wallet on the nightstand.

Rick turned and headed for his bedroom, but he was back in five minutes. "My room looks like yours, clothes tossed about and drawers from the lamp tables on the floor. Are you missing anything else?"

Wearily, Hok held up his left arm. "My watch!" That was a three-hundred-dollar watch. I bought it before I left San Francisco."

Scratching the rough beard on his chin, Rick moved slowly about the clutter while he studied the piles of clothes tossed about the room. *Was this heist for real or make believe?* The thought, which weighed heavily on his mind, prompted him to say, "Hok, despite the value of your personal loss, I believe it was a cover-up. I feel sure the burglar was after the map?"

"Then he or she was most inconsiderate of my welfare!"

Hok's hangdog look was almost comical. Rick hid his smile and said, "If you feel okay, let's report it in the morning. If we report it now, we'll lose a lot of sleep with the questioning."

"That makes sense," Hok replied slowly. "Most of the cobwebs seem to have cleared, and I'm ready for some sleep, the normal way."

The following morning, Rick's early wake-up call was answered with effort. Wearily, he crawled out of bed and headed for the bathroom to revive himself with some cold water to the face. After he returned to the bedroom, he called the harbormaster's office. *Jake had the Valiant and crew right on schedule,* Rick said to himself after he hung up the phone.

An hour later while Rick stopped at the front desk to pay the bill, Hok went to the hotel's area with the safety deposit boxes. The clerk who figured the bill was the same young man who had helped Rick check in yesterday. His clear weather forecast for today in answer to Rick's inquiry had been correct.

When the bill was placed before him, Rick nodded toward the sunshine streaming through the windows and said, "You know your weather."

The clerk's smile was all teeth and half-lidded eyes. "Thank you, Mr. Scanlon. You enjoy stay here?"

"Well, I found one of your guests to be quite interesting, but my partner most certainly has a different opinion about your room accommodations."

"Oh, I sorry to hear that." The clerk's smile faded. "What caused him discomfort? Was bed too hard? Or maybe too soft? Room service?"

"He was mugged in his room!" Rick interrupted curtly.

Deep furrows suddenly lined the clerk's face. This new revelation stunned him to silence.

"My partner was knocked out from a blow to the head," Rick continued while he pointed to the back of his own head. "Then he was robbed of an expensive watch plus his money."

The clerk's face fell in disbelief. "That terrible. Nothing like that ever happened before in our hotel. Is your partner all right? Does he need medical treatment?"

"No he has a hard head," Rick answered, a thin smile creasing his face. "His main concern is the loss of his watch and money."

At the other end of the long desk, Hok, who had just returned from the security box, was engaged in a spirited conversation with an elderly Asian man.

Rick nodded in Hok's direction and said, "That guy down there doing most of the talking is my partner."

"He talking to right man. That is manager of hotel. He will help your partner," the clerk said.

And I think you are being overconfident, Rick started to say, but he didn't. Instead, his thoughts shifted to the mugger. *Is he or she still here in the hotel?* he wondered.

Rick eyed the clerk gravely and asked, "Maybe you can also help. I realize it is early, but have there been any other checkouts this morning?"

"Only two guests," the clerk answered quickly. "Mr. Willoughby and his sister check out about an hour ago."

"Those are the only checkouts? By the way, I met the attractive Miss Willoughby when I entered the hotel yesterday. What did her brother look like?"

"Big man. About your size."

Rick thought about what the clerk had said and then asked, "Would you say they looked like brother and sister?"

The clerk did not answer immediately. His eyes glazed slightly as his thoughts drifted back and he tried to recall any distinguishing features regarding the previous checkouts. "They both had the same colored skin. It was dark but not as dark as Africans or Indonesians. More like … more like," he said and then paused momentarily before he continued, "like maybe they were Arabs. And he had hard eyes."

"What do you mean?"

"The man not smile with eyes. They stay hard."

The clerk's information confirmed Rick's suspicion. *So Broadman and his accomplices are on our trail.* The sobering thought prompted Rick into action. He thanked the clerk, picked up his receipt, and then waved to Hok that he was leaving.

"I gave the hotel manager all the details of my mugging last night," Hok said over Rick's shoulder. "But I'm not too confident of the thief being caught. The manager seemed more pleased that we were checking out early."

"I agree with your reasoning," Rick replied. Then his thoughts shifted briefly to last night. *He would probably never know if the two were brother and sister, but one thing he did know was that she was good at her job.*

CHAPTER 44

After he got into the backseat with Jamila, Rahab growled, "Airport!" to the cab driver. Neither spoke during the long ride to the Kaohsiung Airport. His eyes were fixed in a perpetual glare while a thin line marked Rahab's mouth.

Let the asshole rage, Jamila thought, smiling inwardly while keeping her head turned to look out the window. She had learned the word asshole living in London, and it certainly fit Rahab. She was glad to be returning to her home in Afghanistan.

Last night after Scanlon had left her room, she had called Ahmad Sattar. When she had started to explain about the failure to get the treasure map, he had stopped her. He had already heard the news from Rahab. Surprisingly, he had not seemed too disturbed about the failure in retrieving the map. He had said their plan now was to track the Americans at sea.

Interestingly, it sounded to her like there was someone else making this new plan. But she did not question him about it, feeling it would be unwise to do so. He said that Rahab would stay in the area while he awaited further orders and that she should catch the next plane back to Afghanistan. He would be glad to see her again.

At the airport after security, Jamila and Rahab had only a thirty-minute wait before they boarded their plane for Hong Kong. Less than two hours later, when they got off the plane, she had a connecting flight leaving immediately, and he had a call to make. Their good-byes were brief.

"I hope your luck at sea is better," Jamila said, not bothering to extend her hand.

"It should be!" he snapped and then turned and headed for a quiet place in the airport to make a telephone call.

★ ★ ★

The heading for the *Valiant* was windward as the shoreline of Kaohsiung receded in the background. Rick was on the open bridge. The wind felt good against his face. There was something cleansing about sea air. It flushed out your soul, especially after being exposed for a while to the contamination related to shore duty.

He breathed deeply, filling his lungs with fresh sea air, enjoying its heady affect. *The balmy weather is a soothing tonic to the two large diesels down in the engine room,* Rick thought, feeling the steady vibration under his feet.

Before the ship left the dock, Rick had introduced Hok to Jake Flowers, who would be Rick's first mate aboard the *Valiant.* Twenty minutes later, Jake assembled the crew down in the galley for their introduction to the ship's owner and his partner. Rick met each member with more than a handshake. He was interested in their individual backgrounds and asked lots of questions. The galley coffeepot had to be refilled before the meeting was over. Rick was pleased with the crew's experience and their apparent attitude toward the cruise.

Later, when he and Jake were alone, he mentioned his feelings and thanked Jake for his job in putting the crew together.

With a straight face, Jake answered, "Well, did you expect anything else from me?" Then with a smile cracking his face, he added, "But that's not all. We've got aboard some up-to-date blasting equipment. Just before we left the States, the supplier demonstrated the ease of installing it while claiming the penetrating charges could pierce any metal thickness. The secret is attaching them to the metal's surface."

"Sounds useful," Rick said. "How are these blasting charges detonated?"

"We have two types of charges. One type, its detonator is triggered by an electrical circuit energized from a battery-powered source, which, in our case, is housed in a small water-tight box with a T-bar switch on top. And the wire-connected penetrating charges have special clamping devices to assure a clear underwater wiring circuit from charges to the T-bar trigger. This is strictly state-of-the-art stuff, according to the supplier. The other type is the standard self-contained penetrating charge, each with individual timer. I've shown our crew how to install both types. I'll give you and Hok a lesson when ready."

"Later for me," Rick said. "Right now I've got a more pressing matter." After he turned to leave, he said over his shoulder, "But I'll look forward to the lesson."

Down in his quarters, he studied the report from Hok's grandfather, Asawa Utamaro. During WWII, the Japanese had used Red Cross ships more for shipping materials to feed their factories in Japan than for treating and transporting their wounded. Late in the war, two of these ships had been granted safe passage by the Americans from the East Indies to Japan. During the voyage, the two ships had become separated. One ship named *Jawa Maru* had mistakenly been sunk by an American submarine whose captain would have been court-martialed until the true cargo of the ship had been revealed.

But the other ship, which was named the *Asaka Maru,* was of the most interest to Rick. It had contained the treasure and had been sunk, according to Asawa's speculation, by a floating mine or mines that had been prevalent in the Taiwan Strait area at that time. The ship had probably broken into three sections. The bow section, which contained the treasure in four walk-in safes, had likely come to rest at the ocean floor on top of a plateau, while the other two sections had probably fallen into a deep hole estimated to be twelve thousand feet deep. But what really caught Rick's eye was the fact that the plateau was adjacent to the deep hole.

He put down the report and tried to picture the sunken wreck just as a knock sounded on his door. When he opened the door, he found Hok holding a copy of the report. "Have you read—"

"Come in, Hok," Rick interrupted. "Yeah, that's what I'm doing."

"Have you read about the only survivor from the sinking?"

"No, I haven't got to that part of the report."

Hok walked in and sat down in the only other chair in Rick's compartment. "It's interesting," Hok continued. "My grandfather is claiming that *hari kari*, or some form of it, must have been used by all other members of the crew in order not to have to reveal, if captured, the cargo's contents."

Rick thought about that for a minute and then said, "And this one survivor shows up sixty-five years later with the navigation chart." He paused, reflected on the span of time, and then added, "Or more probably a son or close friend of the survivor's family."

"I'm betting it was a son," Hok said. The report indicates that the Japanese body found floating near the dock at the time Kuang claimed he picked up the chart was a man in his forties. My grandfather has speculated that the lone survivor's reneging of *hari kari* could have been the cause for the long delay in exposing the treasure's existence. The lone survivor was probably drawing his last breath before he passed on his navigation chart."

"Then this lone survivor had to know something about navigation."

"He was the ship's navigator," Hok said.

CHAPTER 45

After Hok left, Rick read the rest of the report and then went back topside and up to the bridge, where Woodrow Schaeffer, a wiry African-American, was at the helm.

"How is she handling, Woody?" Rick asked.

"Like a baby buggy, skipper. She has answered every bell without a whimper since leaving the States."

"Let's hope she answers a few more before we get back there," Rick said, glancing at the clock hanging on the bulkhead. "We had better kick her flank if we are to meet that Chinese gunboat on time." He reached for the phone near the binnacle.

"Whose ears are on down in the engine room?"

"Al Jefferson, the chief engineer," Woody answered.

"Al, this is Rick Scanlon. Let's see what she will do," Rick said into the phone. "All ahead full."

It was late afternoon when Jake and Emory Chang, the other helmsman, came into the pilothouse to relieve the watch. Jake checked the ship's course and then turned to Rick. "We've been airing out the diving gear with a couple of seamen, Sid Warner and Pete Thompson, back on the fantail. You might take a look at those regulators. Some of the valves seem to work a little sluggish."

"Okay," Rick answered from the door. He and Woody had just climbed down to the main deck when they heard a yell. "Hey, skip, when are we gonna get some paint that will stop metal from rusting?" Greg Castine leaned on his chipping hammer. He and another member of the crew's deck gang named Hank Butler were chipping paint from a midship ventilator.

"There is no such paint! That's what you get for being a fuckin' deckhand," Rick replied. Woody's laugh echoed inside the passageway as he and Rick continued on below to the mess room.

After chow, Rick worked on the diving gear back on the fantail with the deckhands Pete Thompson and Sid Warner. Both were single and in their late twenties. After he had met the crew and before they had gotten underway, Jake had filled Rick in on stories about some of the members. Rick, laughing to himself, remembered the one about these two seamen, who apparently would chase anything socially qualified to wear a skirt.

Jake had said that Pete and Sid's lack of discrimination toward the opposite sex was confirmed one night with two floozies in San Francisco's Lafayette Park. The two couples had split soon after they had arrived at the park. But within minutes, there had been a wild yell from Pete. He had come charging out from behind some hedges and bellowed, "Let her go, Sid. Mine is hung like a bull!"

The steady sound of the *Valiant's* wake had a mesmerizing effect on the three men working quietly on the fantail. Each man was sealed in his own world when the thought occurred to Sid while he replaced a defective air valve. "Rick, I hear it is almost impossible to get it up after you've had the bends. Is that right?"

"Skipper," Pete interjected, his face set in stone, "I know what Sid's concerned about. I overheard his Oakland girlfriend say she only liked two things hard, and one of them was ice cream."

Talking agitated Pete's ever-present lip full of snuff. He turned and spit over the side. After he rubbed a hand across his mouth, he continued looking seaward. "Hey, skip! Is that the gunboat we are expecting?"

"Must be," Rick answered. "I had better get up to the bridge and find out." He started toward midship and then hesitated and turned around. "Sid, I hate to say it, but after this cruise, your Oakland friend will probably have to learn to like soft ice cream.

"You guys can go fuck yourselves!" Sid countered, while Pete got rid of more tobacco juice.

Back on the bridge, Rick watched through his binoculars the small warship closing fast from starboard. The red flag of the People's Republic of China rippled from her mast. Asawa Utamaro's report had mentioned the probability of this happening. Although their search area for the treasure was in international waters, China had claimed jurisdiction well beyond the usual twenty-two-kilometer boundary from their shoreline. The reasoning had to do with their claim to a group of islands extending a considerable distance off their coast.

The gunboat slowed her engines and then stopped fifty yards away while members of her crew scurried about and prepared to send over a boarding party.

"I hope she's friendly," Jake said, studying the other ship's armament.

"We'll soon find out, right, Hok?" Rick said, following his partner into the wheelhouse. "Do you have the search permits ready?"

Hok nodded as he laid out the documents on a table. "My grandfather claims this paperwork should grant us the permission needed for the search." He paused momentarily before he added, "He also said he was sure the Chinese will expect a share of the treasure if our search is successful."

"The share document is included in the paperwork to be signed, right?" Rick asked.

"Yes," Hok answered.

An hour later, the gunboat with its visiting party back aboard headed for the China coast while the *Valiant* prepared to get underway again. Near Hok on the open bridge, Rick said, "Hok, were you as concerned as I was about their acceptance of our equal share agreement?"

"Yes, but I really believed you convinced them not to be greedy when you said that after deducting for sailing costs, there would be four equal shares distributed as follows: one for the crew, one for me, one for yourself, and I thought this was the clincher when you looked their leader square in the eye and said that even though our search will be in international waters, one share for China, and that's for any help that we might need."

The afternoon sun had dipped low on the horizon by the time the salvage ship and her crew had reached their destination. Back on the bridge, Rick thought about how they had been guided here. Drafted in a secret code, preserved in a legacy of time, and bloodied with three murders, the navigation chart had directed them to this spot in the ocean. A smile creased his face as he looked out over the water. The site where the sunken treasure ship was supposed to be was occupied by a pod of whales dozing peacefully as the sun disappeared slowly from view.

CHAPTER 46

IT WAS 2:00 A.M. in San Francisco, but the voice of the man who had answered Rahab's call was as crisp as someone's speaking during the afternoon. *Doesn't he ever sleep?* Rahab asked himself, but his musing was cut short by the cold implacability in the voice. "Listen carefully. Do not take notes. What I am about to say is for your ears only." He spoke in chopped sentences as always when he demanded attention. Faisal never wasted words.

"Your target currently is heading in a southeasterly course out of Kaohsiung. It is being trailed by our submarine. A storm is forecasted in three or four days. This could mean trouble for monitoring the target. You go on to Macau, where you have a room at the Metropole Hotel on Avenida De Praia Grande. Buy a boat. It must be seaworthy."

There was a short pause. "Buy deep-sea fishing gear to be used as a decoy. You are to sail that boat in and around the harbor while waiting to hear from me. Keep your cell phone handy at all times. Be alert for my call in two days at the most. Unless I inform you differently, prepare to sail your boat straight east of the lighthouse on the barrier reef at the mouth of the harbor. The sub will pick you up after nightfall. You will trail the American ship until it reaches its salvage site. You will then know what to do with the American ship. That is all!"

Two nights after his call to Faisal, a periscope broke the surface near Rahab's boat. The arrival of the submarine wasn't too soon. His stomach was churning from the sickening roll of the restless sea. Even though his boat was motor-powered, his skills at ocean sailing were limited.

The murky darkness blanketed long, wind-driven swells when he crawled aboard the sub. With a short burst from an assault rifle, a crewman sent Rahab's half-swamped boat the rest of the way to the bottom. At noon the following day, Rahab was in the cramped quarters of the submarine's sail, which housed the conning tower and command center. The wedge-shaped structure, which was located directly above the control room, stuck up from the sub's top and contained slotted windows, one forward and one aft, both near the top of the housing. With all the monitors and gages arranged before the helmsman on the forward bulkhead, there was barely room for Rahab when he intruded on the helmsman and the sub's captain, Alan Taraki, an English-Arabian.

A large wave broke over the sail with little effect on the motion of the submarine. But the wave's impact made Taraki concentrate harder on the job at hand. He had been trailing the American ship until the storm, but he wasn't concerned about being unable to find it again. He had confidence in the up-to-date sight and sound equipment in his submarine.

A thin man with beady eyes and a slack-jawed mouth, he thought about the best way to destroy the ship they were after. He had debated making the hunt from the surface, thinking it was the most expedient way for making a positive identification. Because the shipping lanes in the area were used by many countries, he knew if he sank the wrong ship, it would mean his death knell from Sattar's wrath. And the job would be left to this arrogant son, whose foul breath was rapidly filling the sail's limited space.

Rahab swore silently, trying to see through the slotted window in the rear wall of the sail. *What good is a window in a sub anyway?* he pondered momentarily before he realized it could be used when the sub traveled on the surface. But his only interest was getting to the salvage site as marked by the American ship.

Rahab was aware of the storm that had started during the night. He was awakened this morning by voices from two crew members talking about it. He was mindful that a heavy storm would make the identity of the American ship more difficult to discern. He looked down at the shorter captain and asked, "How soon will the storm pass?"

With its Middle Eastern accent, his voice grated in Taraki's ear. "It'll be 2300 hours before we clear the storm!" Taraki answered without looking at Rahab.

Rahab sensed the animosity behind the captain's words. Since he had come aboard last night, his presence had no doubt added to the crew's strain about their impending mission. And the submarine's claustrophobic environment fueled Rahab's surly attitude. Movement was more than a burden to him. He quickly became exasperated whenever he banged his head or shoulder as he moved along the narrow corridors. And the accompanying hatchways that had been designed for water-tight sealing were another hazard as well as a vexation. In passing through the narrow opening between compartments, when he stooped to avoid hitting his head, he sometimes forgot about the higher threshold and banged his shin on its edge. Sometimes his head would then take the shock when he failed to remember the door's purpose.

Rahab's stay in the tower was short. He turned, climbed down a ladder, and squeezed himself through the floor to the control room. He glared briefly at the three crewmen on duty and then moved over to a hatchway. He stepped through the opening without injuring himself before he headed to the galley.

When he got there, he stayed. His only movement was back and forth to the head to relieve himself. As the hours passed, the frequency of his trips to the head began to match each refill of his coffee cup.

CHAPTER 47

The day broke warm and clear with the *Valiant* poised over the salvage site that was marked with a permanent buoy containing a metal rod attached to its top. When the buoy's anchor reached the ocean floor, the metal rod floated upright. The undersea search would center on this target.

Jake and the crew got the *Valiant* underway to sweep the ocean floor with sonar. A transducer near the ship's keel received the high-frequency pings and fed the information into a recorder.

Meanwhile, the radar scope on the *Valiant's* topmast picked up the target and transmitted a signal down to a screen in the chartroom behind the wheelhouse. Here, Rick started downloading a pattern of the radiating, wedge-shaped grids on his computer. When he shouted the course, Jake, who was at the helm, began steering the *Valiant* back and forth over the area representing one section of the grids. To keep the search confined to each individual grid, the *Valiant* used its GPS.

Ten minutes after they had started the search, the stylus on the recorder began to sketch a steep rise. "Do you think that's it?" Hok asked excitedly as he leaned over Rick's shoulder.

"Could be!" Rick almost shouted. But after a while and with other steep rises becoming transparent that were too long to be a shipwreck, his voice was more controlled. "Don't forget that your grandfather's analysis claimed there will be a bunch of plateaus scattered about the ocean bottom in this area."

"I remember," Hok replied. "And we are supposed to be above a 12,000 foot deep trench extending all the way from the Gulf of Tonkin to the Taiwan Strait." Hok hesitated a few moments and then added, "How close do you think we are to the deep hole?"

Rick studied the screen a few moments before he answered, "About two miles. Right now we are in the area where your grandfather claims the section of the *Asaka Maru* containing the treasure is supposed to be on top of a plateau.

The sweep continued. The *Valiant* shuttled back and forth inside the first grid of the search pattern while other outlines showed on the screen that were too long to be what they were looking for. Then a whole series of rises began to appear. The ocean floor was saw-toothed into hills and valleys.

"Damn it! It's rolled up down there like a big washboard!" Rick swore.

"We have learned one thing," Hok said, his gaze still fixed on the screen. "Our oceanography map of the shelf here is accurate."

"Yeah, unless our sonar equipment is fucked up," Rick answered. He then paused for a moment in thought before he said, "We will continue with it for the rest of the day, and if the pattern remains the same, we'll use what data we have to set up a search tomorrow with our handheld detectors." By the end of the long day, however, the hills and valleys were still there.

Early the next morning, Rick established four separate search areas with his laptop and the use of the GPS—fore and aft plus port and starboard of the *Valiant.* Four marker buoys were prepared for the search areas. More than 250 feet of anchor cable was attached to each buoy before they were taken to their designated positions in a motor-powered workboat by two crew members. Rick directed where each buoy was to be dropped by reading his laptop's search map. He called to Jake on the open bridge when they needed to make the drop. Jake relayed the message through a bullhorn to the men in the motorboat. With a quiet ocean, the work went smoothly.

In preparing for the dive, all members of the crew who were not on watch huddled on the fantail with Rick, Hok, Sid, and Pete, who would make the initial search. They went over dive times and decompression procedures. Each of the respective tanks that the divers would use for their air supply was checked for the proper mixture of oxygen, helium, and nitrogen. Rick wanted the mixture to allow for maximum submergence relative to the depth they were diving.

By midmorning, the four were wearing wet suits and making final adjustments to their scuba gear. Rick was the first to go. He stepped over the side and climbed down a short ladder to a square platform tied to the ship's hull at sea level. He checked his lifeline to make sure it wasn't snagged. He held his metal detector in one hand and gave a thumbs-up with the other. Then he turned and stepped off into the water.

He descended slowly, allowing himself time to adjust to the pressure changes while swimming in the direction of his designated marker buoy. His light, which was attached to the metal detector's shaft, revealed a gloomy underwater world as he continued his descent. When his flippers finally touched the bottom, the murky water instantly changed to a black cloud.

A thick layer of silt covered the ocean floor. *This shit is as thick as molasses,* Rick thought, kicking out with one of his flippers. Another black cloud blotted out all remaining visibility. He switched on his metal detector, and with a pull of his lifeline, he signaled the man tending his line aboard ship that he was starting his seabed search.

Rick moved through a shadowy wasteland occupied by an occasional fish. Its silent vigil was disturbed by the unaccustomed light. But it was the excessive amount of silt that surprised Rick the most. He had expected to find coarser sediment on the ocean floor. *Could the recent earthquake have anything to do with it?* he wondered.

He started a sweep from the crest of one hill down and up to the peak of the adjoining slope, following a similar route along the floor's configuration that the stylus had recorded on the sonar screen. He began his descent back down to the valley again, keeping his detector moving over the ocean floor ahead.

Rick covered the complete valley in a zigzag trail from the crest of one plateau to the top of the paralleled hill. He found no trace of any wrecked ship by the time he had reached the anchor of his marker buoy. He paused and checked his time. He had another five minutes before he would have to start his ascent. *I hope the other divers are having better luck,* Rick thought while he checked his detector for proper operation.

He continued his search well beyond his marker, using up most of his five minutes before he swam back to the anchor cable. He gave four quick pulls of his lifeline and signaled that he was ready to head home. His ascent to the surface would be considerably slower than it had been when had been going down. To help the divers comply with decompression regulations, the crew had tied a piece of line every fifty feet along the marker buoy's anchor cable. By the time Rick had reached the surface after he had spent the allotted time for pressure equalization at each of the four stops, he was ready for a break.

After the other three divers who all had the same luck as Rick were back aboard, the *Valiant* moved to the next GPS coordinates on Rick's laptop. Then another four divers were sent down for the second group's search that morning. Changing positions was a rigorous process, but Rick was pleased with the efficiency of the GPS-laptop system in their search.

That evening in the mess room, Rick listened to the other divers' finds for their first day. The consensus was primarily car wrecks. "Mine were Toyotas, I think," Hok said with a yawn. His back was propped against the bulkhead on the opposite side of the table.

It was only their first day, but Rick could sense the wariness in the divers' voices. After he had seen the ocean floor of the search area, he knew their job was going to be an arduous one. There was a long silence interrupted only by the intermittent clinking of coffee cups against saucers before Rick said with a straight face, "The best piece of tail I ever had was obtained only after I had to spend a lot of time hunting for it."

Sid spoke immediately, "I hope there were no bends in your detector after finding it."

Pete choked on a drink of coffee, and he had just begun breathing normally when Jake entered the mess room. He sat down—no coffee for him—and made sure he had everyone's attention before he said, "You guys had better find something soon."

Rick stared at his first mate. "Sounds like you know something we don't."

Jake looked around the room. He wasn't diving. Rick wanted him aboard at all times to handle the *Valiant.* "I've been tapping the glass all day," Jake said. "The pressure drop is slight, but I believe there is a definite trend on the way."

As if on cue, Jake was interrupted by Herb Renfro entering the mess room. Herb was the ship's radio operator when he wasn't diving. He filled his coffee cup, and when he turned around, he noticed that all eyes were on him and the room had suddenly quieted. Startled and irritated, he asked, "What the hell? Is my pecker hanging out or what?"

"Jake just gave us a weather report," Rick said. "Using sea duty experience as his barometer, he claims we could be in for some bad weather."

"I have to agree with Jake," Herb said on his way to the table. "Skipper, the pressure drop is slight, but the wind has shifted. It's now from the east. My guess is we are in for some rough weather in two or three days at the most."

Rick listened intently. He then put down his coffee cup before he asked, "What do you hear from China or Taiwan?"

"That bothers me. Although the reception's been pretty lousy, there is no indication of any bad weather from either one. I'm thinking since the wind shift was sudden and only a short time ago, this change may still be under the radar of either country's weather system."

"That's what I mean!" Jake said with a smug look on his face. "We are in for a hell of a good blow within the next three days at the most."

CHAPTER 48

By the following evening, the temperature had dropped twenty degrees. The *Valiant* was riding a roller-coaster sea. The rest of the divers were already in the mess room when Rick came in after he had made his last dive of the day. The talk was not encouraging.

"Too much silt down there!" Greg Castine said. "It's like looking for a chunk of coal in an ash pile!" His high-pitched voice had everyone's attention.

"I still think one of those hills down there is hiding the section of that Japanese ship that we're looking for!" Pete said.

"Yeah, but which hill is it?"

Hank Butler handed his coffee cup to Hok, who was standing by the urn, before he stated, "I believe Pete is right. It's in one of those hills and covered with about fifty feet of that shit!"

Jake Flowers quietly entered the mess room. He had a rolled-up piece of paper under his arm. As he balanced himself against the ship's movement, he walked over and drew a cup of coffee before he sat at the table. During a break in the conversation, he cleared his throat with self-importance, twice, but the delay was just enough to prevent him from edging into the spirited discussion, which was beneficial only in relieving a lot of stored-up frustration.

If Jake doesn't sing his own appraises soon, he will pop a safety, Rick thought, watching him from the other end of the table. Rick waited until Herb refilled his coffee cup and sat down again across from Jake before he shouted, "What's the latest on the weather, Herb?" His loud voice quieted the room.

"Storm likely by tomorrow night, but nothing severe." Then he qualified his report. "The reception still isn't good."

"Aha! I have told certain people you can't count on that squawk box of ours!" Jake banged his cup on the table. He never looked in Rick's direction.

"Yeah, what's your prediction tonight?" Herb asked testily.

"I am saying we have barely two more days before we get hit with a big one!" Jake bellowed. By the time he had unrolled a map of the strait, his voice had calmed. "It looks like you blind bastards are going to need some help in finding this wreck before we are buried in the storm."

He set a coffee cup at each corner of the map before he continued. "I have been studying the report that Hok gave us about the history of this sinking. Maybe there is a good reason why none of you have found the wreck."

"Are you saying it isn't down there?" Hok questioned.

Jake smoothed a crease in the map, taking his time, making sure it lay flat on the table before he replied, "No, I'm saying the reason you haven't found it is because it has moved from other earthquakes that have happened during the past sixty years."

Hok stole a glance at Rick before he turned back to the first mate. "Your perception is admirable, Jake. My grandfather cautioned me about this possibility, and Rick and I discussed it before we left Taiwan. But we felt it was a gamble we had to take."

"I understand," Jake said, his arrogance changing quickly to rapt attention of the sketch in front of him. "That's why I've made a rough drawing showing new coordinates for our search area. While the previous owner of the *Valiant* was trying to sell it, I spent my spare time, which I had plenty, in reading the ship's logs. The ship was docked at Manila when that monster tsunami hit Sumatra, Indonesia, in December of '04. The crew set sail immediately on down to the damage site to help in the relief effort. Evidently, this prompted the previous owner to become interested in the history of storms in the South China Sea." Jake paused, allowing himself a long sigh. Then he stirred the contents of his coffee cup before he finally took a drink.

Engrossed in Jake's account, Rick grew impatient and broke in curtly, "So the previous owner has recorded the results of his research on storms in the ship's logs. What's the gist of it?"

"He claims there have been many earthquakes, especially in this area over the past half century. And he claims, they have tended to move in a northeast direction, so I have drawn new coordinates accordingly." Jake finished his story and leaned back in his chair.

Rick got up and moved around the table to look over Jake's shoulder. He studied the rough map, saying nothing while occasionally looking at the crew's existing map of the search area, which hung on one of the mess room's bulkheads. The room remained quiet while Rick completed his study and then returned to his chair at the head of the table. His face turned grim when he looked over at Jake. "You realize your coordinates are putting us close to the big hole."

Jake nodded and said, "I know that, skipper, and I know we can't be sure of these logs' reliability. But we all know we are not having any luck here and with the approaching storm." His face went blank momentarily before he turned to Herb sitting at the other end of the table. "Herb, you are the only one of us that is any kind of a meteorologist. It's written in these logs that the previous tsunami in this area, one of similar magnitude as the '04 one, occurred in 1945. If we assume the earthquake that caused it happened after this ship was sunk—"

"I see what you're getting at," Herb interrupted, "but even though the wreck we are looking for is only part of the ship, I don't believe it's possible for an earthquake to move it that far." He looked over at Rick. "Skipper, didn't you say we were nearly two miles from the deep hole?"

"That's right."

"I also believe the wreck is closer to the big hole but not for the same reason as Jake," Herb continued. "While you guys have been doing the grunt work, I have been studying your grandfather's report." Herb nodded toward Hok. "Let's think about it. This lone survivor, who was the ship's navigator, from his station in the bow area, could have seen his ship start breaking into three sections. Being the navigator he had to be aware of the big hole and his ship's position near it. So he must have felt sure the bow section did not fall into the hole, or he would not have made the chart. Since we have found no evidence of the sunken ship so far, why not search closer to the hole? What I'm really saying is when this survivor drew up his chart, he may have purposely added more leverage than necessary, making sure the bow section was away from the hole.

Rick reflected on what both Jake and Herb had said. He was tired but forced himself to try to think rationally for several moments before he got up from his chair. He drank the last of his coffee and then set his empty cup near the urn before he said, "Since we can't find the wreck at our present location, we will head for the new coordinates as shown on Jake's map at first light." He turned and left the mess room.

CHAPTER 49

By midmorning of the following day, they were at the new search location. Fifteen-foot waves beating against the *Valiant's* hull had slowed their progress. After they had marked new search patterns, they only had time for three teams of divers to do any hunting, but at sundown, voices hardened with exasperation remained the same as previous evenings in the mess room. Hank Butler was the last diver to arrive. After his bleak report, the room quieted until Herb walked in with the weather report.

"A Taiwan station is claiming the storm will hit us late tomorrow evening," he announced.

"How fast is it moving? Rick asked.

"The Taiwan weather station is forecasting winds between sixty and seventy knots, and you know what that means?" Herb answered, looking steadily at Rick.

"Typhoon, right?"

"That's right, skipper, so I hope you will plan on us being in a safe harbor by tomorrow afternoon," Herb replied. A slight smile touched his lips but not his eyes.

"I understand," Rick said. Then he announced to the room, "This means we will only have time for a morning search tomorrow, so we want to spend that time as efficiently as possible." He looked over at Jake, who sat directly across the table, and said, "Let's make a new search pattern right now to use tomorrow morning." He rose abruptly from his chair and headed for the door. "Give me a minute to fetch my laptop," he said over his shoulder. "Herb, stick around. I can use your help."

At the other end of the table, Pete, Sid, Hank, and Greg were not thinking about the weather. They talked in lowered voices.

"If we find it, what are you going to do with your share of the treasure, Pete?" Hank asked.

"I'm going to buy a two-story building," Pete answered without hesitation.

A long silence followed. "I know I am going to kick myself in the ass for asking," Hank said, "but why a two-story building?"

"I'm going to have a whorehouse upstairs and a liquor store below."

There was another long silence before Sid interjected, "You're going to be a fucking drunk, right!"

"You got it!" Pete whacked his buddy on the back.

At daybreak, the *Valiant* was underway, steaming in an easterly direction in heavy seas while following the new course they had charted the previous night. But the sonar screen continued displaying the ocean floor's hilly terrain. Rick checked the GPS coordinates on his laptop in the chart room and yelled the course to Woody Schaeffer at the helm.

Right after they had changed the course to a westerly direction, a large hit was made by the magnetometer. Rick immediately called Woody Schaeffer to stop the engines. While Jake and the seamen handled the anchor cables and used the GPS coordinates as shown on the laptop, the *Valiant* was positioned over the hit.

Back on the fantail, Hok helped the four men who were making the dive get into their scuba gear. The ocean was carpeted with tall, white-capped waves in a brawling race to the horizon's finish line. The waves that were spilling over the ship's hull made the deck as slippery as an ice rink. When the divers were finally over the side, Hok staggered back to the chart room, where Rick kept vigil of the ship's position relative to the hit's seabed location.

"What do you think?" Hok asked after he hung up his slicker.

Rick's eyes never left his laptop when he said, "Let's hope!"

But two hours later, with all the divers back aboard, futility still reigned. The hump on the ocean floor was another pile of junk left to be dissolved by the timeless action of the briny seawater. Weary crew members who were on watch hoisted the anchors, and the *Valiant* continued its relentless search, which was now becoming more perilous by the hour.

The incessant waves slapping the hull steadily grew in intensity while they created new creaks and groans from the ship's structure. The temperature dropped steadily as the wind began screaming through the superstructure.

The *Valiant* steamed ten miles farther, made a 180-degree turn following the search pattern developed the previous night, and started back to the marker buoy but in a zigzag course. Within fifteen minutes, the mag made another hit. Rick was up stretching his legs—or trying to—but the shifting deck discouraged his effort. He returned to his chair just as the hit was made. It was the biggest yet, and it was directly below.

"Stop all engines and drop the fore and aft anchors!" He shouted to Woody at the helm. Rick started back to the fantail, on the double, this dive he would make himself.

By the time the ship's engines stopped and her anchors caught on the bottom, Rick was in his wet suit with help from Hok. The help was necessary, the *Valiant* moving about like a lassoed mustang trying to free itself.

When he was strapping the mask in place, Hok yelled, "Herb says keep your downtime to fifteen minutes!"

Rick acknowledged Hok with a shake of his head. Then he held his arm close to Hok's to synchronize the time on their respective wristwatches. After a final check of his equipment, Rick climbed over the side and slipped down into the water.

He descended to the bottom and stood in the silt near the forward anchor long enough to remove one of his weight belts and hang it through a link in the anchor chain. He strapped a flashlight to another loop. Hok had suggested the extra light to save time in finding the anchor chain after the search had been completed. Rick gave a quick pull on his lifeline and began swimming along the ocean floor.

He went only a short distance when his detector began to buzz, startling a school of curious, snub-nosed fish. Rick felt around in the silt-covered floor and picked up a tin can. When he touched it with his light, the can crumbled into suspended pieces.

He continued on and found another can and then another, but ten feet farther, the detector suddenly quieted. He checked his watch. He had used five minutes. Then he tried to remember how the hit had appeared on his screen aboard ship, but that didn't help down here in the murky water. All he knew about direction was that the anchor chain was behind him. Suddenly, he felt the emergency four pulls on his lifeline. The storm was intensifying.

Another three minutes after he had changed direction, his detector came awake. The instrument's chatter was different, more distinct, and clearer in tone. Its staccato pitch settled into a steady hum. A million needles started tattooing Rick's skin. He kept swimming, trying to penetrate the darkness beyond the range of his light, but he saw nothing except the inky silt. *Damn it! It must be more junk,* he thought while the chattering detector lacerated his nerves.

And then he found the wreck. Unknowingly, he had moved up to the silt-covered bow that had blended into the ocean floor. His detector hit something hard. He reached out and brushed the silt away from metal plating. He shined his light upward. A silhouette of a ship's bow loomed above him. It was huge. From his position and the extent of his searchlight's beam, it appeared to be the entire ship. But when he moved back a few feet, he could see that the bow was buried in one of the hillsides. The angry, disjointed sound of the detector beat against Rick's eardrums. He didn't hear it. The shock of his discovery numbed his mind. All thoughts and feelings were suspended. Then more tugs on his line, this time with greater force, awakened him to reality. He turned back.

When he reached the anchor chain, Rick, who was still galvanized with his discovery, started up to the surface, but he ascended too fast. He felt two quick pulls on his lifeline. He was at the fifty-foot marker. He held onto the chain and looked at his watch. He had an eight-minute stop.

He cheated. After only five minutes, he moved on up. When the slack on his lifeline was taken up, Rick gave the line a quick pull to indicate he was okay. He felt the answering two pulls telling him to stay.

After a two-minute stop, Rick waited no longer, he continued on up. At the surface, typhoon-driven waves slammed against the *Valiant.* The ship rolled and pitched, straining the lines of its anchors. Then it happened. The ship lurched forward when the stern anchor tore loose from the bottom. At that instant, Rick broke the surface and was hit immediately by a thirty-foot wave. In the trough of the receding wave, his face masked cleared enough for him to see the bow of the *Valiant.* He was in its path.

CHAPTER 50

"TWENTY-THREE HUNDRED HOURS ... MY *khra!*" Rahab swore to an empty room. His dark, shaggy features wrinkled into a scowl. *Why don't sailors tell time like everybody else?* He glanced at his watch. There would be another seven hours before the storm passed. He reached for his coffee cup just as a voice crackled over the speaker. "Surface craft starboard at twenty-five degrees and fifteen kilometers!"

Rahab got to the tower ladder just as the sub increased its speed and turned sharply. His movements slowed as he held firmly to the ladder and worked his way up into the sail.

Over the helmsman's shoulder, Taraki had his binoculars aimed toward the slotted window in the forward bulkhead. The sub's powerful searchlight made a visible path ahead of the bow as they plowed through the raging storm.

"Is the craft moving?" Rahab asked, his voice edged with excitement.

"No!"

"Have you got a fix on the craft? It must be logged accurately!" His emotions nearly out of control, Rahab's loud voice blared inside the small sail. "That has to be the treasure site! Have you logged the position?" he repeated.

"That has been done!"

"Has the plan of attack changed any?"

But Taraki did not hear that question. He listened to the message from the control room. "The craft is ahead at two thousand meters!"

If that is our target, it should be radioing its position, Taraki thought. *And as close as we are, its foghorn should be sounding.* He checked again to make sure the switch was on to engage the sub's exterior audio system. *There must be a good reason why there's no warning signal from the ship.* He smiled to himself. *If I were anchored over a billion-dollar treasure, I wouldn't want others to know.*

Similar thoughts were churning in Rahab's brain. He had no binoculars, but over the helmsman's other shoulder, he could see the sub's bow through the small window. His eagerness for action prompted him to ask again, "Is the plan of attack still the same?"

"Yes!" Taraki's reply was instantaneous. *The stupid bastard. I would have informed him of any change,* he swore silently. The plan was simple. When assured of their target and also assured that it was stopped, he would dive and then fire his two forward torpedoes simultaneously. The purpose of the extra firepower was to annihilate the target completely, leaving no incriminating evidence of the marine disaster. His crew, all experienced deep-sea divers, would then salvage the treasure.

"Stand by to dive! Ready torpedo tubes one and two!" Taraki ordered over the sub's audio system.

But Rahab's adrenaline was in overdrive, escalating his impatience to the limits of his sanity. Then he heard it, the mournful wail of a foghorn barely audible above the storm. He leaned over the shorter helmsman, trying for a glimpse of the target through the forward window. The wind-driven squalls created shadowy outlines just beyond the range of the searchlight's beam, and they tantalized Rahab's mind. He sucked in his gut, stood on his toes, and leaned closer while he grazed the helmsman's shoulder.

"Target is moving!" The strident message from control ricocheted in the conning tower like a rifle shot while it jolted Rahab off balance. Instinctively, he grabbed the helmsman, crushing him against the wheel. A flailing arm of the helmsman knocked the binoculars from Taraki's hands. He cursed, "What the hell!" and then the voice over the sub's intercom immediately screamed, "Target dead ahead!"

In struggling to free himself from the hapless Rahab, the helmsman accidently jerked the wheel to hard starboard just before a shuddering jolt was felt throughout the submarine. The impact was followed instantly by a loud screeching sound of metal grinding against metal.

CHAPTER 51

SOMETHING STIRRED IN THE deep bottomless pit of Rick's mind. He awakened just as the *Valiant* was paying off, riding beam to the wind and heavy sea as it drifted to leeward. The ship's violent maneuver brought Rick fully awake. *Something is wrong, but what is it?* The sudden realization flashed across his mind.

He swung his legs onto the deck and started to rise just as the ship made a sudden roll. He fell back in his bunk. *How the hell could I sleep through this storm?* The thought confounded the murky shadows clouding his mind. Instinctively, he reached up and scratched his head. A sharp pain shot through his body. But the breath-catching pain brought back the memory of his contact with the ship's hull. He felt the large lump on the side of his head and was relieved to know his scalp was still in one piece. After he reached for his dungarees, he got up and headed for the bridge.

Rick worked his way along the slippery deck while holding onto the guard rail. The cold sting of the seawater spray from the waves lashing the hull cleared his mind. He needed it when he reached the bridge.

Inside the pilothouse, Jake's swearing curdled the air while a slightly less vocal Woody Schaeffer spun the wheel freely. There was no response from the rudder.

"What happened?" Rick shouted above the roar of the storm outside.

"We got hit by a submarine!" Jake bellowed.

"A what!"

“That’s right, skip. A fuckin’ submarine,” Jake continued. “It rammed us in the fantail, broke our rudder! Al down in the engine room says our port screw is gone, too!”

“Were we sounding our foghorn?”

“Well,” Woody hesitated momentarily, searching for the words. “Not at first—”

Jake interrupted, “What he’s trying to say is there was a brief hitch in the circuitry could have been a relay or switch, but it didn’t take long to free it and we had it working well in advance of the ramming. That sub charged us like a killer whale going after a seal. There was no indication of hearing our signal!”

“How about our radio?”

“Herb could get no response from the sub!” Jake answered. “He feels the rebuff was deliberate!”

“Damn, skipper, how are we going to steer?” Woody cut in. He was still trying to get some reaction from the helm.

Rick looked at Jake. “Can’t we steer with the emergency quad?”

“Al’s got Emery and Sid back there now, rigging the chain falls.”

“Jake!” Al’s voice echoed from the speaker. “The rudder must be gone. We are getting no response with the quad!”

”Stand by, Al, I’m coming down!”

While Jake was putting on his weather gear, Rick asked, “Did you get a good look at the submarine?”

“Yeah, it was definitely a sub!” Jake answered, his voice crusty.

“Damn it. Don’t you think I know—”

“I mean,” Rick cut him off sharply. “Was there anything on its hull like a number to identify it?”

Jake stopped. As he eyed Rick thoughtfully, he said, “Yeah, there was something painted on its hull. It was like a round ball, and in the center was a flag.” Then he left.

Rick remained in pilothouse and got on the phone to Herb in the radio room. “What kind of help can we expect in the area, Herb?”

“Hi, skipper! Glad to hear from you again.” Herb’s voice sounded over the receiver. “About the help, there’s plenty of Chinese chatter. I’m not sure how close, but I can soon find out. Shall I put out a distress call?”

“Yes, and call me just as soon as you know who and where the help is?”

Rick hung up the phone and held onto the back of the helmsman's chair.

"Take the chair, skipper," Woody said and tried to get up when the *Valiant* pitched into the trough of a tall wave.

"Sit still. I'm not going to be here long," Rick answered just as Jake's voice blared over the speaker.

"Skip, our rudder is completely gone! Do you want me to jury-rig one?"

"Not yet, Jake! Stand by. Herb is radioing for help. Let's see how soon it can get here!"

Three minutes later, Herb called over the speaker, "Four hours away, skipper! It's that Chinese gunboat that checked our search papers a few days ago!"

"Will it be able to tow us?"

"I'll find out!" A long pause followed before Herb answered, "I think he said yes. Shall I tell him to come and get us?"

"Yeah!" Rick answered. He had to grab the chair with both hands to stay upright before he added, "And at flank speed!"

When he regained his balance, he reached over and flipped on the all-points speaker switch. "All hands! Help will be here in four hours to give us a tow! Batten down all hatches! Check our searchlights! Make sure they are trained to forward on the mooring bitts! Jake and Hok, come up to the bridge when you have a minute!" Then as an afterthought, he said, "Our situation is not all bad. I found the wreck during my last dive."

"Hey, skipper, you really did find the wreck?" Woody chortled. "Are you sure it is what we're looking for?"

"Well, it was a bow from a big ship. It had all the appearances of—"

Hok's arrival interrupted Rick. He bounded into the pilothouse and slammed the door behind him, but his hasty entrance wasn't forced by the storm. A big grin tugged at his mouth when he faced Rick and said, "You mean our efforts haven't been in vain?"

"Well, as I was just telling Woody, there's a bow down there from a big ship."

Hok reached out to shake Rick's hand and ended up nose-to-nose when the ship rolled abruptly. "A handshake is enough. A kiss is a bit over the top," Rick said with a stern face before it turned into a quick smile. "Hok, what I really called you about … will you stick close to Herb in the radio room? He will need you to help in deciphering the Chinese lingo, especially when that gunboat gets here."

"Okay, I was heading there when you called me over the speaker."

"One other matter before you go," Rick said. "Did you get a look at the sub that rammed us?"

"I sure did!"

"Do you remember any kind of identification lettering on its hull?"

Herb reflected on the question a few moments before he answered, "Yes," and his eyes brightened. "There was a … kind of armiger, I think it's called."

"A what?"

"A coat-of-arms thing. It was round with a flag in the center."

"A flag!" Rick considered this for a while before he asked, "Could you make out any colors in the flag?"

"Yes, now that you asked. Our stern searchlight had that sub square in its light beam. There were three colors in that flag—black, red, and green."

"Thanks, Hok. I have a good idea of the country that uses those colors."

Hok moved to the door, and just before he left, he turned and said, "Yes, I now have an idea myself."

A few minutes later, Jake entered with the same energy that had propelled Hok into the pilothouse. "Skipper, if it wasn't for this damn storm and rudder problem, I'd break open a case of champagne that I've been saving for this occasion. What did it look like down there? Any gold bars flash in your light's beam?"

Rick laughed, suddenly realizing it had been a while. Jake's enthusiasm was contagious. Woody sang, "Gold coins in my pocket," to the tune of "Three Coins in the Fountain."

"Wait a minute," Rick said. "Let's don't celebrate a victory before we play the game. We've got a damaged ship to take care of first. Jake, I want you to prepare the crew for towing the ship. Fabricate a bridle to connect the line to the bow's starboard mooring bitts."

"Aye, skip! And I'll rig some chafing gear for the hawsehole."

"Good! In this storm, that towline will need some protection.

As he kept himself upright by holding onto the idled helm, Woody listened intently to the conversation. A good helmsman and an excellent diver, he was nineteen years old, and he had never experienced this predicament at sea before. His revelry of a few minutes ago had changed when he began to realize the complexity of the pending tow. When Rick mentioned his name, Woody's instantly responded, "Yes, sir!"

"We'll probably need to use our engines to help the towing ship in getting us underway and to alter our heading relative to the weather. However, we will use our own propulsion only if and when called for by the other vessel, understand?"

"Yes, sir! Then I'm to keep our engines on standby only until ordered differently, right?"

"You got it," Rick replied. "I'll have Herb and Hok relay the radio messages from the other ship to you, so be ready to respond accordingly, got that?"

"Yes, sir!"

At the door, Jake said, "I'm leaving, Rick. I'll call you on the speaker when I have the crew ready."

CHAPTER 52

THE GUNBOAT ARRIVED AT 2230 hours. It was on schedule, and it kept in constant radio contact with Herb and Hok, who were relaying the messages to the pilothouse. Slowly, it circled the *Valiant,* which was abeam to the fifty-knot, northeasterly wind and wallowing in twenty-foot waves.

"It's got some powerful searchlights," Jake said, shielding his eyes inside the pilothouse with Rick and Woody.

"And I'm glad of it," Rick said, one hand protecting his eyes from the glare. "The extra light should make our job a bit easier in securing the tow." But his mind was on the messenger line that would be tied to the heavier towline. Would his crew be able to grab the free end of the messenger line, a baseball-sized mass of yarn with a leaded core, if the wind should carry the lighter line to leeward.

Hok's voice over the speaker interrupted Rick's thoughts. "Rick, it sounds like they are saying, 'Throwing appliance across bow.' Could that be right?"

"Yes, they will shoot it across our bow using a high-powered shotgun. That's what I like to hear. Apparently, this gunboat is prepared for rescue work. Ask them to let us know when they are ready to shoot so that our seamen on the bow can take cover."

Waiting for Hok's reply, Rick used the time to advise the rest of the crew what was happening with the rescue vessel. He alerted the seamen who would be securing the towline so that they could take cover when the messenger line was ready to be shot across the bow.

"Here's their plan, Rick!" Hok's voice, which was hoarse with emotion, came haltingly over the speaker. "They will circle once more, and when they start to cross in front, they will shoot messenger line across our bow. When we have secured towline, we be ready to rev our engines!" There was a pause. "Does all that make sense?"

"Good job!" Rick answered quickly. "They want us to help relieve the strain of the initial tug on the towline by pushing forward with our own propulsion."

Rick watched the gunboat begin to circle the *Valiant* again. Then he turned to Jake and said, "You had better help the seamen secure the line, Jake."

"Aye, skipper!" Jake answered. "I'll signal you just as soon as we are secured at the bow."

After Jake left, Rick was on the phone with Al in the engine room. "Al, the gunboat wants a push from us to get started? Can we help or hinder with only one engine?"

"We can't help if we yaw the *Valiant* off course!" Al's gravelly voice grated in Rick's ear. After a short pause, he added, "But damn it! We should try. I say it's worth the gamble."

"Okay Al, let's hope we catch a wave at the right angle to push forward instead of sideways. I'm handing the phone to Woody. He will be giving you orders from now on."

"I'm with you, Skip. We'll be ready in the engine room when you need us."

The gunboat plowed a path through the rolling, pitching sea. It moved slowly up the port side of the *Valiant.* As he stood by the speaker phone inside the pilothouse, Rick could see activity on the stern of the rescue ship. When it was about ready to make its starboard turn, he picked up the phone and announced to the crew, "Stand by. The gunboat is just now starting to cross our—" He stopped abruptly.

The flash of a firefly from the stern of the gunboat jolted him. He didn't expect the line to be shot until they were closer to the *Valiant.* But there it was in the glare of both ships' searchlights. He could barely make out the monkey fist at the end of the small line flying toward his disabled vessel. He recovered quickly. "There it comes!" he shouted. "Be alert on the bow!"

The ball with the line attached flew across the *Valiant's* bow and landed in the water on the starboard. The angled shot from the gunboat had placed the attached line, now lying across the bow's deck, only ten feet from the mooring bitts. It was a perfect shot. "Go for it!" His order wasn't needed. Jake and the four seamen scrambled over the slippery deck to grab the line before it was washed overboard.

From the pilothouse, Rick watched gravely. The taut muscles of his face showed his concern for the men's safety on the treacherous bow. They worked frantically, pulling on the smaller line with its other end attached to the heavier rope coming over from the gunboat. The hawser's eye finally snaked up over the edge of the bow. Jake worked it over the mooring bitt while the seamen secured it quickly with a bridle. When Jake turned toward the bridge and held up both hands, Rick immediately called Herb to radio the gunboat that the towline was secure.

Two minutes later, the gunboat turned and headed straight off the bow of the *Valiant* while it paid out the towline with its stern windlass.

A minute later, Hok yelled over the speaker, "They say rev our engine!"

When Rick nodded to Woody, there was an immediate reaction from the *Valiant.* Rick felt a new vibration under his feet. The *Valiant* came alive, and luck rode with the crew. The push from the *Valiant* coincided with a similar wave that the gunboat was experiencing, and the tug on the towline when it came up out of the sea was slight. The tow was underway.

"I think the gunboat is asking how well the start of the tow went," Hok said over the speaker. "What shall I tell them?"

Instinctively, Rick yelled, "Tell them slicker than a cat's ass!" Then, with a broad grin, he said, "No, tell them it went fine."

CHAPTER 53

Midafternoon of the following day as the towing procession came in sight of Kowloon, two harbor tugboats moved out on a calm sea and relieved the gunboat and its weary crew of their towing mission. Rick and the rest of the crew, except Hok, worked with the harbormaster and his people while he got the *Valiant* into an available dry dock. Hok's job was to call Dr. Yang.

Hok was anxious to talk with him for two reasons. The first one was to learn if he was finally off the hook with the government regarding the SARS situation, and the second reason was that Hok wanted advice on protecting their salvage sight from the submarine predator. Two hours later, Hok got a return call from Dr. Yang. A Chinese gunboat would definitely patrol the area while the *Valiant* was being repaired.

"I'm concerned that they won't try to salvage the treasure now that they have a good idea where it is."

"I ask Dr. Yang about that possibility," Hok said. "But he claimed that we can trust the government; his dealings came straight from the right sources. So it appears they are backing us in our venture." After a slight pause, Hok added hesitantly, "Well, he did sound like he was back in bed with his government."

"I hope so," Rick said. "I have a feeling we are going to need more of his help before we are through."

Grateful for Yang's help, Rick was not that confident in the gunboat's insurance. He remembered the conversation in Broadman's office about the difficulty in identifying a mysterious submarine. He was skeptical that a small gunboat could detect this kind of submarine with the type of underwater-sounding systems usually aboard such vessels. He said nothing, until the *Valiant* was repaired there was not a lot anyone could do about it anyway.

The following day, Rick learned the repair work would take a while. No problem with the rudder, it could be repaired in Kowloon in less than a week, but the new propeller would have to come from Shanghai and would require considerable machining time.

Rick asked Hok to go with Jake to Shanghai and oversee the work. Hok smiled, listening to Rick's rambling explanation of his need to accompany Jake. "The language factor is always a potential problem, and not only that, the influence from your ancestry should help in getting the job done faster. It should aid in avoiding any further delay."

Hok's eyes locked on Rick's. "You wouldn't be planning a flying trip to Beijing, would you?"

"Well," Rick said without looking at Hok, "the thought had occurred to me."

CHAPTER 54

At midmorning, the spring day promised lots of sunshine. Already, there was a reflective glare from the surface of the road winding its way through the countryside close to the Great Wall of China and the seacoast.

Traffic from cars, bicycles, and an occasional horse-drawn wagon was sporadic, which often made the driving both tiresome and precarious. Changing speeds intermittently and running the air conditioner at maximum output were not the best operating conditions for the automobile's engine. As he weaved his rental car around the mixed vehicles, Rick kept a wary eye on the panel's temperature gauge.

He and Pat had started their trip soon after daybreak this morning. When the car started overheating, he pulled off the road and stopped in the shade of a large copper statue of an emperor from the Ming Dynasty. The puffy eyes of the ancient ruler sitting on a huge throne stared illusively down at Rick, who was partly hidden under the hood of the car.

Pat did not moved from the passenger side of the car. Conversation between them had been light although cordial enough when it did occur. But the long silences were not uncomfortable. They traveled in an area known as Shanhaiguan Pass, and she remembered reading that in the early history of China, this land had been extremely important to the defense of Beijing in the east and Xian in the west, which made the area a national tourist attraction.

As she glanced occasionally at Rick, she realized his stillness was not deliberate. He was studying the ancient castles, sections of the Great

Wall, and battlements at the top of defensive structures. As they passed these objects of China's early history, she smiled to herself and realized that his periodic groans were from obstruction to his sightseeing.

Waiting in the car, she thought about how this trip had originated yesterday. She and Francois had just left the surgical ward after another exhausting day and had stopped for a while at the lake to fill their lungs with the cool night air.

"Doctor, I marvel at your skill after three weeks of these twelve-hour days," Francois had begun. Pat listened perfunctorily, her elbows propped up on her knees.

Yes and formality still reigns, she had thought. He still had never called her by her first name.

"And as a doctor, you know better than most. At this pace, the human body can only take so much. What I'm trying to say is you need a break to get away, to recharge your batteries, as you Americans like to say. I have a small house fronting a beach about 250 kilometers from here that is near a sleepy, coastal town by the name of Shanhaiguan. It is in an area where the Great Wall extends eastward to the sea. Take one of the nurses with you."

Why don't you take me? She had wanted to ask, but she had already known the answer from their previous talk here at the lake. Working together day after day, their relationship had developed into more of a brother-and-sister kind than anything more emotional. Then during the night, as if by prescience, Rick had arrived at the hospital unexpectedly. For some reason, she had awakened earlier than usual this morning. Before she realized that no one had awakened her, she slowly stretched her arms and legs, yawned deeply, and luxuriated in the feeling of a long, restful sleep. The aroma of fresh flowers wafting gently throughout her tent was her first recognition that the day was different.

She turned her head. A large vase filled with red roses sat on her bedside table. "Hi, I'm back" was scrawled across the card propped against the vase. After she got dressed, she stepped outside her tent. Francois held the car door open, and Rick was behind the wheel. The car was close enough that she could see a basket of food and a suitcase in the backseat. Surprisingly, it was her suitcase.

"This time, I won't take no for an answer," Francois had said. "This trip to the coast is for medical purposes."

She didn't move. For a few moments, she stared at Rick, who kept his face comfortably expressionless. "I like selecting my own company." Her voice was controlled.

"This is a precautionary measure," Francois had said. "I want no fatigued doctors on my staff. And besides, you will be seeing a beautiful part of China that few visitors get to see. And Rick promised to return you in three days."

Doctor, you are missing the point, Pat had felt like saying. Instead, a recent conversation with one of the nurses crossed her mind: "Dr. Kendall, you must see the China countryside near the coast. There are grass-covered valleys where red shelves of rock look out from hillsides. And there are deep, clear lakes where only a lone fish will sometimes ripple the placid waters."

With a sigh, Pat had gotten into the car.

CHAPTER 55

THE AFTERNOON SUN HAD dipped below the horizon by the time Pat and Rick arrived at their destination. They had driven through the small town of Shanhaiguan and another five miles before they turned east, left the main highway, and traveled a winding road only a short distance to the seashore. Their small house was not the only one fronting the beach that stretched for miles in each direction. The larger houses appeared to be used for year-round living, but the ample space between houses combined with lots of trees and vegetation provided a vacation retreat with plenty of privacy.

Rick was pleased with the setup, but Pat was too exhausted to fully appreciate the amenities of their beach house. After supper, she went to bed in the cabin's only bedroom. The bedspread was turned back, exposing white sheets that appeared to be freshly laundered. A wicker chair, a nightstand, and the one bed were the only furniture, but there was no door to close off the room.

Rick understood the early turn-in. The deepening shadows around her eyes were not from cosmetics. However, the night was not an unpleasant substitute for Pat's company. The ocean mirrored a full moon in countless reflections along the isolated beach.

A jetty extended several hundred yards out to sea in front of him. Its rocks had likely been placed there centuries ago, perhaps restraining a raging ocean to provide Marco Polo's ship a safe harbor. The cool night air and the tide's ebb and flow tranquilized the mind. The moon had started its downward journey long before he went back inside the cabin.

Something disturbed Pat. She woke up, puzzled by the stark furnishings in the moonlit room. Then a breeze stirring the curtains at the window carried a sound in long, whispering cadences. She had no idea of the time, but she felt refreshed as if she had slept for hours. The other side of her bed had not been disturbed. Its pillow, which was still fluffed, seemed poised and ready for use.

A creaking noise came from the living room. Rick was trying to get comfortable on the small couch. *Pat Kendall, you are being very unkind to the man who saved your life,* she scolded herself quietly, but her thoughts drifted. Lately, with her work at the temporary hospital, being intimate with a man had not been on her mind.

Francois had interested her at first. His intellect as well as his consideration for others appealed to her, but the long hours in surgery working with him and being around him had produced more of a familial relationship.

As she thought about Rick in the next room, she realized that she did not have the same feeling about him. She started to call his name; however, something restrained her, and she wasn't sure why. *Maybe I'm not quite ready for this type of man.* Other than high school, her relationships had always been with intellectuals primarily of the medical profession.

But with Rick, it was not his intellect that kept her at a distance. It was something else. Maybe it was those dark, smoldering eyes that read your mind before you wanted him to and the quick, knowing smile creasing his face when you turned away or changed the subject of the conversation. But sleep was playing a tug-of-war with her thoughts, and sleep eventually won the battle. She turned on her side and closed her eyes.

Midmorning sunbeams rode a gentle breeze and entered Pat's bedroom when she awoke the second time. She heard a noise outside just before Rick's face appeared in the opened window.

"Hi! When are you coming out to play?"

She smiled, watching him from her bed. Sweat beads glistened on his forehead while his chest heaved from gulping quick breaths of air.

"Come on out," he continued. "I am getting tired chasing sandpipers."

"Why? Do you think you will have more luck chasing me?"

"I don't know! I haven't tried yet!" His face disappeared from her window.

The day was perfect, and they spent hours enjoying it. Huge powder-puff clouds drifted lazily across the mellow August sky. Seagulls wheeled overhead while the surf washed the beach in long, even strokes of the tide, disturbing the sand just enough to smooth over the tracks left by the sandpiper's scurrying feet. It was a day for lovers, but the only time he touched her was when she reached for his hand as they waded in the deeper surf.

Their last evening began with a light supper. Later, they were about ready to go out to the beach when Pat thought of something. "Go ahead," she said. "I will join you in a couple of minutes."

Carrying a blanket, Rick left while she returned to the cabin with the half-empty bottle of wine. It was the wine's effect that had triggered her memory. She walked into the bedroom and searched briefly in her travel bag. She slipped the tiny package into the pocket of her shorts. *Just in case the mood is right,* she thought as a smile touched her lips.

At the cabin's door, she stopped for a few moments. Fifty yards ahead, Rick sprawled on the blanket, his head resting in his hand. He was watching the surf. It inched toward him, signaling the start of the incoming tide.

Pat felt relaxed. For the first time in the weeks since the earthquake, her responsibilities were entirely forgotten. The balmy weather and the quiet seclusion of their beach hideaway were intoxicating—the type of environment that dreams were made of and promises granted.

She stood in the doorway, allowing her thoughts to drift lazily across her mind. When Rick stirred on the blanket, her thoughts returned to him. *I have to admit,* she thought. *That man has had a lot to do with my peace of mind.*

Noticing the approaching tide almost touching his feet when she walked up prompted her to ask, "Aren't you a little close to the surf?"

"Warm salt water is good for the body and soul," he answered.

"Therapeutic, yes. Spiritually beneficial, I wonder." She looked around before she added, "But we cannot let a wet blanket ruin this beautiful night." When she sat down, she allowed him to use her leg as a pillow for his head.

They were content to watch the twilight change into a ceiling of stars surrounding a full moon. The phosphorescent surf forged from the restless tide continued moving up the beach. The hypnotic sound was mind-stirring.

Pat thought about a recent conversation she had had with Francois. It concerned a letter that she had received from Hok's parents, one inviting her to visit them while she was in Asia. Francois had mentioned that it was an opportunity for her to become familiar with some advanced bone marrow research at Queen Elizabeth Hospital in Hong Kong. She was proud of her work at the field hospital, but it was not the reason she had come to China.

Idly playing with the short hair on the back of Rick's neck, his low murmur interrupted her thoughts.

He cleared his throat and said, "Those are skilled hands. For my surgery needs, I will know who to contact."

"Uh-uh, with you, my knife might slip."

Rick looked up at her. "What a sad day that would be for the women of the world," he said and sighed. "What about your Hippocratic Oath?"

"Short memory!" she answered, leaning back on her hands.

He watched her, trying to see inside her mind. Only the movement of the surf broke the silence, but when he finally reached for her, she was ready. Their tongues searched and teased in a moist embrace. The warm night and soft blanket encouraged freedom—freedom to explore, to touch, and to caress. When clothes got in the way, they removed them.

Rick never hurried. His kisses moved down her neck and along her shoulders, lingering at her breasts. As he moved, he heard a sigh when he stopped for a few moments, and he continued until he felt a hand pressing on the back of his head.

Pat, who was lying on her side, moved her hand along Rick's leg. Fingertips only began touching, stroking, endlessly searching but always moving in one direction. She leaned down just as the incoming tide reached their blanket.

The warm seawater touched them like raindrops from a spring shower, but it went unnoticed. Rick turned and cradled Pat's head in his arm for several moments before he kissed her. Then he reached down. His own fingertips began their search, knowing where to move but in no hurry to get there.

When he started to position himself, she said, "Wait!" After she found the small package among the clothes, she handed it to him.

"Doctor's orders?" he asked.

"Peace of mind!" she answered while a smile played at her lips.

The brief interlude only heightened their excitement. Under a luminous canopy of shimmering stars, he positioned himself over her. Soon, the low moans in his ear accelerated into gasping breaths, spurring him to achieve the ecstasy of pleasure for mutual fulfillment.

As the intermittent surf gently bathed them in its phosphorescent foam, the art of lovemaking was created—only they had ever made love before this night.

CHAPTER 56

A STEADY WHINE THAT the submarine's propulsion system generated echoed in Rahab's ear. He felt caged. The limited space in the conning tower prevented him from any freedom of movement. And time was a factor, although he knew they were ahead of the Americans' ship repairs.

Taraki was sure that the force of the ramming would have damaged the Americans' ship. But had it been extensive enough to put their ship in dry dock? Taraki's reluctance for this assessment had prompted Rahab to call Fuchou and persuade him to watch for any American ship under repair at the Kowloon shipyards. And Fuchou had responded. Rahab knew when the American ship went into dry dock and was kept informed with periodic calls informing him that it was still there.

But the urgency had been escalated with Fuchou's recent call. He had reported a flurry of revived activity at the American ship.

Rahab was bitter when he turned to Captain Taraki and said, "How much longer before we get to the strait?"

"Eight hours."

"Can't this thing go any faster?"

Taraki stared at Rahab before he answered, "Yes, but I do not recommend it. The condenser is running hot. We need more testing time before increasing speed." He paused momentarily. Then with eyes the color and size of walnuts, he added, "The ramming caused more damage than we thought or was called for!"

They were nose-to-nose, eyes stinging darts into each other's glare, but Rahab was first to blink. He admitted his clumsiness had caused the previous debacle with the American ship, but he argued bitterly that Taraki had waited too long to fire the torpedoes. Rahab had heard enough about the sub's damage from the ramming.

The thought still burned in his brain that they had to go all the way to Vladivostok, Russia, for the repair work. According to Taraki, the damage was critical enough that the repairs should be made at the main naval base of the Russian Pacific Fleet. And no amount of wheedling could change his mind. The three-thousand-kilometer trip was the longest Rahab would ever take.

His face cold and hard, Rahab turned abruptly and left the conning tower for the galley. Later, he was in his quarters, trying to sleep when a crew member whispered, "Surface craft flying a Chinese flag overhead."

Back at the conning tower, Rahab confronted Taraki again. "If that is a Chinese Naval vessel above, it is patrolling in international waters, right?"

Rahab's guttural words were a low growl.

A tight smile creased the captain's face when he answered in a normal voice, "Do not worry. Regardless of the type of surface craft, its sounding equipment can only detect the wreck. This sub is designed to defer any sonar signals so we are undetected." The captain hesitated momentarily before he continued, "There is one slight problem. When our sound-deferment system is in operation, our own sonar system automatically becomes inoperative."

Rahab's face was a study in bewilderment. He looked like he had drank from a beer bottle filled with piss. "But how did you know there was a surface craft above? And how did you know it was a gunboat?"

"Our own sonar's range is much greater than that of surface vessels or other submarines," Taraki replied. "The Russian underwater sound technology is the most advanced throughout the world. When we discovered the Chinese ship ahead, we immediately switched to our deferment system without changing course. We are just about at the salvage site." Taraki paused. As he stared intently at Rahab, he added, "Or I should say we will soon be at the site where we rammed the American ship."

Rahab's face went blank for only an instant before he said, "But that Chinese ship has no jurisdiction over us. We are in international waters, right?" he repeated.

"That is disputable by the People's Republic of China. They are claiming control here in the China Sea of coastal waters that extend well beyond the usual twenty-two-kilometer boundary, and keep in mind we are not too far outside that boundary." He returned Rahab's stare. "This is the time for discretion, not agitation."

A slight clicking sound came from the speaker followed immediately by the words, "Captain will you come down to the control room."

Rahab followed Taraki down the ladder to the command center. The navigator, who was seated at his station, was intently studying a monitor in front of him. "Captain, the magnetometer has made a large hit dead ahead, and we are positioned directly over the GPS coordinates where the ramming occurred but—"

"That is good!" Rahab interrupted, his loud voice echoing in the room. "That is what I have wanted to hear!"

"Wait!" Taraki silenced him. His order came with a hard glare before he turned and again leaned over the navigator's shoulder. "Go ahead with your report!"

"The wreck is only five meters from a deep trench in the ocean floor."

"How deep is the trench?" Rahab asked. His voice grated on everyone's ears like nails on a blackboard.

"Four thousand meters."

"What!" Rahab roared. "I was told the depth of the wreck would be no more than ninety meters. What is that hole doing here?" Then his voice grew contemptuous. "How do you know that?"

"There is a deep trench in the center of the South China Sea," Taraki said, his voice firm. "It extends from the Gulf of Tonkin to the Taiwan Strait. We are at the edge of that trench."

"More delays, am I right?" Rahab snapped. "This means we can do no blasting inside the wreck! Any use of explosives might cause an undersea landside that could topple the wreck into the trench! Isn't that right?" Rahab repeated, but he didn't wait for an answer. He whirled and headed for the diving hatch.

In the forward compartment, the crew members who would make the inspection of the wreck were already in diving gear when Rahab arrived. The chief salvager, a tall, slender Arabian in his early forties, listened to a surly Rahab explain the trench hazard relative to the wreck's location.

There was no change of expression in the salvager's face. Problems were part of his job. When Rahab finished his tirade, the chief turned and started through a hatchway that led into a water-filled chamber before he said, "The flame from our cutting torches will have to substitute for any blasting."

The hatch closed on the chief and another salvager. When the pressure inside the chamber equaled the outside pressure of the ocean, a watertight door in the sub's hull opened, and the two divers swam out. Two others followed before Rahab got into his scuba gear and left with the remaining salvager.

Rahab moved stiffly at first, getting used to the change of his environment. After he adjusted his headlamp, he swam along what was left of the sunken ship's hull, noticing how close the keel was to the gaping hole. The wreck lay on its port side, imbedded into the slope of a hill. He silently cursed at the dark cloud of sediment he kicked up with his flippers.

With radios built into their headgear, each salvager kept in contact with one another as well as the sub. During the first few minutes, the talk was limited until the chief's voice broke in curtly, "All the passageways are clogged! We will have to cut through the hull!"

Two members of the crew abruptly swam back into the diving chamber. They soon returned, each pulling a large bundle of wiring harness. All the divers, including Rahab, paired up and worked in shifts, returning to the sub to replenish their special air supply while allowing for decompression time. Within an hour, a string of lights lit the area between the sunken ship and the sub. As they continued their shift work, the divers started to rig a scaffold along the side of the wreck's hull. Despite their frequent trips to the sub for replenishing materials as well as breathing, little time was wasted building the platform.

The chief gave the order to bring the torches immediately after the scaffold was in place. Cutting torches dropped through the diving chamber, and two divers standing on the platform began cutting into the hull of the wreck. Within minutes, a dense cloud of sediment obliterated the ocean floor.

"Stop the cutting!" the chief's voice, hardened with exasperation, sounded over the headsets. "We have got to get rid of the silt!"

Rahab swore silently, though he knew the chief was right. Suddenly, his thoughts shifted to the American salvage crew. A worm of fear wriggled inside his gut.

CHAPTER 57

Seagulls whirled overhead, their eyes searching for anything floating in the *Valiant's* wake that tempted their gluttonous appetite. They would follow until the ship was out of sight of any land before they turned back toward Kowloon.

Through the open porthole in Rick's quarters, the China coastline gradually receded in the background, but Rick wasn't watching the retreating vista. He sat at a small desk against one of the bulkheads, updating his ship's log until a gust of wind blew some papers to the deck. When he picked up the papers, he found a snapshot of Pat among them.

Three weeks ago, he had left her in Beijing. He studied the picture a few moments. Despite their shared intimacy that last night on the beach, she had been more preoccupied than talkative during their return trip to the hospital. What had been on her mind had never been completely revealed in her face.

But another gust of wind interrupted his thoughts. He had a ship to get ready for some salvaging work. He closed the log, got up, and left his compartment.

The *Valiant* met the patrol boat a considerable distance from the logged position on the navigation chart, where the ramming had occurred. As the two ships closed within hailing distance, Rick was relieved to see that the marker buoy for the wreck was still in place. Herb had been keeping track of the weather. There had been two severe storms in this area while they were in port.

Rick picked up his binoculars. He would have felt more comfortable if the patrol boat had been positioned closer to the marker buoy. But the storm hadn't stampeded the whales. Just off the starboard bow, three sperm whales broke the surface. Their curiosity apparently satisfied, they spouted tall geysers and splashed their broad tails.

Crusty gray patches polka-dotted the ocean in a wide area around the *Valiant.* They weren't barnacles stuck to the backs of the whales, Rick decided after he studied the patches for a few moments.

Hok stood near Rick on the bridge. Earphones on, he was in radio contact with the Chinese vessel. All at once, he broke into Rick's thoughts with a loud laugh. "The Chinese captain is standing off this distance from our buoy because of the whales."

"Huh?"

"It's mating season, and our marker buoy is in the middle of the whales' bedroom."

"That's mighty considerate of him," Rick said, "but I'm a lot more concerned with what is happening under the water. Does he ever patrol closer to our buoy?"

Hok relayed the question and then waited several minutes for the answer. "Twice a day, he moves through the pod of whales and past our buoy."

"Okay," Rick acknowledged. "Ask him if he knows what has caused these blotches floating on the surface."

Hok soon had the Captain's answer. "He claims the ocean here near the strait sometimes looks this way for several days after a storm. Earthquakes on the ocean floor can also stir up the silt. But his intention is to keep his gunboat in the area until we have started our salvaging work." Hok paused a moment before he added, "Then I think he said … unless we prefer the gunboat to leave."

Rick thought about that before he said, "I believe we can trust them. We have their signed agreement on the treasure's distribution. With their firepower, there's not a hell of a lot we can do if they decide to take all the treasure."

Then he turned to Woody at the helm and said, "Drop anchor here, Woody." A thin smile tugged at Rick's mouth. "We'll move closer to our marker buoy after the whales have had their fun."

"Aye, skipper," Woody answered with a laugh.

While the *Valiant* was being anchored, Rick's thoughts quickly changed to the job ahead. "Hok, let's you and I go down alone and make the first inspection of the wreck. I've got Jake preparing the crew for the main salvage work."

"All right, what will we need other than lights?" Hok asked.

"Blasting charges."

Hok's features clouded in a frown. "Couldn't the blasting cause the wreck to slide into the deep hole?"

"We'll go slow, experiment with a single charge at a time."

"But is it wise to do any blasting before we know for sure what kind of cargo is aboard the wreck?"

"I know what you mean," Rick answered, "but I've had plenty of time to study your grandfather's report. The bow portion of the wreck down below should have no fuel or ammunition, nothing explosive. It was a hospital ship."

"But was it truly a hospital ship?" Hok persisted. "My ancestors were cunning during that war. Wasn't it larger than most hospital ships, and wasn't it also traveling at a destroyer's speed?"

Rick nodded. "That's all true, but I believe it's worth the gamble in trying to keep the slower torch work to a minimum. The blasting will get us down into the hold, where the treasure is supposed to be, a lot sooner."

Hok reflected on what Rick had said for a few moments before he voiced his agreement. "Your reasoning makes sense. Now tell me how to get ready for the dive."

"We've both been schooled by Jake with the explosives aboard. Ask him to help you prepare the charges with the magnetic strips for fastening to the wreck's hull. Let's use the manual charges that are triggered from the T-bar switch." He paused briefly before he added, "And have Jake break out those special earplugs. They should help to muffle the noise without hindering too much radio contact.

An hour later, Rick went over the side in his diving gear. He carried a bag with his share of the blasting material, and Hok followed close with his share. Their diving masks were equipped with lights, freeing the use of both hands for the job ahead. But it didn't take long for Rick to realize the water seemed murkier than it had on his previous dive when he had discovered the wreck.

He and Hok were in a canyon next to the one containing the wreck. Rick looked at a compass strapped to his wrist and motioned for Hok to follow. They swam upward along the dark face of the slope.

As they neared the top, Rick heard a noise. He thought it was his tanks bumping together. He stopped to adjust the straps when he heard the noise again. This time, it was more distinct. It came from the other side of the hill. He moved on up to the crest and inched his head over it just enough to see the deep valley far below.

"What the hell!" Rick exhaled the words inside his mask as all thought and feeling froze momentarily. His mind returned as questions flashed across his brain. *Is this real?* The wreck was outlined in a glow of lights. *How did the lights get there? And what were they connected to?*

His stare followed the row of lights. The long, menacing shadow alongside the wreck took on the distinctive shape of a submarine. Then he noticed a round symbol with a black, red, and green flag in its center.

CHAPTER 58

REMOVING THE SILT WAS slow, too slow to suit Rahab. But begrudgingly, he admired the salvage crew's ingenuity in building a temporary system to do the job.

Originally, the chief salvager had intended to use a high-pressure jetting nozzle secured to the end of the sub's fire hose. The nozzle was designed to divert some of the water backward to balance the forward thrust of the jet stream and allow the operator to maneuver it easily, but the water turbulence caused the silt to reform as fast as it was removed and nullified the nozzle's effectiveness.

To get the job done, the salvagers cobbled together a vacuum system from the sub's hose supply. A long hose was secured to the sub's air pressure system while the other end, containing a three-way valve system, was located near the wreck. Two men held the flexible front end of the hose, containing the valve assembly, in the silt covering the hull of the wreck. The created vacuum drew the silt into a larger hose, handled by two other men, to discharge the silt beyond the sub.

But after the vacuum system had been placed in operation, Rahab still was not satisfied. "Can't the air pressure be increased to remove the silt faster?" he asked through his headset.

"Yes, but there is a risk!" the chief salvager's voice echoed over Rahab's earphones."

"What risk?"

"The increased pressure could stir the water at the surface directly above us. The crew on the gunboat might get curious," the chief replied.

Rahab thought about that before he asked, "Won't the silt leaving the vacuum system float to the surface?"

"The captain said it would, but he claimed the water around here is sometimes cloudy after a storm. According to our navigator, there have been two rough storms lately."

Jury-rigging the system and the silt removal had required time, crucial time. Each passing day was ratcheting Rahab's nerves tighter. It had taken four days before the chief salvager's order came over the headsets, "Secure the vacuum system. Return to sub and prepare for opening the hull."

★ ★ ★

Rick waited for Hok to swim up alongside him at the crest of the hill. Then he gave Hok some time to recover from the shock of viewing the scene in the valley below. After he nudged Hok's shoulder, Rick pointed to the insignia on the sub's hull. When Hok saw it, he nodded immediately, signaling with hand gestures that it was indeed the sub that had rammed them.

They remained concealed behind the crest of the slope and watched two divers holding a long hose near the wreck's hull turn, and with the hose, they disappear under the bottom of the sub. Moments later, three other divers came into view while carrying sections of larger hose. One by one, they disappeared under the bottom of the sub. When the last one was out of sight, Rick waited for a few moments. He didn't move until he felt confident enough that there were no other divers. Then he swam over the hill and signaled Hok to follow him.

They swam down to the port side of the sub's bow, where Rick grabbed a penetrating-type charge from his bag and fastened it to the hull while using special clamps for underwater blasting. Then he removed a coil of wire from his bag and motioned for Hok to continue setting charges ahead of him.

After the last explosive was connected, Rick continued stringing the wire beyond the sub and up the slope of the hill, but Hok did not follow immediately. One of the charges had loosened from its terminal plate. He swam back to the sub to secure the connection.

Rahab's chest hurt from the pounding inside his rib cage. He paced the sub's narrow passageway, waiting for the cutting torches to be assembled. One of the salvagers using a large wrench tightened some fittings on a hose connection to an overhead valve manifold. His skilled hands were a blur until Rahab, his mind on the expectant payload just outside the sub, brushed past him, oblivious to his contact with the man's arm. The wrench banged on the metal deck, missing Rahab's toe by inches.

"You clumsy bastard!" Rahab swore. "Watch what you are doing!"

The tall, swarthy salvager bristled. Quickly, he picked up the wrench and pointed it at Rahab. "Who you call clumsy!" he roared and stepped toward Rahab, who drew back his fist.

"Enough of this!" the chief said and then stepped between the two. "Rahab, we need help with disconnecting the exterior elbow on top of the sub's hull. The job will get done faster if you work outside!"

Rahab glared at the salvager with the wrench. Bitterness rose like gall in his throat, but when the chief released him, he forced himself to put on his mask. He adjusted it, but his hands soon balled into fists again. In his path, another salvager was meticulously making up some pipe fittings to attach them to a coil of hose. Rahab watched only for a few moments before he snapped, "All right! Get the fuck out of my way!"

Hunched over and without looking up, the salvager replied sharply, "Fuck you too!" But he inched out of Rahab's path.

Rahab left the sub in blind fury. *Arrogant bunch of bastards*, he swore silently while he kicked his legs hard. He was near the stern of the sub when he was suddenly a man warned. That mysterious pain was back in his stomach. This time, the pain was not slight. It was a sharp blow that made his breathing difficult. Something was wrong! He looked about, his concentration total. Almost instinctively, his hand touched the wire.

Is that some debris from the wreck? The question raced through his mind. He started to alert the crew with his headset, but he had second thoughts. *Fuck them,* he swore to himself as he began swimming along the wire.

Hok reconnected the loose wire to the charge and then started after Rick again. Ahead of him, near the stern of the sub, a cloud of bubbles formed and then wildly dispersed when an emerging diver swam past the stern as if someone was after him. When the diver stopped suddenly, Hok instinctively moved closer to the conning tower. The diver seemed unsure about which way to go. After hesitating a few moments, the diver turned and, in measured kicks, disappeared in the darkness beyond the stern in Rick's direction.

Before Hok could move, another cloud of bubbles rose from underneath the sub. A second diver appeared with a knapsack slung over his shoulder. This diver swam in Hok's direction but remained on the other side of the large tower. The diver stopped near the tower and began removing an elbow attached to the sub.

Hok's first thought was to swim around the diver, but it was too risky. The intense lighting covered too much area. He drew his knife and waited.

The salvager faced Hok's direction, but there was a slight current. Would it, as meager as it was, be enough to turn the diver's body? Hok felt the hammering inside his chest as he froze alongside the sub's tower. Slowly, the bubbles leaving the salvager's mask moved in the opposite direction.

When the diver's body turned slightly by the current, Hok waited no longer. He reached the diver who was pivoting back against the current. The diver saw the knife an instant before it pierced his neck.

CHAPTER 59

RICK FINISHED STRINGING THE wire over the crest of the slope and down the opposite side. He set the T-bar switch into a small crevice, anchoring it with rocks. The LED on the face of the switch registered green while he was setting the switch in place, but suddenly, it changed to a red color. *Damn!* Rick swore to himself. He knew this meant one of the charges was not connected properly and would cause a disruption in the wiring circuit. Quickly, he turned and saw Hok's dim light just coming over the crest of the hill.

Rick turned back and continued to study the light on the switch, hoping the circuit's interruption was temporary. Then some discordant impulse flashed a warning in his brain. Instinctively, he turned again just as a slashing knife barely missed his throat. The knife dinged off his air tanks and tore through his shoulder. He twisted out of the diver's grasp and drew his own knife.

Face masks inches apart, there was instant recognition between the two men. Warily, they moved away from each other, which caused them to drift in a tight circle, but the sparring was short. The meeting with Scanlon in Hong Kong burned in Rahab's brain. He made the first lunge, but it was well telegraphed. After he grabbed Rahab's wrist, Rick slashed with his own knife. It missed the Afghan's chest and lodged in his air tank's harness.

Clouds of silt stirred up by their kicking flippers covered the fighters. Rick strained to free his knife while an arm grabbed him around the neck, but his awkward position prevented any leverage to pry himself loose. It was not a stranglehold. The arm had encircled Rick's tank regulator.

They were once more face-to-face. Neither could gain the advantage until Rahab's rage again took control. He released his hold and clawed wildly at Rick's face. The force of the attack ripped off Rick's mask and tore the regulator and hose connections from his air tanks. But it left Rahab off balance while allowing Rick to pull his knife free. He struck hard and buried the blade into Rahab's rib cage.

Hok swam up and over the crest. He continued on down the other side, following the wire. In the glare of his light, two motionless divers entangled with each other were suspended just above the ocean's floor. Rick was easily recognized without a face mask. Quickly, Hok pried Rick loose from the other diver who soon drifted out of sight. After placing his own mask over Rick's face Hok, with his fist, rapped the large buckle at his chest. The harness holding his air tanks released instantly and Rick had a new supply of air.

But Hok was now in jeopardy. He had to find the other body. His lungs began to burn as he swam around a large rock and bumped into the lifeless diver. Hok grabbed at the diver's face mask, but the straps were tangled. Fighting to keep from passing out and with a fireball inside his rib cage, Hok braced his knee on the diver's chest and yanked with both hands. The mask tore away. He clamped it over his face just before a thunderous explosion echoed from the valley opposite the hill.

Hok moved in slow motion. He tried hard, but he could not keep his feet on the ground. A cold chill wracked his body just before he opened his eyes. Endless bubbles streamed before him. Suddenly, two staring eyes were an inch from his face.

Hok's hands searched along the front of the dead diver. When he found the large buckle in the middle of the chest, he pushed it, but the harness did not release. It was caught on something underneath the body. Fearing entrapment here on the ocean floor, Hok yanked and jerked at the harness, but his effort could not free the entangled harness.

The mental torture of his dilemma plus the physical strain of his effort to free himself soon consumed all his strength. Exhausted, he collapsed against the body, his arms encircling it. One of his hands brushed against the T-bar switch handle. With the other hand, he felt a harness strap wrapped around the handle. The discovery was an instant antidote for Hok.

After he unhooked the diver's harness from the switch handle, Hok quickly adjusted the breathing apparatus over his own shoulders. Then he rested for a few moments. The brief respite helped him to realize the irony of the situation. When the body of the dead diver came to rest on top of the switch, it had triggered the detonators of all the explosive charges and blew up the submarine.

Rick jolted awake. By the time he realized where he was, a heavy cloud of silt suddenly engulfed him. When the thick fog began to settle, he headed toward a dim light. Getting there, he found Hok sitting on the T-bar switch box. Hok rose immediately, and with helmets face-to-face, they embraced quickly after recognition. Then Hok, with hand gestures, explained how the unmasked body lying near them had blown up the sub.

After focusing his light on the face of the dead diver, Rick recognized the man who he had fought with at the bar. Nodding his helmeted head, Rick turned and motioned for Hok to follow him back up the hill. At the crest, their lights beamed down into the darkened valley, where the silt had just settled enough to show no remnants of the previous submarine.

They swam down and on over to the wreck on the opposite side of the valley. After inspecting the wreck's hull where it was buried into the hillside, Rick determined what he had feared the most; the sediment along the hull had loosened. The wreck had apparently edged closer to the deep hole when the sub exploded.

After returning to the *Valiant*, Rick and Hok rested on the fantail while explaining to the rest of the crew what had happened below and how the result had created a severe problem for them.

No one said anything. Stunned into stillness, thoughts were on the ocean floor's condition. *The sea never gives up its secrets easily*, Rick thought as he rubbed his neck. It ached from the sling used to patch up his shoulder wound.

"Damn it!" Rick finally broke the silence. "We got a job to do! Let's get underway and find out with our sonar just how much of a problem we have down there." He picked up his binoculars and studied the water ahead. "The whales should have completed their joyride by now."

Thirty minutes of crisscrossing over the water where the wreck was buried, Rick had his answer. The wreck had inched closer to the edge of the deep trench. He turned to Hok standing nearby. "We were right. It has moved."

A long silence followed before Hok said, "What do you think?"

Rick studied the monitor some more before he answered. "Well, to be honest, I don't know what to think, but one thing I do know is that we have got to do something and fast."

Within earshot in the pilothouse, Jake offered, "Why don't we try to get a cable around it?"

"You mean hold the wreck in place with the *Valiant*?"

"Yeah, I know what you are thinking, skipper. That piece of bow down there is probably bigger than our salvage ship, but with both anchors set and our engines on fast idle, I believe we can supply enough torque to the retaining line to hold the wreck in place." Jake waited, his eyes leveled on Rick's face.

As he pictured Jake's plan in his mind, Rick quietly considered all the details involved. When he could find no flaws, he said, "Okay! Let's give it a try!" His eyes flashed a quick sparkle when he returned Jake's stare.

There was little daylight left by the time a cable was looped around the wreck and then secured to the two forward deck bitts on the *Valiant's* bow.

CHAPTER 60

RICK WOKE UP WITH stiffness in his shoulder that reminded him of yesterday. He lay in his bunk for a few moments, thinking about the big guy that he had fought with twice. After destroying a sub and its crew, Rick felt sure there would be some retaliation and no doubt with more tenacity. But for now, the salvaging of the treasure was more pressing on his mind. With a vigorous grunt, he levered himself out of the bunk.

Rick wanted the divers rigged to stay down for long periods of time. He put Woody Schaffer in charge of running an air hose down the anchor chain to a manifold at the ocean floor. The divers could descend with a small tank of air to the manifold and then switch to an individual line leading out from the assembly.

While all the other divers were busy installing high-intensity lights around the wreck, Rick decided to join them. After he suited up for the dive, Jake questioned Rick's judgment of working with his wounded shoulder. "The salt water will aid the healing," Rick had told him just before he had left the *Valiant*. By the time he reached the site of the wreck down below, his prognosis was correct. As he prepared to go to work, Rick wasn't sure if it was the salt water's healing or its chilling that had numbed all his soreness from his shoulder, but he didn't care. He had full use of his arm. He leaned toward the wreck with his cutting torch and started opening a hole in the hull of the wreck.

The gas lines supplying the cutting torches were rigged so two divers could work together. By midafternoon, a large piece of the hull's heavy plating fell away where Rick and Emory Chang had been working.

A bluish white metal filled the opening. It was tin, and because it had a much lower melting point than the hull, they rapidly cut an access hole through this softer metal only to be met with a tangled mass of the ship's structure. By the end of the third day, the only other cargo found besides the tin was a hold filled with rubber.

In the mess room that evening, Jake was first to air his feelings. "There's too much of that fuckin' tin and rubber! I haven't seen anything resembling a walk-in safe." He was hunched over his coffee on the opposite side of the table from Rick. "Skipper, tell me honestly. Do you think we've been had?"

Rick didn't answer immediately. He looked around and wondered if his eyes were as red as the others in the room. "Jake, if I knew that for sure, you would be the first to hear it from me!" As he rose slowly to refill his coffee cup, Rick continued, "All the reports that Hok and I have studied plus the ruckus back in Kowloon appear to make this venture authentic. And don't forget, the people who were here with their sub evidently felt the hunt was worthwhile."

At the coffee urn, Rick only partially filled his cup and then drank it in one gulp. He turned to leave and then glanced over at Hok, who was seated at the other table, before he added, "Hok, how about you and Jake helping me with some log reports?"

Up in the chart room, Rick waited until they followed him through the door. "I didn't want to worry the rest of the crew, but I had the feeling down there today that the wreck has moved slightly. Let's check her position."

Rick picked up a profile map that was made on transparent paper, showing the wreck's original position. He placed the map over the image on the sonar screen showing the current position of the wreck. "Yeah, that confirms my suspicion," he said after he studied the two outlines. "Since we started entering the wreck, it has slid more than a foot closer to the hole."

"Has either anchor changed positions since we started?" Hok asked.

"No, at least we don't think so," Jake said. "I've had a diver check their positions daily."

There was a long silence before Rick finally said, "First thing tomorrow, let's check the cable for any signs of weakening. And Jake, have Herb contact the gunboat tomorrow. I would like to know if it's in the area, should we need extra help."

The following morning, the cable was still holding firm. *Probably stretched a little,* Rick thought as he went back to work with the other divers.

Tunneling through the broken beams of the wreck's hull and searching for the treasure was like traipsing a mine field, carrying a live hand grenade. Two more days, and their luck hadn't changed.

After chow during the evening of the second day, Jake met Rick topside. "The wreck has moved another six inches," he whispered. Pete and Greg were standing within hearing range.

"That wrecked bow is definitely edging toward the hole each day." When Rick said nothing, Jake added, "It's getting damn risky down there!"

"Don't you think I know that?" Rick hissed.

Jake had struck a nerve, and Rick responded in kind when another pain rippled through his gut. They were becoming more frequent. The long hours were taking their toll. Sid and Hank both had severe cases of the cramps. Al had cut a deep gash in his hand, and Woody had a severe burn on his left arm from the time when he had dropped his cutting torch.

Rick knew he should have been more open with his thoughts and what he expected of the crew, but he remained silent, too tired to think. He watched the last rays of sunset dip into the horizon before he said, "We are not quitting yet!" He spoke quietly but firmly, and then he turned and headed on below.

CHAPTER 61

"WE HAVE LOST ALL contact with our submarine! Your plans have apparently cost me a submarine and its crew, which included a son!" Ahmad Sattar's voice rumbled over the phone.

Ed Broadman listened. He had no other choice.

"We believe the Americans are responsible. Any more failures on our part, and the Americans will be short a DEA man in their San Francisco office! Faisal, do you understand?"

"Yes, I do." The bitterness in Sattar's voice reminded Broadman of the taste of gall in the throat.

"Our newest submarine will not reach the salvage site for two weeks! The American ship is not to leave the salvage site! Do you hear me?"

"Yes!" Broadman replied.

"Then what do you need? And this time, you personally had better be sure of the need!"

Broadman needed an answer, but he didn't have one at the moment. He would need a contact in Hong Kong, someone who would not mind doing a dirty job if the money was right, someone who had contacts. He knew the man.

"Arrange an appointment for a Pedro Sanchez to see Fuchou at his office three days from now."

"It will be done!" There was a short silence. "Remember, no more failures!" The phone clicked in Broadman's ear.

The next day, Broadman left for Hong Kong.

The cab ride, Broadman noted, was precisely fifty-five minutes from the Hong Kong International Airport to the Marco Polo Gateway Hotel on Canton Road in Kowloon. He registered as Edward Broadman from San Francisco.

An hour later, disguised as a balding Caucasian with a mustache, Broadman left the hotel. Discernable only to the most perceptive observer, his inclined posture was due to the weight of his briefcase.

He took a cab to Tsim Sha Tsiu's shopping district. At the first luggage shop along his route, he bought two suitcases. He declined when the staff offered to wrap them. While the clerk processed the sale at the register, Broadman opened his briefcase and transferred a heavy dictionary to one of the new suitcases. He inserted the briefcase with another thick book into the second piece of luggage. Then he picked up the two bags and momentarily held them before he placed them back on the floor just as the sales clerk returned with the receipt. Broadman left the luggage shop and walked to the next block, where he hailed another cab and took it to the Dorsett Seaview Hotel on Shanghai Street.

The doorman summoned a red cap who loaded the two suitcases onto his handcart and then followed Broadman into the hotel, where he registered as Pedro Sanchez from Buenos Aires.

The blubbery Fuchou sat quietly behind his desk. His dark eyes, which were buried deep in his face, belied his calm exterior. They darted like a snake's tongue as he watched Pedro Sanchez, who sat across the desk from him.

Fuchou had received a call three days ago from Ahmad Sattar, who had arranged this meeting. Sanchez, a man with a beaked nose separating a bushy mustache and someone who appeared to be in his fifties, had introduced himself as Sattar's new man for the China trade.

So Rahab Sattar is fish food at the bottom of the strait, Fuchou thought happily while he reached up to tap the cockatoo's cage. Sanchez had been candid about his visit. *I wonder which has top priority with Sattar*, Fuchou speculated, *to avenge the loss of a son or to salvage a treasure?*

Either way, this man must have been a confidant of the Afghanistan drug dealer. There had been nothing vague about Sanchez's proposal. Fuchou was to receive five million dollars for taking two hostages who were grandparents of the American ship captain's partner. This plan was calculated to delay the salvaging work long enough for another submarine to reach the strait.

With both the Americans and the drug lords fighting over the treasure, this hostage scheme is the best deal for me, Fuchou concluded, but he was not ready to tell that to Sanchez.

"A maximum time for holding the hostages must be established first," Fuchou declared.

"Seven days maximum."

"And what if you have not taken the treasure and sunk the American ship in that time?"

"You kill the hostages, and the money is yours."

"And the money? How will I be paid?"

The obesity of this Chinese man effectively clouds his cunning, Broadman thought as he realized he had no alternative but to deal with him. Broadman opened his briefcase and set it in front of Fuchou before he answered. "Your promise to do the job is worth a million dollars now."

Fuchou thumbed through the stacks of crisp new bills. It was American money. "And how will I be paid the remaining four million?"

"A courier will bring you two million more the day the hostages are taken. After we have possession of the treasure, you will receive the final two million."

"What if you not take treasure in seven days?"

"You are still guaranteed the final two million."

Fuchou turned around slowly and then reached up and tapped the parrot's cage. He waited until its head appeared from under a wing and then turned back around in his chair. He looked down at the money before meeting his visitor's eyes. "What's to keep me from settling for a million with promise only?"

Broadman slipped one hand in his coat pocket. "You have that option," he answered in a cold, unrelenting voice, "but you will not enjoy it with a bullet in your chest."

CHAPTER 62

IT WAS NOT PAT's intention to stay at the Utamaros' during the week that she was in Hong Kong, but they had insisted.

"We would be offended if you refused our hospitality. For helping to save our grandson's life, we now owe you our lives." Mr. Utamaro had been very persuasive.

The day had gone well for her. Dr. Chen Guofeng, head of the research department of Queen Elizabeth Hospital, had lectured on the latest techniques in bone marrow transplanting. Later, she had the opportunity to examine the results of his work on three patients.

She was in her room, getting ready to join the Utamaros for dinner when she heard some loud voices downstairs. *That certainly can't be my hosts talking*, Pat thought. She left her room and started down the stairs but stopped abruptly. At the landing near the front door, the Utamaros were being held at gunpoint by a tall, nondescript Asian man dressed in a rumpled business suit. Pat whirled, but her movement caught the gunman's attention.

"Stop!" he shouted, pointing the gun at her. "Come down!"

His broken English was guttural but distinctive enough for Pat to obey. When she started back down the stairs, another Asian gunman appeared. He was shorter, but his suit had the same lived-in look as his associate's. When he saw Pat, he yelled something and then raced up the stairs, brushing her against the banister.

"We are being taken hostage!" Mr. Utamaro said, eyes flashing in his drawn face." Mrs. Utamaro was silent, her features only slightly more animated than her husband's.

"B-But why!" Pat stammered.

"No talking!" the taller thug growled in stuttered syllables. The muzzle of his pistol hurt when it jammed into Pat's shoulder.

The second gunman returned, his shoes thudding rapidly on the staircase. He said something to the taller man. Then they both turned and stared wildly at Pat. She felt panic rise in her throat. Their jerky movements prevented them from standing still. They jabbered in voices that sounded unnatural, but that was not Pat's main concern. They kept staring at her.

Suddenly, the taller gunman motioned everyone toward the door. Outside, there was a car in the driveway. The Utamaros were crowded into the backseat with the taller gunman while Pat was forced to sit in front with the hoodlum who was driving.

Asawa's passive features concealed the thoughts racing through his mind. He felt sure this kidnapping had something to do with his grandson's search for the treasure, but what? And these captors, he recognized their dialect as Korean, but who were they working for? He thought about their surprised look when they had discovered Dr. Kendall. It was obvious her presence had been unexpected.

They traveled in an area of Kowloon that Asawa had never been to before. The buildings were more desolate. Junkyards and automobile salvage businesses were numerous. The few people there were dressed in dirty clothes.

The gunman who was driving slowed the car and turned into a narrow street leading to an area with a security fence. They continued on inside the enclosure until the car skidded to a stop in front of a two-story, brick building with long cracks in the mortar joints. A wooden door that was wide enough for an eighteen-wheel tractor-trailer blocked their path. The only identification for the building was a faded sign above the door. Barely recognizable in the splintered boards was the number thirty.

That number! It stirred Asawa's memory just before he was jerked roughly from the car. With his wife and Dr. Kendall, he was hustled inside the building through a small entrance door.

The building was used as storage for hundreds of pallets built with wooden side racks. Forced to move rapidly toward the far end of the building, Asawa noticed various symbols painted on the slats of the portable platforms that were stacked in long rows extending the length of the building.

The letters CU were on the sides of the pallets containing reddish brown metal. Asawa knew that CU was the symbol for copper. Another section of pallets that were identified with the letters ZN contained bluish white metal. Asawa assumed this was stored zinc. An adjacent section had the letters SN, which Asawa knew stood for tin.

Narrow passageways bisected the stacks approximately every twenty feet. As they were forcefully marched along one of the aisles between the stacks of metal, the image of the building's number burned in Asawa's mind. He looked around, but the stacked pallets blocked his view until he reached the end of the long row.

There was an open space where all the rows ended and a plywood partition that extended across the back of the building. Against the back wall, there was a flight of stairs that led up to a second floor. A chair hung from the wall at the base of the stairs. Asawa, following along behind his wife and Pat, saw the chair just before they were pushed through a doorway in the partition wall.

His memory sharpened instantly. His grandson had been here. Hokusai had inspected some metal for purchasing by his firm before it was shipped to America. He had told Asawa about seeing a chairlift in one of the warehouses. He said that the owner of the metal salvage company was too fat to climb stairs and needed the chairlift to get to the second floor of the building. The owner was Fuchou.

After getting the three hostages inside the rough-built room, the taller Asian locked the door. Then he called Fuchou on his cell phone. When Fuchou heard that the kidnapping was complete, he immediately called Sanchez.

"You have done well!" Fuchou heard the elation in Sanchez's voice. "Your description of the blonde woman identifies her as a friend of the American salvage ship's captain and his partner. Proceed with the communication phase."

CHAPTER 63

At Stone Cutters Island near Kowloon, a cargo ship that was long overdue for a coat of paint was being prepared to get underway. The grungy crew scurried about on the main deck and the adjacent dock, removing the mooring lines while Wu Thou watched from the bridge. A short, muscular, middle-aged Chinese man, Wu Thou was owner and captain of the small freighter that had become a fishing trawler when the freight business had eased off.

Those were the two legitimate uses for his rusty ship. During their voyages, he and his crew never missed the opportunity to board any small boat that happened to stray far off the China coast. Wu Thou always made sure the valuables that were taken from the hapless passengers of the smaller boats were divided equally among his crew.

His ship backed away from its berth and headed out into the main harbor and on past Green Island's lighthouse located off the southern coast of Hong Kong Island. Wu Thou had cargo bound for Shantou, but it would be late in arriving.

As he sat alone in his cabin, Wu Thou looked around at the radio equipment shoved into every corner of the small room. Radio had been his hobby since he had first heard a voice come from a faceless box. And when he had accidentally turned a dial and the voice changed into music, he had become addicted.

Growing up, Wu Thou had been a member of a gang that made their money stealing cargo from the Kowloon docks. He used his share to continually improve his transmission and receiving set.

Wu Thou's wrinkled face lit in a smile as he reached for the volume control. Another member of that gang was Fuchou, who would pay him twenty-five thousand dollars for making this trip.

★ ★ ★

"Rick and Hok, wait up!" Herb yelled from the radio shack. He reached them before they went over the side for their first dive of the day. "This message just came over the radio!" he said, holding up a piece of paper in his hand.

When he noticed the deep furrows lining Herb's forehead, Rick said, "Go ahead. Read the message. I can tell already it is not good news."

"No, it's not!" Herb replied. He looked at the paper and started, "We are holding Asawa Utamaro, his wife, and Dr. Patricia Kendall as hostages. For more information, go to the Utamaros' residence on Perth Street in Ho Man Tin, Kowloon. Use door key under entrance mat. Do not contact the police, or you will not see them alive again."

"Who sent that?" Rick snapped.

"I don't know!"

"Whatta you mean, you don't know?"

"When I request acknowledgment, all I can get is a repeat of the message!"

"Can't you radio the coast?" Hok asked, his voice hoarse with emotion.

"My radio signal is jammed. I can barely reach the gunboat's radio."

"Come on!" Rick called. He whirled and started in the direction of the radio shack. "Hok, this could be a trap just to get us away from the salvage site!" he yelled over his shoulder.

"I was thinking that!" Hok answered breathlessly. "But we've got to make sure."

"Do you read me? Acknowledge, over!" The radio signal from the *Valiant* was loud and clear in Wu Thou's cabin. By 0800 this morning, his ship was close enough but still out of sight of the American ship and the Chinese gunboat to jam their radio frequencies. Wu Thou watched the clock above his transmitter. The time would soon be ready to repeat the hostage message.

"Nothing!" Herb said, banging his fist on the desk in front of his radio.

"How about the gunboat?" Rick asked quickly. "Is its radio having the same problem?"

"I don't know," Herb answered. "The signal between us is so damn fuzzy it's hardly recognizable." He switched two dials and started sending.

Rick swore silently. He could guess who was behind this hostage scheme. He thought about using wireless communication, but the radio message's warning stopped him. Any use of the cell phone or the Internet might risk involvement of the Hong Kong authorities. Hok's grim features prompted Rick into a quick decision. He waited no longer for confirmation by the *Valiant's* radio. "Hok, will you go over to the gun—"

"I'm on my way!" Hok shouted, rushing out the door.

Thirty minutes later, Hok called through a bullhorn from the deck of the gunboat. "Radio jammed! But the captain will take us to Hong Kong!"

A misty fog shrouded the dock lights when Rick and Hok stepped off the gunboat near Shan Street. An hour later, Hok jumped out of the cab as it rolled to a stop in front of his grandparents' home. When they entered the house, they found the message on the kitchen table.

"It is written in my grandfather's handwriting," Hok said, his voice trembling. He cleared his throat and continued. "Furnish our captors with five million dollars in unmarked bills by Thursday at 9:00 a.m. Meet a courier at kiosk with money in suitcases at Haiphong Road and Kowloon Park Drive. Hokusai, you are to offer a light to a man standing on the corner with an unlit cigarette. He will bring you to a house where your grandmother, Dr. Kendall, and I will be the only three. Failure to comply means we will be zero."

"Well, one thing's for sure," Rick said after Hok had finished. "These kidnappers think we have already found the treasure."

"Yes," Hok answered while he sat in one of the chairs at the table. "Under the circumstances, it will be exceedingly difficult to convince a bank that we are worth that much money." There was no smile on his face. He spoke haltingly while his stare remained fixed on the message.

Only a ticking clock broke the silence. *This drug organization has all the daring and cunning of a hungry wolf,* Rick thought. Absorbed in thought, he realized he was assuming a drug organization was behind this entire embattlement over the treasure find. *But considering the circumstances starting with the navigation chart, who else would be as interested in salvaging this particular treasure?* he asked himself. He now realized they had been tracking his progress ever since he had checked out of his room in Kaohsiung.

Hok raised his head. Then he spoke just loud enough to be overheard. "My grandfather is as precise in his writing as he is articulate in his speech. Several of these sentences are poorly structured, which means the message is in code. I must put into practice some of the code games he played with me when I was a child." He paused briefly, raising his head as if he was looking back in his memory,

He reached for a pencil only after he had added just above a whisper, "Except this one is no game."

CHAPTER 64

All things considered, it could be worse, Pat thought while she looked around the windowless room. She sat on a hard bench across from the Utamaros. One bare lightbulb hung from the ceiling and provided the only light for the room. There was a bathroom of sorts in one end of the narrow room. Empty wooden shelves from floor to ceiling stood along one wall.

I wonder how much of the five million dollars I am supposed to be worth, she thought. *More importantly, how much will Rick think I am worth?* Mr. Utamaro had filled her in on the details of the treasure hunt. The unflinching attitude of the Utamaros toward their captors was a calming influence, but the occasional laughter from just outside the room was disturbing.

However, she was hopeful of being rescued and soon. She knew about the coded message. After Mr. Utamaro had been forced to write the ransom note, he later revealed to her how it had been written. Her sense of helplessness concerned her the most. She had inspected every inch of the room, looking for something that she could use to defend herself. With each passing hour, the scurrilous laughter convinced her of the need for a weapon.

Asawa sat beside his wife, listening to the voices of the men outside the room. When Dr. Kendall glanced repeatedly at the door, he whispered, "They are discussing how to spend the money." In truth, the talk from the two thugs was getting bolder. They were intending to satisfy their lust for the beautiful doctor before "the boss" arrived at the warehouse. Asawa assumed the captors were talking about Fuchou.

Back at the house, Hok jumped up from his chair. "That is it! That has got to be it!" His voice was louder than normal when he turned to Rick. "Spell out the words with the letters I have highlighted," he spoke excitedly, pointing to the message.

Rick leaned over the table. The featured letters made a diagonal line across the message, beginning with the first letter of the first word in the first line and then going to the first letter of the second word in the second line and so on until reaching the last three lines. There, whole words were underlined with the same diagonal pattern:

> (F)urnish our captors with five million dollars.
> In (U)nmarked bills on Friday at 9:00 a.m.
> Meet a (C)ourier at telephone booth with money
> In suitcase at (H)aiphong Road and Kowloon Park Drive.
> Hokusai, you are to (O)ffer to a man standing
> on the corner with an (U)nlit cigarette a light.
> He will bring you to a (house where) your mother, Dr.
> Kendall, and I will be the only (three) people.
> Failure to comply means we will be (zero).

Rick spelled out Fuchou's name before he pronounced it fully. "But 'house where' and 'three' and 'zero?'" Rick said. "That doesn't—"

"That means warehouse thirty, and I have been there!" Hok beamed. "I have inspected some scrap metal at that warehouse. Let's get started!" He turned and headed toward the kitchen door.

Caught up in the excitement, Rick hurried after him, but at the door, he grabbed Hok's shoulder. "Wait! Let's think about this for a minute! We don't want to endanger your grandparents and Pat any more than they already are!"

"What do you mean?" His voice tore at Rick.

"This house is probably under surveillance right now. Fuchou or one of his henchmen wanted to be sure you would enter the house to read the note. Doesn't that make sense?"

Hok finally nodded, but his features remained etched in a frown.

"And the phone is probably tapped, so we had better not call the police."

"But we can't wait," Hok said and hesitated for a few moments. As he looked directly at Rick, the intensity in his voice ebbed. "I understand.

Fuchou probably has friends on the police force. I don't trust anybody but ourselves for this job."

"Then let's make our plans carefully. How far is this warehouse from here?"

"About twenty kilometers."

"We will need a car."

"We can use my grandparents' car. It should be in the garage." Hok paused, and a thin smile crossed his face. "No, we would be seen leaving, and the note indicates that we have five days before meeting the courier."

"Can we leave the house from the back without being detected?"

"Yes, there is an alley back there and no streetlights. But what about a car?"

"We will rent one. Let's go upstairs and turn on some lights so that it looks as if we are going to bed." Rick reached for a revolver in his pocket. "Better check our guns now," he added.

CHAPTER 65

FUCHOU SAT QUIETLY. His bulbous figure took up most of the front seat in his Mercedes. He waited another thirty minutes after the lights had gone out on the second floor of the Utamaro's condo before he started his car.

He drove rapidly along Argyle Street, heading in the direction of the Mong Kok district of Kowloon. Nervously, he tapped the steering wheel with his ring finger. Now came the long wait. He did not expect Scanlon to raise the five million unless his crew had already found the gold. But that was unlikely since, according to Sanchez, their ship was still at the site.

Fuchou had read Utamaro's note after one of the kidnappers had given it to him. Next Friday, when the five days were over, instead of a man with an unlit cigarette on Haiphong Street, there would be two men with orders to use their guns inside his warehouse.

Fuchou breathed easier. The taking of the hostages had gone well. After Tai Nam and Lui Wuhan had arrived from Pusan yesterday on one of his freighters, Fuchou had provided them with a car. They had already made a practice run from the Utamaro's home to the warehouse while Fuchou had observed in a separate car. They had used radios to keep in contact.

The two Koreans were loyal. They were his best drug runners, but the dope was rapidly becoming their master, especially when it came to the shorter one, Liu Wuhan.

Fuchou stopped at the gate in the security fence surrounding his warehouse. Two Doberman Pinscher's flashed their teeth in the beam of his car's headlights. The snarling sounds quieted when the lumbering figure with a paper bag in his hand got out of the car. Dog biscuits hurled over the fence disappeared in midair. The snapping jaws cracked like pistol shots.

Fuchou unlocked the gate and drove a short distance inside the enclosure. When he got out to lock the gate, the first thing he did was open the back door of his car. The two dogs were sitting calmly in the backseat when he returned from fastening the gate. He took them for a short ride to a parking place near the building before he let them out. He used a key to unlock the entrance door to the warehouse.

Just as he stepped inside, a noise came from the back of the building. Then there was a shout. "Crazy woman!" Scuffling sounds followed.

Fuchou labored on in that direction, his short legs moving as fast as their top-heavy burden would allow.

He stopped at the end of a long row of stacked pallets and glanced around the corner. Blood ran down the side of Wuhan's face. His free hand ripped at the front of the blonde's dress.

"Take your hands off me, you kidnapping junkie!" Pat screamed. Tears washed her eyes as she hit Wuhan in the head with the spiked heel of her shoe.

Fuchou could see inside the small room. The taller Korean, Tai Nam, leveled his gun at Utamaro, whose bloody head was cradled in his wife's arms.

"Stop!" Fuchou shouted in Korean. "Wuhan, put woman back in room! Tai Nam, get out of room!"

When Pat was released, she rushed back into the smaller room. When he had tried to protect her, Mr. Utamaro had lunged at the gunman, who had been much too quick for the elderly man. He easily sidestepped away from the attack, and then he hit Utamaro back. The barrel of his gun had made a sickening crack against Utamaro's head.

The taller gunman was slow when he left the room. He also had thoughts about the white woman, who was now attending to the old man lying on the floor. The front of her dress had been torn away. A lot of bare skin was now showing. He liked the way she looked. He took his time leaving the room.

Pat kneeled down to examine Mr. Utamaro's wound. She pushed back his eyelids. If he had a concussion, it had to be slight. When she went into the bathroom to wet her handkerchief, the sprayed water hit sensitive skin. She took only a few moments to tie her ripped shirt across her breasts before he returned to the Utamaros.

"His eyes are open," Mrs. Utamaro said. "He will be all right, won't he, Dr. Kendall?" Her troubled face failed to hide the firm set to her jaw.

"Yes, since his pulse is beginning to beat normally, I believe he has had only a minor concussion."

Asawa motioned for silence by raising a limp. He was staring at the door.

Outside the room, Fuchou waited, which infuriated him more. He did not want to be seen by the hostages. When he heard the door slam, he moved out from behind his cover. "You stupid pigs!" he raged. He had drawn his gun and started waving it at the two Koreans. "Do you want to ruin the deal? We have to wait till the treasure is taken."

"How long that be?" Wuhan asked.

"Six days, no longer."

That must be Fuchou, Asawa thought, but then the talking stopped abruptly.

Eight blocks from his grandparents' house, Hok and Rick rented a car at an all-night car rental place. "Tell me again about the warehouse?" Rick asked when they headed out into the traffic while Hok drove.

"It looked like any other warehouse from what I can remember," Hok answered. He had to wait for the light to change at Nathan and Shan streets. "We entered through a large roll-up door. There must be a rear door, but I don't recall seeing one."

"Was there a security fence around it?"

"Yes!" Hok was grateful for the reminder. "And there was a gate. It was wide enough for a large truck to pass through the fence.

"Some warehouses have guard dogs? Did you see any?"

"No, but the gate was open. If there were dogs, they would have been locked up."

They traveled for a while in silence. The space between the buildings on each side of the street gradually widened.

"The warehouse is ahead of us around the next corner." Hok's voice was barely audible.

They left the car parked on the street and felt their way along a dark alley. The backside of the tall warehouse loomed ahead of them. Rick was in the lead. He moved forward, his footsteps silent. Twenty feet from the building, he bumped into a steel fence.

Two thunderbolts with blazing eyes and barred teeth hit the fence opposite Rick's head. Long, silver fangs blurred into snarls filling the midnight air. Rick was only two steps behind Hok when they both reached the car. "Well, we know about the dogs," Hok gasped.

Rick waited for his breathing to slow before he answered, "Yeah, we are going to need something to distract them, something more tender than my ass."

CHAPTER 66

The time was 1:30 a.m. when Hok walked back up the alley with a bag of dog biscuits. Rick, carrying a tire iron from their rented car, circled around to the front of the warehouse. He waited in the shadows of the front gate until he heard the dogs barking at the rear of the building. Then he climbed the fence. He dropped to the ground on the other side, picked up the tire iron, and started for the building a hundred feet away.

In the meantime Hok's breathing returned to normal when the savage sounds on the other side of the fence quieted to salivating grunts and scampering paws thudding against the turf. Despite the darkness, most of the biscuits he tossed over the fence never hit the ground. Those that did rolled only a short distance before they were scooped up in flashing teeth—all except for one biscuit.

It must have hit a rock, the thought flashed in Hok's mind while he nervously watched the white biscuit roll out of sight along the hard ground toward the front of the warehouse. Hok could hear one of the dogs giving the treat a long chase before running it down. Anxious moments passed while Hok, his ear pressed against the fence, listened for the dog's return, but that sound never came.

Rick's shoulder touched the building. When he started moving toward the entrance door, his shoe kicked a loose rock. It rattled against the building. He paused for a few seconds before he started forward again. He was almost to the door when a blurring shadow turned the corner of the warehouse. The only sound from the dog was its paws striking the ground, but two dilated eyes were blazing coals burning brighter with each charging leap toward him.

Inside the building, Fuchou and his two henchmen listened in guarded anticipation to the loud barking outside. But when the dogs soon quieted, they relaxed in their silent vigil. An hour later, the same sharp outburst was repeated, except this time, only the barking stopped. Fuchou could hear the sound of the dogs running in the loose gravel. When the movement continued, he motioned for Wuhan to look outside.

The shorter gunman started in the direction of the back door, but Fuchou stopped him with a stern shake of his head. With his gun, he gestured to investigate from the front of the building.

Wuhan turned and plodded toward the front of the warehouse. He cursed under his breath. Why had Fuchou returned when he had? Wuhan still felt the pain from the pelting that white bitch had given him earlier, but she would not leave his mind. She had fought like a tiger, and that made him want her more.

It was the first time he had seen a white woman's breasts. Except for color, hers was no different than others he had seen, but he hadn't gotten his hands on either one. Fuchou had arrived too soon.

The boss will not stay much longer, he thought as he reached to unlatch the three-foot-wide, walk-in door adjacent to the roll-up door. The smaller door was hinged to swing outward. Just as Wuhan pushed it open, eighty pounds of fury slammed against the inside of the door. An instant later, as if by instinct, Wuhan's gun discharged into the Doberman's neck.

Rick fired two quick shots at the outline in the doorway. The bullets entered Wuhan's chest from point-blank range. Another fleeting shadow came from around the corner. It leaped for Rick's throat. He pivoted, avoided the dog's lunge, and swung the tire iron. The blow stunned the dog long enough for Rick to get off a shot. It hit the second Doberman behind the ear.

"They are here!" Pat whispered excitedly after she heard the shots. She helped Mr. Utamaro to a sitting position before she moved closer to the door. A long silence followed the flurry of gunshots.

With the first shot, Fuchou immediately motioned Tai Nam to the front of the building. He started along a narrow corridor of the stacked pallets while Fuchou moved along the opposite side from Tai Nam. The only lit area inside the warehouse was in the back near the hostages' room. With his path soon in darkness, Fuchou cursed under his breath. The light switch was in the front of the building.

When Rick heard Hok's footsteps moving rapidly along the outside of the fence, he ran back to the front gate and waited. Watching Hok's dim outline come into view, Rick motioned for him to climb over the fence. They moved quickly to the opened front door and stepped over the still forms of the dog and the gunman as they entered the warehouse single-file.

The only light inside came from the back of the building, but it was just enough for Rick and Hok to see that there was a wall of racked pallets in long rows reaching all the way back to the lit area.

With the tire iron still in his hand, Rick used it to nudge Hok to the nearest corridor leading to the back of the building. "I'll take the opposite corridor," Rick whispered to Hok. "Let's go."

CHAPTER 67

THEY MOVED QUIETLY TOWARD the back of the warehouse. Twenty feet from where he started, Rick felt an opening in the row of stacked pallets. Quickly, he moved through the narrow passageway to Hok's side and whispered his name.

"Yes!" Hok exhaled with a choking gasp in his throat.

"Stay put for a few seconds," Rick murmured. "I am going to throw this tire iron toward the back of the building on my side of these stacks."

"Go ahead! I'll wait!" Hok whispered his reply.

Rick felt his way back to a corner of the long corridor leading to the rear of the building. Quickly, he stepped around the corner and threw the iron rod as hard as he could in the direction of the lit area. Then he moved back around the corner in the narrow passageway.

Immediately after the rod clanged against the concrete floor, there was a loud groan followed by three shots that whined near Rick's head.

As he held his gun around the corner, Rick returned three answering shots. A raspy cough sounded just before something hit the floor.

Fuchou heard Tai Nam's body hit the floor hard. When he realized his only other henchman was probably dead, Fuchou turned and plodded to the back of the warehouse. Quickly, he unlocked the door to the room containing the hostages. Seeing the old Japanese man lying on the floor and his wife attending to him, Fuchou grabbed the white woman and jerked her toward the door.

"You fat slob!" Pat shouted. "Take your hands off me!" After she was forced outside the room, she yelled, "Rick, is that you?" But her voice was muffled.

"Keep quiet!" Rick whispered to Hok. "We don't know how many others are here!" He motioned Hok to continue along his side of the stacked pallets.

They moved out into their respective corridors leading to the back of the building. But Hok was not as fearful for his own safety as he was for his grandparents'. *Why hadn't they called out? Has this fat pig, Fuchou, harmed them?* Hok moved ahead, almost in a run. As he approached the back of the warehouse, he could see a wall. He rushed ahead and stumbled beyond the protection of the stacked pallets.

"Drop it!" Fuchou ordered, staring at Hok, who was thirty feet away.

Hok froze. Fuchou stood behind Pat and held a gun to her head. His other hand covered her mouth.

"Drop it now!" Fuchou repeated. He pressed the gun barrel against Pat's temple.

"My grandparents!" Hok fought the sickening feeling in his stomach. *Why had he been so careless?* "Where are they?" He looked around.

"We are here, Hokusai!" His grandfather's voice came from an open doorway three feet from Fuchou and Pat.

"And grandmother! Is she?"

"I am all right, Hokusai! I am with your grandfather!"

His grandparents' voices steadied Hok. His gun clattered on the hard floor.

Fuchou's eyes kept glancing back and forth along the row of stacked pallets. "Where is your partner?" He motioned with his gun hand for Hok to move into the room with his parents.

"He is dead!" Hok answered.

Fuchou's sharp "drop it" order surprised Rick. A moment later, he tripped and almost fell over a dead body before he continued on toward the back of the warehouse. He stopped at the end of the row and inched his head around the corner.

Can Rick really be dead? Pat asked silently. She fought the fear consuming her. With effort, she pushed the thought away. Instead, she watched for some sign from Hok. His head was downcast, but he kept talking. For Hok to talk so much was unusual.

Pat hated her helplessness. And her chin hurt where Fuchou held her with his hand. Suddenly, the pain was forgotten. Rick appeared for an instant at the corner of one row of stacked pallets.

Guardedly, she watched for Rick to reappear. When he did, his lips were parted, but his teeth were clamped together.

"After the noise of the shooting, don't you know the police will be here soon?" Hok said, continuing his slow pace to the opened door.

"Shooting sleeping pigeons from the rafters is not unusual," Fuchou replied. "Pigeon stew ... my favorite—" But as soon as he started speaking, Pat bit him hard. "Ouch!" he bellowed.

When Fuchou released her, she dropped to the floor instantly. Two shots sounded. One bullet whistled by Hok's shoulder and burrowed into a pallet of scrap metal an inch above Rick's head. The other tore through Fuchou's left eye.

CHAPTER 68

BROADMAN WAS GOING THROUGH his usual morning routine in his hotel room. He was in the bathroom shaving. The early morning news was on the TV in the next room. He was paying little attention; however, when he heard Fuchou's name mentioned, his hand jerked, and he accidently cut himself.

"What's that?" Broadman said to his own image in the bathroom mirror. Blood oozed through his shaving lather as he whirled and rushed back into the bedroom.

Fuchou's name had been mentioned in connection with a kidnapping. The Hong Kong newsman described how a local businessman with a police record was an apparent fatality. An American ship's captain and his partner, whose grandparents were two of the victims seized, had aborted the kidnapping scheme. Also mentioned was a Dr. Kendall, the other freed hostage who was described as a heroine to the earthquake victims of Beijing. The reporter switched to news of a department store fire just as Broadman's telephone rang.

"What went wrong?" Ahmad Sattar's loud voice exploded over the receiver."

"I don't know!" Broadman answered disquietly.

"When I first heard the news, it was good that you weren't where I could get my hands around your throat!" There was a pause before Sattar continued in a lower voice, "Faisal, what has saved your ass this time is that our new submarine should be at the salvage site in three days."

Broadman breathed easier. He did not answer immediately while he searched his mind for a way to convince Sattar that he was still involved with the situation. "Will the crew of the new sub be trained well enough to salvage the treasure?"

"They won't have to be if the treasure is pirated. The new sub will stay submerged until the treasure is aboard the American ship. I suggest you be in the vicinity of the salvage site—possibly aboard a freighter of some kind. Understand?"

"But can we trust the Russian crew?"

"Yes, you can trust Captain Maxim Babel and his crew." The phone was silent for several moments before Sattar continued, "Find a way to meet him and the submarine near the salvage site. I am sure I won't have to tell you to be incognito at the time." The phone clicked in Broadman's ear.

Thoughts started racing through Broadman's brain as he hung up the phone. He decided he would meet the new submarine just beyond the horizon of the salvage site. Wu Thou would take him.

During the planning of the recent salvage attempt by the original submarine, Broadman had met Wu Thou. When the importance of the aborted radio communication had been discussed, Fuchou had offered Wu Thou's services. But Broadman had hesitated about including anyone else in the scheme without assurance of the person's loyalty. That was when Fuchou had taken Broadman to meet Wu Thou aboard his weather-beaten freighter. The plans for the radio interference had been finalized in his private quarters.

Broadman did not trust Wu Thou and his sleazy-looking crew, but they were an expedient partner. Because they were already accomplices, he knew that the extra help might prove useful in pirating the treasure. Should greed suddenly become a factor with Wu Thou during the transfer of the treasure to the new submarine, Broadman felt that the new submarine's crew should be able to handle that possibility.

CHAPTER 69

At the salvage site, the balmy weather reflected the serenity of the Luzon Strait's placid water. Suddenly, it erupted into a huge bluish gray shower of water. A bull whale that was fully-grown at eighty-five feet and 150 tons broke the surface, squirting water from his blowpipe. But that was the only disturbance at the surface. Below was different.

It was now around-the-clock salvaging work. Only one crew member at a time took a break from the grueling workload. After the warehouse incident and the following police reports, Rick and Hok had taken his grandparents and Pat back to the Utamaros' home in Kowloon.

Asawa waited until his wife and Pat had gone to bed before he warned Rick and Hok of the impending danger with the drug people at the salvage site. But Rick was thankful for the continued help from the Chinese. Because their gunboat was now in dry dock, they returned him and Hok to the *Valiant* by helicopter.

Rick sat alone in the mess room of the *Valiant.* If Asawa's information was correct, Rick knew he had only one more day before the drug people would return. *Probably in another submarine*, he thought.

The crew was unaware of the imminent threat to their safety. Hok had said nothing, and Rick's own silence was a cloud on his mind. He glanced once more at the clock, and when he rose from the table, he upset his half-filled cup. The splattered coffee went unnoticed as he left the mess room.

After he descended to the wreck again, Rick started to light his cutting torch when Hok swam up close. His eyes were twice their normal size while he peered through his face mask. With his hand, he motioned for Rick to follow him back to a jagged hole in the main deck of the wreck's bow.

Hok freed his oxygen line from around a silt-covered deck bitt before Rick followed him down the hole. When they reached the bottom, a low, grating noise sounded an instant before Hok stumbled against Rick, who grabbed a metal stringer to balance himself.

But thoughts of the wreck's movement were soon forgotten. Wedged under two twisted beams beneath their feet was a large metal box.

Suddenly, Rick's mind was freed of all worry. He felt like doing a dance on the beam he was standing on. *Eureka! Eureka!* The words raced across his brain. But his elation was mingled with fear of the wreck's movement. Rick gave Hok a quick jab on the shoulder before he adjusted the flame on his cutting torch. He started clearing away the overhead.

In his cumbersome diving gear, Woody Schaffer climbed over the slippery deck to where Rick and Hok had disappeared. The beam of his light found them and what was beneath their feet. Quickly, he turned and went to find Greg and Sid, who were in the forward hold at the front end of the bow.

The work was slow and hard. Including stops for decompression time at the surface, it required over half the day for the five men to free the first safe from the wreck and send it up to the *Valiant*. An hour later, an adjacent safe followed the first one, but there were no more safes. Rick and Hok started up out of the hole when the wreck moved again. There was more movement this time before the *Valiant's* retainer cable stopped it.

At the wreck's main deck, the five men moved in the opposite direction from the bow. They found Pete and Hank emerging from a hole near what was once the engine-room level of the dead ship. Both divers were listless. They had overstayed their downtime.

Woody immediately switched their air hoses to receive a new supply of air and then tugged on their lifelines and started them topside. Before he left, Hank Butler reached out for Rick with one hand, and with the other, he held up two fingers and pointed a languid arm toward the hole in the deck where he and Pete had been working.

Rick waited until the two divers were on their way topside before he moved over to the hole they had vacated. With his light, he could barely make out the two additional safes entangled in the wreck's substructure. As he stood on the main deck thirty feet above the safes, Rick was now well aware of the tugging on his lifeline, and so were the others standing motionless, watching him closely. But the lure of the treasure was now an addiction.

With the beam of his light, he motioned for the others around him to start widening the top of the hole while he ignored Woody, who was approaching through the turbid water. He was waving frantically for everyone to surface.

Rick used his torch to clear away a hanging piece of channel iron. When he dropped down the hole, he removed a twisted piece of angle iron extending across the first safe. By that time, Sid had joined Rick. Fifteen minutes later, the safe was hoisted from the hole and on its way up to the *Valiant.*

The last safe was now clear of any debris except for a beam wedged across its top. As he stood with Sid at the bottom of the hole, Rick glanced upward and saw Woody's light moving rapidly while he signaled them to surface immediately. But above Woody's head dangled the shackle attached to the derrick's hoisting cable.

Yeah, Woody, but damn it. There is only one more safe, Rick said to himself. He signaled for the cable to be lowered, but it wasn't lowered. It was dropped, landing on top of the safe, barely missing his boot. The image of Jake yanking the derrick throttle flashed through Rick's mind.

Rick reached for the shackle, and ten minutes later, he had it secured around the safe. Then he turned and waited for Sid to finish cutting through the beam.

Sid was about halfway through the beam when the wreck started moving again and then stopped abruptly. The suddenness of this shifting maneuver caused Rick to tumble over Sid, who had to do some quick juggling with his torch to avoid being burned. When they both regained their balance, Rick ordered Sid out of the hole, his eyes flashing.

Back in a kneeling position on top of the safe, Rick began completing the cut through the beam. When he felt the hoisting cable begin to tighten, he unconsciously wrapped his other arm around the cable as his torch made the final cut through the remaining flange of the beam.

Suddenly, the derrick's power snapped the beam in two, causing the safe to lurch upward. The abrupt movement jerked the torch from Rick's hand. As he fought for balance and clutched the cable with both hands, he and the safe began to ascend rapidly just as the wreck shifted again. But ten feet from the top of the hole, another beam snagged the corner of the safe.

Rick frantically kicked at the beam, but it wouldn't budge. After he braced his feet against it, he wrestled with the hoisting cable and tried to pry the corner free while twisted metal along the sides of the hole loosened.

Briefly, the wreck seemed to shudder before its movement suddenly quickened. *Has the Valiant's retaining cable snapped?* Rick thought. He glanced upward and could see the opening to the hole beginning to close.

But luck rode with Rick and the safe. The wreck's movement gradually tipped the safe from under the beam. His arms aching, Rick felt the safe move slightly. He mustered his last reserve of strength and fought with the shackle cables. It was just enough for the corner of the safe to slide by the beam, freeing him and the safe from the metal protrusion.

The movement of the bow section accelerated. Billowing clouds of silt and bubbles engulfed the rusty wreck as it tore at the ocean floor on its way to the trench. A long abrasive screech of metal rubbing against metal echoed in Rick's eardrums as the bow's insides tore free. The sound signaled the dead ship's final burial. It momentarily teetered on the edge and then plunged over the lip of the trench into the deep ocean's bottom. *The final resting place of the wreck made a hell of a headstone for the drug people,* Rick thought while he began his upward movement to the surface.

The ocean floor was sealed again in silence. The sudden stillness had a heady effect on him. Standing on the safe while stopping at the decompression stations was like riding on top instead of inside an elevator. The bizarre contrast crossed his mind. But his thoughts quickly changed as to what was inside the safes and then to a feeling of apprehension. The *Valiant* was not yet in port.

CHAPTER 70

After the last safe came aboard, the *Valiant* immediately hoisted both its anchors and headed for the China coast, but the ship was not alone. The family of whales followed, stopping only to feed and play while supervised by the harem leader.

A young female with a large white spot near her left eye frolicked among the young males. Occasionally, she swam away from the group only to return when none of the younger bulls followed her. But the harem leader hadn't missed the flirtation. The third time she left the pod, he followed. Only this time, one of the younger bulls who was as large as the leader finally understood the female's maneuvering. He started after her, but the older bull quickly cut off his approach.

The young whale stopped, unsure whether to continue or not, but his hesitation was brief. He charged, slamming his muscular body against the leader. The older whale, momentarily stunned from the blind-sided impact, whirled in the direction of the younger bull. But the younger animal was ready for a fight. He rotated his flippers and bent his tail flukes upward until his snout rose above the surface.

The eyes of the harem leader flashed. His wide tail slapped a shower of water into the sky just before he dove. Moments later, a mid-ocean geyser erupted above his huge black head. He emerged, treading the water with his flippers and tail, looking for the challenger who had started his charge from the choppy wake of the lone ship.

At full throttle, the *Valiant* steamed toward Shantou, China, the closest port of call from the salvage site. Every pair of binoculars aboard the *Valiant* had been put in use. From the bridge in the fading daylight,

Rick scanned the waters directly ahead. Jake and Hok also searched for any sign of a periscope off their port and starboard.

Other crew members with the same duty were stationed on the bow and fantail. Greg and Sid watched from the mid-deck while Herb used the sonar's earphones pressed hard against his ears. All lookouts were wearing headsets connected to the ship's loudspeaker.

Rick made sure the *Valiant* was underway before any of the safes were opened. Any celebration of their contents was deferred with his announcement of a possible attacked by a submarine.

His words, spoken to the crew assembled earlier on the fantail, kept echoing in his ears. "Here is what Hok and I think we have brought aboard. The value of the two safes of gold ingots over six tons should be worth close to five hundred million dollars. The one safe with well over three tons of platinum and the last safe with all the uncut diamonds and some artwork, we really don't know their value, but we are estimating the total cargo to be worth slightly less than a billion dollars."

Rick's musing was brief, and then Hok moved over from the other side of the bridge. "Are we still in international waters?" he asked.

"It's questionable. To the rest of the world, we are. To China, no."

A short burst of static came from the loudspeaker followed instantly by Greg shouting, "There is something beyond our stern!"

"It looks like a sub!" Sid's voice blended with Greg's.

Rick was outside the bridge in seconds, with Jake on his heels. They swung their glasses aft.

Jake's chuckling voice broke the tension when he said, "Don't sound the alarm yet, skipper. Those are whales playing." He paused, studied the whales' movements, and then added, "Or fighting."

"Suits me," Rick exhaled slowly. "They can play or fight or fuck at our back door all the way to port."

CHAPTER 71

IMMEDIATELY AFTER HE ENTERED the submarine's command center, Captain Maxim Babel asked, "Our speed?"

"We are still maintaining twenty knots, captain," answered a mustachioed navigator who sat at a long desk mounted to the bulkhead. Four other crew members were at their stations. One sat adjacent to the navigator, while two men sat at a similar desk but on the opposite side of the command center.

The last member of the watch, the helmsman, sat at the front of the room with both hands on the helm, which was only slightly larger than an automobile's steering wheel. The bulkheads in front of each crew member contained a mass of monitoring screens and gauges.

Deep furrows lined Babel's face. The voyage had been late in starting. They had barely left the choppy waters of the White Sea bordering the northwestern Archangelsk Region of Russia, where the new Lada-class diesel-electric submarine had been built, when one of the circulating pumps on the cooling system developed a severe vibration. They had turned back to the Severodvinsk Navy yard for repairs. Both shaft bearings had to be replaced. Now into the third week of their cruise after they had sailed the Arctic and North Pacific oceans, they were nearing the Taiwan Strait.

The submarine burrowed a watery tunnel under the East China Sea at flank speed. To meet the scheduled arrival time after the delayed start, the sub pushed hard. *Too hard*, Babel thought, turning his head and listening to the sound of the circulating pump. More time should have been taken in aging the new bearings.

But there had been a telephone call from the man who was paying Babel's salary and not in rubles. He had no choice but to get underway as soon as possible. And now because of the long period at maximum speed, the pump had developed a high-pitched whine that reverberated throughout the boat.

The ocean's surface was clear in all directions when Babel secured the periscope back inside the sub. Two days ago, when they were cruising by Japan, Babel was contacted on his cell phone by Ahmad Sattar with new plans. A freighter with Sattar's representative, Pedro Sanchez, aboard would meet Babel's sub near but out of sight of the American salvage ship. Sanchez would direct the pirating of the treasure.

When they finally arrived at the rendezvous area, there was a two day wait before any movement of the ship was evident at the salvage site. Because the ship was beyond the horizon, Babel's crew had kept track of its movement with the GPS aboard the sub.

The steely-eyed Sanchez was tall and thin, with more hair under his nose than on top of his head. He carried a holstered Beretta 92 and appeared capable enough to carry out his part of the plan, which was the most hazardous. With a group of heavily armed men from the freighter, Sanchez would board the American vessel and hold its crew at bay while the treasure was transferred to the sub.

With the transfer complete, Sanchez would board the sub while the armed men would return to their freighter. Then when the sub sank the American ship, the firepower of their four forward torpedoes would obliterate the vessel and leave minimal evidence of the ship and crew, even on the sea floor.

But Sanchez was no fool. He realized the peril, because they would make easy targets for that ship's crew. With a stern face, he had asked, "How are you going to cover me and my men?"

At the time, they were standing on the starboard side of the freighter's main deck while they looked down at the sub tied up alongside them.

"See the two humps forward and aft on the sub's topside," Babel had said and gestured with one arm."

"Yes."

"Those are concealed RPG gun mounts used for surface firing. While you and your men are approaching in your launches, we will rake the salvage ship's superstructure with steady firing. Probably knock out the bridge completely."

Now cruising at twenty-three knots, the sub closed fast on the slower salvage ship, but the distance was still too great for a positive identification. Babel left the periscope station and moved over to study the coordinates on the screen in front of his navigator. It was important for the attack to take place in international waters.

When the American ship left the salvage site, Wu Thou got his freighter underway along with the sub. He was supposed to block the salvage ship's path, while Babel would time his sub's departure to arrive at the salvage ship and board it from its port side.

But during the meeting aboard his freighter, Wu Thou had cautioned both Sanchez and Babel that he was unsure that he could catch up with the salvage ship.

"Don't worry," Babel had said. "I will close, submerged at an angle, and knock out its rudder with a well-aimed torpedo."

Edward Broadman, who was standing on the open bridge of Wu Thou's freighter, sighted his binoculars on the distant American salvage ship. His scalp itched from the thin-haired toupee, which was fitted skin-tight over the top of his head, and the gray mustache, which was taped above his upper lip, was so thick that it tickled his nose. *This job can't be over soon enough*, he said to himself while he stifled the urge to scratch the irritated places. But his thoughts quickly returned to the approaching confrontation.

Broadman kept in touch with the sub by phone. He had just finished speaking with Babel—or trying to. There was a distinct sound over Babel's phone that made his voice difficult to hear clearly. "What's that background noise?" Broadman asked.

"Just the normal sound of the cooling pump," Babel answered. At this particular time, he was not about to confess to any problem with his sub. During the long voyage to the strait, the steady sound had had a mesmerizing effect. Now, with the crew at their battle stations, the high-pitched hum was annoying. Any additional noise signaled an instant alert to each crew member.

"Bearing of the target is two five zero. Range is five thousand meters, captain," the navigator broke the tension once more. On his left sat the fire control officer, who studied the electronic data flashing across another monitor directly in front of him. The computers aboard were programmed with data-relating blip configurations to the known warships of all other nations in the world.

Within seconds after he heard the position of the target, the fire control officer hunched his shoulders. "Captain," he said, his voice shrill. "The target is not a warship, and it is smaller than a normal oceangoing freighter!"

Babel was convinced it had to be the American salvage ship. "Maintain course and speed for another five. Then slow to one third!" he ordered.

★ ★ ★

The younger bull rolled quickly on his side and charged, snapping his jaws viciously. The leader turned at the last second, avoiding a head-on collision, but the impact of the huge mammals slamming together sent a shower of water skyward. Broad tails and flippers churned the water into white foam around the whales. Twisting and fighting, the two sank into a whirling sea. They broke apart, rose to the surface, and swam in opposite directions.

As if by a signal, they turned around and then accelerated their speed. They raced toward each other, but the leader was caught off guard when the younger bull suddenly dove. An instant later, a tall geyser shot into the sky and churned into a billowing cloud of water. The surging fountainhead disappeared and left a calm sea in its wake.

The young bull gradually rose to the surface and then lay as still as death in the water. His back was broken.

CHAPTER 72

"WHAT THE HELL!" BABEL shouted when his face was suddenly jammed against the periscope. The sub's abrupt speed reduction threw the other members of the crew out of their chairs and tossed them about like bowling pins. The control center was an instant din of shouting, cursing men.

When the helmsman was jammed against the steering controls, he accidently engaged the surface switches, causing the sub to surface. The vessel breached in a cascade of foam, generating a large wave across the placid ocean as the prow surfaced.

"Slow two thirds!" Babel yelled. He rubbed the hurt from around his eyes while he swung the periscope aft. There was a large gray mound off the sub's fantail. He intently studied it for a moment before he shouted, "Holy Christ! We've rammed a whale!"

After he sighted the periscope again on the salvage ship, its American flag now visible, Babel ordered, "Stay surfaced! Keep with our plan."

★ ★ ★

Pete called from his forward lookout station, "There's a ship heading our way from starboard! It's still too far away to see its flag!"

In the pilothouse, when Rick trained his glasses on the distant vessel, a warning flashed in his mind. "I don't like the looks of this!" he said to the others in the pilothouse. "That ship appeared too abruptly after we got underway." He called to Herb, "See if you can get the Chinese gunboat on the radio! I don't care if it is in dry dock!"

Minutes passed. "No luck, skipper! Static problem again!"

Three seconds after Herb's negative report, Hank Butler's shrill voice came over the loudspeaker. "Holy hell, skipper! Submarine off our port side! And it's a big mother!"

Rick turned to his left, and with his glasses, he saw the distant submarine immediately. With both Jake and Hok in the pilothouse watching the approaching vessels, thoughts raced through Rick's mind like angry bees. "Jake, we still have plenty of those timed charges, right?"

"Yes, we do!"

"We've got to try to scuttle these marauders. Here's what I want you and Hok to do! Call Pete and Sid, and the four of you get into your diving gear! Do it quickly while trying to stay out of sight of these approaching vessels! Jake, you and Pete blow the sub! Hok, you and Sid handle the ship! Make your dives from—"

Rick was interrupted when a hail of shots sprayed the pilothouse, causing everyone to duck from flying glass.

"I'll get our guns, skipper!" Jake yelled, crawling over to the door.

"No!" Rick ordered, seeing smoke rising from deck guns mounted to the sub's topside. "That sub has too much firepower!" Then he reached for the speaker phone. "Stop all engines! Al!" He turned back to Jake and Hok. "Make your dives from the fantail. To give you guys enough time to set the charges, I'll be doing my damnedest here topside to keep these bastards' attention."

After Jake and Hok left the pilothouse, Rick turned to Woody at the helm. "I'll take the wheel, Woody! I want you to spread the word among the rest of the crew about our scuttling plans! Make sure each man is armed and to stay hidden until orders from me or the first explosion. Understand?"

Woody nodded his confirmation while he headed for the door.

"And tell Greg to come up to the pilothouse on the double!" Rick called after the departing helmsman.

As he locked the wheel in place, Rick went back to the radio room, where Herb was still trying to make contact with the Chinese gunboat. "I gave up on the radio, skipper." Herb's voice was strained. "They must be jamming us, but I did get the dock master at Kowloon with the cell phone. He is now trying to contact a gunboat." He paused, and a fleeting shadow of doubt crossed his face when he added, "I think that's what he said."

Rick caught the uncertainty but said nothing as he hurried into an adjacent room and rushed to a large locker. He unlocked the door and reached behind the weather gear. The first gun he picked up was a military-issue AK-47 with two firing modes—semi- and fully-automatic. He made sure it was fitted with a thirty-round banana clip with tracers loaded every five rounds. *That baby should do some damage*, he thought while he laid it on the deck. Then he removed a twelve-gauge Remington automatic, and a Glock 17 pistol. He made sure it was fully loaded with fifteen bullets in its clip.

While he checked each gun and made sure they were ready to fire, a conversation with Jake flashed across Rick's mind. Weeks ago after they had left Kaohsiung on their way to the treasure site, Jake had shown Rick where all the guns were stored in the various lockers aboard the ship.

Surprised at the amount of armament aboard the *Valiant,* Rick turned to Jake and said, "You either expect trouble on this venture, or you hit a gun sale someplace."

"Just preparing for the worst."

"Does the crew know how to fire these guns?"

Jake grinned. "We had a lot of free time getting here from the States. I made sure each man had plenty of practice." Jake paused momentarily before he added, "I know you can handle a gun from our days along the Gulf coast, but is Hok familiar with this kind of weaponry?"

Rick thought about that before he answered, "That's a good question. I'll make sure we both get some practice."

Rick slammed the locker door shut and started to lock it from force of habit, but then he shook his head. *Easy access might help create an atmosphere of minimal resistance to the pirates*, he thought. Then he turned and yelled through the open door to the radio room, "Herb, I'm leaving you the shotgun and a box of shells! Hide the stuff at your option!"

Rick whirled, ran back to the helm, and noticed the freighter was still a long distance away, but the sub's deck guns continued their intermittent firing. Each salvo was spraying the *Valiant's* superstructure.

The diving crew in full scuba gear crawled along the deck of the fantail and headed for the protection of a tarp-covered launch. They concealed themselves from the two approaching vessels by staying close to the short wall of the starboard rail. The small motorboat sat on its cradled supports three feet above the deck near the stern of the *Valiant.* Greg had purposely loosened the large canvas covering, allowing part of it to hang over the outside of the rail just above the ocean surface.

When the diving crew met up with Greg under the launch, Jake immediately began distributing the explosives while explaining the scuttling plan. "Notice these are the individually timed charges."

"I noticed!" Pete interrupted. "But what time do we set for them to explode?"

"I've been thinking about that ever since I picked them up on the way here." Jake rattled his reply. "It's got to be done and as quickly as possible." He looked at his wristwatch and said, "Synchronize your watches using regular time, which, according to my watch, is twenty till four. Set all charges to blow at 4:15."

When all divers' wristwatches were set, Jake continued, speaking rapidly while meeting each listener's eyes, "Do not jam the charge against the hull! The sonar systems are highly sensitive! Remember that each charge has a magnetized fastening device. Rely on it!"

As he watched the approaching pirate ships through a slit in the canvas covering, Greg interrupted Jake, "The freighter looks like it's going to block our course, and the sub is coming in on our port side."

Jake reflected on this before he said, "That must be their plan. The sub will tie up on our port side to receive the treasure while the freighter will be used to stop us from moving. Hok, that means you and Sid will have a longer swim to get to the freighter, so you guys set your charges at 4:30, got it?"

"Yes," Hok and Sid both answered.

"All right, let's put on our helmets and get at it," Jake ordered. "And Greg, be sure our pistols are handy when we return from setting the charges."

CHAPTER 73

THE SEA WAS PLACID, not even a ripple to mar its surface. The calm water was belying the tension that surrounded the meeting of the three vessels. As he stood on the open bridge of the freighter, Broadman counted twelve of Wu Thou's crew on the main deck, their assault rifles firing sporadically at the American vessel, which was stalled in the water.

There was no return fire from the American ship. Knowing Scanlon, Broadman was surprised. *However, he is smart enough to know,* Broadman thought, *he has no chance against us.* The lack of any retaliation caused Broadman to speculate on the possibility of stealing the whole ship and avoiding the hassle of off-loading the treasure at sea. *But then there is still the problem of getting rid of the ship and its crew. This way is best*, he decided as he watched two men working on the sub's topside hatch, through which the treasure would be transported.

Broadman's stomach churned nervously, watching the sub prepare to tie up to the salvage ship. One member of the sub's crew tossed a line with a hook secured to its end at the American ship's rail. But it missed, and the crewman was taking a lot of time trying to retrieve it from the ocean. However, Broadman was pleased with the firepower exposed on the sub's topside. Besides the manned guns on the deck, there were six other men with AK-47s aimed in the ready position at the salvage ship. With grappling hooks, the sub's bow and stern finally began inching closer to the salvage ship.

* * *

"Where the hell is Hok and Sid?" Jake growled in a low voice while he crouched in a pool of water and watched the sub's activity through a slit it in the tarp. He and Pete had been back for several minutes.

"We should blow that sub before it ties up to us, right?" Greg whispered to Jake.

"Hell yes!" Jake muttered, his low voice edged in irritation. "Now with the sub's lines attached, we've got to cut those lines after the sub explodes, or we could go down with the sub!"

Greg thought about what Jake had said before he stammered, "But won't the explosion affect us?"

"I don't think so. We're using small penetrating charges. The explosive power should be just enough to take out the bottom of the sub. Probably jar us a bit, but that should be about all." Jake spoke rapidly while he continually checked his watch.

Under the marauding freighter's keel, Hok and Sid had started setting their charges at the ship's bow and were now amid the ship. Sid led, setting his charges far enough apart so that Hok would set his own in between. At the freighter's fantail, the murky water, even with his headlight, was still hazy enough to cause Sid to swim between the two silent propellers without seeing them. When he reached the rudder, he realized immediately that he had swum farther aft than he had intended. Quickly, he reached out with his last charge to set it against the freighter's hull.

But at that moment, the unanchored freighter churned one of its propellers while the rudder moved slightly for repositioning the ship. The movement was just enough to clamp Sid's hand with the charge between the top of the rudder and the keel while the backwash from the propeller jammed him hard against the steering gear.

By the time Hok reached the fantail, the propeller was again still, but he found Sid hanging lifeless by one arm with his hand in a viselike grip at the top of the rudder. As he drew near, Hok saw that Sid's hand was clinched around an explosive charge.

Hok immediately began trying to work Sid's hand loose from the rudder, but his flippers allowed him only minimal leverage. Hok glanced at his watch. He had five minutes before the charge would explode. Quickly, he moved back down and pounded on Sid's harness. Goggles against goggles, Hok tried shaking him but got little response. There was only one way.

Hok unsheathed his knife and moved back up near the top of the rudder. He decided to do the job with a quick stab. With his left hand he gripped Sid's arm and drew back his right hand with the knife. An instant later, the rudder moved slightly to reposition the freighter, causing Sid's hand to slip from its holding crevice. Sid's limp body started sliding down the surface of the rudder, which prompted Hok to drop his knife and grab Sid with both hands before he sank out of sight.

But the sudden movement had caused Sid's hand to release the charge. Hok worked the limp body over one shoulder and then frantically began searching for the explosive. But the weight of Sid's body limited Hok's movement. With one hand, he held onto the rudder while twisting himself and using his headlight to search the gloomy water around him. But time was short. He had to get away from the freighter.

Then he felt Sid move his head. It nudged Hok's side, causing him to look down. And there was the charge. It had lodged under Sid's hose connection to his tank. When Sid began slowly kicking his flippers, Hok slid him off his shoulder and grabbed the charge with his free hand.

Quickly, Hok moved back up and clamped the charge to the freighter's keel near the rudder. When he returned to the slowly sinking Sid, Hok grabbed his shoulder harness with one hand and vigorous kicked his flippers. The agitation fully awakened Sid from his stupor. With one arm dangling, he started pawing the water with his good arm while moving his flippers. They headed for the *Valiant.*

CHAPTER 74

RICK WATCHED THE SUB inch closer to his ship. He was on the open bridge but out of view from the freighter. The sub's crew began securing the bow and stern lines to the *Valiant* as gangplanks appeared from inside the sub, and other crew members stored them on its topside.

If we can blow the sub before those gangplanks are set in place, we've got a better chance, Rick thought, and then it happened. His thought was interrupted by a muffled explosion. The throttled eruption seemed to raise the submarine for a few seconds before it dropped sharply, toppling the sub's crew like tin pins.

Although it was anticipated, the explosion combined with its result froze Rick and his own crew momentarily. Emory Chang, the one of all his crew he least expected to respond first, grabbed an ax. With one well aimed blow, he cut the sub's line tied near the *Valiant's* bow. And then he headed aft to cut the line attached near the stern.

That was all Rick needed. He dove for the door of the pilothouse and not a second too soon. The *Valiant* was raked with the first salvo of rifle fire from the freighter.

"Stay low, Herb!" Rick ordered as broken glass from shattered windows peppered the air inside the pilothouse. From a hidden receptacle, he grabbed the pistol, and after he shoved it inside his belt, he then reached for the AK. Through a broken window, Rick sprayed the freighter with answering fire. With his shotgun smoking because of rapid fire, Herb kept any of the sub's crew from boarding the *Valiant.*

Another muffled explosion sounded, this one with less intensity than the previous one, but it had enough force to cause several of the freighter's crew to drop their assault rifles. The suddenness of the jarring impact aboard the freighter stunned its crew, and the delay proved useful. Rick heard the increase in answering fire from the *Valiant.*

An oil slick that was growing bigger by the minute had replaced the submarine. The members of its crew who had originally stood on the sub's topside with AKs were now swimming furtively about. Some even used the gangplanks as armrests for firing their weapons. The Russians' semiautomatics, which men fired from the awkward angle of the floating gangplank's surface, were only effective in limiting the Americans' firing rate. But when each well-hidden crew member of the *Valiant* did get off a shot, it was accurate. The ranks of the swimming Russians gradually dwindled.

After he inspected the damage to his freighter, Wu Thou headed back to the bridge by keeping on the port side of the ship's superstructure and out of view of the American salvage ship. He moved quickly, controlling the anger seething inside him. This type of resistance from the Americans had not been part of the deal he had made with Sanchez. Bitterness consumed Wu Thou as he moved up to the bridge, where his betrayer, holding an assault rifle, fired steadily at the American vessel.

"Will we stay afloat?" Sanchez asked while he paused to reload his weapon.

"Yes!" Wu Thou snarled his reply from his crouched position on the bridge's open deck. "All emergency hatches are closed!" He paused momentarily and then said, "But the repairs are going to be costly!"

The undercurrent of Wu Thou's answer was clear to Broadman. He sat down on the deck and used the high rail surrounding the open bridge for protection against the Americans' return fire. As he watched the sub sink below the ocean surface, he felt a twinge of pain hit his stomach when he realized that Wu Thou and his crew now had him cornered.

The two men, who were only twenty feet apart, ignored the gunfire around them and stared at each other. *That look of violence coming from the back of your eyes isn't new to me,* Broadman thought. *But I'm saving a bullet aimed between your eyes before you aim one between mine.*

"Tell your crew," Broadman hissed, "each member gets a share of the treasure just as soon as the Americans are put down."

For several moments, the only movement from Wu Thou came from his eyes. They blinked once through his fixed stare. Still lying down, he slid around on his stomach, crawled over to a ladder leading to the deck below, and disappeared.

The intensity of the firepower coming from the raiding freighter seemed to be increasing. The blasting crew, who were still in their scuba gear, remained hidden under the tarp-covered motor launch at the fantail of the *Valiant*, but their angle for any effective firing at the freighter was minimal. Even more frustrating, was getting to a strategic position, which was almost suicidal, given the length of time they would be exposed to the freighter's guns.

Jake chafed at their futility while thoughts raced through his mind for a way to be helpful. Suddenly, he had an idea. "Greg, how many extra explosives do we have?"

"Six," Greg answered. "They are stored with our guns up in the launch."

"Can you get to them without being seen from the freighter?"

"I think so. I stored everything while the rest of you were planting the explosives."

"Good! Here's what we're going to do. Greg, get to the stuff and hand everything down to us. Hok, you and I will plant the remaining charges on what's left of the freighter's keel. I think I know about where the fuel storage is located on a freighter of this type. We'll plant all the remaining charges near its location. Hopefully blow a big enough hole to sink the freighter. Sid and Pete, get your helmets back on. Everybody, pack a gun in your belt. Greg, I want you to help Pete get Sid to the starboard side of the *Valiant* and board out of sight of the freighter. Any questions?"

Everyone was silent, but four pairs of eyes were staring eagerly at Jake when he added, "Okay, let's get at it!"

CHAPTER 75

From Rick's vantage point on the *Valiant's* bridge, the gunfire from the freighter's crew was continuous and deadly, while the answering fire from the *Valiant* was sporadic at best. Word had been passed up to Rick that Emery and Hank had leg and shoulder wounds respectively. But he also learned their wounds were not keeping them from returning fire.

Amid the uproar of ricocheting bullets, smoke, and rifle shots, Rick heard the discerning sound of a motor starting. He shouted to Herb, who was ten feet away and lying as flat as Rick on the deck of the open bridge. "They're coming over on a motor-powered boat!"

"Maybe not!" Herb answered, holding his Remington over the rail and aiming in the direction of the freighter. Immediately after he got off a round with the shotgun, another explosion came from the freighter. This time, the blast was much sharper in its sound than the previous eruption. The unexpected detonation instantly silenced the freighter's gunfire, prompting Rick and Herb to chance a quick look over the rail.

The suddenness of the jarring blast had upended the riflemen who had been sprawled along the freighter's deck. They were scrambling to retrieve their weapons and get back behind their cover, but the motor launch caught Rick's eye. Its coxswain at the stern and another man at the bow had just released the davit's shackles when the explosion occurred. The eruption pitched the two overboard and caused the launch, its engine idling, to move away from the freighter and head in the direction of the *Valiant.* The two swimmers were now all arms and legs, trying to reach the launch. With a blast from his AK, Rick made sure they never reached the boat.

Wu Thou was halfway up the ladder to his bridge on the freighter when the second explosion occurred. The jarring impact caused him to fall back down the ladder and hit his head on one of the steel steps. Motionless, he remained sprawled out on the deck, blood oozing from a gash on his forehead. Then he pulled himself up, and with the ladder's handrails, he slowly got to his feet. When he regained his senses, he became aware that all the firing was now coming from the American ship. Anger seethed inside him like smoldering embers. He directed his rage toward one man.

He stumbled his way up the ladder and on into the pilothouse. His helmsman's beady eyes were popping out of his head. "Both engine rooms are taking on water!" he babbled. After he reached for the wheel, he spun it easily. "And our rudder is gone!"

Realizing his ship's perilous condition, Wu Thou fumed. Then he saw Sanchez move from his kneeling position behind the bridge's rail. With a deep-throated howl, Wu Thou jerked a .38 from his belt, whirled, and ran through the open door of the pilothouse.

The yell drew Broadman's attention. Stunned, he watched Wu Thou charging toward him with a drawn revolver. Blood from his head wound blinded Wu Thou's aim. He fired two shots. One hit the rail near Broadman's head, and the other splintered the deck, barely missing his legs.

Still coming, Wu Thou was unable to get off a third shot. Broadman aimed his rifle and fired at point-blank range. The bullet took out Wu Thou's good eye. He fell face-first only two feet from Broadman.

The sharp, stinging, cacophonous sound of gunshots stopped suddenly. A tomblike silence pervaded the area.

The freighter's helmsman was not deterred. After he watched his captain go down, he picked up his rifle from the deck and aimed it through one of the broken windows of the pilothouse. But the barrel of the gun touched a sheared piece of glass hanging loosely in the window frame, knocking it to the deck.

The noise drew Broadman's attention to the weapon pointing at him from the pilothouse. Pure reflex saved his life as he rolled to the left an instant before the bullet from the helmsman's rifle burrowed into the deck where Broadman had been. Quickly, Broadman returned the fire. His bullet didn't miss.

While he watched the empty motor launch approach the *Valiant*, Rick heard the four sporadic shots. Their echoing sounds indicated they had been fired from within the freighter. The long silence that followed stirred his curiosity, especially when he noticed that the freighter appeared to be slowly sinking. "Herb, cover me!" Rick ordered. "I'm going down to the main deck to try to grab that runaway boat. I want to go over to that freighter before it sinks."

"Wait, skipper!" Herb said. "Why not let it sink? What good is it to us?"

"Herb, I know it's damn risky, but I want to know for sure who is trying to take our treasure."

"Then let me go with you."

"No!" Rick ordered. "You can do me more good from your position right here." He moved over to a ladder, and he was soon down on the main deck. In a dead run, he headed for the port side of the *Valiant*, where he expected the motor launch to be.

His rapid footsteps startled Greg, Pete, and Al from behind their cover. "What's up, skipper?" Al called in a low voice.

"I'm going over to the freighter!" Rick answered over his shoulder. "Help me grab their motor launch!"

Carrying their rifles, the three followed. Pete, who was directly behind Rick, yelled, "Why, skipper! There's still armed men aboard that thing!"

Rick didn't answer. The unmanned launch wasn't where he had expected to find it. "Damn it," he swore. "I'll have to swim for it." Then he turned. "Pete, I think I know who is aboard that freighter, but I want to know for sure before it sinks."

Rick started to remove his shoes, but Greg said, "Wait, skipper! I think I can get it with a line!" The deckhand ran over to a locker and grabbed a line containing a small iron hook. When he quickly moved back to the rail, he shouted, "Give me some room!" He swung the hook over his head in a circular motion before he tossed it at the empty launch. His throw was two feet short of the craft.

"Shit!" he stormed while his hands worked frantically to retrieve the hook. He threw again. This time, he arched the hook higher and gave an extra effort in his throw. It hit inside the boat with a thud, prompting Al's droll comment, "You may have a leaky boat ride, skipper."

When they pulled it alongside the *Valiant* and the launch showed no ill effects from the retrieval, Al said, "Let us go with you, skipper. There's plenty of room in the launch."

"All right, but I won't need all of you. Greg, I want you to steer the boat and bring that line with you. We may need it to board the freighter. And Pete, you come with us." Rick gave the orders rapidly while he made sure his revolver was fully loaded. He then turned to Al and added, "Alert the rest of the crew about what we are doing and have everyone forward with their weapons at the ready to cover our boarding the freighter!"

"Okay, skipper," Al answered.

While he moved down a small ladder that hugged the side of the *Valiant*, Rick gave his final order, "And Al, have our motorboat ready to launch if we need help!"

CHAPTER 76

BROADMAN KNEW HE WAS in deep trouble. All the riflemen along the main deck of the freighter were down. Most didn't move. As he studied the carnage down below from behind his cover on the open bridge, a seaman with a cigarette in one hand and a rifle in the other appeared at the door of the boatswain locker. He took only a quick glance at the dead and wounded before he looked up and gave the bridge a long, cursory stare. When the man spotted Broadman, he quickly ducked back out of sight into the locker.

Shocked, Broadman suddenly realized he now had both the Americans and the freighter's crew—or what was left of them—to contend with. Surrendering to the Americans was out of the question. It would mean revealing his true identity, which would eventually result in his death or a lifetime incarceration.

He forced himself to think clearly. Without any knowledge of the bedraggled freighter's latest condition, he decided to remain aboard as long as possible. It was late evening when he looked at his watch. It would be dark in another hour. If the Americans sunk the freighter, it would be nighttime, and he could steel aboard a lifeboat among the freighter's debris.

His immediate problem was that he didn't know how many of the remaining crew members he would be forced to deal with. Quickly, he counted all who were in sight lying on the main deck below. He estimated there couldn't more than two or three able-bodied seaman left, including the man he had just seen.

He started to leave the bridge when the sound of a motor approaching the freighter distracted him. After a glance seaward, he saw three men in a motor launch almost to the port side of the freighter. Broadman immediately recognized Scanlon as one of the passengers. He realized they had command of the boat that he had prepared only an hour earlier to take him over to the American ship.

But he had little time to dwell on such irony. He crawled over to a ladder and climbed down to the main deck of the freighter while he remained out of sight of the advancing launch. He ran along a clear deck on the opposite side of the hiding riflemen and quietly opened a door to a storage locker. The narrow room spanning the width of the freighter's superstructure was crammed full of hawsers, shackles, and other riggings hanging from wall-mounted hooks. Cans of paint were stacked in one corner.

Broadman moved silently across the locker while he crouched under the hanging equipment to prevent any noise. As he neared the other side, Broadman saw a deckhand with the one he had spotted before leaving the bridge. Both men were kneeling and watching the American ship. They would have to turn to see who was behind them.

The time it would take for them to recognize him gave him the advantage. He fired his Beretta twice, his aim deadly. When the seaman smoking the cigarette tumbled headfirst to the deck, his rifle discharged into one of the paint cans.

After he left the locker in a run, Broadman headed aft to a hatchway leading down to the deck below. Then he moved to another hatchway between the ship's machine shop and electric shop. His destination was the engine room one deck below, but when he arrived at the horizontal hatchway, its passageway was blocked. The large metal door covering the opening in the deck was dogged tight.

Damn it! Broadman swore to himself while he felt a pounding inside his chest. Frantically, he positioned himself on top of the metal door and spun a wheel attached to the small escape hatch.

Water spurted out of the fluid-tight joint around the circumference of the hatch before it was half-opened. To prevent flooding the compartment, he pushed hard on the wheel while he turned it in the opposite direction. When the small hatch was closed again, Broadman rested momentarily to catch his breath.

In the brief silence that followed, he heard a noise. It came from the machine shop. Broadman froze. Icicles pricked the back of his neck.

He didn't move from his kneeling position. Only his eyes searched the lathes, grinders, and other power tools in the gloomy atmosphere of the grime-encrusted shop behind the chain-link partition.

For the first time, he noticed that all the lights were out. The sunshine spilling down the main deck's hatchway covered the interior with just enough light to distinguish the areas' contents. His searching gaze rested on a tall, free-standing drill press. Something looked suspicious about the machine, which stood in a shadowy area of the long room. The instant he realized a man was hidden behind it, a shot rang out. Even though it was a rifle shot from an enclosed area, the sound reverberated into a roar. But Broadman never heard the raucous echo. The bullet had creased his skull with enough force to knock him over backward, stunning him.

A long silence pervaded the area before a man finally stepped out from behind the drill press. His rifle held at the ready, he inched forward quietly through an opening in the partition wall toward where Broadman lay on his back, his head concealed. When the rifleman reached the sprawled Broadman, he stepped closer to look at his kill.

As he studied the still form intently, he accidently kicked the small wheel attached to the escape hatch. The sound, although slight, was enough to bring Broadman's mind back to reality. Behind his eyeballs, shapes started to form, but they were erased immediately by a sharp pain in his head. His eyelids fluttered open.

The rifleman, absorbed in watching for any movement in Broadman's body, failed to catch his eye movement in the dark shadows. At the same time the rifleman poked Broadman's midsection with his gun barrel, he instinctively gazed in the direction of Broadman's head. Only the whites of Broadman's eyes were visible, but the recognition came a second too late.

When Broadman had been knocked off his feet by the rifleman's bullet, he had unconsciously held onto his pistol. It was wedged against the side of the large hatchway door and his body. His sprawled position had left him with his pistol now pointed at the rifleman's chest. The bullet from Broadman's gun entered the rifleman's heart an instant before his own trigger finger could react.

CHAPTER 77

Rick was first to board the freighter. He did it cautiously. On the way over, he had heard two shots, audible above the boat's motor noise. He could tell they had come from the freighter. While he waited for Greg and Pete to follow after him, he was startled by another shot, and this one came from the bowels of the freighter.

They secured the motor launch, and the three hesitated briefly on the freighter's main deck. They were studying the wounded and dead bodies sprawled along the main deck when a second shot shattered the silence. The muffled report sounded as though it came from the same place as the previous shot.

"What do you make of that, skipper?" Greg asked in a lowered voice.

Rick started to answer, but a groan from a wounded body ten feet away distracted him momentarily. "I don't know, but I'm going to find out. I want you and Pete to remain here on the main deck in sight of our ship. Tend to the wounded as well as you can. I'm going to search this old tub's below decks and try to find a reason for that gunfire."

Before Rick could move, Greg stopped him with a hand to the shoulder. "Keep your eyes peeled, skipper. If you aren't back in say … twenty minutes, how about I come looking for you?"

"I'll buy that," Rick answered. "Be sure you make plenty of noise and call out my name, okay?"

"I got you."

Rick left, using the starboard side of the freighter away from the wounded. An open door swinging on its hinges beckoned Rick. As he stood beside the opened door, he took a quick look inside. The interior revealed a boatswain's storage locker. He started to move on but spotted two bodies lying on the deck inside the room. With his pistol at the ready, he eased into the locker room, where there was enough light from the two opened doorways to reveal no one else hiding behind any of the riggings hanging from the walls.

He stooped to touch the bodies. The warm flesh let him know they hadn't been dead very long. Then an unusual smell drew his attention. When Rick lifted his head to sniff again, he detected fresh paint. It was coming from one of the cans stacked in the corner of the room, but he failed to notice the lit cigarette lying on the deck in the path of the paint spill.

Leaving the storage locker, Rick headed aft to an open hatchway. He studied the hatchway for a few minutes and then walked by and continued all the way to the stern, making sure there were no other entryways to the deck below on that side of the ship. From his knowledge of these types of cargo ships, he was sure the crew's quarters were near the stern. He felt sure those last shots he heard came from below the main deck. He returned to the hatchway and started down, taking one slow step at a time.

CHAPTER 78

Broadman sat up. After the sharp explosion of his shot, he shook his head to clear the heavy fog enclosing his brain. He reached for his handkerchief to wipe the blood from the side of his face, but the bleeding had stopped. He stood up, and after he took a few steps, he felt relieved to discover he could move. Suddenly, he heard footsteps on the main deck above.

Broadman turned and headed toward the stern, moving to a bulkhead hatchway he knew led to the galley. He listened intently. When he heard nothing, he unlatched the door and stepped through the opening, pulling the hatch closed behind him.

Instantly, a strong vaporous odor assailed his nostrils, prompting him to look over at the large stove against the opposite bulkhead. Each of the room's sides contained a porthole that provided enough light to show him the unlit gas stove was not the source of the pungent smell.

As he glanced upward, he detected smoke appearing around one of the ceiling diffusers from the ventilation system. But when he heard a noise behind him, Broadman was more anxious to find a place to hide. The sound had come from the area on the other side of the wall where he had just been.

Stealthily, he moved on across the galley and stepped through a bulkhead hatchway leading to the crew's sleeping quarters. After he dogged the hatch, he turned and moved along a narrow passageway separating sleeping compartments. The only light came from an opened doorway of one of the rooms. Broadman hesitated there, briefly studying the opened porthole, but it was on the side of the freighter in view of the American ship.

The freighter, which rocked slowly to the gentle waves, was shrouded in deadly silence until interrupted by a voice. Broadman remained calm. He determined by its echoing sound that the voice came from a distance behind him. But as the voice continued, he realized that the person was moving in his direction. It caused Broadman to move to a ladder leading back up to the main deck.

When Rick reached the deck below, he was met by a raging fire rapidly consuming a dead body lying near a horizontal hatch. The fire spread quickly throughout what appeared to be repair shops. A vertical pipe leading from floor to ceiling had no termination. It simply extended through an oversized sleeve in the overhead and through the same kind of sleeve in the deck thirty feet from where Rick stood. The vertical pipe acted as a torch, carrying its flaming message to each deck of the ship.

"There's smoke coming from some place on this tub!" Greg yelled from the main deck. He was stationed at the hatchway's entrance, where he had seen Rick disappear earlier.

"Yeah!" Rick barked his response. "It's coming from down here!" Through the smoke, he saw a hatchway in an adjacent bulkhead. As he ran for it, he yelled, "Stay topside! I'm moving on aft!"

The latches were hot to his touch, but he soon got them opened. After he stepped through the doorway, he turned and closed the hatch, dogging it tight with only one latch. When he faced the room again, he could tell it was the ship's galley, which was beginning to fill with smoke.

After a quick look around the stove area, he moved on and entered a hatchway leading to an adjacent room. He closed the hatch behind him and kicked open the first door on his right. The sleeping compartment, its interior lit from daylight through a porthole, was empty. A quick check of each adjacent room on each side of the passage way revealed no lurking gunmen. By the time Rick finished his search of the area, a smoke cloud was rapidly filling the narrow passageway. His choking cough forced him to take a ladder leading to the upper decks.

As Pete sat on the rail along the main deck with the dead and injured crew members, he noticed the water line creeping up the freighter's hull. When he saw Greg approaching, he yelled, "This old bucket is sinking like a ruptured duck with its feathers on fire!"

"I know!" Greg replied while he stepped over the scattered bodies in his path. "How many of these are still breathing?"

"Only two, one with a shoulder wound and the other with a broken leg."

"Good! Let's move them over near our launch. You've searched them for weapons, right?"

"Yeah, they're clean, but how about Rick?" Pete asked.

"He told me to stay topside."

CHAPTER 79

At the top of the ladder, Broadman stopped inside the doorway leading to the starboard side of the freighter's main deck. He made sure no one was in sight before he stepped outside. When he did he immediately smelled smoke. A quick look over the rail, he noticed flames coming out of portholes. He turned and moved quickly to a ladder leading back up to the open bridge.

The door to the pilothouse was standing open. Keeping low, he moved on inside. Then, with his eye level barely above the bottom of the large window fronting the pilothouse, he studied the scene below. Movement near the bow caught his attention. Two men were dragging what appeared to be wounded bodies along the main deck.

Broadman immediately recognized the victims as crew members from the freighter. The group stopped near the motor launch, which was moored to the freighter's rail. The launch was floating only a few feet below the top of the rail. He now realized the freighter was not only on fire but slowly sinking.

The pain of his predicament seared through him like a knife, but he had no time to dwell on his misfortune. He had to think about getting off this freighter. It was now twilight, which was a good thing for him. It would be dark by the time the ship was completely underwater.

He remembered that a lifeboat was secured above the pilothouse. The nearest land was the Penghu Islands. He knew the direction there, and he had a compass on his wristwatch. He moved with surprising dexterity despite his impaired leg. He limped through the chart room and radio shack and moved into the captain's sleeping quarters.

Quickly, he glanced around the room while the strain of uncertainty prompted the eel of fear to wriggle in his gut once again. A floor-to-ceiling locker in a corner of the room caught his eye. He rushed over and jerked open the door. It was filled with scuba gear. Broadman remembered Wu Thou saying that he was a shallow-water diver, not the deep-sea kind.

Thoughts raced through Broadman's mind. The scuba gear could be useful. He had to get off this freighter without detection. When he turned for another look at the room, he saw a straight ladder fastened to the opposite bulkhead, one leading up to a hatch in the overhead. It was the only access to the top of the bridge. It was Wu Thou's private lounging space. Quickly, Broadman climbed up the ladder and opened the hatch just enough to see outside.

The only distraction on the open deck forming the roof of the captain's quarters was the lifeboat secured just beyond the railing on the port side, which was to Broadman's advantage. It formed a shield to hide him from the freighter's port side, where he had seen the men from the American ship.

Broadman had an idea. He would get inside the lifeboat and release it just before the freighter sank. Should the lifeboat be sucked into the down draft of the freighter's sinking, he would be prepared for it. He scrambled back down the ladder and started gathering the scuba gear from the locker.

Rick's search for anyone still alive below decks was futile. To keep ahead of the fire's heat and smoke, he was forced to continue climbing upward through the freighter's superstructure. He was soon back on the open bridge. In the rapidly darkening night, he remained quiet while he waved to Greg and Pete, who were still waiting with their injured on the bow. When asked with hand gestures if they had seen any other members of the crew, their shaking heads gave him his answer. There was one more place to look before he knew he had to get off this firetrap of a ship. He was determined to find out who had been behind this pirating venture. With a wave of his hand, he pointed to the pilothouse and then moved inside the windowed room.

With his pistol still at the ready, he moved on through the vacant pilothouse and into the adjacent chart room, but he found no one behind the door or under any map tables. There was a hatchway in the opposite bulkhead. With light footsteps, Rick advanced over to the hatch. As he examined the steel door with its gasket edging, he found it was dogged with only one latch. *Could the last man through have been in too much of a hurry to dog all the latches?* Rick questioned himself.

He used extreme care in loosening the latch and then opened the door an inch at a time, making no sound as he stepped through the opening. He knew by the room's contents and its location near the bridge that he was in part of the captain's quarters. An open locker door swinging gently from the ship's movement was the only item in the room that seemed out of order. The locker was adjacent to a small head or bathroom. After a quick look, he found that it was vacant.

A straight ladder secured to one of the bulkheads caught his eye just as a noise broke the stillness. He froze. The noise had come from the overhead, and it sounded like something scraped momentarily on the deck above. Quietly, he moved over to the ladder and climbed up to a round hatchway in the overhead. A small wheel in the center of the hatch was geared to a series of latches around its perimeter.

While Rick turned the wheel an inch at a time, his ear close to the hatch cover, he heard more movement just beyond the hatch. The sound was not continuous. It came in spurts as if extreme care was being used to muffle the source. Rick tried to conceal his approach by matching his effort with the sudden bursts of activity above.

The noise grew louder after he cracked open the hatch, but all he could see was the bottom of a lifeboat just beyond the rail that surrounded the roof of the small room.

The partially opened cover blocked his view of the small deck's entire area. By now the flames, which were spurred by exploding cans of paint, had climbed up the freighter's hull, engulfing the ship's superstructure in a blazing fire.

Rick could feel the heat intensifying as he gradually opened the hatch, but the movement on the opposite side of the hatch had suddenly stopped. As he held the hatch cover with one hand, he removed his ball cap with the other and eased it around the cover's edge.

CHAPTER 80

Quickly, Broadman removed his disguise for both convenience as well as comfort before starting to put on the diving gear. To prevent exposing himself to the two men on the bow, he struggled into the scuba gear while lying on the deck. He had just strapped on his tanks when he saw a shower of sparks shooting skyward. The brief spectacle caused Broadman to glance in that direction.

The hatch cover drew his attention. The small opener in the center of the cover was now at an angle. He thought that maybe he had forgotten to secure the hatch properly. His eyes widened when he realized the cover was slowly being opened.

He froze momentarily and then noticed the opening of the cover had stopped. Someone was there. His thoughts shifted quickly to prepare for the intruder. Even when he deliberately scraped his oxygen tank on the deck, the cover continued to inch open. *He knows I'm here!* The thought flashed through his mind. Broadman rolled over on his stomach, purposely making more noise while deliberately aiming his Beretta at the cover. As he held his breath, he waited.

Rick moved only the bill of his cap past the edge of the hatch cover, which was now fully opened. An instant later, a bullet shredded his visor, tearing the cap from his hand. The loud report of the shot fired from close range deafened him, but he recovered quickly. As he held the hatch cover as a shield with one hand, he quickly drew his own pistol from his belt with the other hand and aimed the pistol around the edge of the cover.

He fired only one shot before the force of another bullet flung the gun from his hand. The sharp burst of the shot ringing in his eardrums plus his numbed fingers forced Rick to drop the half-opened hatch cover.

Dazed from the noise and the numbing pain in his hand, he clung to the ladder but only briefly before he slid down to the deck in the captain's quarters. He massaged his right hand vigorously to restore circulation, but he still heard shots being fired from both close and distant range. When the above hatch began to open, he scurried for cover in the adjacent room barely ahead of three bullets that splintered the deck behind him.

When Broadman shot the gun from the intruder's hand without thinking, he stood up suddenly to move over to the hatchway. His first shot had alerted the two men on the bow. Exposing himself drew fire from the bow, and Broadman had to drop back to the deck. From a prone position, he fired six quick shots in the direction of the bow.

It silenced the return fire, giving him time to move over to the hatch. He jerked open the cover and emptied his Beretta, spraying the remaining four shots all around the captain's quarters while exposing only his arm through the hatch's opening.

The click on the gun's empty chamber alerted Broadman that he was out of ammunition. Savagely, he clawed his way back to where he had left his clothes. There was an extra cartridge clip in one of the pockets.

Rick also heard the click after the last round of shots had been fired. Abruptly, he ran back into the captain's quarters and scrambled up the ladder. After squeezing through the hatchway, Rick remained in a crouched position and faced the back of a man twenty feet away. The man was on his hands and knees, searching furiously through clothes strewn around the deck.

Rick drew his knife from its holster fastened to his belt. By the time he had flexed his fingers momentarily to assure a firm grip on the handle, the man had stopped his searching and spun around.

"I thought I would find you!" Rick said his voice steady. "It's why I came aboard. I had to know." Then his voice sharpened when he said, "But why are you involved?"

"Your ways are not my ways." Broadman answered in iced syllables as he quickly unfastened one of the tanks, strapped to his shoulder, and heaved it at Rick, who dodged it easily.

The noise of the tank hitting the deck brought Greg and Pete from behind their cover on the bow. The ploy had maneuvered Rick between his men and Broadman, who had dropped his empty gun and now clutched a knife that was part of the scuba gear.

Rick was fired up. He started to attack Broadman but hesitated, not because of his knife but because of what he had said. "It sounds like I'm facing a traitor!" Rick spat the words while he squeezed his knife handle.

"You Americans should never have interfered in Afghanistan's war with Russia," Broadman replied, and his dark, hooded eyes bore into Rick from across the open deck.

The statement caught Rick by surprise. He studied Broadman gravely, unable to conceive of the statement's relationship to the existing confrontation.

His eyes glazed and his voice growing shriller, Broadman went on doggedly, "When Afghanistan formed a Marxist government purely for the sake of much needed land reform, my country began to prosper with more freedoms for its people and the abolishment of farmer's debts. But it happened during the Cold War, and your country could not abide the threat of more Communistic expansion."

CHAPTER 81

"WHAT THE HELL HAS that got to do with you being a DEA agent?" The whole thing confused Rick. He wanted to hear more.

"I was born an Afghan and always have been an Afghan under the guise of an American." And Broadman wasn't through ranting. "Your CIA together with Pakistan and Saudi Arabia began to provide the Muslim extremists who had migrated to Pakistan with military aid. These *mujahedin* or freedom fighters soon numbered in the thousands and began to attack various parts of my country. This brought in Russia to stop these invaders, and the US took advantage of this intervention by encouraging these Muslim fanatics to declare a holy war against the Russian infidels who were desecrating Afghan soil."

Broadman paused. His babbling dissertation had left him breathless. When he continued, his words slowed into a clearer voice. "Ironically, out of all the aid from your country, the Taliban was born, eventually leading to the 9/11 catastrophe and our resolve to defeat American imperialism." Broadman was silent, squeezing his mouth shut until his lips compressed into a thin, straight line.

Rick had scrambled onto the open deck, ready to kill this assailant, but after he recognized Broadman and finished listening to his tirade, he hesitated out of confusion. However, his uncertainty was short-lived.

"Imperialism my ass!" Rick's voice echoed like cold steel striking concrete. "Evidently, you have never read our constitution. It has been in effect for nearly 220 years. It starts with, 'We, the People,' and since we are a government of, for, and by the people, we do make mistakes. But when we do, like this foreign policy error you are harping about, our government officials who made the mistake are usually replaced by the voting rights of the people. That's a democracy, a type of government that fanatics like you don't understand and—what is more obvious—don't *want* to understand."

Rick was interrupted by the fire. Smoke poured out of portholes in the freighter's superstructure rising above the deck behind where Broadman stood.

"Drop the knife!" Rick ordered. "We've got to get off this ship!"

"I am getting off and over your dead body," Broadman replied. Then he leaned down and picked up a shirt from a pile of clothes that was on top of two oxygen tanks in front of him. His glowering stare never left Rick while he wound the shirt into a ball around his left hand.

Rick made the first aggressive move. He sidestepped a few feet to his left, deliberately exposing Broadman to Greg and Pete at the bow.

But Broadman was not fooled by the maneuver. He remained in a crouched position and matched Rick's movement. Suddenly, Rick moved backward a couple of feet and then sideways. Then he returned to his original position. Again, Broadman, who remained in a crouching position, matched Rick's every movement, but this latest maneuver placed the pile of clothes and tanks directly behind Broadman.

With his knife held in a chopping position, Rick lunged at Broadman and struck at him blindly, keeping his eyes glued to Broadman's knife. The sudden movement placed Broadman in a defensive position, both of his hands extended, allowing Rick to grab Broadman's wrist of the hand holding his knife. But the ploy quickly subsided to a standoff. Rick's own knife was now caught in Broadman's balled-up-shirt shield.

Faces inches apart, arms straining to be released, their bodies rammed and twisted against each other, they were momentarily at a standoff, but Rick had the advantage. With two strong legs, he gradually inched Broadman backward until he abruptly tore his knife free of the makeshift shield and struck downward at Broadman's chest.

When Broadman stepped backward to avoid the knife stab, his foot struck one of the oxygen tanks lying on the deck, which caused him to trip over backward. Rick's knife barely ripped through Broadman's shirt. Off balance from his knife thrust, Rick clung onto Broadman's right hand and fell heavily on top of him.

Instinctively, Rick broke his hold to catch himself. It gave Broadman an opportunity for a quick jab with his own knife before he landed on top of his clothes pile. The knife tore through Rick's shirt and sliced into the side of his shoulder. The minor flesh wound failed to distract him. He still aimed his knife at Broadman's unprotected chest, but Broadman twisted an instant ahead of the plunging knife, which Rick buried into the side of Broadman's neck just above the collar bone. The maneuver tore the knife from Rick's hand. It fell to the deck as they both scrambled to their feet and again faced each. The superstructure behind Broadman was now a wall of fire.

Rick was now unarmed. He grabbed an oxygen tank from the deck while Broadman reeled. With blood beginning to stream down the front of his shirt, he raised his right hand and threw his knife at Rick, who barely had time to deflect it with the oxygen tank.

As Rick advanced, Broadman moved backward, unaware of the fire behind him. For a few moments, his lackluster eyes cleared and locked on Rick's while he moved his hand to locate whatever was causing the pain in his neck.

To Rick's amazement, Broadman's discovery of his wound seemed to resurrect his strength. He looked upward and shouted in a strong, clear voice, "Jihad forever!" Then he deliberately stepped backward, ignited himself in a ball of fire, and disappeared into the blazing inferno.

A moment later, Greg's head popped through the deck's hatchway. "Are you okay, skipper?" He had to yell to be heard above the roaring fire.

"Yeah!" Rick answered. "Let's get the hell off this burning wreck before she sinks!"

The ocean was almost up to the main deck by the time they got the wounded crew members off the freighter and into the borrowed launch. On the way to the *Valiant*, Pete, who was at the motorboat's controls, said, "Look … our escort is here." The gunboat had finally arrived.

CHAPTER 82

RICK SAT ALONE IN the pilothouse. After the *Valiant's* arrival in Shantou with the Chinese authorities present for the opening of all the safes, three hours of celebration had followed. Now with all the revelry over, everyone gone, and the crew turned in for what was left of the night, the following stillness had left Rick in a melancholy mood, and he wasn't quite sure why. When the treasure had finally been divided according to the search permit's agreement, he knew that he could pay off his debts and still be a rich man.

Maybe I am numb from fatigue, he thought, leaning back in the helmsman's chair. He stretched out his legs, propping his feet on top of the instrument panel in front of the helm while thinking about the recent problems getting the *Valiant* safely into port.

But his depression persisted. He felt like a mountain climber after he had reached the top, knowing there was only one other direction to go. He was beginning to realize that his newfound wealth was not going to be as self-satisfying as the hunt for it had been. The challenge was gone.

Then dockside movement distracted him. The austerely lit pier was a dim pathway for a crippled old man. His clothes were little more than rags as he walked with the aid of a wooden crutch that had replaced a missing leg. While the bent figure disappeared into the night, Rick thought about the earthquake victims. The thought shifted and soon became an inspiration. The Chinese authorities here for the opening of the safes had told him of a major celebration to be held three days from now in Beijing. The observance was in recognition of Dr. Kendall's care for the earthquake victims and for the success of the treasure find.

I wonder what her true feelings for me are? he questioned himself quietly. He certainly hoped she had enjoyed their last evening together at the seaside retreat, but on their return trip to the field hospital, he hadn't really found out either way. Although pleasant in her conversation, her attentive answers to his various questions made him feel that she was not always revealing what was truly on her mind.

His money worries now at bay, he considered bringing an end to his solitary lifestyle. The thought surprised him. Since he had left the service after Desert Storm, he had spent little time thinking about anything else except his shipping business. *Must have had something to do with my never developing any lasting relationship with a woman,* he thought.

But Pat intrigued him. And it was just as much her intellect as her appearance. She definitely had a mind of her own as well as the ability to know when to use it. *Well, it's going to be interesting seeing her again,* he said to himself when he got up from his chair.

Three days later in Beijing, Rick and Pat soon learned that the Chinese knew how to stage a celebration. "That is the Museum of History. It is popular place here in Beijing." The young Chinese driver turned his head slightly while he spoke to Rick and Pat in the backseat. He pointed out of the car window at the large gray building. As they neared the center of China's capitol complex, they were second in a parade of cars containing the rest of the *Valiant's* crew plus some government officials. Dr. Yang's head was visible in the backseat of the car directly in front of them.

Crowds of people had multiplied on both sides of the street until the caravan was forced to a slow crawl. Many waved little Chinese and American flags at the motorcade. Liberally sprinkled among the flags were waving pieces of white cloth. The cars, which were going slow enough to be touched, passed between two multicolored ribbons that danced in the afternoon sunlight. The cheering would increase immediately after Rick and Pat had been recognized.

"A person could soon learn to like this," Rick said, reaching out to the people. "Better than any medicine, right, doc?"

"I will include it with my next prescription," Pat replied while she waved to the people lining the street on her side of the car. Actually, she was surprised at Rick's mood. Two hours ago at the airport, instead of talking about the treasure find like the rest of his crew, he had asked her all kinds of questions about her work at the hospital and how it was functioning. She remembered, well, the variety of jobs he was able to do around the hospital. Once when the lights went out in surgery and after he arrived, one of the nurses said, "All is well. Rick is here." She was right. The lights were soon back on.

And now his sense of humor was much more in evidence. After each segment of two or three questions about her hospital work, he would add, "I'll bet any of your free time was spent thinking about me, right?" Or he would say, "Surely moonlit nights filled your dreams about me."

Several days ago, she had made plans to fly back home and had informed both Dr. Yang and Colonel Cheung accordingly. Her departure date was tomorrow. And Rick had surprised her by saying he would be accompanying her tomorrow on the plane trip.

She also noticed that while the caravan was being assembled, he had spent time talking with Dr. Yang and Colonel Cheung plus other government officials who were hosting the parade. Rick must have been informed of her flight plans by the colonel, she thought. She had received a personal invitation from him to attend the festivities today. The colonel claimed he was acting on behalf of China's president, Hu Jintao.

CHAPTER 83

"We are near Tiananmen Square," the driver said, interrupting Pat's thoughts. He had to shout to be heard above the crowd.

"Tiananmen Square," Rick said, leaning forward in his seat to make himself heard to the driver. "Always reminds me of the tank man who faced off a column of tanks singlehandedly during the Pro-Democracy Movement." He paused momentarily in thought. "It doesn't seem possible, but that was around twenty years ago. The size of this crowd amazes me, and the enthusiasm of your people is contagious," Rick said, a broad smile creasing his face.

"Chinese love celebrations. Our Dr. Yang is taking advantage of your treasure find, captain, and your popularity, Dr. Kendall. Being restored to all his government posts, Yang is staging this celebration to return in triumph. He is what you Americans would call a politician, am I not right?" An impish grin tugged at the driver's mouth.

But Pat was thinking about what Rick had said. "Did you know the young man who stopped the tanks?" she asked.

The driver shook his head. "Who he was and what became of him still is mystery."

When they arrived at the square, the caravan inched across the acres of paved surface and through an opening in the ranks of the cheering people standing elbow-to-elbow. The channel through the crowd led to one side of the square, where a huge picture of Chairman Mao covered a high wall forming the Gate of Heavenly Peace.

When their car finally came to a stop, a man in a Chinese Army uniform opened the door on Rick's side of the car. Another uniformed guard then led Rick and Pat through an archway separating the square from the Imperial City. They walked up a flight of marble stairs opening onto a terrace that overlooked the vastness of Tiananmen Square. The terrace, which was thronged with elderly men dressed in dark business suits, was full of broad smiles, especially on the faces of those closest to Dr. Yang, who was talking animatedly in the middle of the group.

While the others applauded, a dark-haired, middle-aged man put his arm around Yang and drew him to the front of the terrace. The guard with Rick and Pat leaned close and said, "The one with Dr. Yang is President Hu Jintao."

The guard's words were drowned out by a hundred thousand cheering voices as the square erupted in a sea of fluttering red flags.

It looks like a giant carpet of autumn leaves rustling in the wind, Pat thought, but she had little time for fantasizing. When the crowd quieted, Yang said something to Hu Jintao, and then they surprised Pat by turning in her direction and motioning for her to step forward. *Why me?* The thought flashed through her mind. With her strained smile clearly visible, she glanced uncomfortably at Rick, but if he knew what was happening, he gave no clue.

Paralyzed, she stood for a few more seconds and then walked slowly toward the two men. President Hu Jintao appeared hesitant when she was introduced. He held one of her hands in both of his before he bowed. While he continued to hold her hand, the president turned and spoke to the people.

Because his words were in Chinese, Pat could only assume she was being introduced, even though the introduction seemed a bit lengthy to her. But when it was finished, a thunderous applause sprang from the people, and the crowd magically changed from red to a sea of white.

Pat felt the tightness inside her chest melt away as she acknowledged her appreciation with a wave of her hand and the repeated words, "Thank you."

Rick stood ten steps behind Pat and watched the color rise in her cheeks while the applause continued.

"News of Dr. Kendall's work has spread throughout all of China," the escort officer shouted in Rick's ear. "Presently, she is the most popular foreigner in our country. Sorry, captain," the grinning officer continued. "Despite your success in finding the treasure, you and your crew only rate second to Dr. Kendall."

The ovation continued. Pat, who was starting to feel self-conscious, looked around at Rick, who had a jovial expression on his face and a sparkle in his eyes.

When the cheering finally quieted, Dr. Yang signaled for Rick and Hok to step forward with the rest of the crew. Yang made the introduction to the people in the square, but when they started to applaud, he hushed them with an uplifted hand. He continued his rapid speech, turning often to face Rick. The response from the people grew louder as Yang beamed with pleasure.

Pat watched the impetuous Yang. An instant after he had finished speaking, a deafening roar came from the crowd. Hok, who was smiling broadly, shook Rick's hand while jubilant government officials quickly gathered around him.

Pat edged over to Hok. "What is all of this about?" she shouted.

"Rick has donated a large amount of his share of the treasure to help build a new hospital here in Beijing, and Dr. Yang said it will be built in your honor," Hok answered.

The American flags waving below were a blur, but only for a moment. Thoughts filled her mind. Rick's generosity had caught her by surprise. She remembered his duplicity when he had retrieved the navigation chart and the way he had tried to hide it from her. Later, she had learned from Hok about the risk Rick had taken in recovering the last safe of treasure. The complexity of this man made him difficult to know, but it also made him interesting. As a woman, she was curious as to why he had never been married. When she had asked him, his answer had been simple, "My seafaring life doesn't fit well with marriage." That conversation had happened during their return trip from the seaside vacation. His brief comments would be interspersed while he studied intently the ancient Chinese landmarks as they drove past.

Her thoughts were distracted as Rick reached down and picked up a box of Chinese flags from the floor. Quickly, he passed them out to his crew. With the crowd's applause still ringing, he regarded Pat with a broad smile and handed her one of the flags. As he raised his flag high above his head, Rick faced the people in the square. The rest of the crew and Pat automatically followed Rick's lead.

An instant later, the noise level of the crowd doubled. The ovation continued until Yang finally summoned Hok, who briefly listened to the Chinese leader before he turned to Rick and said, loud enough for Pat to hear, "Dr. Yang wants you to speak to the people!"

For a few moments, Rick appeared undecided. Then he seemed to gather his thoughts before he slowly raised his hand. "Thank you," Rick stammered, but his voice was firm when the applause quieted. "President Hu Jintao, Dr. Yang, Colonel Cheung, government officials, ladies, and gentlemen of the People's Republic of China, we Americans are overwhelmed by your welcome." He paused for the interpreter before he continued, "The building of the emergency hospital here in Beijing and the salvaging of the treasure was a Chinese-American effort that we hope will initiate a better understanding between our two great countries. Although we are thousands of miles apart, our friendship must never be encumbered by distance or distrust. Thanks again for your warm reception."

That evening there was a banquet in a huge building called the Great Hall of the People. Pat discovered that toasting was a favorite custom of the Chinese. "Bottoms up" soon changed to the livelier *gan-bei*. When there was a pause from the Chinese in their long toasting ceremony, Rick, who stood between President Hu Jinta and Dr. Yang, raised his glass. "May our troubled yesterdays be as forgotten as our friendly tomorrows will be remembered."

We will see, Pat mused, thinking about her plane trip with Rick tomorrow when they would be heading for home.

CHAPTER 84

"BEIJING HAS MANY RING roads that encircle center of city," the driver said. He was the same driver that Rick and Pat had had yesterday when they had entered the city for the celebration. He was still acting as a tour guide for them as they rode in the backseat on the way to the airport. Today, they had an additional passenger. Adjacent to the driver was Hok, who was going to spend some extra time with his Grandparents down in Hong Kong.

"You must also work for the city's public relations department," Rick said with a chuckle.

"You three are popular in Beijing," the driver replied. "I want you to leave with good memory of our city."

"We are indeed," Pat said ardently, bending forward in her seat to be heard by the driver. When she noticed a park they were passing, she asked, "What is this area of Beijing called?"

"Chaoyang. It not most historic part of city, but if looking for nightlife, it is place to be," the driver answered.

"I'll remember that on my next trip to Beijing," Hok said, his face creased in a smile.

When Pat sat back in her seat, Rick's hand reached for hers. The movement was instinctive and so lackadaisical that neither noticed the cozy gesture while they both were looking at the park as they drove by. But when the intimacy of the act became evident and they looked at each other, he did not release her hand, and she didn't want him to.

For a while, they sat quietly, saying nothing while focusing their attention on each other. *There certainly is very little not to like about this woman,* Rick thought. The few tiny freckles that were barely noticeable under blue eyes that seemed to spark an interest as to what was behind them. Her high cheekbones covered with flawless skin that was tinted a light brown, not from the sun or makeup. No woman had ever affected him the way she did. And to his surprise, he had never felt more comfortable with anyone.

Strange, but this man is not the type that has filled my dreams, she thought. The intellectual, a doctor or a lawyer possibly, had always been in her vision of the one for her. Never a man with the physique of a pugilist and a face that could be either chiseled out of stone or carved from the sun's rays and beaming at her now.

Opposites do attract. The adage flashed across her mind as Rick's face inched closer to hers. She didn't resist his kiss, which was long and lasting.

The sudden silence from the backseat prompted the driver and Hok to glance quizzically at each other. Hok moved closer to the driver and spoke in a low voice, "They should enjoy their trip back home, right?"

The driver's quick nod accompanied his broad shining face.